La Muliga

Cameron Lally

authorHOUSE®

AuthorHouse™ UK
1663 Liberty Drive
Bloomington, IN 47403 USA
www.authorhouse.co.uk
Phone: 0800.197.4150

Published by AuthorHouse 03/25/2019

ISBN: 978-1-7283-8650-8 (sc)
ISBN: 978-1-7283-8648-5 (hc)
ISBN: 978-1-7283-8649-2 (e)

Print information available on the last page.

This book is printed on acid-free paper.

Contents

1

Raging Battle

The battle between the Ramada Organisation and the Coven of the Great Witches roared on. The fighting was on the doorstep of the witches' fortress. The witches had the upper hand. A huge mistake and a large gamble made by the organisation had led to this deadly confrontation. The forty-eight-year-old leader of the organisation, Abu, stood in the middle of the battlefield. He was wearing dark clothes, had a long silver beard, and was looking for the leader of his enemies. All around him the witches were killing his soldiers. Not a single witch had been killed.

He ran through the fighting, and the enemy's fortress came into view. A tall dark building that housed some of the most evil creatures on the planet, the fortress was on full defensive mode. Abu ran faster and stopped when he saw the door of the fortress open. Emerging from the building was Great Witch Emerald, the leader of all the witches in existence. A calm but fierce witch when appropriate, always dressed in red, Emerald was the greatest of all the witches.Emerald scanned the battlefield and located her target. She was in front of Abu in a matter of seconds. Abu looked into the eyes of the monstrous witch and couldn't believe who he was face-to-face with. He gasped, "You know why I'm here."

Emerald knelt and looked Abu directly in the eyes. "Yes, and if your plan had worked, it would have killed some of my witches in the area. You had to be stopped." Abu thought back to last week, when he had made the decision to attack the witches. His main objective was to kill the two Great Witches, Emerald and Diamond. He was ready to complete half of his mission.

Abu began shooting at Emerald with his machine gun. Emerald stood still and smiled as the bullets hit her. Abu carried on firing, and Emerald carried on smiling. Abu eventually stopped, after seeing that it would take more than bullets to kill the most powerful witch in the world.

He threw his gun to the floor and sprinted away, desperate to leave the war zone. Emerald's second in command, Great Witch Diamond, appeared beside her. A more sinister and ruthless witch who was always dressed in blue, Diamond's enormous power was second only to Emerald's. "Do you want me to go after him?"

Emerald considered the implications of her decision. After careful consideration, she decided. "No. Let him go home and tell the rest of them that they lost this battle. That will make them think very carefully about their actions in the future."

Diamond wanted, more than anything, to chase and kill Abu, but Emerald's word was law. She reluctantly returned to the fortress, followed by Emerald.

Abu ran as fast as he could. He witnessed the deaths of nearly all his soldiers and did not look back once he had passed them. Eventually, he was away from the battle, away from the witches' dominion, and away from death. A burning desire for revenge against the Great Witches came over him as he returned to his own base.

2

The Holiday

It was one of the hottest days of the year. The sun was shining above the city. Every house had some sort of breeze passing through the walls to cool down the people living in the houses. Most of the people outside were appropriately dressed for the weather, with the occasional exception of business people in suits. Two fifteen-year-old boys were enjoying a peaceful walk in the sun, on their way to the local shop to buy cold drinks. The two were friends, James Turner and Richard Evans.

James was of medium height, had short hair, and was wearing shorts and a T-shirt. Rick, as Richard was commonly known because he hated his real name, was small, had fairly long hair, and was wearing his long red coat and bright blue jeans. James constantly asked Rick if he was too hot, but he insisted he was fine.

They planned to stop by their grandparents' houses to collect some money for the shop. As their shadows danced with them past houses on Central Road, the road where Rick's grandmother, Nora, lived, Rick started to talk. "Nice weather, but it'll probably be better when we go on holiday to La Muliga. Where did you find out about it? You never did tell me."

James answered him. "I found it in a brochure that my Biology teacher, Mr Taran, gave me." Rick then asked when the holiday was being booked.

"My dad's booking it tomorrow. We'll be going for four weeks," said James.

"And who else is coming?" asked Rick.

"So far me, you." Rick interrupted James to say that his mother, Angela, would bring the money tomorrow.

James continued. "Fred Johnson has paid. Mr Taran paid this morning. There might be some other people coming, though we won't know for certain until tomorrow."

The boys reached the broken gate at the front of Nora's cottage. Rick pushed the gate. It fell off its last hinge and clanged loudly on the path. "She's had this gate for thirty years," explained Rick.

Rick pushed the gate to the side and walked down the concrete path, which was covered in cracks. They walked past Nora's dead cherry tree to get to the door. Rick knocked on the door.

Instantly, the light in the hallway came on. Nora's face appeared at the polished glass panel in the door, and the letter box opened. The front of a single-barrelled shotgun came through it, aimed at Rick.

Rick panicked as the gun touched his coat. He shouted, "No, Grandma! It's Rick! Not the rentman!"

Nora apologised, and the gun went back inside as the door opened. Nora was short, in her seventies, and had white curly hair. She placed the gun behind the door.

"Sorry lads. I thought it was the rentman by the way you knocked on the door. I've not paid the rent for nearly a year, but I can't keep avoiding him. I'm just on my way out shopping," said Nora.

Rick, breathing steadily, asked her for some money for the shop. Nora gave Rick a two-pound coin and locked her door. After walking down the path, she headed off to do her shopping.

The boys crossed the road to get onto South Hand Avenue, where James's grandparents lived. They approached the house. His grandparents' red Mitsubishi was parked on the drive. The boys entered the house, and the smell of roast chicken flooded their noses.

James's maternal grandmother, Doris, was in the kitchen. She was wearing a clean apron, had her hair tied back, and was in the middle of cooking a roast dinner. The living room had a proper fire as well as two armchairs and a settee. A large white fan was spinning in front of the fire.

"Hello!" said Doris when she saw the boys.

Suddenly, someone jumped up and landed on the floor with a deafening thud. Footsteps were heard coming towards them. A man came around the corner of the living room and stood still. It was James's grandfather, Graham. Graham was a tall, big man. He was wearing his work clothes; his boots had made the loud noise. He towered over everyone as he greeted the boys.

Doris looked at James and asked him what he and Rick were doing there.

"We're going to the shop. So please can I have some money?" asked James. Doris nodded and went to get her purse.

Graham turned to the boys. "I hear you two and some other people are going on holiday. Why haven't you invited me?"

The boys started laughing, but they stopped once they realised that Graham wasn't joking. "I'm being serious. Why haven't I been invited?" repeated Graham.

James was shocked. "We didn't think you would want to come to La Muliga with us."

"Well, guess what? I do" said Graham.

Doris returned with some money. She gave it to James, and having heard what Graham had asked, she said "you want to go to La Muliga with James and his friends? Are you being serious?"

"I'm being very serious. James, are any other adults coming?" asked Graham.

James answered that Mr Taran was the only adult going, and Graham was delighted at the news that another adult was coming. "If Mr Taran's going, I can go."

James asked Doris if she wanted to go, feeling obliged to ask her, as Graham was now going.

"No," answered Graham straight away.

"I was going to decline anyway. You lot have fun and I'll have a nice four weeks to myself," said Doris. "Now, I must get back to the kitchen. I'm making dinner for me and your grandad, and he's going to take Great-Gran Betty her dinner." With that she went back into the kitchen to all the steaming pans. Graham said he would give James's father, Paul, money for the holiday tomorrow, knowing that's when it was being booked. Graham asked the boys if they were going anywhere after the shop.

"No, we're only after cold drinks from the shop," replied James.

"Well come back here, and I'll drop you two off as I'm taking Gran's dinner round to her," said Graham, echoing what Doris had said.

James thanked him and decided to leave. He said goodbye to his grandparents, and he and Rick left the house.

As they were walking, Rick moaned about Graham coming on the holiday. "He'll probably be like, 'Can you feel the pain?' and strangle me if I steal his shoe again."

They laughed as they remembered this particular occasion. Rick had hidden one of Graham's shoes, after Graham had called him Richard. When Graham had noticed it was missing, he'd put his arms around Rick's neck and screamed, "Can you feel the pain!"

They carried on walking until they reached a row of shops which included a hairdressers', cafe, post office and the local Premier shop. A bell rang as they entered the shop. They found cold drinks and chocolates, paid for them, and left.

The boys walked back the way they had come. As they were walking, Rick asked if there were any specific plans for the holiday.

James replied that they would probably go to the beach, visit a water park, and eat in the hotel and restaurants. "I wonder if they'll sell any of the genetically modified seeds," wondered James.

Rick said "Sorry?"

"Have you learnt in Biology about a scientist called Stefan Nance?" asked James.

"I don't know," said Rick.

"Specialist in genetic modification?" asked James, thinking this information might trigger Rick's memory.

"Can't remember," said Rick.

"Nance died a few years ago, and after he died, seeds were found in his house. Nance had genetically modified them to make them grow quicker. No one knows how he managed it, but they're really popular now. And because they can grow so quick, they cost pounds a packet," said James.

Rick shrieked at how expensive the seeds were. With that outburst, they found they were now outside Doris's house and they re-entered it. Graham was standing in the dining room holding a plate wrapped in foil, as if he had been standing there waiting for the boys to get back. Doris was nowhere to be seen.

They got in the Mitsubishi. Graham drove up two streets and along a main road until he reached the street where his mother lived. He parked the car outside the house and everyone walked down the drive towards the house. As they got nearer, they could see Betty Miller, a very small elderly woman, sitting in a chair, in the living room, wearing glasses and reading a newspaper.

As soon as they entered the house, Graham and the boys felt like they had just entered a freezer. The air conditioning was on full. Betty put down her newspaper, looking totally unaffected by the low temperature in her house, and smiled at her guests.

Graham took Betty's dinner into the kitchen. Betty looked at James and smiled. She had never met Rick before. She turned to him and asked, "Are you Rick?" Rick confirmed his identity.

"Tell Rick what it's like to be ninety eight gran," said James.

"It's great," said Betty. "You can't do much of what you want. You can't walk properly. But I'll be ninety nine soon, so I only need to wait another year to get a telegram from the Queen when I'm a hundred."

The boys sat down, and James spoke to Betty about the usual things they spoke about; visitors Betty had had, how other family members were, and whether anything interesting had happened. Graham reappeared, and they prepared to leave. Betty, however, told James to go into the kitchen, as she needed to tell him something important. She didn't say what it was, only that it was better if she told him before he went on holiday.

James and Betty went into the kitchen and the other two wondered what she was going to tell him. The two were in the kitchen for about ten minutes, and when they came back into the living room, Graham immediately asked, "What was all that about?"

"You'll find out soon," promised Betty.

They left the house, and Graham asked the boys if they wanted a lift home. The boys said they would walk and talk instead.

"Okay. Tell your dad I'll bring my money round tomorrow. And if I don't see you, Rick, before the holiday, I'll see you when we go to La Muliga," said Graham, and he got into the car and drove home.

James and Rick began walking, and Rick asked James if he was doing anything when he got home.

"I'll tell my dad that my grandad is coming to La Muliga. Then I'll call on the Johnsons to see Fred and tell Scott a bit more about the holiday," answered James.

They eventually reached Rick's house, where Rick departed. James made a solo journey to the street where his house lay: Cutlass Avenue. His house was number five. James entered his house and told his father Paul, a heavily built black-haired man, about Graham going on the holiday and that he would be paying the following day.

James decided to go and see the Johnsons, who lived at the end of Cutlass Avenue. As he was making his way there, someone shouted James's name. It was Megan Edwards, the sixteen-year-old brunette girl who lived three doors down.

"James, I'm letting you know that I'm coming to La Muliga and I'll bring my money round tomorrow," said Megan.

Megan bid James farewell, and he continued to the Johnsons' house. He walked around the lawn and rang the doorbell. Fred's father, Scott, let James in. Scott was of medium height, average build, and nearly bald. He had raised Fred on his own for ten years since his wife and Fred's mother passed away. He told James that Fred was upstairs and that he would get him to start packing his bag soon.

James went upstairs and entered Fred's room. Fred was thin, had curly blond hair, and was on his computer.

James and Fred started talking about what they were going to do at La Muliga. Fred had a love of books, and he was looking forward to writing some of his own stories on the holiday.

Later on, James checked his phone and saw that it was quarter to four and decided to go home. When he entered his room, his mother Helen pulled up with his younger twelve-year-old sister Holly. Helen was a small red-haired woman, and Holly was the same, only younger. They had been on a shopping trip.

During the following day, Saturday, money was brought for everyone who was going on the holiday. There were now six people in total going. It was 2 p.m. when Paul, with all the money next to him, started booking the holiday. He went onto the EasyJet website, chose La Muliga as the holiday destination, typed in the names of everyone going on the holiday, and made the leaving and returning dates 24 July and 21 August respectively.

He announced, "It's booked. Everyone will leave on 24 July and return on 21 August. The flight to La Muliga will be about two hours, and everyone will be staying in the Los Playas hotel."

Two days later, Monday, was a school day for James. He attended City High School. He left the house and got the bus to school. When he arrived, he went straight to the yard and joined some of his friends; Alice Rivers, Emma Fisher, and Fred.

Alice had long black hair, was very athletic, and was on the school athletics team. Emma was a blonde girl who was the most intelligent of the group. Fred was the class clown, who never listened to his teachers. The four of them had met when they'd started high school and had remained close ever since.

At 8.30 a.m., the bell rang, and everyone headed to form. The four friends were in different forms, so James made his way to the other side of the school on his own and reached his form room.

The class was told there was an assembly so everyone went up to the hall. In the assembly, the headteacher, Mr Nelson, spoke in a loud voice about bullying and how he would not tolerate it at the school.

When the assembly ended, James got his coat and bag from form and went to his first lesson, History. His next lesson was Biology with Mr Taran, the same Mr Taran going to La Muliga. Some of the students in his Biology class were Fred, Emma, and Wasem Askar. Wasem was small and very quiet, but hiding behind the silence was a boy who could be very mischievous at times. Mr Taran's lesson focused on genetic modification and mentioned Nance's seeds.

At the end of the lesson, the bald, clean-shaven, tall, smartly dressed Mr Taran said, "Guys, you need to revise for your exam tomorrow. If you don't do it I will beat you up in the car park after school. I'm only joking."

Every student left the room except for James and Emma because James wanted to talk to Mr Taran about the holiday. Wasem was the last one to leave, and he closed the door behind him.

James confirmed that the holiday had been booked, and they would leave on 24 July and return on 21 August.

"That sounds good. I'll enjoy four weeks abroad," said Mr Taran.

Emma interrupted him and said, "Are you going to La Muliga Mr Taran?" Mr Taran nodded.

Emma looked a bit confused about this, wondering why a teacher was going on holiday with some of his students. "Why?"

James answered instead, realising he needed to tell Emma something. "Sorry Emma, I don't think I've told you Mr Taran went to school with my mum, Helen, so we know him on a personal level."

Emma apologised, and Mr Taran asked her if she was going on the holiday.

"I wasn't invited, sir," said Emma, shooting an evil glare at James with her blue eyes.

"You can come if you want," said James.

"I might surprise you" said Emma.

"Are any other adults coming?" asked Mr Taran.

"Yes, my Granddad Graham." James was curious about where Mr Taran had gotten the brochure for La Muliga, as he had never heard of it before Mr Taran had told him about the place.

Mr Taran confirmed that, in class one day, he was saying how much he really wanted to go on holiday because his last holiday had been five years earlier. "After class, Wasem told me about La Muliga. I liked the sound of it, so he gave me the brochure," said Mr Taran. Fred and Megan then entered the room.

Everyone started talking, mainly about the holiday, and the people who were going said what they were looking forward to. Fred was looking forward to eating in restaurants and getting away for four weeks. Megan was more interested in sunbathing on the beach. But all of them liked the general idea of going on holiday for four weeks.

When it was time for lesson three, English, James, Emma, and Fred, being in the same English class, went together. The English lesson lasted until the bell rang for lunch. James, Emma, and Fred arrived at the canteen and ate their lunches. When they'd finished eating, they put their rubbish in the bins and went out to the yard. They ran into Alice, who said she had decided to come on the holiday.

"That's good Alice. Book yourself on tonight to leave on 24 July and to return on 21 August" said James.

They stayed there talking until it was time for their last lesson, Chemistry. In Chemistry, they went over what they needed to know for the science exam until the bell went, signalling the end of the day.

James, Emma, and Megan got on the same bus because they lived close to each other. At home, James did quite a lot of last-minute revision for the exam. He got a text message from Alice, saying, "I've booked it."

The total number going on the holiday was now seven. He messaged her back saying he was pleased and went to bed early for the exam.

The following day, James and the rest of Year 10 sat the Science exam, and they found it really hard. They would get the result on 22 August, a day they were now dreading after the difficulty of the exam. Everyone in Year 10 was allowed to go home after the exam as a treat.

3

An Unexpected Arrival

The rest of the school term flew by. City High School broke up for summer on 19 July. The summer holidays got off to a good start, and the weather was brilliant. There was an atmosphere of excitement as the holiday to La Muliga drew nearer.

On the night of 23 July, the day before they were due to leave, James packed his bag. The flight was at 1.p.m. Everyone was coming to James's house to get the minibus to the airport at about 10 a.m. He went to sleep thinking about all the things he would be doing when he arrived at La Muliga.

The next morning, James woke up early and got ready. Helen, Paul, and Holly woke up and went downstairs to wait for the guests. As this was happening, the first person going on the holiday arrived. It was Rick, with his mother, Angela. Angela was tall and pale and had come round so she could wave goodbye to Rick. Fred then arrived with Scott after the two had walked from their house.

The next person to arrive was Graham who arrived in the Mitsubishi with Doris. Graham told everyone he'd packed his diving gear and would therefore be going diving in La Muliga. Alice and Megan were next to arrive with their parents.

Finally, Mr Taran arrived by taxi as the minibus arrived. The driver opened the back, ready for the suitcases. Those going on the holiday helped the driver put all the suitcases in the back.

"We'll say our goodbyes. Give us five minutes," said Graham to the driver. The driver nodded and went back into the minibus to wait for them.

Once everyone had said their goodbyes, they all took their seats in the minibus. Graham sat in the passenger seat, and everyone else sat in the back. The minibus left Cutlass Avenue and was now en route to the airport. During the journey, the people on the minibus were in conversation, mainly with the person they were next to.

They arrived at the airport at 10.30 a.m. and stopped in a lane outside an entrance to the departure lounge.

Everyone took the suitcases out of the back and got trollies for them. Each put their suitcase onto their own trolley, and thanked the driver. who said, "You're welcome. Now I'm off to pick up someone else, who's also going to La Muliga."

The group entered the airport, and Graham said they would be checking in their suitcases and having them weighed first. He went to the front to lead the way. The others queued up, and one by one, their suitcases were weighed and checked in.

Mr Taran was the last person to be seen. Everyone waited at the side for him. Whilst Mr Taran's suitcase was being weighed, the female assistant put a tag around his suitcase. She asked, "Where are you and your friends going?"

"La Muliga" answered Mr Taran.

The assistant gave him a confused look. "La Muliga? Is that the type of place you'd like to go on a holiday?"

"Yes. Why not?" asked Mr Taran, curious about why the assistant didn't think highly of his holiday destination.

"Oh no. Don't listen to me. I forgot about the two rules that the head pilot has brought in. One is that what is discussed in the airport stays in the building and is only discussed with the staff. The second rule is that the staff can't question anyone about their holidays or question why someone chose a holiday. Forget what I said before. I will lose my job if the head pilot finds out," explained the assistant.

"I take it La Muliga isn't the type of place you'd go on holiday," said Mr Taran, laughing.

"No. It isn't." The assistant laughed too, shaking her head slowly as she said it.

The assistant took the suitcase and put it on the conveyor belt. Mr Taran joined everyone else, and they all made their way to passport control. On the way, Graham asked Mr Taran what the assistant had asked him. Mr Taran told him about her questions about La Muliga and about the new rules at the airport. Everyone wondered why the assistant wouldn't go to La Muliga for a holiday and why the new rules had been made at the airport.

At passport control, their belongings were put into a basket, which went onto a conveyor belt and through an X-ray machine. Then one by one, they went through the metal scanner. Once they did this and got their stuff back, Graham led the way to the food court.

When they got to the food court, Graham said he was going to the bar and asked if anyone else was coming. Mr Taran said he would go too. Graham asked the others where they were going.

"We're going to Burger King," said James.

The men went upstairs to the bar, and the kids found a table. James and Fred decided to get the food. They took everybody's order, walked over to Burger King, and joined the queue. As they were queuing and talking about La Muliga, Fred asked, "Did Rick say please when he told you what he wanted?"

"No I don't think he did to be honest," said James. "But everyone else did."

"The cheeky kid. I wouldn't get him anything if I were you. We're good enough to get him his food, and he doesn't even have the decency to say please. I won't forget it," said Fred. James had a feeling that Fred would pursue the issue and that Rick was going to wish he'd used some manners.

James and Fred were served together, and they ordered the food and paid for it. Everyone ate their food within ten minutes. Some offered James money for buying their food, but James declined the offer, saying it was his treat. Fred noticed that Rick didn't offer James any money towards his food. This made Fred's blood boil even more.

James checked his phone. The time was 12.25, time to get the others from the bar. The adults were sat together talking and having a laugh, so the others joined them. At 12.30, James went back down the stairs to check the intercom; it said the flight to La Muliga was boarding at Gate 1 in Terminal 1, now!

James went back to the bar and told everyone what the intercom had said. Everyone got up from the table and went to the terminal. When they got there, they were told by two assistants standing at the walk-on that the flight would be boarding in two minutes.

A man of about sixty came over and stood behind them. He was bald, tall, and wearing a holiday cap. He was also waiting to board the plane. James looked at the man and realised that it was Mr Harry Barton, the previous headteacher of City High School, who had retired. James decided to say hello.

Mr Barton recognised James and held out his hand. "How are you, James?"

"Fine, sir," said James, shaking Mr Barton's hand.

Mr Taran heard Mr Barton's voice. Having been a teacher at City High School while Mr Barton was headteacher, he came over, shook Mr Barton's hand, and said, "Good to see you, Harry. Are you coming to La Muliga?"

"I certainly am!" replied an excited Mr Barton.

"How did you find out about it?" asked Mr Taran.

"I was visiting City High School on the day of the science exam. After the exam, a brochure fell from the bag of one of the students leaving the hall, and I picked it up. The brochure told me everything I needed to know to book a holiday to La Muliga. I took it home and booked for myself to leave on 24 July and return on 21 August. I brought the brochure back to reception the next day." Mr Barton added that the boy whose bag the brochure had fallen from was called Wasem Askar.

"Wasem, he's a character," said Mr Taran.

Mr Barton confirmed he was travelling alone and staying at the Los Playas hotel.

"We're staying there too, all seven of us," said James.

Mr Barton was introduced to everyone else. One of the assistants then said, "Can all eight passengers follow us onto the plane."

"We make seven and Mr Barton makes eight. Are we the only people going to La Muliga?" asked James.

The same assistant said, "Yes. It's only the eight of you."

Everyone in the group wondered why they were the only eight passengers. Graham suggested Mr Barton sit with them, as they were all booked in the same hotel.

The assistants started to walk through the walk-on. The passengers followed the two assistants onto the plane.

4

The Shock

The eight passengers took their seats at the front of the plane. James sat on the second row next to the window. Rick was about to sit at the end, but as he reached it, Fred ran and sat there.

Before Rick could do anything, Graham and Mr Barton walked over to them. Graham put his hand on Rick's shoulder and said, "Don't worry Rick you can come and sit with me and Mr Barton."

The three of them sat on the front row to the left.

Once everyone was seated with their seatbelt fastened, the pilot introduced himself. "My name is Michael Hopkins, I'm the head pilot at Manchester Airport, and I will be your pilot for this flight, the flight to La Muliga will be about two hours. During that time, you will have the opportunity to buy food and drinks. You will find your suitcases in the holders above you. The reason for this will be explained when we reach La Muliga. The plane will now prepare to take off."

The air-crew made sure everyone had their seatbelt on and, that all phones were either turned off or on flight mode and then went through the emergency procedures.

The plane began to move slowly around the runway. It then sped in a straight line and rose into the air.

For the first hour of the flight, all of the passengers spoke with whoever they were sitting next to. Rick was listening to music but he had it at a low volume so that he could also listen to Graham and Mr Barton's conversations.

Graham was telling Mr Barton about his career as a builder. Mr Barton described his teaching career. "I started off as an English teacher and worked my way up to a deputy head at City High School. When the headteacher, my wife Margaret Barton, was offered a job at another school, I applied for the headteacher position. And after my interview, the chair of governors told me that I would be succeeding Margaret and becoming headteacher in September 2000. I really enjoyed my thirty years at City High School. We retired last summer, and now the headteacher is Mr Gerald Nelson. I now spend a lot more time with Margaret."

The air-crew came around with the food trolley. Some bought snacks. James asked one of the air crew why their suitcases were in the holders above them. "Mr Hopkins will explain everything before we reach La Muliga."

Later, Mr Taran asked what the time was. James answered. "It's half past two, sir."

"James, we're going on holiday. You don't have to call me sir. Call me Sahid instead," said Mr Taran.

"Same with me, James. Don't call me sir. Call me Harry," said Mr Barton.Towards the end of the flight, Michael Hopkins spoke again. "We're close to La Muliga. Air-crew, prepare the passengers for landing."

The passengers assumed the crew would be checking seat belts were on and doing general security checks. But instead, they went to the back of the plane and came back with parachutes. The passengers were very alarmed. The crew gave each passenger two parachutes.

"What are these for?" asked Fred.

"Mr Hopkins will explain in a moment," said one of the crew.

Hopkins then came out of the cockpit. He was a middle-aged man with white hair and was wearing his pilot uniform. All the passengers gave him a frightened look when they saw him, immediately thinking no-one was flying the plane. Hopkins knew what they were thinking. "Don't worry. The plane isn't flying by itself. My co-pilot is flying the plane. You're all going to have to parachute off the plane. You'll need to attach one parachute to yourself and the other to your suitcase. I would advise you to put your hand luggage into your suitcase. You have to use parachutes because there isn't an airport at La Muliga," said Hopkins. The passengers were now extremely alarmed.

"If we have to parachute off because there's nowhere for the plane to land, how on earth are we supposed to get back on a plane to come back home?" enquired Rick rather fiercely.

"A ferry will come to collect you after your four weeks holiday," said Hopkins.

The passengers hurriedly prepared their parachutes, some clearly shaking, with fear rushing through their bodies. Hopkins went over to one of the exits and opened the door. "Come on, everyone."

One by one, they threw their suitcases out and jumped out of the plane. Once their parachutes were open, it took them fifteen seconds to reach the ground.

Each landed on a beach and looked around to see the others were there too. It was very hot, and the sun was shining above them all. The air was tranquil, and the only sound that could be heard was the noise of the departing plane fading away.

When everyone looked ahead, they got the biggest shock of their lives. All they saw were tall green trees.

La Muliga wasn't a holiday resort at all. It was an island. They were on an island.

5

Survival

The sea brushed up the sand and touched their feet. The tide went back out and returned, sometimes coming farther up the beach than it had previously. At that moment, they weren't too concerned about a bit of salt water in their shoes. They looked at the trees, the trees they feared held nothing behind them. They saw no signs of life, no buildings, nothing. This seemed an uninhabited island.

Taran was checking his phone, he said. "I'm going to beat up Wasem in the car park when I get back, giving us a brochure to go to an island, and my phone has got no signal!" No one's phone had a signal.

"What are we going to do if we can't ring anyone?" "Will the ferry actually come at the end of the four weeks?" "I hope so. Otherwise, we'll be staying on this island forever."

They stood still and stared at the trees, all thinking the same dreadful thought; what if they did stay on this island forever? There were so many unanswered questions.

They continued staring at the trees, and more questions came into their heads.

Eventually Graham said, "We're not going to achieve anything standing here looking at trees. If we're going to be here for four weeks, we need to look around and see what's here." He began walking into the forest, and everyone else followed him.

The trees cast a long shadow over them, blocking the sunlight. Without the sun, it was still warm. When they walked past the first trees and over branches, leaves and sand, with flies buzzing around them, James said that the assistants, air crew and Hopkins must have known that La Muliga was an island. Everyone agreed.

They came across two hammocks. Ahead of the hammocks was what appeared to be a used campfire. Graham observed the area; there were two shovels, a few bricks, a ladder, scrap metal, a bow and arrow, and clay. "This seems like a suitable place to camp. If we don't find anywhere else, we'll come back."

Everyone agreed with him about the place being suitable, and they all dropped their suitcases before continuing to explore the island.

They came to a little stream. The water was flowing over stones and rocks in an easterly direction. It looked like it continued into the sea. They crossed over the stream and decided to come back to see where it was coming from.

After walking past bunches of trees, they came to a small and strange-looking building. The building had two windows with a door in between. James took the lead and approached the worn-out door. The door had a rusted gold plaque on it that read. "Laboratory of Stefan Nance."

James took a step back and said, "I don't believe it. This is Nance's lab."

"Nance as in Stefan Nance who we study in Biology and who developed the genetically modified seeds?" asked Mr Taran.

James was compelled to see what was in the lab. He entered and everyone else followed. The lab was a single large room on one floor. At the back were shelves of books and chemicals and a sink with rusty taps and plugs. Packets of seeds were also on the shelves.

A desk was towards the left. On the desk were a calorimeter, a journal, a picture lying face down, and stacks of seeds. Some of the seeds were in packets, but others were simply piled on the desk. Everyone showed some interest as they looked around the lab, but James was the most fascinated by what he saw.

He walked over to the desk and picked up the picture. The picture was of Nance and his wife. James had seen a picture of Nance's wife before, so he knew it was her in the picture. He put the picture down and looked at the journal. He flicked through the journal and noticed that only the first page had been written on. Part of the second page was missing; this made James wonder what Nance had written on it.

He read the first page: "I've done it. I genetically modified the carrot, banana, apple, and peach seeds, and it took them five days to grow! My test trees outside are the result. I will take the seeds home. Everyone will be proud."

As soon as he'd read the journal entry, James went outside. Right in the corner were four test trees, one of each fruit and vegetable.

Everyone else came outside and looked at the trees. James said, "In his journal, Nance said these test trees were grown from his five-day seeds."

The group were intrigued, but all agreed they needed to explore the rest of the island and see where the water in the stream was coming from. On the way up the stream, they saw a deer galloping along.

Eventually, they saw a cave and realised the stream was coming from it. Megan led the way up a path and into the cave. The path in the cave was a circle around a lake and the water from the lake was flowing out of the cave. Walking around the lake, they noticed a little oven door in the wall. Megan opened the door and saw a metal rack inside and fire stoves underneath it. There were matches and a pair of oven gloves next to the door.

Megan said, "We can use the matches on the stoves to get a fire going, and then it'll do what an oven does." All agreed and decided to further explore the island.

The next thing they came to was a five-by-five metre patch of soil. The only thing there was a watering can. Fred asked what the time was.

James took out his phone. "It looks we're one hour ahead of British time. It's half past five, Fred." They continued searching the island.

By half past six, the group had explored the whole of La Muliga, and nothing else interesting was discovered, apart from a few more animals. After the island had been explored, they went back and sat around the campfire, contemplating the island.

Everyone looked at Graham and waited for their next command, knowing that he was bound to come up with some new orders eventually. He said, "This wood is useable, has anyone got any matches?"

Megan pulled some matches out of her pocket, revealing she'd brought them back from the cave. She lit a match and put it to the wood, starting the campfire. The fire glowed in the middle of them, and with the heat, everyone felt like sleeping. Everyone started talking about how the holiday they were expecting had been too good to be true. They agreed that La Muliga was unexpected but also interesting because of Nance's lab. They guessed he had genetically modified the seeds there and that no-one knew his lab was here. They believed that the oven in the cave would be useful as well.

"It will. And it's not every day you find an oven in a cave. The world is changing fast," said Megan.

"It's fine saying what's good about La Muliga, but don't you think we should be thinking about survival?" said Graham.

The thought of survival then dawned on them. No one had even thought about how they would actually survive for four weeks. They didn't know what to do.

"The water in the lake appeared to be clean. So we'll need to drink from the lake, especially with this heat. Does anyone have any food?" asked Graham.

James mentioned the seeds in the lab and suggested they could be grown. Graham agreed. After being told there were a few snacks left from the plane, he said, "We'll eat the snacks tonight. The seeds will be good, but they'll take five days to grow. I'm afraid it looks like we're going to have to eat the animals in order to survive until then."

Everyone else nodded their heads, hating the thought of killing and eating animals but knowing it needed to be done.

"We need to survive for four weeks. But I reckon there are other things on this island that may be useful or just interesting. Some of you may have a job at home that would be useful to do while you're here. Or you may have a very good skill. Think of a skill that you're good at and come up with a job you can do for four weeks," said Graham.

There was silence as the adults thought about their jobs, and the young people thought of a skill they believed would be useful.

After a minute of thinking, Mr Taran was the first to speak. "Before I became a teacher, I was a miner. I took part in the miners' strike in the 1980s. So with one of the shovels, I could dig a mine and see what I find. I might find old pieces of metal, buried treasure or other useful artefacts. Who knows?"

Graham thought about Mr Taran's previous job and said "I didn't know you took part in the miners' strike. What was that like?"

"Quite bad," said Mr Taran "Margaret Thatcher was closing down pits, and our pay was being restrained. We went on strike from 1984-1985, but it was very violent. I dropped out of the strike when I found a job as a teacher with my degree from university."

Everyone was quite intrigued by Mr Taran's story. He then said, "I also have a lot of medical knowledge as a Biology teacher, and I always bring my first aid kit with me wherever I go. It's here in my suitcase. If anyone gets injured or has an illness, I can use the first aid kit and my medical knowledge to help them get better." Everyone felt relieved.

James was next to speak. "I can grow the seeds in Nance's lab in the soil patch," he said. "We can eat them after five days, and I can keep growing them. I could also look around the lab and see what else I discover."

Rick then spoke about his idea. "I'm quite a good builder. I played with a lot of Lego when I was five, and I've built sheds in my garden. So I could, with a bit of time, build a building here, let's say a small hotel, using this." He pulled a box out from behind him. The box was transparent, so everyone could see that it contained a small amount of concrete, glass, rail, bricks, and everything else needed to build a hotel.

"This was behind Nance's lab. There are still fifty more boxes there," said Rick. "It'll take me a maximum of four weeks to build the hotel. But first I'll build some wooden huts for us to sleep in until I've finished the hotel. I'll start building the huts now." He stood up, took some materials out of the box, grabbed the ladder on the floor nearby and walked away to start building three wooden huts around the circle.

Fred said, "I'll hunt the animals for food using the bow and arrow and cook what I get in the oven. Also, I've written four short funny stories. People at home have said they're good. I have a pen and paper in my suitcase. I'll let you read them and I'll tweak some of them and multi-task."

Megan had an idea. "At home, one of the jobs I do is washing the dishes. I know there aren't any dishes here yet, but our clothes will need washing. If anyone wants clothes or dishes, if we get any, washed, tell me, and I'll wash them in the lake."

The only people who were left to say their job were Graham, Mr Barton, and Alice. All eyes were on them when Graham said, "There's clay that I can shape into dishes, metal into knives and forks, and heat them up in the oven in the cave." The others couldn't think of a job so they decided to help someone else. Mr Barton would help Graham, and Alice would help build.

"Also, I'm not saying you can't build Rick, because clearly you can. But Harry and I could help you after we've made dishes and cutlery. We'll only need eight, and they can be washed every day by Megan. If we help you then the hotel will be built much more quickly" said Graham. Rick said he would be grateful for the help.

"Now that the jobs are sorted out, has anyone got any towels?" asked Graham.

Graham had brought four, and everyone else had brought one each. James asked Graham why he had brought four.

"I thought we were going to a proper holiday resort in Spain and these towels were meant for the beach," said Graham. He asked if anyone wanted an extra one to act as a pillow. The group decided who would have extra towels as pillows and who would sleep in which hut. Half an hour later, Rick got down from his ladder and announced that the huts were done. Three small circular wooden huts were around the fire. The roofs were cones of wood, there was a gap at the front of each that acted as an entrance, and they all had wooden floors inside.

Night had now fallen, and it was time to sleep. The group went into their huts and took the parachutes with them. When they stepped into their huts, they looked around at the walls. There was a smell of fresh wood and, in each hut, a small room at the back, which was for people to change clothes privately. Everyone became extremely tired and fell asleep instantly.

It hadn't been two hours when Rick woke up in pain screaming. "I can't sleep on this floor! It's too hard! I'm going onto the hammock!" He left the hut with his towels. Some were woken up. They heard Graham say, "Shut up, Rick."

Fred jumped up and began rolling up the sleeves on his dressing gown. "I'm going to teach Rick a lesson!"

"Leave it, Fred," said James. "He's gone now."

"I know, but that's three times in one day that he's been an idiot. First he doesn't say please. Then he doesn't offer money for his food, and now this. If he does one more thing that pisses me off, I'm going to attack him," said Fred. They went back to sleep.

James's alarm went off at 8 a.m. He got dressed and took his toothbrush and toothpaste out of his suitcase to clean his teeth. The only place where he could spit out the toothpaste was in a hole in the ground. The group gradually all got up.

Graham walked over to Rick, who was fast asleep on the hammock. Graham pulled the hammock, causing Rick to fall out and wake up. "Time for work, Rick," said Graham.

Rick got up, rubbed his eyes, and walked over to his hut, cursing Graham under his breath. He later came out dressed and cleaned his teeth. Graham gave everyone a small box of cereal which he had brought with him.

"Now that everyone's here and had breakfast, it's time to survive. Go and do your jobs, and I'll catch you all up later," said Graham and everyone went off in different directions to do their different job.

At 12.30 p.m., Graham and Mr Barton were near the campfire. Between them, they had shaped eight pieces of clay into plates and dishes.

"I'm just going to take four pieces of clay to the oven and check how everyone's doing," said Graham.

He got up with the pieces of clay in his hands and matches in his pocket and walked to the cave. He checked on a couple of people on the way. Mr Taran had made a four-foot deep hole with the shovel and said he hadn't found anything yet. Fred hadn't had much luck finding animals and would probably go to the sea later and get some fish.

When Graham entered the cave, he lit a fire on the stoves and placed the pieces of clay onto the rack. Megan was knelt by the lake washing some clothes. She pointed at eight pairs of socks and five T-shirts next to her, which she'd washed. Graham left the cave and went to the soil patch. James was there with a watering can, pouring water over the patch. He had planted some seeds and would plant more and see what he got in five days.

Graham came to where Rick and Alice were building the hotel. The floor for the hotel appeared to be nearly finished.

"How's the hotel going?" asked Graham.

"It's good. We've nearly done the floor, and we'll start on the walls tomorrow," said Rick.

An hour later, Graham went to retrieve the four pieces of clay, which were now plates. Mr Barton decided to take the rest of the pieces of clay to the oven.

When it started to go dark, Graham went around La Muliga shouting for everyone to get back to the campfire and bring anything that might be useful. Soon, everyone was back, and a big discussion began.

Fred brought back two fish, which he had caught in the sea. He took them to the oven to cook. Megan brought back the clothes that she'd washed. Fred returned and passed his first book around. It was about a wedding that turned into a food fight and the book ended with someone walking towards the wedding cake. The people who read it didn't find it that funny but were laughing to keep Fred happy. Fred said he would let them read the rest tomorrow.

Graham was the last person to read Fred's book. "It's good, Fred. This will be the routine every day until we leave the island. Work during the day and bring back anything we need. Your fruit and vegetables can come every five days James. Keep building the hotel, Rick and Alice. Harry and I will help you tomorrow."

Graham and Mr Barton handed out the cutlery and plates they had shaped and put into the oven. Fred went back to the oven to get the fish. He returned with the fish on a plate and cut the fish into even slices. He gave everyone a slice and they began eating.

They found the fish quite pleasing for their first dinner on the island. The plates and cutlery were handed back to Graham and Mr Barton. Megan asked if they needed washing.

"Please Megan. Then Harry and I can help with the hotel," said Graham. "We'd better be going to bed. Everyone needs to be up at eight again tomorrow." They all made their way to the huts.

As Rick went towards his hut, Mr Barton ran over to him. "Rick, I know you go to Northump Academy. Is it as good as the headteacher makes out?"

"No. It's the worst school ever. I wish I went to City High," said Rick.

Mr Barton laughed. "I'm asking because, as a former headteacher, it's interesting to see what people think of other schools. People who I've asked about City High School are happy with it, and students from other schools aren't happy with their schools. So I must have done something right when I was in charge of City High School."

Night fell and the group slept for the second time on this mysterious island.

6

The Ancestry Story

Nearly a week had passed and things were starting to look a lot better for the temporary residents. Mr Taran had managed to dig a huge mining pit. There were two ladders to get in and out, and along with metal, he had found clay and bricks, which helped in building the hotel.

James's first lot of fruit and vegetables had been grown and eaten and everyone looked forward to this seasonal food every five days. He still hadn't had a proper look around Nance's lab because he had been constantly growing and watering seeds in his vegetable patch.

Half of the hotel had been built. But even with help from Alice, Graham and Mr Barton, Rick felt he was missing something that would allow the hotel to be built more quickly.

Fred had been bringing back birds as well as fish to eat; Fred hoped to catch the deer one day after seeing it again, galloping near the cave.

The whole of Fred's first story was read by everyone. The first story involved a food fight at a wedding, which ended with the destruction of the wedding cake. He didn't tell anyone much about his second story, only that it was about a man who came across a talking mouse.

During the first week, all of them found that they could get really hot working in the blazing sun all day. So they decided to have a break from 12 noon to 1.30 p.m. every afternoon. During the break, they would go in the sea and on the beach. Graham had told them not to swim too far out, as there are sharks in the sea. "So don't try and swim home either," he instructed.

After the introduction of the break, Fred decided to hunt until he found food. Then, he would help with the building of the hotel after 1.30. His contribution helped half of the hotel to be built in the first week.

On 30 July, Mr Barton was helping to build the hotel when he dropped a brick. He slid down the ladder to get the brick, which had landed on a pile of clothes. He noticed that the pile of clothes were the ones he had meant to give to Megan to wash but had forgotten.

He picked up the clothes, strolled over to the cave, and told Megan he had more clothes that needed washing.

"Leave them here, Harry. I'll wash them once I've done these," said Megan, who was in the middle of washing some of Rick's jeans.

Mr Barton left the cave, and as he was walking along the stream, he noticed Fred aiming an arrow at a deer. It was the same deer Fred had seen and hoped to catch for dinner. Mr Barton decided to stay and watch what happened.

The deer was happily eating some grass until it saw Fred. Sensing danger, the deer started galloping towards Fred. Fred wasn't quick enough with his arrow, and the deer knocked him clean off his feet. He landed by a tree and hit his head on the trunk, knocking him out cold.

The deer was gone and out of sight. Mr Barton ran over to Fred and picked him up, deciding that the best thing to do was to take him to Mr Taran.

When Mr Barton arrived at the mining pit, Mr Taran noticed the unconscious Fred. He ran over, saying, "What happened?"

"A deer knocked him right off his feet, and he hit his head on a tree," said Mr Barton.

"I'm going to beat up the deer in the car park," said Mr Taran as he checked Fred's pulse. "His pulse is pretty strong, and he's breathing. There's no wound on the back of his head. He'll regain consciousness in a few minutes."

Just then, Fred began coughing and woke up. "Where am I? What happened?"

"The deer that you've been hoping to kill knocked you over, and you hit your head on a tree," said Mr Barton. "You're by the mining pit now."

"I'll get back to work then," said Fred, standing up.

"Fred, I think it's best if you rest," said Mr Taran.

"I'll be fine, Sahid. Someone needs to catch the animals." Fred strolled back to his hunt.

That night, everyone had heard about Fred's incident and that he had made an excellent recovery. Despite his injury, he had managed to catch two birds and two fish for dinner. After everyone had dinner, they went into their huts and to bed.

The next day, 31 July, the group had their break from 12 to 1.30 p.m. and spent it in the sea and the beach. At 1.30, they changed back into their work clothes in their huts.

The silence outside was interrupted by the sound of a plane coming closer and closer to the island. As the plane flew across the beach, three suitcases were thrown out of the plane on parachutes. Then three people parachuted off the plane and landed on the beach. The group walked past the hammocks and trees and onto the beach.

Three females were unstrapping their parachutes. James recognised one of them as Emma, true to her word about surprising James. The others were two older women. Doris, James's nana and Graham's wife, was one of them, but the second person wasn't recognisable yet.

"You said you'd come, Emma," said James.

"I told you I'd surprise you, James," said Emma, smiling at him.

"And how come you're here, Doris?" asked Graham.

"I decided to come and surprise you," said Doris.

Mr Barton looked closely at the other woman. She was short, and had white hair and tanned skin. He couldn't believe his eyes. "Margaret? What are you doing here?"

"I went onto our computer and found out the place you were going to was La Muliga, so I booked myself on to see what you were up to and to have a nice holiday," said Margaret. Margaret introduced herself to everyone else as Mr Barton's wife and his predecessor as headteacher of City High School.

"I thought we were going to a Spanish-owned holiday resort. I even brought binoculars. Why are we on an island!" said Doris, expressing her disappointment about where she'd ended up.

"It turns out that La Muliga is actually an island. The brochure was given to Mr Taran by a boy called Wasem Askar. Who was the pilot on your plane?" asked Graham.

"Some idiot called Michael Hopkins, and he mentioned a ferry picking us up," said Doris.

"Let's just hope it does turn up in three weeks," said Graham. Emma complained when she realised her phone had no signal.

"None of us have a signal, Emma. But we've improved the quality of the island. We'll show you around. Follow me," said Graham.

The new arrivals picked up their suitcases and followed the others. Emma asked James what it had been like on the island.

"It's not been that bad. You'll see some of the things we've found," said James.

They were now at the campfire. The newcomers put their suitcases down and introduced themselves to the people they didn't know.

Graham pointed at the huts. "These are the huts we're sleeping in. Rick built them, and he's the only person who doesn't sleep in them. He sleeps in one of the hammocks over there because he's an oddball, and this is the campfire we light up at night."

Some of the group looked away when Graham called Rick an oddball. Emma hid her face on James's shoulder and laughed into it. Rick stuck a finger up at Graham's back. No one except Fred saw it. He felt angry that Rick had done it when Graham wasn't looking.

They proceeded to Mr Taran's mining pit. "This is where Sahid has been mining and finding metals and bricks," explained Graham. They crossed the stream to reach Nance's lab.

"This is the lab of late scientist Stefan Nance," explained Graham. "He genetically modified some seeds, and now they only take five days to grow. James is growing some. There are test trees over there."

They were then shown around the cave, where they saw the oven and the lake, followed by James's vegetable patch and the half-finished hotel.

Once they were back at the campfire, Graham said, "Harry and I made the dishes and cutlery, and Fred writes his stories here. So, newbies, which job suits you?"

"Hang on, Graham. You haven't mentioned food," said Doris.

"We've had no choice but to hunt and eat the animals here and cook them in the oven in the cave," said Graham. "I know it's horrible, but we have to do it. Right, new people, which job will suit you?"

"First, we need to decide which huts we're staying in," said Doris.

Graham stood still for a moment, staring at Doris. They agreed who would sleep where.

"Now, for the third time, what job will suit you all?" asked Graham again.

They decided on their jobs. Emma would help with growing the vegetables. Margaret would help with the building of the hotel. Doris would make some more dishes and cutlery and then aid with the building of the hotel.

The new people went into the huts to unpack. Fred confirmed he had caught more birds and fish and would be making an early dinner. Mr Barton lit the campfire, and the group sat around and ate dinner.

Darkness fell during dinner, and it was soon time for bed. Everyone stood up. Graham faced Doris with a strange evil grin on his face. "Did any of you bring any towels?"

"I did," said Doris, and the grin faded from Graham's face. "I have five."

Margaret had two, and Emma had one. The towels were evenly distributed. In the huts, they lay their towels down in different parts of the huts and lay down to see what it was like.

Everyone was up the following morning by eight thirty. They went off to work at nine, and this time, some had helpers.

When Rick and Margaret arrived at the half-finished hotel, Rick said. "Margaret, I feel as though I'm missing something that would allow me to build the hotel much quicker. Any ideas?"

"Do you have any blueprints?" asked Margaret. Rick shook his head.

"There's your answer. I can draw some for you if you want," suggested Margaret.

"Please. Fred should have a pen and paper," said Rick.

Margaret got a pen and paper from Fred. Rick started climbing the ladder and said, "Meet me at the top Margaret." When Rick got to the top, Margaret was already sitting down with her pen and paper ready to sketch her first blueprint. Rick confirmed the building would have two floors.

She was halfway through drawing the first blueprint when she acknowledged it was a brilliant and remarkable achievement to build half of a hotel in a week.

"I played with lots of Lego when I was young, and I've built lots of sheds in my garden, and my great-great-grandfather was one of the builders of the Empire State Building," said Rick.

"That's fascinating!" exclaimed Margaret.

Alice then appeared and decided to help Rick with his building. They started talking, and he told her how his mother, Angela, had raised him on her own for his whole life. Alice admired that and asked who Rick's father was.

I've never met him. Mum told me she was with him for about a year until he found out she was pregnant with me," explained Rick. Alice wondered whether Rick would ever meet his father.

The topic of conversation then moved to high schools and how they both missed their primary schools. They started talking about primary schools and Alice asked if he had a favourite primary school teacher.

"It would have to be Miss Taylor, she was a great teacher," said Rick.

At the vegetable patch, Emma was busy watering vegetables. James had gone to the lab to get more seeds. He came back with more apple seeds and planted them into the soil.

Once he'd finished, Emma voiced her strong opinion about Rick and how she thought he was rude, but she thought Fred was sweet. She asked James how long he'd known the two of them.

"Since I moved to Cutlass Avenue," answered James. "By the way, I found out something quite interesting the other day, something that links some of the people on the island."

"What do you mean?" asked Emma.

"Do you want me to tell you how some of my ancestors met some of the other people's ancestors?" asked James. Emma nodded.

"In AD 242, my ancestor Claudius Turner travelled to England on a boat, and the person who sailed him there was a mysterious man called Benjamin Johnson who was Fred's ancestor. Benjamin said he was a survivor of the Trojan War. He'd fled during the war and came to and stayed in the river," said James.

"But the Trojan War was around 1180 BC. How on earth was he still alive in AD 242?" asked Emma.

Apparently, he was cursed by Zeus to live another 1,500 years," said James "Claudius reached England and settled in the country. During the Black Death, Christopher Turner became very ill. He nearly died. It was during that time when he met Elizabeth Rivers," said James.

"Alice's ancestor!" said Emma.

James nodded. "And the rest is a story for another day," said James.

"What? Are you being serious?" asked Emma. James nodded at her.

"Why?" asked Emma, keen to here more of the ancestry story.

"Another day," said James, and it was no use. James would not say what happened next until another day.

Graham shouted. "Time for your break." They went back to the hut. Emma was disappointed.

They walked to the beach, and James whispered. "Keep the story a secret for the time being, and don't worry. I will tell you the rest." Then he went into the sea.

Emma lay down on the beach. While sunbathing, she was thinking about all the things that could have happened once Elizabeth Rivers came on the scene and how James knew about the ancestry he'd started telling her about. She decided she would ask him once he'd told her the rest of the story.

7

A New Arrival

Five days later, due to the teamwork of the builders, the hotel was completed. It was a huge building with two floors. The first floor had five comfortable rooms; each room could accommodate four people. Each room had four small beds, which had been made by the builders in the process. The second floor was like an attic and was used as a storage room. The ground floor had a long dinner table, and the kitchen was underground. The lights were powered by the sun. The hotel had stairs but no elevator. The builders had decided to build a terrace on the roof, which would take about a week to complete.

The hotel brought about a lot of beneficial changes. The residents at La Muliga moved into the rooms in the hotel with proper beds. Dinner, which was differing animals, was prepared every night by Fred in the kitchen, and the whole group ate together at the dinner table. After dinner, they sat around the campfire every night until bedtime. Apart from that, life at La Muliga stayed the same.

On 7 August, exactly a week after the new arrivals had come to La Muliga, James decided to tell Emma the rest of the ancestry story. "During the Black Death, Christopher Turner was seriously ill from the plague. He nearly died, until Elizabeth Rivers came along. She was a doctor, and she saved Christopher from dying. Elizabeth and Christopher fell in love and they married. The next big thing was in the 1800s."

At that moment, Graham was heard shouting, "Time for your break!"

As James and Emma made their way to the hotel, Emma turned to James. "Don't you dare leave me on a cliffhanger again, James," she said, pointing at him.

"Don't worry. I'll tell you the rest after the break," said James.

When they got to the first floor of the hotel, they entered the room where they slept. The room was a good one because it was large and comfortable. It was kept clean, courtesy of the tidy inhabitants. They went into the bedroom to get changed, and once they'd finished, Megan came into the room, followed by Fred.

"What's it like washing the clothes?" asked Emma to Megan.

"It's not that bad," said Megan.

Once James, Fred, Megan, and Emma were changed, they walked to the beach and sea where everyone else was.

After an hour, Graham called out, "Right back to work!" Doris asked for one more minute.

"No. Back to work, Doris," said Graham, and he pulled the towel that Doris was lying on, causing Doris to spin in the sand. She cursed at Graham, and everyone laughed.

When James and Emma returned to the vegetable patch, Emma immediately told James to continue with the story. "It was during the Victorian era. Henry Turner met your ancestor, Priscilla Fisher. (Emma became excited). She was well known as the sister-in-law of Queen Victoria. She had a lot of money and was seen as the figurehead of London. She married and had a falling out with her husband's sister, Mary Ann Nichols, who stole £20,000 from Priscilla in 1887 and was found murdered in 1888 in Whitechapel."

Emma said "Whitechapel? 1888? That was the place and year of the Jack the Ripper murders."

"Correct," said James, smiling because Emma had seen the connection. "It's unlikely that Priscilla was Jack the Ripper, seeing as four other women were murdered in the same way. But it's very strange. In that same year, after the murders, Priscilla was responsible for killing a witch who had been terrorising London. Her death made everyone feel safer" said James.

"Witches are real?" asked a shocked Emma.

"They were, but it sounded like this witch was the last of her kind," answered James. "Priscilla died in 1889. During the 1920s, Seth Evans, Rick's great-great-grandfather, helped build the Empire State Building under the guidance of Les Miller. Les went on to marry a woman known as Betty Arnott."

"Betty, that's your great-gran's first name," said Emma.

"That's right, and what would she have been called after marrying Les?" said James.

"Betty Miller. Ooh! It is your gran. So Les was her husband, which means he was Graham's father," said Emma. James nodded and revealed the story had now concluded.

"Have you told anyone else the story?" asked Emma.

"No. Only you. I'll probably tell everyone else later. But for now, let's keep it to ourselves," said James, and they started planting and watering seeds.

Emma asked, "James, how did you find out about the ancestry story?"

"My Great-Gran Betty went onto Ancestry.com and found lots of old documents, which told her the story starting from AD 242. She told me the story when I went to visit her" said James.

On top of the hotel, Rick was building more of the terrace and Margaret was in the middle of drawing a blueprint. Graham, Alice, Doris, and Mr Barton were building a toilet in the dining room.

Rick turned around and realised he had run out of bricks. Margaret told him he could get more from the mining pit. He slid down the ladder and saw Megan walking back to the cave after returning some washed clothes.

Megan suddenly fell into the ground. Rick panicked and ran to the hole. He looked down and saw Megan lying in a three-metre-deep hole surrounded by leaves. She wasn't moving. Rick realised he could get to the spot where Megan was lying through the mining pit.

He ran to the mining pit, went down one of the ladders, and observed the pit. There were five tunnels at different sides of the pit. Mr Taran was by the tunnel that would lead them to Megan.

"Quick, Sahid. Megan fell down a pitfall trap, and you need to see her now!" cried Rick. "She's through this tunnel."

He and Mr Taran ran as fast as they could through the tunnel and reached the unconscious Megan.

"I'm going to beat up whoever made this pitfall trap in the car park," said Mr Taran.

Mr Taran examined Megan and concluded she had injured her leg but would need to wait until she woke up. "Take her to the campfire. It'll be warmer for her there."

Rick did as he was told, and Mr Taran followed him. Once he'd put Megan on the ground near the campfire, he returned to the mining pit, worried about Megan but remembering he needed more bricks. Rick got more bricks and took them to the hotel.

When he returned to the campfire everyone else on the island was there. They had seen a circle of people around Megan and decided to come and see what had happened. Mr Taran had told the others that Megan had fallen through a pitfall trap and that Rick had carried her to the camp.

With Megan still out cold, Doris said, "Which of you decided to make a pitfall trap?"

"I'm afraid that was me, Doris," said Fred. "I've been trying to catch that deer for a week, so I decided to use a different tactic, the pitfall trap. I've only made one, but I won't be making anymore now."

After some time, Megan opened her eyes, much to everyone's relief, and said her leg hurt. Mr Taran asked if she could walk on it. Megan got up and started to walk. She had a limp every time she took a step with her right leg.

"You can walk on it, so it's not broken. You'll be fine," said Mr Taran.

Everyone turned when they heard somebody shout. "Hello!" They looked past the hammocks and stared at the trees that shadowed the beach. Footsteps could be heard, along with the snapping of branches and crunching of leaves. Someone came out of the trees, walking towards the group. The group could make out that the person was a man. It was only when he reached the hammocks that many of the group realised it was Fred's father, Scott Johnson.

"Scott! How'd you get here?" asked Graham.

Scott explained that he had gone to Manchester Airport because he was concerned after failing to make contact with Fred. "I asked an assistant when the next flight to La Muliga was, and she said there were no more flights. I started to panic until Michael Hopkins, who said he was a pilot, suddenly appeared and assured me that everyone who went to La Muliga was fine. He then said that he would take me there to see Fred. I couldn't understand how he knew everybody was fine. He told me to go home, and arrangements would be made for me to travel.

This morning, a helicopter arrived, and Hopkins was the pilot. He explained that the helicopter would take me to France, to a pier in Marseille. From there, he would take me to La Muliga on a boat.

The helicopter took me to Marseille. I boarded a little boat with Hopkins. After half an hour, this island came into sight. Hopkins explained it is a small island full of interesting places. Hopkins drove the boat right up to the beach. I got off, and Hopkins told me to look around. Here we are."

Fred appeared from the shadows, delighted to see his father.

The group confirmed they were very suspicious of Michael Hopkins and also of Wasem Askar, the boy who had shown Mr Taran the brochure for La Muliga all those months ago. Hopkins had said that a ferry would collect the group on 21 August, which was two weeks away, time enough for Scott to explore the island.

Graham showed Scott around and met the others on the beach. Nance's lab and the cave had been the most interesting, and Scott was amazed at how quickly the hotel had been built.

Graham introduced him to those he didn't know, and they discussed jobs. Scott outlined food he had brought and said he was happy to cook.

"So what will you make us tonight?" asked Graham.

"I was thinking of cooking pasta in a proper sauce. But as a quick starter, I'll make some carrot soup," said Scott.

"It's getting dark. I'll end this break, and we'll get dressed and wait at the dining table. You and Fred can make our dinner in the kitchen, right! Come on, everyone, time to get changed!" shouted Graham.

Everyone obeyed the master and went back to the hotel. When everyone was dressed in smart clothes, all of the La Muliga hotel residents made their way to the dining table, and the cooks went to the kitchen. The kitchen was fairly large and included a sink, refrigerator, conventional ovens, and a few cupboards.

Doris was arranging drinks to go with dinner. Everyone on the table started talking about their excitement to be getting a decent meal. Doris returned carrying a tray of drinks. Scott and Fred arrived. Each held a tray filled with bowls of soup. The soup was followed by pasta with sauce.

Everyone was merrily drinking and really enjoying the meal, and before long, it was half past eleven. Some decided to skip pudding, because they were tired from a hard days work and a hearty meal.

Graham was very grateful to Scott for the food and outlined his role for cooking and serving food at set times during the day for the remainder of the time on the island. Scott was more than happy with that and asked Fred if he would help with the preparation, now that they had enough supplies without him killing any more animals.

Fred accepted the request but indicated he would continue his "battle" with the deer, much to everyone's dismay.

Everyone except Graham, Scott, and Fred went upstairs to their rooms. After the table was cleared up and the dishes were washed, Scott said, "I'm a bit curious Graham. How come you're one who gives out orders and keeps control?"

"We need to have order and control because we're on an island. If we didn't, everything would be all over the place. It would be very chaotic, and no one would know what to do. With order and control, we're in a routine that is stuck to by everybody. So someone needs to keep order and control, and seeing as no one else can, I decided to," said Graham.

8

The Incident of Scott

Another week went by at La Muliga. Nothing much happened in that week. The terrace was finished on the hotel so the builders were now working on building a huge cellar to keep them working. The idea to build the cellar came from Rick. The terrace was ideal for resting and contemplation during breaks and after dinner. Even though most of the group had enjoyed La Muliga and had had a good laugh, they couldn't help feeling relieved that there was only a week left until the ferry was said to be collecting them. But they still had to get through one more week.

It was on 14 August when James, realising there was only a week left, decided to tell the story about how most of their ancestry was connected. That night, after everyone finished dinner, James said, "Stay sat down for a minute, everyone. I have an interesting story to tell you."

When everyone was ready to listen (even Emma, though she knew what was coming) James began. He told the others the story about Benjamin Johnson sailing Claudius to England and how Benjamin claimed to be a survivor of the Trojan War and cursed by Zeus to live another 1,500 years. Scott was very intrigued by that story.

He told the rest of the story in order: Christopher Turner's near death because of the Black Death and his being saved by Dr Elizabeth Rivers, the murder of Mary Ann Nichols by Jack the Ripper, Priscilla Fisher killing the witch, and Seth Evans in America. He ended by revealing that Les Miller married Betty.

Once the story was finished, everyone said it was strange and coincidental and asked James how he knew it all.

"My Great-Gran Betty discovered it on Ancestry.com. Then she told me the story," said James.

"So that's what she told you in secret the day we visited her," said Graham.

Everyone sat silent. Now that there was an element of proof about this revelation, it all started to sink in.

"So my ancestor really was cursed by Zeus to live another 1,500 years," said Scott.

"That's a matter of opinion, Scott, as to whether your ancestor was telling the truth or not," said Rick.

"Have you told anyone before today?" asked Graham.

"Only Emma two weeks ago, and we can tell the story to the rest of the family if we get back," said James.

"I wouldn't be surprised if Betty has already told the whole family. Fancy that, my own mother not telling me, arrogant woman," said Graham, and everyone laughed.

There was a short silence until Scott stood up and started clearing the table.

Once the table was clear, everyone automatically went up the stairs to the terrace. They sat on the terrace for about thirty minutes, each in deep thought about what they had just been told. At the end of the thirty minutes, they retreated to their rooms and went to sleep.

The next day, 15 August, proceeded normally at first. The La Muliga group worked, had a break, and then went back to work. At about 2.30 p.m., they were all doing their jobs when everyone heard someone shouting. The shouting was so loud that the whole of La Muliga could hear it.

Rick and Alice had been talking about the possibilities of Priscilla Fisher being Jack the Ripper when they heard the shouting.

Everyone heard Scott shout, "Bloody hell! I've left my lighter on the beach!" Scott came stomping past the hotel and went through the trees to the beach.

Moments later, they heard a big gasp of breath. "OOOOOO!" The sound came from where Scott had gone. Everyone abandoned their job and went onto the beach to investigate.

Scott was on the floor gasping for breath. He looked as if he was having a fit. Mr Taran ran over to him, with the others following behind.

Mr Taran got on his knees, took one look at Scott, and shouted, "He's having a heart attack!"

Mr Taran took control of the situation. "Someone try and get Scott to sit up so he's more comfortable," he instructed.

Fred grabbed Scott and lifted him up. It was no use. Every time Fred managed to get Scott to sit up, he just collapsed back onto the floor due to his shaking and gasping.

Mr Taran and Fred grabbed Scott and started running with him toward the campfire. The others followed.

Once they were at the camp, Mr Taran took a packet of aspirin out of his first aid kit and took a tablet from the packet. "Chew on this, Scott."

Scott took the aspirin using his mouth and nearly took Mr Taran's hand with it. He chewed the aspirin and his gasps of breath disappeared. He slowly shut his eyes. Mr Taran checked Scott's pulse, and then put his hand on his chin. "This is very strange."

"He has narcolepsy" said Fred, "that sleep disorder that makes you fall asleep. Do you think that might have caused his heart attack?"

"No" said Mr Taran straight away. "It explains why he's just gone to sleep. But the cause of his heart attack is very strange. From my experience, I have discovered that a heart attack is usually caused by a build-up of plaque in the arteries, which blocks it and stops the heart from getting oxygen. Scott's heart attack hasn't been caused by that because he was fine after taking the aspirin. If his heart attack had been caused by a blockage in his arteries, then it would take more than just aspirin to make him feel fine. There is only one explanation. Scott has seen something that has scared him, causing him to have the heart attack," said Mr Taran.

Scott's eyes then opened wide, and he glared around at the others. He looked terrified.

"What's wrong, Scott?" asked Mr Taran. Scott shut his eyes again and slowly shook his head. Mr Taran decided to ask Scott what he had seen that frightened him.

Scott started shaking his head much faster with his eyes shut. He didn't want to tell them what he saw. "What was it you saw Scott?" repeated Mr Taran.

"OOOOOO!" gasped Scott as his heart attack began again.

"He's having another heart attack!" cried Mr Taran. He gave Scott another aspirin, which aided his recovery for the second time.

Scott had fear in his eyes that was clear to everyone. Scott then closed his eyes and went to sleep again.

Mr Taran explained that he had gone into a narcoleptic coma, which meant he was asleep because of his narcolepsy but in a coma as well because of his heart attack. Mr Taran was concerned about Scott's condition and requested the others not to ask him again what he had seen if he woke up. He said he would stay with Scott to monitor his condition and told Rick to build a gurney for Scott to lie on, telling the others to go back to work. They dispersed.

9

The Bomb

The following day, 16 August, Scott still hadn't woken up and was lying on the gurney that Rick had built. Everyone was starting to worry about him, but it was Fred who was most affected by it. Throughout the start of the day, Margaret was getting bored of hearing Rick and Alice talking about the ancestry story; Priscilla Fisher; and Rick's favourite teacher, Miss Taylor. So she decided to go and help Fred cook and see how he was getting on.

When she entered the kitchen, Fred was busy cooking the dinner. Margaret asked if he needed any help and how he was getting on. He said he was fine. Margaret was not convinced, and she looked carefully at Fred. She saw a tear spill from his eye and fall to the ground. "What's wrong Fred?" asked Margaret. Fred wiped his eye with the sleeve of his shirt.

"Sorry, Margaret. I shouldn't be crying like this, but my dad's the only person I have in my family since my mum died. I'm worried because he's been lying on that gurney for the past nineteen hours or so, and he doesn't seem to be close to waking up. What is wrong with him?" sobbed Fred. Margaret put her arm around him and tried to reassure him that Scott would be fine. Rick was secretly watching them.

"But even Sahid can't explain what caused his heart attack," said Fred.

Margaret desperately tried to change the subject and said, "I think it's about twelve. So let's go for our break."

Luckily for Margaret, Graham's voice was heard shouting, "Break time." Rick quickly ran away.

Everyone went to the rooms. Fred got changed into his swimming shorts but kept his shirt on because he had no intention of going into the sea today. He walked down to the beach where the others were. He walked along the sand and stood still so that the tide just about touched his feet.

James and Rick tried to cheer Fred up by reminding him of some funny memories, like when Rick nearly got shot by his Grandma Nora because she thought he was the rentman and when Graham tried to strangle him. Fred usually found those events funny, but he didn't today. He walked away along the beach with his hands in his pockets.

"What's wrong with Fred?" asked Rick as he and James swam away from the beach.

"He's upset about Scott," said James. "No one can say if Scott will wake up, and with him having a strange heart attack and no one knowing what caused it, I can understand why Fred is feeling down."

The break was ended when Graham's booming voice shouted, "Break's over. Back to work!"

Graham decided to go to the test trees, as he wanted some apples to snack on.

Once dressed, everyone went back to work. When Alice stepped onto the hotel roof, she heard something rather mysterious. "What's that noise?" Everyone stopped and listened.

There was a plane flying towards La Muliga. The plane got nearer and nearer. Doris put the binoculars she had brought for sightseeing against her eyes to have a closer look at the plane as it came closer. When it was close to flying right above them, Doris lowered the binoculars and said, "I don't believe it! That nob-head Michael Hopkins is flying the plane. I bet he's dropping another bunch of innocent people to their doom."

The plane was now flying to the other end of the island, and when it was above the hotel, the doors opened. Once the plane was above the test trees, something was pushed from it. Everyone looked at the object and could make out that it was large, round, and black.

Many of the La Muliga group wondered what it was. Doris suddenly shouted, "Everyone, run! That's a bomb!"

The bomb hit the ground right in the middle of the test trees and exploded. The test trees were completely destroyed, apart from two that managed to survive. The blast only went as far as Nance's lab. But then Doris remembered something.

"Graham went there!" she shouted. "Quick! We need to make sure he's all right!"

She sprinted towards the test trees with the others following her. They came to Nance's lab and looked at the spot where many test trees had stood. Graham was nowhere to be seen. "No! Don't frighten me! Where is the control freak?" shouted Doris.

"In here," called a voice that sounded like Graham's. It was coming from Nance's lab. Doris ran into Nance's lab and everyone heard her say, "Thank God you're all right!"

Luckily James had moved some apples to Nance's lab the previous day. Otherwise Graham would have been killed by the bomb. Doris was very concerned and reminded the group that four bad things had happened. Fred had been battered by a deer, Megan had nearly died after falling through a pitfall trap, Scott had had a heart attack with an unknown cause, and now Hopkins had dropped a bomb on the island. "Why did he do that? Is he trying to kill us?" asked Doris.

"Doris, if you look at where the bomb was dropped, we may have an answer about whether Hopkins is trying to kill us," said Graham. "The bomb has shattered most of the test trees and has also made a large hole. After the blast, I saw the hole. From where I was stood, I could see stone steps that led down the hole. Why don't we go over to the hole and see where the stone steps lead us. Then we may have a reason for why Hopkins dropped the bomb."

Everyone followed Graham to the hole. When they got there, they saw that Graham was correct about the stone steps. The steps led down the hole, but when the steps ended, there was a large metal door.

Graham went down the steps and approached the door. The door had no handle. All that was there was a sort of keyboard and a small screen attached to the door.

"The door doesn't have a handle, so I assume it requires a password to open it, and the password must have to be typed in using the keyboard. The password could be anything, but we need to find out what's behind the door. Let's try, La Muliga," said Graham.

He typed in "La Muliga" on the keyboard; the letters came up on the screen as he typed them. Once he'd typed the word, he clicked on the enter button, and a computerised voice said, "Access denied."

Graham then tried "island." "Access denied."

At Doris's request, he tried "Hopkins" and "Michael Hopkins." "Access denied."

Mr Barton suggested "Nance" and "Stefan Nance." "Access denied."

"This is stupid," said Graham. He tried another ten passwords and they were all followed by an, "Access denied."

"Fuck this. Let's get back to work. We haven't got a clue what the password is," said Graham.

With no other choice, the others followed Graham's orders and went back to work, wondering what the password was and what was behind the door.

James and Emma were at the vegetable patch picking fruit that had been grown. They agreed that La Muliga was getting more and more strange as the days went by.

They contemplated the why Hopkins had pinpointed that exact spot to drop the bomb and concluded he must be aware of the door and that he would return to the island.

"That may be true," said James. "But there may be a way to find out the password and possibly what's behind the door. If we have any chance then I think there's only one place to search for answers. Nance's lab. I've been saying since we found this lab that I'll have a good look around it, but I've only been in to collect seeds. I'm going to go there and search for answers." He walked towards the lab. Emma went with him.

When they reached the lab, the door was closed. James looked at the plaque that read "Laboratory of Stefan Nance" and reached out for the handle to open the door.

10

The Discoveries

James and Emma entered Nance's lab. They looked around at the shelves of books; the different chemicals; and Nance's desk, on which sat the calorimeter, more chemicals, and more seeds. They decided to search the shelves first.

They looked at the books and saw that Nance had been very interested in science in general. The books that stood out were about evolution and psychoanalysis. Clearly, some of Nance's interests were in the fields of Biology and Psychology.

James then turned his attention to Nance's desk, and read the journal he had read the first time he had entered the lab. The desk had four drawers that could be pulled out. He looked in the drawers; all were empty apart from one.

The drawer contained a voice recorder. Emma looked at it. James picked up the recorder and pressed play. Nance's voice said, "At last, my seeds are ready to be taken home so that I can show everyone. I shall take them home in a few hours and hide them in the cupboard and reveal my discovery. However, the cancer is making me more and more tired. I know I haven't got long left, but let's hope I can make the journey home. Throughout all my years as a scientist, I've been interested in what makes a human being unique. I reached a huge milestone when I genetically modified the seeds. After that I decided to do further research, research about human strength and the brain."

James paused the recorder so that he and Emma could take some time to think about what they had just heard. It was clear to them that Nance was working on another experiment after completing his work on the seeds.

James pressed play again, and Nance's voice returned. "Human strength is an interest. I find it fascinating that some people have very little strength, yet some have lots of it. People can gain strength, usually by building muscle mass. I have tried to find other ways in which a human can gain strength. In my opinion, you are able to defend yourself better with more strength.

"After reading books on evolution, I have determined that it's clear that, when humans were apes, they had greater strength and defended themselves better. Now the brain, a human brain is about the size of two fists. But the brain of animals such as whales and elephants are much more expanded than a human brain. The expansion comes from the frontal lobes in the cerebral cortex, the layer of tissue that covers the brain and is associated with memory, vision, and self-control. So if we had a bigger brain with a larger cerebral cortex, then surely we would have a better memory and vision and more self-control. I have been researching possible ways in which a person can gain a better memory and vision, along with more self-control, without having a larger brain."

James paused the recorder for a second time and allowed what Nance had said to sink in. He and Emma could gather that Nance had been researching different ways to make his hopes come true because the obvious ways were impossible to achieve.

James played the recorder for the last time. Nance's voice rang out, "With all my research, I have found a way to have more strength without gaining muscle mass and a better memory, vision, and more self-control without the brain being enlarged. If you want to find out how I've made it possible. Take the picture of me and my wife out of the frame. You'll find a key. Use the key to unlock my safe, which is behind my books on the bookshelf." The recording ended.

James put the recorder back into the drawer and picked up the picture frame. He took the picture out of the frame and saw the gold key. He took the key and looked around the bookshelf, moving books around until he saw the safe. The safe was in the shape of a silver square, and there was a little hole for the key.

James put the key into the hole and unlocked the safe. He and Emma stared at what was in the safe.

During the next day, 17 August, Rick and Alice were talking nonstop. Rick was talking about a particular memory he had that involved his favourite primary school teacher, Miss Taylor, the very memory that contained the reason he loved Miss Taylor so much. Rick had been accused of assaulting someone who he didn't like. The truth was that Rick hadn't assaulted anyone. Rather, the person who made the accusation told his friends to be false witnesses, so with this "evidence" against Rick, the headteacher was considering suspending Rick for a day.

Miss Taylor had saved Rick. She had overheard the boy who'd made the accusation, Bradley Mispon, asking his friends to be false witnesses. Once Miss Taylor told the headteacher what she'd heard, it was Mispon who was excluded and not Rick.

Rick and Alice then started to talk about Priscilla Fisher, particularly how a woman who knew very important people and had lots of money could have been a notorious serial killer. Although Rick and Alice personally didn't believe that she was Jack the Ripper, there was still a chance that she was. After they'd finished talking, Alice reached out and grabbed Rick's hand. Rick looked at Alice's hand and then at her. They maintained eye contact for a few seconds, but they were both distracted when someone shouted, "Are you sure this is La Muliga?"

"I'm very sure," came another voice.

"Who's that?" asked Alice. She let go of Rick's hand and looked around to see who was talking.

"I don't know, but the second voice sounded like Hopkins," said Rick.

Along with Rick and Alice, several others heard the two voices. They made a move from the hotel to the beach and looked at what the commotion was about. Betty Miller, James's great-grandmother and Graham's mother who had told James the ancestry story, was on the beach. On a boat driving away was another person. Even with his back to them, they knew the person on the boat was the mysterious pilot who had brought them to La Muliga, Michael Hopkins. He drove the boat away from the island with a look on his face that suggested he would be back.

"What are you doing here, Mum?" asked Graham.

"Everyone's been worried at home because we couldn't get hold of anyone. I rang Manchester Airport and asked about the holiday to La Muliga. Michael Hopkins was given the phone and said he had flown the plane on both flights to La Muliga and asked me if I wanted him to take me to La Muliga. I said yes. So I packed my bags, and Hopkins took me to Barcelona on a helicopter. We got on a boat and he brought me here. I assume there's no TV here?" enquired Betty.

"No there isn't" said Graham.

"It's kicking off in the UK," said Betty.

Betty had everyone's attention, and all those who have been on the island for these past weeks (except Scott) listened intently.

"On 28 July, a Russian civilian was killed in Russia by members of the Ramada Organisation. The Russian government began to search for the organisation and they were found on 3 August. Three Ramadas were killed, but the rest managed to hijack a plane and flew out of Russia. It was on its way to the United States. The US president found out that a plane full of Ramadas was flying towards America, and the plane was shot down. It landed in California. No one was injured. Seven Ramadas were killed, but the rest managed to escape and go into hiding.

"On 8 August, they hijacked a helicopter and again escaped. They headed for the UK. The prime minister ordered the plane be shot down, and the terrorists went into hiding. The army was instructed to find them. They were discovered yesterday, but they got on boats and headed for France. Just after Hopkins picked me up, I heard on the radio in the helicopter that the French president was asking for help," finished Betty.

Everyone stood silent, astounded at Betty's story, astounded at what they had missed.

"Well, we have missed out," said Graham, sounding disappointed. Graham explained about La Muliga and what jobs each person was responsible for. He told Betty that Scott was very ill, having had a heart attack a few days ago. Betty volunteered to help with the washing and cooking.

"What's actually wrong with Scott?" asked Betty.

Graham explained that the cause of Scott's heart attack was not known. "Sahid reckons he saw something that scared him," he added. "He's been lying asleep on a gurney by the campfire in a narcoleptic coma ever since."

Mr Taran said Scott may or may not wake up.

"And Hopkins dropped a bomb on us yesterday," said Doris.

"A bomb!" shrieked Betty.

"And there's a door that requires a password to open it where the bomb was dropped, and we have no idea what the password is," said Doris.

"Let's get back to work. Mum can unpack in the hotel and start work. Don't worry about more bombs being dropped or anyone else having heart attacks. I doubt anything else like that will happen," said Graham.

By 6.30 p.m., everybody was at the dining table waiting for dinner. It was being cooked by Fred and Betty. Betty had cleaned all of her pile of clothes that needed washing, so she'd gone to the kitchen to keep herself busy. A Sunday dinner was being made. Fred was peeling the carrots and potatoes, mixing the stuffing, making roast parsnips, and cooking the meat, which was beef and chicken.

Betty was pouring the drinks, boiling the gravy, and preparing the dessert. The dessert was chocolate fudge cake with cream. She poured out cider into glasses. The cake was setting in the fridge, and the gravy was boiling.

Once the meat was on the plates, Betty took the drinks to the dining table. Fred then brought the dinner to the table, and everyone ate their food.

The conversation centred on Graham telling Betty the ancestry story. "But you'll know all about it, Mum, as you're the one who told James. If we get home, we'll be having words about you not telling me," he added.

After the meal, the chocolate fudge cake with cream was served. Everyone enjoyed this dessert. They then decided to sit on the terrace until 9.30 p.m., when they all went to bed. Betty was in a spare room.

As they went to bed, everyone was thinking about what would happen in four days time, when the ferry was due to collect them. They were also thinking about Scott and his heart attack, the bomb being dropped, the secret door, and what Betty had told them about the terrorists.

Unbeknown to the group, at that particular moment, the terrorists were in hiding, deep within the streets of Paris, near the Eiffel Tower, with the intention of reaching Marseille before or on 20 August.

11

Terrorist Attack

It was 20 August. Three days had past since Betty had arrived at La Muliga. The island group had to wait just one more day before, hopefully, they would be taken back home. However, they all agreed that La Muliga had been very interesting and exciting. It had also been quite scary, but on the whole, the visit had been enjoyable.

On the other hand, everyone was very grateful about going back to the United Kingdom. The cause of Scott's heart attack was one of their primary thoughts, especially because Scott was still lying in his narcoleptic coma on the gurney.

A plan had been made for when they got back. They would take Scott to a hospital straight away, alive or dead, and would hopefully find out what had caused his heart attack. Then they were going to inform the police about La Muliga being an island and about the door that required a password. They were going to report Michael Hopkins to the police for taking them to La Muliga and for dropping the bomb. In the process, they would probably hear the latest news on the terrorists, and the location of Nance's lab would be revealed. But there was still one day left on La Muliga.

There wasn't a need for any more work to be done and the inhabitants decided to relax, reflect, and enjoy their last day. On the terrace, they started talking about what they liked best about La Muliga. Betty joined in, although she'd only been on the island for a few days. Most said they liked Nance's lab and the hotel and said they would miss the island when they got back.

At about two thirty, Graham gave a loud burp. "Pardon me."

"What's that?" asked Mr Barton.

"Sorry, Harry. That was me. I burped," Graham said, apologising.

"I know what that was, Graham. I mean what's that?" repeated Mr Barton, pointing to the sea.

Everyone stood up and looked out at sea to where Mr Barton was pointing. There was a boat coming towards La Muliga.

The boat stopped on the beach, and around forty people disembarked from the boat. From where the group were stood, at the top of the hotel on the terrace, it looked like there was an army of ants.

"Oh no," said Betty as the people from the boats started walking past the trees and to the campfire. "I know who these people are. It's the terrorists who were in hiding in the UK!"

With this shocking revelation, they looked at the new arrivals and realised Betty was right. The terrorists were armed with guns and were wearing long tunic shirts and loose-fitting pants. Two of the terrorists went towards Scott lying on the gurney by the campfire. The terrorists then looked directly at the others.

All the others started running towards the hotel and the two near Scott got hold of the gurney and pushed Scott to the hotel.

Everyone wondered what to do. They almost froze in fear, anxiously waiting until the terrorists reached them.

Within minutes, guns were pointed at everyone.

"Put your hands in the air!" shouted one of the terrorists. Everyone listened to him and raised their arms. The terrorist lowered his gun and smiled. Betty asked where Scott was.

"He's that guy on the gurney, isn't he?" asked the man.

"Yes" said Fred, anxious to hear what the terrorists had done to his father.

"He's downstairs. I've given orders to search the hotel and find somewhere for you and Scott to wait until our leader arrives," said the man.

A terrorist came up to the terrace. "We've found a cellar with prison cells." The man pointed his gun at the group and ordered them down to the prison cells.

"Whose idea was it to build prison cells?" asked Fred.

"Mine" admitted Rick.

"Rick, why on earth did you decide to build prison cells!" asked an angry Fred.

"I ran out of ideas on what to build, and I needed something to build," said Rick.

Fred huffed as they walked to the door with their hands in the air. Down the stairs they went, past the rooms, and into the cellar. The cellar had a small wooden table in the corner, with a set of keys on it. There were six cells along the back. The captives were put into the cells. The cells were locked.

Scott was pushed on the gurney and wheeled into a cell. Throughout the entire racket, Scott stayed in his coma. The people in his cell shouted, "Scott!" at the same time. But Scott's eyes didn't open.

"Scott still hasn't recovered from his heart attack then?" asked one of the men.

"No. He. Wait, how do you know he had a heart attack?" asked Mr Taran.

Either the man didn't hear Mr Taran or he was ignoring him. Just then another terrorist came down and told him to bring everyone up to the terrace. The boss was about to arrive any minute.

The cells were unlocked, and the prisoners came out, and everyone was led up the stairs. A terrorist got the gurney and pushed it up the stairs. Everyone was led back onto the terrace.

All the chairs had been put to one side so there was a lot of space on the roof. A helicopter appeared and slowly landed in the space. The side door opened. A man stepped out of the helicopter. He was wearing a black hat, a black and white shirt, and long pointy black shoes. He looked like he was in a circus.

"I know you," said Graham. "You're Monsieur Lapom from the Belgian government."

"That is correct," said Monsieur Lapom.

Another man then appeared from the helicopter. To the mild surprise of the prisoners, Michael Hopkins came out of the helicopter wearing his pilot uniform.

"Hopkins, so you're the leader?" asked Doris.

"Not quite the leader yet, Doris," replied Hopkins.

A third person came out. He was recognised by a lot of the people on the roof. It was Wasem Askar.

"Ohhh, Wasem, why are you on the helicopter with Hopkins?" asked Mr Taran.

"Be quiet Mr Taran. And now, our leader is coming out" said Wasem.

A man then came out wearing slightly darker clothes than the other terrorists. He also had a long silver beard.

Mr Taran stood staring at the man, bewildered, and then quietly said, "Abu?"

"Hello, Sahid" replied Abu.

12

Mr Taran's Past

All eyes were on the man called Abu.

"This is Lord Abu Askar, leader of the Ramada Organisation," announced Lapom.

Upon hearing the name Askar, Mr Taran asked, "Are you related to Wasem, Abu?"

"He's my son," replied Abu. The prisoners gasped at this revelation.

"So you, your son, and this pilot were all in on this?" asked Emma. Abu nodded.

"But it sounds as if you know this man, Sahid," said Graham.

"I did, a long time ago. We were friends until Abu joined the Ramada Organisation. I can't believe I didn't see that you and Wasem were related. I was a bit suspicious when Wasem first came to City High School, but I checked the system. According to the school's records, Wasem's father was called Neil Askar," said Mr Taran.

"A clever fake identity" said Abu.

"So you did all this. You told your son to give Sahid the fake brochure?" asked Graham.

"That's right," replied Abu.

"Well what's the big idea? Why are we here and why are you here?" asked Graham.

"It all started in 1991 when Sahid and I went on a trip to Russia. You remember that, don't you, Sahid?" asked Abu.

"Yes, I remember it well. Is that why you're here?" asked Mr Taran.

Abu explained. "In 1991, Sahid and I went on a trip to Russia. On the last night, we heard someone say that Comrade Rasponov had gone to a meeting in a building close by. We went to the building. There were guards at the entrance, so we went around the back. Sahid suggested he go through an air vent to listen to their meeting, as Rasponov was a dangerous man. He could speak Russian, as he'd spent a year in Russia during his university course. I had grave concerns and decided to wait outside for him."

Mr Taran was now shaking. Fear could be seen in his timid eyes.

Abu continued. "Sahid snuck through the vent and made his way to a spot above the room where Rasponov was having the meeting. He listened intently to what Rasponov and the others were saying. Rasponov wanted Russia to annihilate the United States of America, and he knew something that would achieve that. It was top secret, and few people knew about it, about Chasov's secret weapon.

"In 1989, Vladimir Chasov decided to build a nuclear weapon to destroy America. Only two people knew about it. Chasov himself and his right-hand man Rasponov. The weapon was finished in 1990 and secretly secured. Chasov died that year. In 1991, Rasponov called the meeting that Sahid was listening to. Rasponov told the people about the secret weapon and that he intended to use it to destroy America. He told them that the weapon was secured behind a door that required a password to open it. He had found some documents written by Chasov, one of which contained the password. He read out the password and Sahid heard it. As he was about to declare where the weapon was, American and British soldiers attacked, destroying the building. Rasponov was the only one who escaped.

"Sahid managed to crawl back the way he came in, where I was waiting. Two soldiers came out of the building. One of them asked, 'Did you discover where the weapon is?' And the other replied, 'It's on an island called La Muliga.'"

As Abu revealed this detail, everyone gasped.

Mr Taran looked around; about twenty pairs of angry eyes were looking at him.

"Are you telling me," said Graham, "the door that was revealed after Hopkins dropped the bomb, the door that requires a password to open it, is hiding the secret weapon?" Abu nodded.

"And you knew the password all along, Sahid, and you didn't tell us! We'll be beating you up in the car park!" shouted Graham. His eyes joined the forty that were staring at Mr Taran.

Mr Taran was panicking. "No, I had no idea that the weapon was behind the door. I didn't even know it was here!"

"He's telling the truth," said Abu. "After the soldiers revealed the location of the weapon, they went away on a helicopter, I waited for Sahid. He came out and told me about the soldiers attacking the place and Rasponov escaping. He didn't mention the weapon or the password and I didn't mention what I heard.

"When the soldiers returned to their countries, General Vinny Leonard and Sergeant Arthur Hughes were told about the weapon. Hughes and Leonard decided to visit La Muliga secretly. The soldiers were sworn to secrecy. They travelled to La Muliga in late 1991 by helicopter. When they arrived, they saw the scientist Stefan Nance. Nance said he had been on holiday in Spain in 1990 and he had gone exploring on a boat and had found the island. He'd searched the whole place and had found a sign saying that the island was named La Muliga. Nance had decided to use the island as his secret lab. When he began using the lab, he started working on secret experiments. Years later, one such experiment would be the seeds that he genetically modified.

"After Hughes and Leonard heard Nance's story, they told him about the weapon. The three searched for the weapon but couldn't find anything, so they agreed to keep it a secret to avoid causing panic. Nance asked the sergeant and general to keep his lab and experiments a secret.

"In 1992, Rasponov was poisoned. Russian President Dimitry Valtev knew that Rasponov wanted to use the weapon and feared it would destroy the world. At that point, I gave up looking for the weapon. In 1999, I joined the Ramada Organisation and became leader of the organisation.

"This April, I decided to seek the secret weapon to get revenge on people who I'll tell you about later. I knew that, if I had a chance of finding the weapon, I would have to hack into files made by Arthur Hughes that were kept secret with the British government. As a computer genius, I hacked into them and found out that the weapon was located on La Muliga. I learned that Hughes and Leonard had visited the place and about Nance having his lab there. But the one thing that was missing was the password for the door.

"I knew that, if it wasn't in the files, the only way I could get it was by getting hold of my old friend Sahid Taran. My son Wasem had recently moved schools and told me his Biology teacher was called Mr Taran. It was confirmed that Mr Taran at City High School was the same Taran I had known when Wasem showed me a picture of him. So how was I going to get hold of him? I didn't want to directly kidnap him. People would notice, and I needed him here. Wasem told me that Mr Taran wanted to go on holiday. I came up with a plan.

"I asked my ally and assistant Michael Hopkins, who is secretly a member of the organisation, to set up a website and brochure showing La Muliga to be a beautiful holiday resort. As a senior person at Manchester Airport, Hopkins has the authority to introduce new rules at the airport. I told him to introduce a rule that ensured what was discussed in the airport stayed in the building and to make sure staff didn't ask people about their holidays. If either of these rules were broken, then the staff member would lose their job and never work again. These were introduced so that no one would discover the truth about La Muliga.

"It went to plan at first. Wasem gave Mr Taran the brochure. He liked the look of the place. But he handed it to James Turner. And in July, seven people were booked to leave for La Muliga. As Sahid was one of them, I let it go ahead. I realised that, if the holiday brochure was discovered, more people might book. I told Wasem to retrieve the brochure. I panicked when Wasem came home the day he had his science exam without the brochure.

"That night a man called Harry Barton booked to leave for La Muliga on 24 July. Thankfully, when Wasem went into school the next day, he found that Mr Barton had returned the brochure to reception, and it was given back to Wasem. Everything went according to plan. Eight of you went to the airport, and weeks before your flight, Hopkins went to see the ferry company to ask if they would collect you all on a ferry on 21 August, with the reason being that no planes would be able to get to La Muliga on that day. They agreed, and Hopkins asked them to keep quiet about it because it would be embarrassing for the travel company. Hopkins flew the eight to La Muliga.

"I had planned to get to La Muliga before today, but complications arose. My wife Lady Askar was in Russia, and I needed to retrieve her. Whilst we were there, we were spotted by a civilian who knew that we were members of the Ramada Organisation. We shot the civilian. Russia retaliated, so we fled to the United States. Whilst there, Hopkins phoned telling me he had flown Emma Fisher, Doris Miller, and Margaret Barton to La Muliga on 31 July, and now he was taking Fred Johnson's father to the island because he was wondering where Fred was. We fled from America to the UK. "I realised that getting to La Muliga would be difficult, and I couldn't waste time trying to dig up the secret door behind which the weapon is located. I contacted some members of the organisation and told them to go to La Muliga with a tracking device to place on Mr Taran. They drove to La Muliga on a boat and put a tracking device in Mr Taran's pocket. As they were leaving, they were seen by Scott Johnson, who was so shocked when he saw the Ramada Organisation's emblem on their clothes that he had a heart attack."

Before Abu could continue, Mr Taran shouted, "So that's what caused Scott's heart attack! It would've scared him when he saw the terrorists."

Everyone looked at him. He put his hand into the pocket of the only jacket he had on the island and pulled out the tracking device. He threw his head onto his knuckle.

"We put a tracking device on Mr Taran because Hopkins had a bomb prepared to drop on the island. The idea was to reveal the door that the weapon is behind to save us digging for it. We needed to make sure it was dropped while Sahid wasn't within its blast path. Otherwise he would've been killed, and I'd never find out what the password is.

"Hopkins dropped the bomb and the hidden door was revealed. After the bomb was dropped, Hopkins told me the news. I had to get to La Muliga before the ferry arrived. But now Betty Miller was concerned and ringing Manchester Airport. I told Hopkins to deal with it, because I couldn't waste anymore time getting to La Muliga. He brought Betty to the island, we moved out of the UK and into France, and most of us got on a boat at Marseille. We hijacked a helicopter and made our way to La Muliga. Here we are."

Silence followed when Abu finished. Everyone was speechless about all the revelations.

Finally, Graham asked, "So why are you here?"

"Mr Taran is going to tell me the password so I can open the door and get the weapon," said Abu.

No I'm not," said Mr Taran, letting out a laugh.

"You will. If you don't tell me, I will torture you until you do," replied Abu with an evil smile. "Tell me what the password is, Sahid."

"What do you want the weapon for?" asked Mr Taran.

"I want the weapon for revenge against the Great Witches, people who we've hated ever since they disarmed a bomb that we planted in the London Underground at the start of this year. I was angered by it so I, along with most of the organisation, stormed the witches' fortress in Greece. I was the only one who survived. I am going to use the weapon to take down those vile beasts who dared to mess with us. It will be justice for my fallen soldiers and a big two fingers up at Lady Gananthia," Abu sneered.

Everyone scoffed at him and asked if he was insane, speaking as if witches were real.

"You may not believe they exist, but trust me when I say they do," said Abu.

"We've learnt from an ancestry story that witches did exist," said Graham. "But I assumed they died."

"No. There's a group of them living in Greece" Abu said.

"If those witches disarmed a bomb that you set up, they sound like decent people. I don't trust you and your terrorist group with a weapon like that. I'm not telling you the password," replied Mr Taran.

"I thought it would come to this," said Abu. "One more time, Sahi. What is the password?"

"One more time. I'm not telling you," replied Mr Taran.

Abu ordered his men to take the group back to the cells, except for Mr Taran. Michael Hopkins said he would help. He pulled out a gun and aimed it at Doris.

Doris swore loudly at Hopkins for aiming the gun at her. At gunpoint, the group walked down the stairs, through the hotel and down into the cellar. They filled up the cells, and the cell doors were locked.

After Hopkins locked his last cell, he placed his key on the table and walked out. Once the terrorists were gone, everyone started talking about their shock at Wasem and Hopkins being allied with terrorists and being after a weapon that the Russians had hidden years ago.

"And now we know that it was those bastard terrorists who caused my dad to have a heart attack and who might cause his death," said Fred.

Scott was lying on the gurney fast asleep in the same cell as Rick, Alice, and Fred. However, as soon as Fred finished speaking, Scott suddenly woke up. "OOOOOO!"

Everyone instantly looked at him. Fred shouted "Dad! You're awake! You're alive! Thank God!"

Scott got up and said, "Quick everyone. I tried to tell you before. Terrorists are on the island!"

"We know, Scott. Fred, fill him in on the details," said Graham. Fred told Scott everything that had happened whilst he'd been asleep and what they now knew.

"And Sahid used to be friends with Abu and knew about the weapon all along?" asked Scott.

"He didn't know it was on La Muliga, so we can't blame him," said James. He was interrupted by a loud scream, followed by an evil laugh.

For the next minute, all they could hear was the scream followed by the evil laugh. They also heard the zapping of electricity and realised Mr Taran was being electrocuted. Then, everything went silent.

"Don't tell me they've killed him!" said Doris.

After another minute had passed, Mr Taran came down the stairs slowly, followed by Abu, Wasem, Lapom, and Hopkins. Mr Taran had bruises and burns on his face. It was clear by the look on Hopkins's face that Mr Taran had told them the password.

"Now I can put my master plan in action," said Abu.

Wasem picked up the keys, unlocked a cell and threw Mr Taran in it. As he was locking it, Graham asked, "The password has been a mystery to us all. What is it?"

"Mr Taran told us the password is Hovacs," explained Abu.

"Hovacs? What is that?" asked James.

"I was wondering the same thing, until I realised it's an anagram of, Chasov," said Hopkins.

13

The Plan

It didn't take long for the minds of the prisoners to rearrange the letters of the word 'Hovacs' and realise it was an anagram of Chasov.

"So what are you psychopaths going to do with us after you've got the weapon?" asked Graham.

"You'll be returning to the UK in coffins!" Hopkins laughed. Doris swore at Hopkins.

The five terrorists walked up the stairs out of sight. Everyone looked at Mr Taran and asked what the terrorists had done to him.

"They tortured me, beat me, electrocuted me, and threatened to shoot me," said a shaken Mr Taran. "I had no choice."

"We understand, Sahid," Graham assured him. "But I don't know what we're going to do. We need to stop the terrorists. But how can we get out?"

Suddenly, a bright light was shining in Graham and Rick's eyes. The light shifted out of their eyes, and they saw Fred outside the cells holding a torch.

"Fred why are you shining. Wait, how have you got out?" asked Rick.

I put a bit of paper into the lock. When Hopkins was locking the cells, mine didn't lock properly, and he didn't realise," explained Fred.

"Get the keys and let us out," said Rick.

Fred picked up the keys and unlocked the cells. Everyone stepped out.

"What do we do now? We don't know if any terrorists are in the hotel," said James.

Rick opened a drawer and found a remote. He pressed a button on the remote, and the wall above the desk opened to reveal hidden cameras.

"I put four cameras up in the kitchen, dining room, the corridor where the rooms are, and the terrace. Look, Abu is sat at the dining table with some other terrorists. If we listen carefully, we'll be able to hear what they're saying."

Everyone focused on the cameras and listened to the conversation.

Abu rose from the table and said, "I'd better get to the door and get the weapon."

One of the terrorists asked, "Are you sure you don't want anything from the banquet that will be made, Lord Askar?"

"No. I need to get the weapon as soon as possible," said Abu. "Where have my other men gone?"

"Two have gone to look around Nance's lab with Wasem and Lapom. Three are patrolling the corridor where the rooms are. One has gone down to check on the prisoners. The others are roaming the island," came the reply Abu and two terrorists left the hotel and made their way to the door.

A further two got up from the table and went down to the kitchen to prepare the banquet. They were seen on the camera in the kitchen looking in the cupboards.

A terrorist came in through the entrance. He was told to go up to the second-floor storage room, find Hakim, and ask him if he had programmed the controls for the main door into his laptop and to lock the door.

"This will ensure the prisoners don't escape, even if they manage to get out of the cells."

He went up to the rooms and was seen on the camera leaving the corridor to go to the storage room to tell Hakim to lock the main door. The prisoners heard a sound of the lock clicking into place. Looking at the cameras, the group saw that only some of the terrorists sitting around the table were armed with guns. The rest were not.

Graham turned to everyone. "We need to get out of the hotel and stop Abu from leaving La Muliga with the weapon. To do that, we need a plan. When we first arrived at La Muliga, I told you all to pick a job that you could do to match your skills. Now you need to think of something to do to help with the escape, whether you use your skills or the job you do."

As everyone was thinking, the terrorist who had been sent to check on them appeared. "What are you doing out of your cells?" he exclaimed.

Graham walked towards him, saying, "Can you feel the pain?" and snapped his neck.

Everyone looked at the dead terrorist and then at Graham, stunned at what he'd just done.

"I didn't know you're an assassin, Graham," said Fred.

"I'm not an assassin. I just thought I'd kill the terrorist. Anyway, any ideas for the escape?" asked Graham.

Mr Taran said, "I can help anyone who gets injured during the escape."

James was next to speak. "I have an idea, if Emma doesn't mind."

Emma confirmed she was willing to do anything to help.

"There's a cupboard in the kitchen where we put the vegetables once they've grown, and the terrorists are probably going to use them for the banquet. If me and Emma can sneak down to the kitchen and poison the vegetables, that'll kill the terrorists," said James.

Betty and Scott said they would assist with the poisoning. Betty added that the two terrorists in the kitchen would need to be killed. Once they were, she and Scott would disguise themselves as the terrorists and bring the food up to the rest of them.

Fred spoke. "I have an idea to help us get to the kitchen. I've written four short funny stories. The first was about a disastrous wedding. The second was about a man who comes across a talking mouse and the mouse says sexual things to him. The third is about a dove that goes to the doctors. And the fourth is about an incident in KFC. All my books are funny. But they're in my room, so we can sneak up to the rooms. I'll get my books and give it to the terrorists at the table to distract them while those of you going to the kitchen sneak down."

Megan said, "I can't really use washing clothes to help with the escape. But, since Hakim has control over the doors up in the storage room, why don't I go there, deal with Hakim, and unlock the door."

Mr Barton spoke next. "After retiring as headteacher of City High School, I became a voluntary examiner for the OCR Exam Board to mark GCSE English Literature papers. Just before coming to La Muliga, I marked most of the papers that were assigned to me, and the exam questions about literary heritage novels weren't answered well by the students. Some of the other examiners and I were at the OCR headquarters marking some of the papers, and I mainly gave out F's on the literary heritage novels. The significance of this is that when I gave an F, I said F, F, F, F!"

Listening to Mr Barton, the others looked surprised. When Mr Barton said, "F, F, F, F!" he said it with a deeper voice and sounded exactly like a dog barking.

He continued. "When any of the other examiners gave an F, they also started saying F, F, F, F! The reason I'm telling you this is because when we get to the floor with the rooms, I can turn the lights off so that the terrorists can't see, place cloths on the floor in the hope that they slip, and shout F, F, F, F! to distract them. Then they'll look for me."

"Good ideas," said Graham. "Now for my part. Has anyone heard me say, 'Can you feel the pain?'"

"Yeah, you did it to me when I stole your shoe, and you just did it to the terrorist," said Rick.

"What does that mean 'can you feel the pain'?" asked Mr Barton.

"It means I'm going to strangle you, and you're going to feel pain," replied Rick.

"You deserved it, Rick. I did it to you messing around. But I'm going to be doing it properly to the terrorists, at every possible opportunity, I'm going to say, 'Can you feel the pain?' and literally snap their necks," said Graham. "Also when the front door unlocks, I think a lot of terrorists are going to run in and try to kill us. But we'll be ready for them. Those at the table have weapons. So when they're dead, we'll get guns and kill the terrorists.

"One more thing, Doris, Rick, Alice, and Margaret haven't told me how they're going to help with the escape," said Graham, trying to name and shame.

Rick said, "I can't take part in the escape. So I'm going to lie on the gurney, and someone will have to push me." He lay down on the gurney. Everyone else was annoyed.

Doris decided to assist Megan. Alice and Margaret, who had helped build the hotel, decided to assist by leading the way during the escape.

"I thought you were trying to get out of taking part, Doris, and if you had, you'd be very sorry," said Graham.

"Graham, if you carry on like this, you'll be going to hospital if we get back to the UK," said Doris.

"Hospital? What for?" asked Graham.

"Serious and life-threatening injuries," replied Doris rather frighteningly.

Graham didn't know whether or not Doris was joking. The fact that Doris wasn't laughing made him think she wasn't, and, for the first time on La Muliga, he was scared. He was seriously worried that his wife was going to murder him back at home. He felt very relieved when Doris smiled and said, "I'm only joking, Graham."

"Oh, phew, good. Now we'll begin the escape," said Graham, his voice was shaky but happy.

Mr Taran walked over to the gurney that Rick was lay on and pushed it towards the others, planning to do something later on. They were ready to put the plan into action.

14

The Escape

Margaret and Alice began led the way to the dining room. They stepped over the body of the dead terrorist and headed up the stairs. Graham reminded everyone that Abu, Wasem, Hopkins, and Lapom would need to be killed. Abu was the priority target because they needed to make sure he didn't get the weapon.

They walked down the corridor that led to an archway that would take them to the main door and dining table. Continuing past the archway would lead them up the stairs to the rooms.

Alice and Margaret stopped next to the archway and everyone else did the same. Margaret peeped around the corner to see what was going on. She turned back around. "They're still at the table. The banquet isn't there." Everyone ran past the archway and up the stairs.

Meanwhile, upstairs, terrorists were patrolling the corridors of the rooms. Suddenly, all the lights went out, and all the rooms were in darkness.

Two of the terrorists walked towards the switch. As they did, they slipped on cloths and fell over. "Why are there cloths on the floor?" asked one of the terrorists, feeling the wet cloths with his hands.

More terrorists came to see what was going on and they too slipped over the cloths and fell over. Then they heard someone shout, "F, F, F, F, F!"

"Who's that?" asked a terrorist.

No one replied and the lights came back on. Many cloths were on the floor. At the other end of the corridor was Mr Barton sitting at a table. He had managed to get across the corridor in the dark, throwing cloths on the floor.

Mr Barton began again. "F, F, F, F, F!" This time, he banged on the table with his hands.

One terrorist said, "Isn't he a prisoner?"

"Yes," replied another. "So how did he get up here?"

"Get him," said a third.

All the terrorists walked towards Mr Barton, who was still shouting, "F, F, F, F, F!" They started running. Mr Barton got up from the table and ran from room to room, saying, "F, F, F, F, F!"

Graham appeared from the shadows and said, "Can you feel the pain?" He grabbed one of the terrorists and snapped his neck. The terrorist died instantly.

Mr Barton was running in and out of the rooms shouting "F, F, F, F, F!" while dodging the terrorists.

One terrorist didn't know whether to kill Graham or Mr Barton or go and ask for help downstairs. He looked at Graham, who was slowly walking towards him, and at Mr Barton, who was shouting, "F, F, F, F, F!" in his ear. In the end, he decided to punch Mr Barton.

He missed, and in that split second, Graham managed to grab his neck, say, "Can you feel the pain?" and kill him.

The other terrorists started to lunge at Graham and Mr Barton. Graham shouted, "Attack!"

The others appeared and started attacking the terrorists. Graham killed two more terrorists, snapping their necks, after saying, "Can you feel the pain?"

Once the terrorists were dead, Fred got his books and Emma started walking to the room that she stayed in. She went over to her collection of perfumes on top of the drawers. She picked up a bottle of perfume and a cup of water. She sprayed some of the perfume into the cup. She went into another room and returned with a bottle of bleach. She was making the poison. She poured the bleach into the cup. She opened the drawer and got a test tube and poured the water/perfume/bleach mixture into the test tube. Mr Taran had found the test tube in the mining pit and had given it to Emma, saying it might be useful one day. She put a cap on the tube to seal it and put it in her pocket.

Fred came out of his room with his four books to distract the terrorists.

"Now, Doris and Megan, go up to the storage room and deal with Hakim. Once he's dealt with, wait fifteen minutes. That should give us enough time to poison the terrorists downstairs, and use Hakim's laptop to unlock the main door and come down," said Graham.

Doris and Megan walked up the stairs at the end of the corridor. The rest walked to the other end of the corridor to go down the stairs they had come up.

When they were descending the stairs, everyone walked behind the gurney as Mr Taran wheeled it down the stairs.

Upon reaching the bottom, Graham held his hand up to indicate that everybody should stop. He looked at the table. Everyone who had been there previously was still there, but there was no banquet on the table.

Fred walked through the archway and stood by the table to distract them whilst the others went to the kitchen.

The main terrorist said, "How did you get out of your cell?"

"Never mind that. Read my books. They're very funny" said Fred, waving his four books at the terrorists. The main terrorist picked up his gun and shot Fred. Fred fell back, and his books landed next to him. He remained absolutely still.

The others standing at the archway gasped.

The main terrorist put his gun on the table, looked at Fred's body, and said, "Did that fool really think we'd read his books? We need to check the cells and see how he got out."

"We could," said a terrorist. "But first, why don't we read his books and see what he wrote about?"

The main terrorist picked up three of the books and put the fourth book on his seat. He gave the other three books to the other terrorists.

The terrorist reading Fred's first book started to laugh, saying, "What a disastrous wedding." Once he'd finished the book, he fell onto the floor laughing.

The terrorist reading Fred's second book fell off his chair because he was laughing so much as well. "That mouse is just a legend!" he exclaimed.

The terrorists who were reading Fred's third book also started laughing and also fell off their chairs laughing.

The main terrorist was reading the fourth book. He looked at Fred and said, "Fred, are you dead?"

Everyone looked at Fred. Now was the moment of truth. Fred's mouth moved. "Yes," he said.

The prisoners were relieved but then realised the terrorists might now actually kill him.

"No you're not," said the main terrorist. "Otherwise, you wouldn't have spoken. Come over here. I want to ask you questions about your book."

Fred stood up and limped towards the table, rubbing the spot where he'd been shot.

The main terrorist said, "So two guys went to KFC. Whilst they were eating, one noticed a maggot inside his chicken." The main terrorist then stopped talking and he too burst out laughing and fell on the floor.

With all the terrorists now laughing on the floor, Fred turned around to the others and nodded to tell them to run to the kitchen.

However, the main terrorist stopped laughing and said, "There's more."

Only Alice and Margaret had started moving to the kitchen, but they quickly ran back.

"After that, the guy threw the maggot to someone else, and the KFC just became infested with maggots." The main terrorist fell back on the floor in stitches again.

Everyone quickly ran past the laughing terrorists and went down the stairs to the kitchen. Mr Taran slid down the stairs on the gurney with Rick gasping. The terrorists were laughing so loudly that they didn't hear them go down.

Fred was debating whether to stay or disappear. He decided to sit at the table. The terrorists stopped laughing and sat back at the table.

In the kitchen, Graham said, "Can you feel the pain?" to the two terrorists who they found there. He snapped their necks. A lot of food was on plates on a table in the middle of the kitchen. It looked as though the banquet was ready.

Emma put a bit of poison from her test tube into some other test tubes so James, Scott, and Betty could assist her. They began poisoning the banquet.

Upstairs, Doris and Megan had reached the storage room. Doris opened the door to the storage room slightly and peeped inside. Hakim was sitting on the floor with his laptop on his lap.

Doris closed the door and whispered to Megan, "I can see Hakim. After I've finished speaking, we'll run in. I'll kill the bastard, and you can sort out the laptop. Then we'll wait fifteen minutes. Let's go."

Doris kicked the door open, and they ran in. Megan grabbed Hakim and wrestled him to the floor. Doris picked up a piece of rope and wrapped it around Hakim's neck and strangled him. His lifeless body went down, and Megan got the laptop. After doing lots of hacking and programming, Megan had control of the doors. "Fifteen minutes left," said Megan.

The food and drinks for the banquet were now poisoned. Betty and Scott were in disguise as the terrorists Graham had killed, whose bodies could not be seen. A hand poking out of a cupboard was a strong clue as to where they were though. Betty and Scott managed to get hold of plates full of poisoned vegetables and other poisoned food, like bread and cake. They reached the top of the stairs and took the food and drinks over to the dining table.

"Dinner is served," said Betty.

"Finally. What took so long?" said the main terrorist as food and drinks were put in front of each terrorist.

The terrorists picked up their knives and forks. The main terrorist stuffed his face with carrots. The other terrorists did the same.

After five seconds, all the terrorists started choking.

Mr Taran laughed, "I was going to beat you up in the car park. But now you're dead!" And all the terrorists fell to the floor, dead.

Back upstairs, Megan looked at the laptop and suddenly wondered if it had been fifteen minutes. She and Doris started to look a bit panicked.

"I'll run downstairs and see if they're ready. If they are, I'll come back and tell you," said Doris. She ran out of the room.

Downstairs, Mr Taran said, "Why's the door still shut?"

"I might have to go up and see what's going on," said Graham.

"No need, Graham," said Doris as she appeared around the corner of the archway. She saw the dead terrorists. "You've dealt with these then. I'll tell Megan to unlock the door."

As Doris sprinted upstairs, Graham turned to everyone and said, "Doris is gone. Everyone get into position for when the doors open. I can see some terrorists outside." Five people grabbed five guns from the dining table.

Doris sprinted up to the storage room at 15 mph. She opened the door, looked at Megan, and told her to open the door. Megan got hold of the mouse and moved it towards the switch.

Downstairs, the crew waited with tension. The main door opened. Thirty terrorists ran into the hotel, firing bullets. Margaret, James, Emma, Fred, and Alice started shooting at the terrorists, occasionally taking cover. Betty and Scott went down to the kitchen to get changed into their normal clothes. Mr Barton jumped onto the floor with his hands over his head. Graham tried to snap some of their necks, but he couldn't get close enough. Every time he tried to approach them, they shot bullets at him. So he took cover behind the archway. Mr Taran was hiding behind the gurney. Rick was terrified as he lay on the gurney, and bullets were narrowly missing him.

Mr Taran observed the soldiers fighting around him. He noticed that the shooters had very little cover, meaning any of them could die at any second. He thought of something that would benefit himself as well as the shooters but not Rick. He strapped Rick to the gurney. Rick tried to get up, but the straps were too tight.

Mr Taran grabbed the gurney and started pushing it towards the terrorists. "Come on Rick" laughed Mr Taran. "No Sahid!" screamed Rick.

Mr Taran pulled the gurney up so that Rick was practically standing up. The shooters saw this human shield and ran to take cover behind it. The terrorists started shooting, and ten bullets hit the gurney, narrowly missing Rick. Fortunately, all ten ricocheted back to the terrorists and killed them. Rick fainted.

Another terrorist fired at the gurney and knocked it down. The shooters ran back to the little bit of cover available to them.

Alice dived and landed near the table. A terrorist shot her in the arm. She yelled, and at that second, Doris and Megan appeared at the archway and hid behind it with Graham. Mr Taran, seeing that Alice had been shot, ran over with his first aid kit, leaving Rick by himself.

"Sahid! Come back, you idiot! I'm still strapped in!" shouted Rick. Terrorists walked towards the gurney, but those with guns fired nonstop at the remaining terrorists. After a minute, all the terrorists were dead. Mr Taran went back to the gurney and unstrapped Rick. Alice was now fine.

Graham shouted, "Come on, everyone. Get ready to leave the hotel. We need to deal with the senior terrorists." Rick decided to get up and walk as he was "feeling better."

Everyone followed Graham out of the hotel. It was dark outside. They all observed the area around them. Wasem and Lapom were standing by Nance's lab, and Abu was going down the stone steps to get the weapon.

Graham said, "We need to stop Abu from getting the weapon."

Before anybody could move, Doris shouted, "Wait!" Everyone turned around and gave her a bewildered look. "Where's Hopkins?"

15

The Chase and the Journey

Now panicking, they looked around to try and spot Hopkins. They heard a noise that sounded like helicopter propellers. A silhouette of a helicopter was flying towards the island. The helicopter was flying across the beach when its headlights came on. They shone on the trees between the campfire and the beach, blowing trees as the helicopter passed.

The light was shining on the group and, Hopkins was heard through a megaphone saying, "Lord Askar! The prisoners have escaped and are standing outside the hotel."

Doris called Hopkins a snake. The helicopter flew past the hotel and landed next to Nance's lab. Wasem and Lapom got into the chopper, and it rose back into the air, flying back in the direction it had appeared from.

When it passed the hotel, Hopkins said, "See you all tomorrow when we'll have killed the witches in Greece. If you're alive, that is!"

"No! That oddball can't get away with Wasem and Lapom!" shouted Doris.

Three terrorists arrived from the beach. Alice shot them. "Get to the beach and try and shoot down the helicopter," said Graham.

They walked past the trees and onto the beach. The helicopter was far away. They knew it would be useless to shoot at it. They saw the boat that the terrorists had arrived on. It was possibly their only hope of escape. Graham said they would deal with Abu and then go hom.

They ran off the beach, past the hotel, and over the stream and stopped at Nance's lab. Alice shot the two terrorists by the lab. James ran into the lab to see what the terrorists had done. He saw a few open books and concluded that the terrorists had only looked at those books.

When James came back out of the lab, everyone followed Graham to the stone steps. The metal door was still open. They ran down the stairs and entered the secret room.

The room was fairly big and felt like a chamber. The walls were made of stone, and in the middle was an empty cabinet, presumably where the weapon had been kept. At the other end was a tunnel, which looked like it ran underneath La Muliga.

Two terrorists were standing at the other end of the chamber. And there, next to the tunnel entrance, was Abu Askar.

Margaret shot the two terrorists and Abu ran away, disappearing through the tunnel system.

They ran as fast as they could to the tunnel to stop Abu. They saw that the tunnel stretched far and wide at a distance of about twenty metres. They heard the sound of someone climbing on ladders and knew it was Abu.

They ran into the tunnel, knowing they had to stop Abu. There was a trapdoor at the top of the ladder. Abu pushed it open, and a faint light shone on him. Those with guns fired at him, but he made it through the trapdoor and closed it behind him.

Mr Taran led the way to the ladder. He quickly climbed it, followed by the others. He pushed the trapdoor open and jumped through. He held it open for the next person and observed his surroundings. He was in a small building with seeds, drawers, a calorimeter, and other scientific material. As Graham came through the hole, he realised he was in Nance's lab.

Mr Taran hurried to the door and saw Abu disappear into the trees. He ran after him, and the others followed in a line. Branches slapped their faces, dirt was splashed on their clothes, everything they had built flew past them, and eventually they heard the sound of a helicopter.

James threw his gun to Mr Taran. He ran through a final set of trees and stepped onto the beach. The helicopter was right next to the sea; Hopkins and Wasem were in the front, and Lapom was in the back telling Abu to hurry up. Mr Taran aimed his gun at Abu's legs and fired.

Abu collapsed to the ground and clutched his bleeding leg. Wasem let out a scream, Lapom froze, and Hopkins turned pale. Abu looked at his colleagues and nodded, Hopkins knew they would have to leave their master behind.

The helicopter rose into the air just as Doris arrived, ready to shoot Hopkins. She saw the helicopter flying away and shot at it in vain. There was still one mystery that was not yet solved.

Abu crawled around to face his enemies. Mr Taran approached him and aimed the gun at him.

"Where is the weapon?" he demanded.

Abu laughed maniacally. The group were worried that it was on the helicopter with the three survivors. Abu's laughter then turned to a look of sadness and disappointment. "It's not on the helicopter."

A wave of relief swept through the group. "Where is it then?" asked Mr Taran.

"I really don't know," Abu revealed. "When the door was opened I went into the chamber, and the weapon was not there. I saw the tunnel and walked through it, went up the ladder, and came to Nance's lab. I realised that the scientist must have found the weapon and hid it somewhere. We searched his lab looking for clues as to where it might be, but we found nothing."

Everyone felt a sense of relief at Abu's revelation and a strong sense of gratitude towards Nance.

"I'm glad he did. We've got you now. Your plan fails, and the Ramada Organisation will be without a leader," said Mr Taran.

"This may be the end for me. But if you think it's over, you're mistaken. Whoever replaces me will try and find the weapon," Abu assured them.

"Good luck to whoever it is," said Mr Taran. With that, he fired five bullets into Abu's chest.

After the fifth bullet, Abu stopped moving. Graham put his hand on Mr Taran's shoulder and thanked him.

"It had to be done. He was my friend, but in the end he was a psychotic terrorist. If he had managed to use that weapon, then all hell would have broken loose. But where did Nance move the weapon to?" asked Mr Taran.

"Or did he move it? He could have destroyed it," said Scott. Everyone thought about Scott's suggestion in silence. There were two possible things that had happened. Either Nance had destroyed the weapon, or he had moved it somewhere else. The group wondered whether it was safe from the hands of the terrorists wherever it was. "I don't know what Nance has done with it. We'll have to tell the police if we get back," said Graham, pausing so that he had everyone's attention. "The boat that the terrorists arrived on is here. We can't swim, as there are sharks in the sea. It may take a while for the ferry to arrive. No one has a signal to contact anybody. I think we should take the boat home."

Everyone agreed and decided to start packing. All of them went up to the hotel and packed their stuff, including the blankets they had each been given. Everyone except James and Emma returned to the beach. Emma asked James if he was going to tell the others about what they'd found in Nance's lab. "What? The experiments or the notes?" asked James. "Both" said Emma. James thought and decided. "On the way home." They finished packing and went to the beach, where everyone else was waiting. To everyone's delight, the ferry was there. It was like a beautiful floating hotel. The back had been pulled down like a walkway, ready for everyone to step on. A man was standing next to the walkway, and he introduced himself as the ferry "Please enter," said the driver, and they stepped into the ferry up. He led them through a door to a staircase, with another door just in front of them. "These stairs lead up to the captain's quarters, and they lead down to the toilets," explained the driver. "We're going to the pier in Marseille and then to Marseille Provence Airport. You are all booked on a flight that departs at 2 p.m. It's 10 a.m. now. Did Hopkins not tell you all that?"

"No, he told us a ferry was picking us up on 21 August to take us back to the UK," said Graham. The driver went up the stairs, and the others went through a door. They were looking at a magnificent lounge. There was a bar, comfortable seats, and one long table. There was a pool table with the balls and cues on top. Graham pointed out a radio on the bar and turned it on. "I'll get you all a drink," said Graham. Scott decided to help him. The others took a seat around the table just as the ferry started moving. Betty confirmed her boat ride had taken forty minutes to get to La Muliga. "Well what an intriguing four weeks this has been. I didn't know what I signed up for the day James came to my house and I decided to come on the holiday," said Graham. He and Scott brought the drinks over and sat down. Rick said, "I remember that day well."

"Why?" asked Alice. "Me and James went to my grandma's house, and Grandma aimed a shotgun at me through the letterbox because she thought I was the rentman," said Rick. Everyone burst out laughing. Doris giggled, "It's a good job it wasn't the rentman, Rick. The rentman would be in heaven, and Nora would be in prison." The laughter died down, and Graham continued. "There are a lot of things that made our four weeks at La Muliga unique. But I never had a chance to have a good look around Nance's lab." Emma looked at James and gave him a look to indicate now was a good time to tell them. James decided to reveal the secret at last. "There's something I have to tell you about Nance's lab. I found a few things in the lab." Everyone listened intently to James. "The day Hopkins dropped the bomb, I thought about the places that may tell us what the password was, and I thought of Nance's lab. I had a good look around, but there was nothing that told me what the password was. I found a voice recorder. Nance had made a recording literally a day or two before he died. In the recording, he spoke about how he was interested in human strength and the brain. He said he had found a way to have more strength right away and have a better memory, vision, and self-control without an enlarged brain. At the end, he behind a picture of him in a frame was a key that would unlock a safe in the lab behind books on the bookshelf.

"I found the safe, opened it, and looked at the contents of the safe. First was the missing page from Nance's diary, which said that Nance himself built the oven in the cave to heat and cook food that he brought to the island. Lastly, there were two items, two results from experiments on human strength and the brain. They were two implants." "Implants are items you can put in your boobs to make them bigger," said Alice. "They are. But in this case, they are objects inserted into a person's wrist," said James. "Ah, one would give a person more strength, and the other would give a person a better memory, vision, and self-control?" said Mr Taran. "That's correct, and there were post-it notes on the implants to identify which was for strength and which was to improve the brain. I left the page in the lab, and I have got the implants with me," said James. He opened his suitcase and pulled out the two implants. The post-it notes were there, labelling them "strength," and "brain." Graham took them and had a look. They were passed around to everyone else. All looked at the implants thoroughly. They eventually got back to James. Graham asked, "You say that you found the implants the same day Hopkins dropped the bomb, but that happened five days ago. Why has it taken you so long to tell us?" James explained that he'd waited because everybody had been stressed. "Scott had had a heart attack and was asleep on the gurney. Hopkins had dropped a bomb. We were thinking about what had caused Scott's heart attack, what was behind the door, and what the password was. Then the terrorists turned up and we were forced to save ourselves. It was one thing after another."

"And you told Emma. First the ancestry story. Now this. Is there anything else you two know that we don't?" asked Graham."Yeah, I've not told you what I intend to do with the implants," said James. Graham turned the radio off so that he could listen to James without getting distracted. "I think it would be wrong for us to keep hold of them because they're not ours to keep. When the authorities search La Muliga, they're going to find Nance's lab and the voice recorder. When they find the safe is empty, they'll know we have them. I think the best thing to do is to hand them over to Nance's family," said James. "Good idea, James. Pass them to me. I'll make sure they get them," said Fred.

James handed Fred the implants and he put them in his suitcase. "I have something to tell you all too," said Mr Taran. Everyone shifted their attention to him.

"I've been finding random stuff in the mining pit. Yesterday, before the break, I found a box full of money. I put it in a safe place and can tell you that the amount is £60,000!" "Sixty grand!" shouted everyone.

"Oh my God!" "I counted it up yesterday, and I was going to tell you all when we were sat on the terrace. But the terrorists arrived, and I didn't want them to know. Luckily they didn't find it in the rooms," said Mr Taran. "It's in my suitcase." He opened his suitcase and pulled out the money wrapped in an elastic band. It consisted of £50 and £20 notes.

"There are thirteen of us, and I want the money to be shared equally," said Mr Taran. Graham suggested each receive £3,000, which equalled £39,000, leaving £21,000 for Mr Taran because he had worked to get it. Everyone agreed. "It's ten forty, so we have twenty-five minutes left, and we've not had a game of pool. Who wants a go against me?" asked Fred. Mr Taran said he would. The two of them set up the pool table as the others came over to watch. Mr Taran won the game, so Rick decided to take him on. Fred went over to James and said, "James, go over there, I need to tell you something." They walked to the bar where no-one could hear them. "Do you know who Tom Harris is?" asked Fred. "Not personally," said James, though he had heard of Tom by name. "He's my friend. He got excluded from Northump for spraying pepper spray into Bradley Mispon's eyes. Then Bradley sent his friends round to beat up Tom while he was at mine. My dad sent Bradley's friends away. Also every four days, he goes into a rage and destroys things in his house. He's behaving this way because he started smoking weed. Since then, he's become paranoid and developed distrust towards other people. Whenever he takes it he goes into one of his rages" said Fred. "And he's your friend?" asked James.

"Yeah but don't say anything, James Just keep it quiet," said Fred. He walked back to the pool table, and James stayed where he was. Emma approached him and asked if he had any plans for when they got back. "Probably just going to enjoy what's left of the summer holidays. You?" asked James. "I'm going to look up a bit more of my ancestry, because I want to know if Priscilla Fisher was indeed Jack the Ripper," said Emma. James told her to tell him if she found out. Everyone heard the sound of a bird tweeting and saw it had come from Fred's phone. He got his phone out of his pocket and saw it was a reminder about results day tomorrow. "Wait, if you've managed to receive the message, does that mean you've got a signal?" asked James. Fred nodded. James got his phone out but realised that the battery had died. Everyone else who had phones got them out, but most batteries had died. It was now 10.58 a.m. "We only have seven minutes left, so that'll explain the signal," said Graham, adding, "That also means BBC Radio News at 11 Live will be on in two minutes."

He turned the radio back on and switched to BBC radio just in time for the headlines at 11 a.m. The headlines were that it had been just over twenty-one hours since members of the Ramada Organisation hijacked four boats and a helicopter and were believed to be heading for an island called La Muliga. The British Prime Minister was on his way to Marseille to discuss the potential terrorist threat with the French president. "We're in the news!" said Rick excitedly. Mr Taran suddenly got up and walked out, telling the others he was going to the toilet. Mr Barton and Margaret slowly walked away from everyone. They desperately needed to talk to each other without anyone hearing. They found a spot, looked around to make sure no one could hear them, and started talking. "What are you thinking, Margaret?" asked Mr Barton. "The terrorists were after the weapon that we are protecting," answered Margaret. "My thoughts exactly," said Mr Barton. "I need to call Gerald." He pulled out his phone and made a call to Gerald Nelson, the current headteacher of City High School. "Harry, I've been expecting a call from you. Are you all right?" said Gerald. "I'm fine, Gerald. What do you know?" asked Mr Barton. "That members of the Ramada Organisation went to La Muliga," said Gerald. "Well the organisation was after the weapon," said Mr Barton. "The weapon, as in the weapon that you and Margaret, along with me and the others are protecting?" asked Gerald. "Yes. Let the rest of them know that the organisation was after it," said Mr Barton. "Okay. Let me know when you're home, and we'll meet and discuss it further," said Gerald. The ferry stopped in Marseille. Everyone collected their suitcases. The driver showed them the way out. They followed him through the ferry, and he opened a door to their side. It took a single jump to land on the pier below. One by one, the La Muliga crew jumped and walked up the pier. As they were walking, there were flashing lights from cameras, and a limousine pulled up at the end of the pier. The driver stepped out and opened the backdoor. The prime minister came out, followed by the French president. The prime minister walked down the pier towards them and asked if they were the people who had been on holiday to La Muliga.

"We are!" shouted Graham. "Thank goodness you're all safe. Did you encounter terrorists? And if so, where are they?" asked the prime minister. "Dead," shouted Rick. Fred walked over to the prime minister with the implants in his hands and asked him to give them to the family of Stefan Nance. Fred was relieved he had handed them over.

The prime minister took the implants. "So Nance finished another experiment before he died?"

"Yes. Hang on. Did you know that Nance's lab was on La Muliga?" asked Fred. "Of course," said the prime minister. "The British government is in possession of documents made by Arthur Hughes after he and Vinny Leonard visited La Muliga. The documents contained information about Nance's lab being there. He wanted it kept quiet, and we did so. But," his voice then reduced to a whisper, "they also said that Chasov's secret weapon was on La Muliga. I assumed the terrorists were looking for it. I didn't tell the citizens because panic would have been caused. Please tell me. Did the terrorists try and get the weapon?" "Yes," said Graham "Abu Askar wanted to use it to kill some witches. But the weapon is missing, and Abu is dead." "Witches? I didn't know they were still around. It's a relief Abu's dead and that the weapon hasn't been found. But the island should still be searched fully." The prime minister turned to the French president. "Would you be able to bring some troops to help search La Muliga?" he asked. The French president immediately started making arrangements, and the prime minister confirmed La Muliga would be searched first and then Nance's family would be given the implants. "Also, Prime Minister," said Doris, "three members of the Ramada Organisation managed to get away. One was Abu's son Wasem; one was a guy from the Belgian government called Monsieur Lapom; and the other was that terrible, dreadful, awful man Michael Hopkins. He took us to La Muliga and dropped a bomb on the island. They all, especially Hopkins, should go to a place in the sky." The prime minister assured Doris that the trio would be found. The French president returned and confirmed soldiers were on their way to accompany them to La Muliga. "Our plane leaves Marseille Provence Airport at 2 p.m. It's 11.13 a.m. now so we need to start making our way there," said Graham elderly people came off the coach. The French president spoke to the driver and asked him if he could take the group to the airport and then return to pick up the elderly people. The driver confirmed he could. "We'll need to ask you all some questions when we get back. But you've all had a tough night and want to get home, so I'll be in touch tomorrow," said the prime minister. The group acknowledged this and went to the coach. The driver came out and opened the side of the coach, and the suitcases were put into the empty space. Everyone got on the coach. As the coach began moving, the French president's soldiers were seen arriving. Meanwhile, on Central Road, the rentman was collecting rent from his tenants. He was dressed like a postman, but his uniform was blue. He had a blue cap to match. He reached the cottage, opened the gate, and walked down the path with cracked tiles. He knocked on the door. "Mrs Evans, it's the rentman," said the rentman. He waited for a minute. No one answered the door. He knocked again and called, "Mrs Evans, I know you're there. You've not paid rent for a year, so you now owe £12,000." He waited for another minute, and there was still no answer. The rentman started walking back up the path. But halfway from the gate to the road, he heard the letterbox open. The rentman turned around, and to his horror, the front of Nora's shotgun came through. The rentman backed away, and Nora shot the rentman. He fell to the ground. Nora opened her door, ran outside, grabbed the rentman by his foot, and dragged him into her house. Back on the coach, Megan and Alice were chatting about their experiences over the past four weeks and how they were looking forward to getting home. Alice asked Megan how her boyfriend was weeks," said Megan, looking at her phone as if she was about to receive a text from her boyfriend any second. "What's his name?" asked Alice. Megan whispered into Alice's ear, "Bradley Mispon." "The kid who tried to get Rick excluded from primary school?" asked Alice. "Yes, he's got a past with Rick and Fred's friend Tom Harris. He tried to get Rick excluded from primary school by saying that Rick assaulted him and got his friends to be false witnesses. But a teacher called Miss Taylor found out. She saved Rick, and Bradley got excluded. As for Tom, he sprayed pepper spray in Bradley's eyes at Northump, causing him to get excluded. Then Bradley sent his friends to beat up Tom," said Megan. "Why are you with him? He sounds like bad news," said Alice. "I used to love him, but we've grown distant," said Megan. After another forty-five minutes, the coach arrived at Marseille Provence Airport. Everyone got trolleys for the suitcases. They entered the airport and went through the same procedure as they had at Manchester Airport. First, their suitcases were checked in and weighed. Next they received their boarding passes and went through passport control, which took them to 12.45 p.m. They agreed to have a wander around the airport and meet by the intercom at 1.40 p.m. James, Fred, Emma, Rick, Alice, and Megan walked to WH Smith to get snacks for the plane. Rick and Alice went inside, and the other four stayed outside. While Rick and Alice were in the shop, James noticed a woman of around fifty years of age looking at the newspapers. She was tall and wearing a long yellow summer dress. He thought she looked very familiar. Then he realised she was Miss Taylor, Rick's favourite teacher who had saved him from being excluded. James told Fred. Megan looked uneasy. "Wow, it is Miss Taylor!" said Fred excitedly when he saw her. "Should we go up to her?" asked James. "Let's tell Rick first," said Fred. He told Rick that Miss Taylor was standing by the newspapers. Rick looked, and when he saw her, his face lit up like a baby boy who had found his favourite teddy bear. He started walking towards her and the others followed him. "Miss Taylor!" shouted Rick. Miss Taylor looked over and smiled. "How nice to see you all again. I've been in Marseille for a week and am now going home. What about you lot?" Rick told her everything that had happened at La Muliga. "They were an interesting four weeks. Was Bradley Mispon there?" joked Miss Taylor. "No, of course he wasn't. You remember saving me then?" asked Rick. "Yes, that little brat tried to get you excluded. But I discovered the truth, and Mispon got excluded," said Miss Taylor.

Megan tried her best not to look at Miss Taylor. "I'll never forget it," said Rick. "I'd better get going. My plane leaves soon. It was nice to see you all again, and I'll see you soon," said Miss Taylor. She paid for her newspaper and left the shop. It was after she had gone when Rick wondered whether she would be on their plane. Once the snacks were purchased, they ran to the intercom. The others were already there waiting. With everyone now together, Graham led them to the gate. Passengers were going onto the walk-on to board the plane. They joined the other passengers, and on the plane, they sat close to each other. Doris said, "If Hopkins is the pilot, I'm going to strangle him." The pilot then spoke. "Good afternoon ladies and gentlemen. My name is Andy Dawson, and I will be your pilot for this flight. The flight to Manchester was going to be one hour, but due to the wind, it's likely that we will arrive thirty minutes later. During that time, you will have the opportunity to buy food and drinks from the food trolley. A film will also be on during the flight. Now, ladies and gentlemen, the plane will prepare to take off." The air-crew made sure everyone had their seatbelt on and that all phones were either off or on flight mode. The crew went through the emergency procedures, and the plane started moving around. It circled the runway, and then shot down it and rose into the air, en route to Manchester.

Once the plane was airborne, everyone heard James ask Graham what would be happening once they got to the airport. Graham's response was that family members should be there. Half an hour later, Miss Taylor approached James and told him Bradley Mispon was on the plane, sitting in front of her, and saying vile things about his girlfriend. James knew that Megan was his girlfriend.

"He called her a tart and was boasting about how he hates her and has been seeing other girls behind her back," explained Miss Taylor. "But when he mentioned that she'd gone to La Muliga, I realised she must be on this plane. Where is she?"

James led Miss Taylor to Megan. He told her that her boyfriend was on the plane, and Miss Taylor told her what she had heard him say about her.

Megan immediately stood up and stormed down the plane's aisle to find her cheating boyfriend. Miss Taylor grabbed Rick and pulled him out of his seat. "Come and watch this!" James, Miss Taylor, and Rick followed Megan through the plane. Eventually she found who she was looking for. Bradley was a short boy with a comb of gelled brown hair. He was sitting with his friends. "Megan!" Bradley gasped, shocked. "What are you doing here?" "I'm a tart, am I? You hate me, do you? You've been cheating on me, have you?" shouted Megan. She slapped her boyfriend across the face. Miss Taylor and Rick laughed hysterically.

"Won't lie to you, Megan," said Bradley. "I'm not the type of person who sticks to one girl." "Well you've just lost a type of girl who sticks to one lad," said Megan. Bradley felt embarrassed on the plane. He was insulted by his girlfriend dumping him in front of a plane full of people. "Don't speak to me again," ordered Megan, and she walked back to her seat. Bradley noticed Miss Taylor and Rick and realised one of them was behind his public embarrassment. "Miss Taylor and Richard Evans, what a coincidence you two are here as my girlfriend dumps me," Bradley snorted. "You obviously didn't listen to me at school, Mispon," said Miss Taylor. "But I can still teach you things, so I hope today I've taught you to be a bit nicer to girls." Rick and Miss Taylor returned to their seats and watched the film. Just after the film finished, Dawson confirmed they were commencing their descent. The plane landed at exactly 3.30 p.m. All passengers got off the plane and walked across the runway to enter the airport. They immediately went to the baggage collector to get their suitcases. Miss Taylor and her husband found their suitcases, waved a final goodbye to their acquaintances, and left. The group from La Muliga had their suitcases within five minutes.

Graham led everyone out of the baggage collection area. They walked past shops and came to the arrivals lounge. Nearly thirty familiar faces were there waiting for them. Paul, Helen and Holly were standing farthest to the left. In a line going to the right were Angela and Nora (Rick's mother and grandmother). The rentman was not there. Parents, partners, and family members of the other people were also there.

The arriving passengers went to the waiting family and friends, and there were lots of hugs and kisses, as well as a lot of exclamations of, "Thank God you're all right," and, "We heard what happened on the news," being made. Everyone said something to everyone.

Rick finished telling Angela and Nora everything that had happened at La Muliga. Rick was curious why his grandma was at the airport. Nora said she had come to see them arrive home and that she had a bit of business to take care of. Rick and Angela wondered what business Nora had been taking care of, as she was acting suspicious.

James's phone began to ring, and he saw it was Emma calling. He looked around and saw her holding her phone to her ear. She mouthed, "Answer it." James answered the phone.

"James, where's Mr Taran?" asked Emma.

James looked around for Mr Taran. He couldn't see him. He saw Mr Taran's wife, but he wasn't with her. She was looking confused too. He looked back at Emma. James realised something was wrong. He ran to Graham and asked him to get everyone's attention because something was very wrong. Graham suddenly yelled, "Oiiiii!" at the top of his voice. He then quietly said, "James wants to say something."

Everyone gathered and looked at James. He nervously said, "I don't know what's happened, but something's wrong. Where's Mr Taran?"

16

The Last Mission

Silence loomed in the lounge at the airport. Everyone turned around and looked in all directions. But no one could see Mr Taran. Confusion and fear was evident in the face of Mr Taran's wife. She was shaking as she looked around the lounge for any sign of her husband. Many people recalled where they'd last seen Mr Taran. James said he had definitely on the ferry. Scott remembered him going to the toilet. Graham asked if anyone remembered seeing him on the coach.

No one said anything. The silence was scarier than somebody saying they hadn't seen him on the coach. Mr Taran's wife covered her mouth as she gasped. Her fear was that her husband was still in Marseille.

The British prime minister then appeared, followed by the French president. The prime minister explained that British and French soldiers had searched La Muliga, while others had searched the ferry. "On La Muliga, we found Nance's lab, a cave, a mining pit, a hotel! and."

"But what did the men find on the ferry?" interrupted Mr Taran's wife. "They didn't see your husband, but they found this letter," said the prime minister. Graham held out his hand, so the prime minister gave him the letter. Graham unfolded it and read it out loud:

"Dear bastards, You thought you'd won because my father's dead. Well, this is far from being won. After leaving La Muliga, Lapom, Hopkins, and I landed. We contacted some members of the Ramada Organisation to come to La Muliga straight away. Lapom got off, and Hopkins and I made our way back.

We saw a ferry coming away and we were told that Abu had been found dead, meaning the organisation needed a new leader. Of course the new leader was going to be me or Hopkins. But because I'm Abu's son, it's going to be me. Whenever a new leader is appointed, he must kill an enemy. I jumped off the helicopter, swam around the back of the ferry, and entered it. I saw Mr Taran going to the toilet so I knocked him out. Hopkins will come back to the ferry using a boat. By the time you've read this letter, Mr Taran will probably be dead in the secret room. You know which room I mean.

Signed, Wasem Askar." Mr Taran's wife sat down and put her head in her hands. Scott piped up, "So, Wasem and Hopkins have Sahid."

James said, "But surely, Prime Minister, you or someone from the French president's army would have seen the terrorists and Mr Taran at La Muliga."

"You'd think. But we didn't see them. They could have been behind that door," said the prime minister.

"What door?" asked James. He and everyone else who had been to La Muliga listened very carefully to the prime minister.

"There was a metal door that we couldn't open because it required a password, and we had no idea what the password was," said the prime minister.

"Hovacs! The password is Hovacs and Chasov's weapon was behind the door," said James.

Some of those standing there started to look confused, wondering what Hovacs and Chasov's weapon were.

Graham said, "We need to go back to La Muliga and save Mr Taran. I'm going. Who's with me?"

Everyone who had been to La Muliga walked towards Graham and stood next to him. Rick's grandmother Nora announced that she was going as well. Angela asked her mother if she would be all right at her age.

"I own a shotgun, remember," said Nora.

"When was the last time you shot someone, Mum?" asked Angela.
"Today. Umm, ummm, I mean, I've never used it before, just threatened people with it," said Nora with an innocent smile.

The French president offered to take them to La Muliga in the military jet that was always on emergency standby. It would take twenty to thirty minutes to get to La Muliga on the jet. The group were curious how the jet could get them to La Muliga in twenty to thirty minutes when the trip had taken a normal plane two hours. But before anyone had a chance to ask him, he told everyone to follow him. He started running through the arrivals corridor, followed by everyone who was going to La Muliga.

Andy Dawson, the pilot who had brought them to Manchester, was walking down the corridor holding a plastic cup of coffee. The French president grabbed Dawson's ID badge and ripped it from around his neck. Dawson nearly dropped his coffee.

"Sorry, this is an emergency," said the French president. He needed the ID badge to get through the security doors. He led the way through doors, down the stairs, and finally onto the runway. He ran to the jet, and the pilots were standing smoking. He said, "Retournez sur le plan. Son urgence" (Get back on the plane. It's an emergency). The pilots threw their cigarettes on the floor and ran onto the jet with the others following behind.

The pilots started up the jet, and it started moving. It circled the runway and went shooting down the runway and into the sky. The speed of the jet dramatically increased. The passengers were forced back against their seats. There was a turbo booster at the back of the jet.

Emma then needed the toilet. James stood up to let her pass and held onto the seat in front as he walked onto the aisle. If he hadn't been holding onto the seat, he would have flown to the back of the jet. Emma got past James, James was about to sit back down when Fred ran and sat in Emma's seat.

"James you've not told anyone about Tom Harris, have you?" asked Fred.

"No, Fred. But why are you friends with him?" asked James.

"Because we've been friends for ages," said Fred, shrugging his shoulders.

Emma returned from the toilet, so Fred got up and walked back to his seat. James felt Fred was making a mistake by being friends with Tom Harris.

Later, the French president went to the back of the jet. He came back with guns, which he handed out to all the passengers.

Once all the passengers were armed with guns, the French president explained how the jet was going to land. The pilots announced that the plane was landing. It landed on the sea. The jets wheels had gone in, and in their place were gliders so that the jet floated on the sea. The jet slowed down, turned sideways and eventually stopped. The doors on the right of the jet opened and everyone unfastened their seatbelts. Everyone stepped off the jet and onto the beach of La Muliga. A boat was next to them and something was lying on the sand, dead. Most of the people had seen it before. But it was Fred who had the best memory of it. It was his nemesis, the deer.

Lying dead before them was the deer that had knocked Fred off his feet, the deer that Fred had vowed to kill, the deer that Fred had never managed to kill. Now someone had beaten him to it. "How's the deer dead? I was supposed to kill it," said Fred.

"I also wonder where the deer was hiding all this time. But quick, to the door," said Graham. The body of Abu Askar was close to the deer. Everyone ran past the body, past the campfire and hotel, over the stream, and past Nance's lab and reached the stone steps. Graham, with the others behind him, ran down the steps. The door was closed, so he typed "Hovacs" on the computer, and the door opened.

Looking inside the chamber, they could see the backs of approximately forty terrorists. Doris, Mr Barton, and Scott were standing on the steps, which gave them an advantage as they could see past the terrorists. They could see Mr Taran on his knees, with Wasem and Hopkins on either side of him. Wasem was holding a gun, aimed at Mr Taran. Michael Hopkins saw that the door was open and, therefore, saw that they had guests. "Oh look," said Hopkins. "The cavalry has arrived!" The terrorists all turned around and the "cavalry" started shooting. The terrorists didn't have guns, so they ran around trying to dodge the bullets. Amid the shooting, Hopkins said, "Quick, Wasem, kill Mr

Taran and replace your father as leader of the Ramada Organisation." The French president heard Hopkins, and he was armed with a sniper. He shot Wasem's gun, which broke and flew out of his hand. "Quick, use my gun!" said Hopkins as he handed his gun to Wasem. Doris saw this and, with very good aim for a pistol, shot Hopkins' gun, destroying it. Mr Taran dived forward into the crowd. Ten seconds later, all forty terrorists were dead. Mr Taran ran to safety to the others. Everyone aimed their gun at Wasem and Hopkins. "Just so you know, I shot the deer," sang Hopkins. "You bastard, I was supposed to do that," said Fred. "You never were good at anything, Fred. That's why the deer managed to survive for as long as it did," Hopkins laughed. "Hopkins, you're an asshole, and how you became a pilot, I'll never ever know," said Doris, and she pulled the trigger on her gun. Hopkins jumped sideways and then forward. Everyone else started shooting at him. Hopkins headed to the tunnel. Doris tried her best to kill the man she hated so much, but her bullets missed and Hopkins went through the tunnel. He shouted, "You missed, Doris!" Wasem was left on his own, weaponless. "Why didn't the terrorists have weapons?" James asked him. "We didn't think we'd need them," said Wasem. "Fool, you did need them," said Mr Taran, now holding a gun. He shot Wasem, who fell forward. "Good, Sahid. Now Wasem's dead," said Graham. "But Hopkins isn't. We need to prevent him from getting away again" said Doris. She ran up the stairs, and everyone followed her. As they were running, a couple of the group asked Mr Taran if he was all right. He said he was just shaken up.

The group came to Nance's lab. They knew that the tunnel ended there, having chased Abu before. Hopkins was nowhere to be seen by the trapdoor, but he had to have been through it. They reached the beach and saw that the boat was gone. They knew that Hopkins had escaped.

"No! Hopkins has gotten away!" shouted Doris. "I wouldn't worry, Doris. At least Wasem's dead. So the world will be a safer place," said Graham. "The world will never be a safe place as long as Michael Hopkins is alive," said Doris. They all got back on the jet to be taken home. An hour later, a woman arrived at La Muliga. Her boat hit the beach, and she emerged from it, running through the trees to find him, way ahead of her guards. If he was dead, they would be very sorry. Killing her husband was bad enough. But if they had killed her son as well, there would be a bloodbath. She came to the door and saw the keyboard. Hopkins had told her the password was Hovacs, so her fingertips bounced on those letter keys. The door opened, and she ran into the chamber. The bodies of the terrorists were scattered all over the floor. But where was he? She turned the bodies over but didn't see him. She turned around and saw Wasem holding his wound, blood escaping through the gaps between his fingers. He smiled at his mother, and she returned her smile.

Lightning Source UK Ltd.
Milton Keynes UK
UKHW010608050519
342118UK00001B/19/P

9 781728 386508

FROM SABBATH TO SABBATH

Returning the Holy Sabbath to the Disciples of Jesus

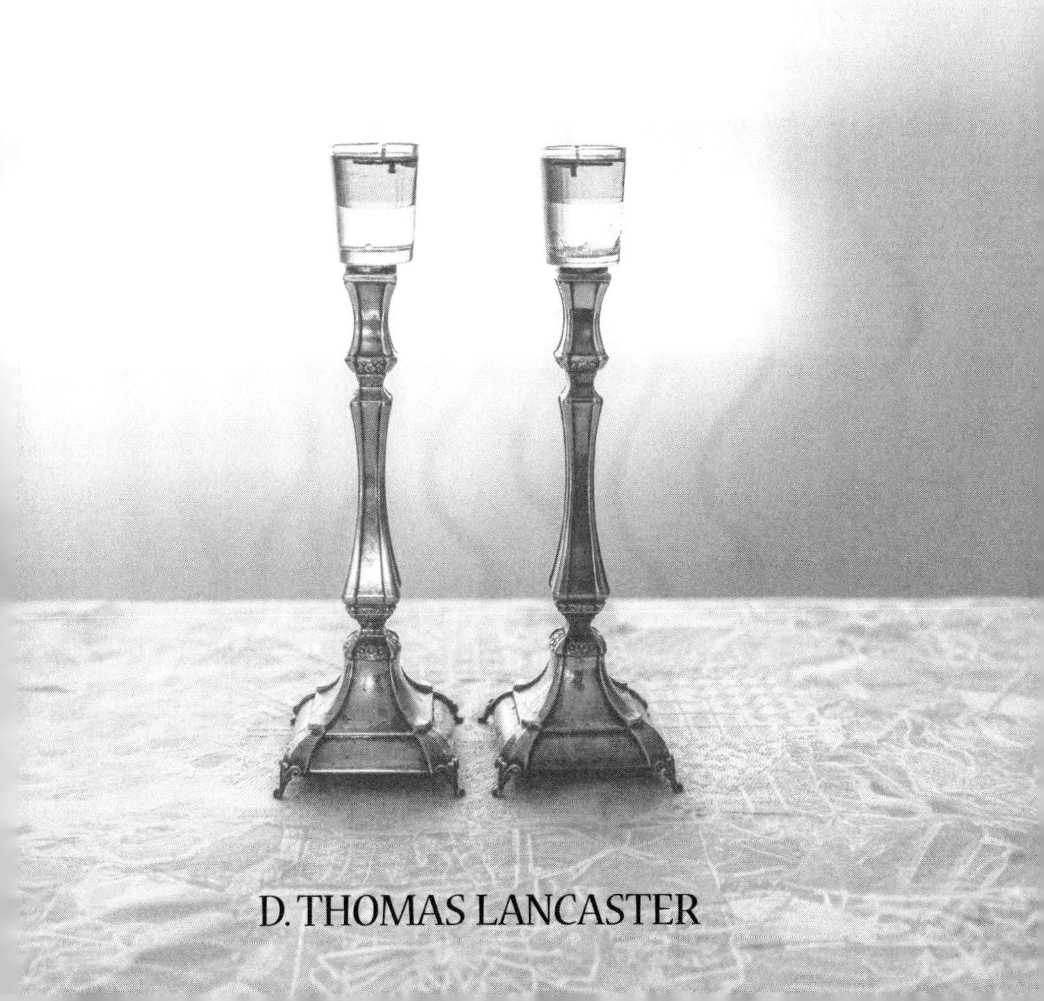

D. THOMAS LANCASTER

FROM SABBATH TO SABBATH

Returning the Holy Sabbath to the Disciples of Jesus

D. THOMAS LANCASTER

FIRST FRUITS OF ZION

FIRST FRUITS OF
ZION

First Fruits of Zion is a 501(c)(3) registered nonprofit educational organization.

Printed in the United States of America

ISBN: 978-1-941534-74-8

Cover design: Boaz Michael

Quantity discounts are available on bulk purchases of this book for educational, fundraising, or event purposes. Special versions or book excerpts to fit specific needs are available from First Fruits of Zion. For more information, contact ffoz.org/contact.

First Fruits of Zion

Israel / United States

PO Box 649, Marshfield, Missouri 65706–0649 USA
Phone: (417) 468–2741 Web: ffoz.org

Comments and questions: ffoz.org/contact

To Maria Anne

אשת חיל

and soul companion

CONTENTS

INTRODUCTION

Why Christians Might Consider Keeping the Sabbath

Why would disciples of Jesus keep the seventh-day biblical Sabbath? The Sabbath is its own reward. The reward for keeping the Sabbath is that we get to keep the Sabbath. The biblical, seventh-day Sabbath creates a weekly cycle of encounters with holiness. Once a week God beckons us to enter into a sanctuary in time where our souls can find spiritual rest and nourishment in his presence. On the Sabbath we can set aside the cares and concerns of daily life and focus on the things of the kingdom of heaven. The Sabbath allows us to slow down enough to spend quality time in God's presence, learning the things of his Word and plugging in to extended periods of prayer, study, and worship. On the Sabbath we spend time with our families and reconnect with fellow believers, fellowshiping under a pervading sense of the holiness of the day.

SPIRITUAL RECHARGE

In this way the Sabbath functions as a spiritual recharge from which we can draw new energy and fresh stamina. We can use that weekly infusion of spiritual refreshment to carry us through the coming week. We use the recharge of the seventh day to sustain us in the mundane world of the other six days of the week.

The laws of the Sabbath force the Sabbath-keeper to submit his will to God and to rest in his provision. Ceasing from our labors reminds us that God is our provider and sustainer. He is the true Creator.

If we choose to ignore the Sabbath, we do not in any way diminish the holiness of that day. God himself has declared the Sabbath holy and blessed. The Sabbath is still the Sabbath whether we participate in it or not. By failing to keep the Sabbath, we only exclude ourselves from it. We forfeit the blessing and holiness that Sabbath has to offer.

WHY KEEP THE SABBATH?

Why would New Testament believers keep the Old Testament Sabbath?

One could simply argue that the Sabbath is a commandment in the Bible. In fact, it is one of the Ten Commandments. It's also one of the Bible's most oft-repeated commandments. It's God's holy day. It seems natural that Bible-believing people will want to keep the Sabbath.

This is a good reason, and it's all the reason many believers need. But there's an even greater significance to the Sabbath than just the keeping of a commandment. This significance is drawn from Jewish tradition, which gives us a prophetic reason for keeping the Sabbath. Jewish teaching says that the seventh-day Sabbath provides a glimpse of the future, a foretaste of the kingdom of heaven. It prefigures the Messianic Era.

Moses revealed that God created the heavens and the earth in six days, and on the seventh day he rested. Yet the early rabbis did not view the story of the seven days of creation merely according to its literal reading. They viewed the story of the seven days of creation as a blueprint for the future, a broad outline for human history, as the Scripture says, "For a thousand years in your sight are but as yesterday when it is past, or as a watch in the night" (Psalm 90:4). The rabbis compared each of the six days of the creation week to a millennium of history. The seventh day, the day of the Sabbath, represents the seventh millennium—the Messianic Era.

In the poetic words of the rabbis, the Messianic Era will be "the day that is altogether Sabbath."

The rabbis envisioned a one-thousand-year era of Sabbath rest, so to speak. The New Testament refers to the "thousand years" of Sabbath rest as the era of the kingdom of heaven. In fact, the biblical idea that history works together toward a final culmination and era of redemption is based on the weekly cycle of six days followed by the Sabbath rest. One might even say that the whole concept of an end-times redemption and kingdom era hangs upon the observance of the Sabbath.

So the Sabbath is not just an Old Testament idea. The Sabbath is all about the future. It's all about the coming kingdom.

WHAT IS THE "KINGDOM OF HEAVEN"?

Every disciple of Jesus is obligated to seek first the kingdom of heaven: "Seek first his kingdom" (Matthew 6:33). All other concerns that pertain to this material world are irrelevant when compared to that one, single, overarching goal—but what is the kingdom of heaven?

Contrary to popular belief, the kingdom of heaven is not a matter of going to heaven when you die. The kingdom of heaven is the reign and rule of God through his righteous Son the Messiah. The kingdom refers to the Messianic Era when the knowledge of the LORD will fill the earth and the revelation of God will become universal. In that day there will be no agnostics or atheists. The existence of God and his presence in the world will be obvious to everyone.

When the kingdom comes all nations will ascend toward the light of Messianic Jerusalem where the righteous Messiah son of David will sit upon the throne of David and administer justice to the entire world. He will teach the Torah (Law) of God to all nations, and the Torah will go forth from Zion, the word of the LORD from Jerusalem. The kingdom will bring an era of universal peace. Then the wolf shall dwell with the lamb, and the leopard shall lie down with the young goat, and the lion and the calf together (Isaiah 11:6). The Prince of Peace will rule the government, and he will judge between nations. They will not make war against one another any longer. Swords will be beaten into plowshares. Spears into pruning hooks. Resources once spent on creating weapons will be spent on worthy ends.

The Messianic Era will blossom in an age of miraculous fertility. "In that day the mountains shall drip sweet wine, and the hills shall flow with milk, and all the streambeds of Judah shall flow with water" (Joel 3:18). In that day there will be no poverty because everyone will sit "under his vine and under his fig tree" (Zechariah 3:10), an indication that everyone will be self-sufficient. The LORD will make the land "like Eden … like the garden of the LORD; joy and gladness will be found in her, thanksgiving and the voice of song" (Isaiah 51:3). There will be no more hunger, starvation, or plague. Everyone will have enough.

In the kingdom of heaven God will raise the righteous to eternal life, and man will be able to reach his true spiritual potential. The Spirit of God will subdue man's evil inclination and recreate man's inner nature. Man's evil inclination will submit to the good. Satan will be bound with chains. He will no longer hold sway over men's minds.

In the kingdom the righteous resurrected will sit at the table of Abraham, Isaac, and Jacob, and will dine with King Messiah. Then the Messiah will drink of the fruit of the vine again with his disciples. Then it will be said, "Blessed is everyone who will eat bread in the kingdom of God" (Luke 14:15).

Our holy teacher and rabbi, Jesus of Nazareth, taught us to diligently seek the kingdom. Every disciple of Jesus should be living for the sake of entering the kingdom. Our Master taught us that if we will believe in him and cling to him—like a branch growing from a vine that does not let go—he will bring us into the kingdom. Not only in the future to come, but right now as well. We can take hold of the kingdom of heaven now. We do not need to wait until the Messiah comes to enter the kingdom; in a spiritual sense, we can experience the power, peace, and perfection of the kingdom right now. He said, "The kingdom of heaven is at hand."

The true disciple of Jesus lives his whole life for the kingdom—both for the future and for the experience of the kingdom right now. Every day, he prays, "May your kingdom come and may your will be done on earth as it is done in heaven." He seeks to prepare himself for the reward of the kingdom by his service to God in this age, and he seeks to bring the kingdom into this world through his attachment to the Messianic King and the presence of the Holy Spirit of God. This is a full-time endeavor.

DAY OF THE KINGDOM

The rabbis claim that the Sabbath offers a foretaste of the kingdom and the World to Come. How so? The weekly Sabbath provides us with a preview of the Messianic Era by devoting an entire day to the LORD every week—a day of peace and tranquility dedicated to rest, to prayer, to Bible study, to festive meals, and to the things of the kingdom.

Moses Maimonides (Rambam), the great codifier of Jewish law, summarizes the kingdom of heaven with these words:

> And in that time there will be neither hunger nor war, neither jealousy nor competition, but goodness will spread over everything. And all the delights will be as common as dust. And the whole world will have no other occupation, but only to know the LORD. And therefore Israel will be great sages and knowers of secret things, and they will attain a knowledge of their Creator as far as the power of man allows, as it is written [in Isaiah 11:9], "For the earth will be full of the knowledge of the LORD as the waters cover the sea." (Maimonides, *Hilchot Melachim* 12:5)

That beautiful description of the kingdom also applies to the Sabbath. The kingdom will be an era of universal peace. On the Sabbath we set aside the sorrows of daily life and enjoy the Sabbath peace *(Shabbat shalom)* of the holy day. We experience the peace of God on the Sabbath, and we live in peace with one another on the Sabbath, setting aside all conflict and strife.

The kingdom will be a time of satiation, abundance, and universal prosperity. There will be no hunger or starvation. Although we may hunger during the rest of the week, we eat well on the Sabbath, for there is no hunger on the Sabbath. Although we may eat sparsely and dress humbly during the rest of the week, we set out the best foods on the Sabbath and don our best finery because, on the Sabbath, "delights" are common, and we "call the Sabbath a delight" (Isaiah 58:13).

In the kingdom the chief occupation of humanity will be to know the LORD. Although we may strive, compete, and undergo all manner of stress, pressure, and angst during the rest of the week, on the Sabbath there is no war, jealousy, or even competition. Although we have many pursuits to occupy us during the rest of the week, on the Sabbath we have no other occupation except "to know the LORD." On the Sabbath we occupy ourselves with prayer, with the reading of the Bible, and the study of the Word. This is how we come to "know the LORD."

The Sabbath offers a weekly foretaste of the era of peace and rest when Messiah will rule the earth. By celebrating the Sabbath, we can participate in the kingdom of heaven on earth even now. The Sabbath can be compared to a down payment on the coming age of Messiah. The rabbis say, "We rest on Shabbat to symbolize the peace that we will have in the days of the Messiah" (*Tz'enah Ur'enah*).

If for no other reason, disciples of Jesus should keep the Sabbath because the Sabbath is all about the kingdom, and Jesus teaches us to seek first the kingdom.

Still, even were it not for this prophetic significance, the Sabbath remains a commandment of God—one of the big ten.

THE TEN COMMANDMENTS

Most people in Western society know about the Ten Commandments, even if they are not able to list all ten. God spoke the Ten Commandments at Mount Sinai and carved them into two stone tablets. Moses wrote them into the holy scroll of the Torah. Cecil B. DeMille made them into a major motion picture starring Charlton Heston. Up until recently, the Ten Commandments adorned the walls of American courthouses. In 2005 a split decision of the United States Supreme Court ruled that the Ten Commandments cannot be displayed in court buildings or on government property. Why? Because they represent Judeo-Christian faith. They uniquely symbolize the whole Bible, and the United States government attempts to separate itself from endorsing any particular religion.

The Ten Commandments summarize God's Law. Like a top ten list, the Ten Commandments catalog the top ten of God's 613 commandments. Christians generally agree that we should all keep the Ten Commandments. Even most Christians who maintain that Christ came to abolish the Law agree that the Ten Commandments are still valid. But not all Christians believe we should keep all Ten Commandments. For example, Martin Luther taught that Christians should not keep the commandment of the Sabbath: "Remember the Sabbath day, to keep it holy" (Exodus 20:8).

Depending on who is doing the counting, the Sabbath ranks as either the fourth commandment (Judaism, Orthodox Christianity, Reformed Christianity) or the third commandment (Roman Catholicism, Lutheranism). Martin Luther felt strongly that Christians should not observe the commandment of the Sabbath. He wrote a book called *Against the Sabbatarians* in which he argued that Christians should not keep the Sabbath—not on Saturday (as the Jews do) nor on Sunday (as the Christians do) nor on any day of the week. He believed that Christ abolished the Sabbath and that when Christians try to keep the Sabbath, they do Christ a disservice.

Despite Luther's opinion about the Sabbath, many Christians believe in keeping the Sabbath on Sunday, the first day of the week: The Christian Sabbath. Some say that it does not matter what day you observe as the Sabbath, so long as you keep *a sabbath* once a week. It could be Tuesday. It could be any day, so long as you take a day off once a week. After all, we all need a break once in awhile, right?

This type of confused thinking about the Sabbath is a symptom of a much larger problem: the church's confusion about the role of Torah and the Jewish people. It wasn't always like this.

Long ago, in the days of Jesus, no one had any questions about what day was the Sabbath or whether or not we should keep it. In those days a different Christian Sabbath did not yet exist, and no one had abolished the Law. Jesus was a Jew. His Hebrew name was Yeshua (we will use his Hebrew name throughout this book). Yeshua warned his Jewish disciples, "Do not think that I have come to abolish the Law," and as an observant Jew himself, Yeshua kept the Jewish Sabbath on the seventh day. The Bible says that he went to synagogue every Sabbath. He was so concerned about the proper way to keep the Sabbath that most of his arguments with other religious leaders pertain to the Sabbath. He even told his disciples they should pray that they would never need to flee from persecutors on the Sabbath. His apostles kept the Sabbath. Even Paul kept the Sabbath.

Today, things are different. Most Christians do not know which day is the biblical Sabbath. Those who do know are usually not certain about the reason they do not observe the Sabbath. This book is about why Christians and disciples of Yeshua might want to think about celebrating the biblical Sabbath in some way or another.

SABBATH FOR JEWS AND GENTILES

Let me put all my cards down on the table, face up. I am a Gentile Christian "Sabbatarian," a Sabbath-keeper, but I did not grow up that way. I grew up going to church on Sunday. My father was the pastor of an Evangelical, Bible-believing church. Today I am a teacher in Messianic Judaism, even though I am not Jewish. My wife and I have been practicing Messianic Judaism for more than twenty years, and we have raised our four children in the Messianic Jewish movement. We have found the Sabbath to be a source of great spiritual blessing, and we want to offer the Sabbath to other disciples of Yeshua.

We are Sabbatarian, but not because we believe that we have to keep the Sabbath to earn our salvation or to find favor with God. We choose to keep the Sabbath because it offers us a foretaste of the kingdom.

The Sabbath is not about legalism. Observing the Sabbath does not earn salvation. As I mentioned above, the reward for keeping the Sabbath is the Sabbath itself. This book will not condemn you or make you feel less spiritual if you do not keep the Sabbath.

If you are a Jewish believer, I am going to try to convince you that the biblical Sabbath belongs to you, and that it is something you should take seriously. It is part of your heritage, part of your rich inheritance as a son of Israel.

If you are a Gentile Christian, I am not suggesting that you are sinning if you do not keep the Sabbath, nor do I suggest that worshiping on Sunday is wrong. My goal is to explain the origin and significance of the Sabbath and to try to convince you to keep the Sabbath too. I believe that Gentile Christians are not obligated to keep the Sabbath in the same way that Jewish people and Jewish believers are obligated to the Sabbath, but I also believe that we should all, at the very least, remember the Sabbath and do our best to sanctify it, whether we are Jewish or Gentile.

God gave the Sabbath as a special gift and a sign to the Jewish people, but the Sabbath can also be enjoyed by Gentile disciples of Yeshua. Yeshua teaches, "The Sabbath was made for man" (Mark 2:27)—that is, for humans. He did not say, "The Sabbath was made only for Jewish people." Isaiah the prophet says that the Sabbath is also for "the foreigners who join themselves to the LORD, to minister to him, to love the name of the LORD, and to be his servants, everyone who keeps the Sabbath and does not profane it" (Isaiah 56:6).

ISN'T THE SABBATH CANCELED?

By now the Christian reader has probably raised some objections: "Wasn't the Sabbath canceled? Didn't it get changed to Sunday to celebrate the resurrection? What about keeping the Lord's Day instead of the Sabbath? Isn't that why we worship on the first day of the week, the day Jesus rose? Didn't Jesus break the Sabbath and free his followers from observing the Law?"

These objections are all based upon the venerable tradition of Christian interpretation regarding the Sabbath, but I believe that the tradition reflects a misinterpretation of the good news of Yeshua. The Messianic Jewish perspective reflects a different interpretation: that the gospel and the new covenant function in continuity with the Torah (the Law of Moses). The death and resurrection of the Messiah, the proclamation of the gospel, and the institution of the new covenant did not cancel the Law, its ceremonial commandments, or its holy days. Therefore the seventh-day Sabbath remains the day of rest and a day set apart as holy to the LORD. Sunday has not replaced it, nor has grace canceled it.

In the earliest days of Christianity—the days of the apostles—all believers honored the Sabbath because the Sabbath was the weekly day of worship. Less than a century later, as Gentile Christianity left Judaism, it also began to leave the Sabbath behind. For most of Christian history the Sabbath has been lost and forgotten. This book is about finding the Sabbath again and putting it back in its rightful place.

To accomplish that objective, I have divided the book into four parts. Part One, "A Taste of Sabbath," introduces the broad concepts of the biblical Sabbath and its observance. Part Two, "Yeshua and the Sabbath Conflicts," examines the conflict between Yeshua and the religious authorities of his day regarding the Sabbath. This material originally appeared in *Chronicles of the Messiah* and my booklet *The Sabbath Breaker: Jesus of Nazareth and the Gospels' Sabbath Conflicts*. Part Three, "Other New Testament Objections," takes a look at select passages from the Epistles that are commonly cited as objections to Sabbath observance. Part Four, "From Sabbath to Sabbath," tells the story of how early Christianity lost the Sabbath and how modern Messianic Judaism is finding it again.

SHABBAT SHALOM

In this book I will make the argument for restoring the Sabbath to its place of prominence among the disciples of Yeshua. I will argue that we should keep the Sabbath as a foretaste of the kingdom of heaven after which we daily seek and for which we daily pray. I will argue that we should keep the Sabbath, as best we might be able, in obedience to the precept.

At the same time, I admit that many brothers and sisters in the faith will disagree with my arguments; others will fail to be completely convinced, and still others will find numerous obstacles that prevent them from entering the Sabbath. I do not want readers of this book to feel in any way pressured or coerced by my arguments, and I certainly do not want anyone to feel condemned for not keeping the Sabbath. Every soul has his or her unique path to fulfill, and ultimately, our Father in heaven will direct our paths if we are open to the leading of his Spirit. We are all in different places, different circumstances, and we may well come to different conclusions. The world has already seen enough religious people throwing stones at one another, and throwing stones is not appropriate on the Sabbath day.

The Sabbath is about peace. That's why Sabbath-keepers greet one another with the words, "Shabbat Shalom," which means, "Sabbath Peace." Whether or not you decide to enter into the world of the Sabbath, I sincerely hope that you will nonetheless taste a little bit of the Sabbath Peace—the Shabbat Shalom of the coming kingdom, "the peace of God, which surpasses all understanding" (Philippians 4:7).

PART ONE
A Taste of Sabbath

CHAPTER ONE

Sanctuary in Time

> A rabbi once hosted an important Roman dignitary on the Sabbath. The Roman asked him, "Why does this food taste so delicious?" The rabbi replied, "We Jews have a special spice we use." The Roman said, "Give me some of this spice to take home. I will pay you whatever the cost." The rabbi replied, "The ingredient to which I am referring is called 'Sabbath.' It cannot be bought, nor can it be used by one who does not keep the Sabbath. The Sabbath adds its own extra flavor to all its dishes." (*Midrash Rabbah*)

Every Friday night, as the sun sets, something spiritual happens. The Sabbath begins. Whether we observe the Sabbath or not makes no difference at all. The Sabbath begins with or without our permission and with or without our participation. Over the next twenty-four hours or so, a spiritual peace rests upon the world, and the day of blessing offers its bounty and rest to the weary.

A Taste of Sabbath

In Sabbath-observant homes people prepare for the Sabbath on Friday before the holy day begins. Food is prepared ahead of time—enough food for Friday night and all day Saturday. Bright Sabbath candles are already glowing on the table before the sun sets. The best dishes, the finest silver, and a clean tablecloth adorn the tabletop; shimmering red wine awaits the blessing. From the kitchen wafts the warm smell of fresh hot Sabbath bread and a delicious chicken soup. As guests arrive for the Sabbath meal, they are greeted with the words, "Shabbat Shalom!" Soon everyone is seated around the table, singing Sabbath songs, prayers, and blessings. Conversations about the Scriptures and the weekly Bible portions continue late into the night, until at last the workweek is a distant memory.

The next day the Sabbath continues with prayer and worship services at which the community gathers to hear the weekly Bible readings and to study the Word together. Sabbath morning services are followed by a quiet afternoon, more festive meals, visits to friends, games with the children, gentle walks through the neighborhood, maybe a nap, and always an exalted sense of the day's holiness. It's much more than a day off from work. It's a day with the LORD.

Finally, at the end of the day, after the sun has set and the Saturday night stars have begun to appear in the sky, the Sabbath ends. The Sabbath-keeper bids the holy day farewell as the Sabbath departs and the regular weekday resumes.

I have had the privilege of spending many Sabbaths in the holy city of Jerusalem and experiencing the *Shabbat shalom* that settles over the city as the Sabbath begins on Friday night. Shops and stores close early on Friday afternoon. People head home early from work. Traffic on the ordinarily swollen and jammed streets decreases to a trickle. The incessant honking of horns falls hushed. In some religious neighborhoods traffic disappears from the streets completely. Shortly before sunset the Shabbat siren sounds to indicate that the time for lighting the Sabbath candles has arrived.

A sweet spirit of quiet descends as the light of the western sun fades and the cool breezes of the Mediterranean Sea begin to whisper across the city. The sidewalks fill with people dressed in their Sabbath finery as people head out to synagogue for prayers, to welcome the Sabbath at the Western Wall, or to visit friends for the evening. They exchange greetings of "Shabbat Shalom" as a deep peace ensconces the transformed city.

Saturday morning the sun rises over the Mount of Olives and all is quiet. Most people are enjoying a morning to sleep in, but others can be seen out on the sidewalks on their way to and from synagogues. Later in the afternoon families stroll in the parks, enjoying a Sabbath day walk. Neighbors are chatting. A sense of holiness hangs in the air.

That night, as the stars begin to appear in the sky, the city wakes from its slumber. Stores open. Lights go on. Cafés and restaurants fill up. Music plays. Traffic returns to the streets, and the city returns to normal as holy time comes to an end.

THE WEDDING GIFT AND THE BRIDE

God gave the Sabbath to the Jewish people at Mount Sinai as a sign of his covenant with the children of Israel. The rabbis compare the covenant ceremony at Mount Sinai to a wedding between God and Israel. Along the same line of thought, the Sabbath can be compared to a wonderful wedding gift. Wrapped up in blessing and holiness, this gift continues to radiate the love of God every week.

People on the outside of the Sabbath sometimes think of the Sabbath as part of the bondage of the Law, something difficult and unpleasant—a heavy yoke. In Messianic Judaism the Sabbath is our delight; it is our joy; it is our treasure; it is our most prized possession. It is the oldest heirloom of the family of God.

Out of all time and space and all energy and matter and all the things that comprise this incomprehensible vast reality that we know as the universe, the Sabbath was the first thing that God set apart as holy:

> For in six days the LORD made heaven and earth, the sea, and all that is in them, and rested on the seventh day. Therefore the LORD blessed the Sabbath day and made it holy. (Exodus 20:11)

On the Sabbath, when we are relieved of the burdens of the secular workweek, we spend extra time in prayer and study, enjoying the holiness of the Sabbath day. It is not just a day off from work. By keeping the Sabbath, we enter into that special blessing and holiness that God bestowed upon the Sabbath day.

The Sabbath stands from the beginning of time as the first institution of godliness, before man made the first temple or altar, before God gave the Bible or a single commandment, before David wrote a single psalm or any man prayed a single prayer. The rabbis say that the Sabbath was the last thing God made, but the first thing he intended:

> This may be compared to a king who made a bridal chamber, which he plastered, painted, and decorated. What did the bridal chamber lack? Only a bride to enter it. Similarly, what did the world still lack after six days of creation? Only the Sabbath. (*Genesis Rabbah* 10.9)

Jewish liturgy compares the Sabbath to a beautiful bride. The Jewish people are the bridegroom. Every Friday night, as the sun goes down, worshipers in the synagogues turn to face the setting sun, which symbolizes the approaching Sabbath day. They sing, "O come my beloved, to greet the bride. Let us welcome the presence of the Sabbath!"

REMEMBER THE SABBATH

The Ten Commandments tell us to "remember the Sabbath day, to keep it holy" (Exodus 20:8). In the Bible, "to remember" can mean to act in accord with one's obligations. For example, God "remembered" Noah in the ark. He remembered Abraham when he spared Lot. He remembered his covenant with the forefathers when he redeemed Israel from Egypt. In a similar sense, to "remember" the Sabbath means to honor one's obligation to keep the Sabbath.

The rabbis explain that we should remember the Sabbath all week long by preparing for it. For example, if a person comes across a nice article of food or drink during the week, he should set it aside for the Sabbath.

The commandment to remember the Sabbath applies every day, even on Sunday, the day after the Sabbath—which is also six days before the Sabbath. Judaism numbers the days of the week according to their relationship to the Sabbath. Sunday is called the first of the Sabbath; Monday is the second of the Sabbath, and so forth.

The Sabbath-keeper remembers the Sabbath even when he is busy and does not have time for a day off, because the Sabbath comes with or without our permission. Our busy schedules do not dictate God's universe or his appointments. We remember the Sabbath even when we feel far from God and do not want to keep his day. When the sun sets on Friday night, Sabbath IS. The Sabbath is not like going to church, which a person can choose to attend or not, nor is it like television, which we can choose to turn on or leave off. Sabbath happens, whether we remember it or not. By choosing to forget the Sabbath or by electing not to keep the Sabbath, we do not in any way diminish the Sabbath; we only exclude ourselves from it. The banquet is still set out on the table whether we accept the invitation or not.

SANCTUARY IN TIME

In his book *The Sabbath,* Jewish philosopher Abraham Joshua Heschel writes about the Sabbath as a sanctuary in time. Just as there are holy places in the world that we might regard as sanctuaries in space, the Sabbath is a holy day, and it creates a sanctuary in time.

The concepts of Sabbath and Sanctuary intertwine. The Torah hints about the relationship between God's Temple and the Sabbath. Before beginning to instruct the children of Israel about all the work of building the Tabernacle, Moses first reminds them of the commandment to rest from work on the Sabbath: "Six days work [on the Tabernacle] shall be done, but on the seventh day you shall have a Sabbath of solemn rest, holy to the LORD" (Exodus 35:2). Before they can build God's Sanctuary in space, they must enter his sanctuary in time.

A sanctuary consists of defined holy space. In the days of Moses, as soon as a person set foot within the Tabernacle he had entered into holy space. Levitical guards watched over the boundaries and guarded the gates of the Sanctuary to prevent people from inadvertently profaning the holy space. Like the Tabernacle, specific defined limits demarcate the holiness of the Sabbath. Specific borders mark off the beginning of the Sabbath and the ending of the Sabbath, setting it apart from the normal day. As the sky darkens on Friday night, the Sabbath has begun, and we have entered into holy time.

Those entering into the holy space of the Tabernacle did so expecting an encounter with God. They entered his courts seeking after his presence. In the same way, when we enter the Sabbath, we should enter with the expectation of encountering God on his holy day.

Many of the rituals of the Sabbath allude to the ceremonies of the Temple. The lighting of the Sabbath candles can be compared to the kindling of the menorah. The double portion of fresh Sabbath bread can be compared to the bread of the Presence, which the priesthood ate on the Sabbath. The double portion also alludes to the continual burnt offerings, which were doubled on the Sabbath day. We salt the Sabbath bread in accordance with the command to salt the offerings in the Temple before offering them on the altar. The Sabbath table is likened to the altar within the Sanctuary; the kiddush cup of wine is like the cup of libations, which the priesthood poured out over the altar in the Temple.

The Bible says that the Temple is the LORD's earthly dwelling place, a reflection of his heavenly abode. The Sabbath functions in the same manner. As a day given over to the things of God, it becomes a day filled with the Dwelling Presence of God.

A HOLY DAY

The Sabbath is a holy day, but what does "holy" mean? In modern English we use the word "holy" as a vague synonym for words like "spiritual," "religious," and "moral," but in the Bible, the word "holy" implies something that has been set apart for the exclusive service or honor of the LORD. Something that has been set apart for the LORD cannot be used for normal things.

The opposite of holy is not evil. An unholy thing is not a wicked thing. An unholy thing is a normal thing that can be used for normal purposes. The English word "profane" refers to something common and normal—the opposite of holy:

HOLY: set apart for the LORD

PROFANE: normal, common, ordinary

I'll give you an example. The Torah gives us a recipe for making the specific type of incense used in the Temple, but then it warns us, "You shall not make it for yourselves. It shall be for you holy to the LORD. Whoever makes any like it to use as perfume shall be cut off from his people" (Exodus 30:37–38). That particular combination of spices and fragrances is holy, so it cannot be used for normal purposes, such as perfuming the air in your home.

A sanctuary is holy space. It consists of a specific plot of ground set apart for the LORD. The holy space within the boundaries of the Sanctuary is dedicated to the worship of the LORD. The Sabbath is similar. God made the Sabbath holy, and likewise he commands us to make it holy. An object becomes "holy" or "sanctified" when it is set apart and reserved for ceremonial or divine service. A place becomes holy when it is set apart by clear boundaries, and dedicated exclusively for ceremonial, divine service. How can time be made holy?

Judaism sanctifies time by setting a period of time apart with clear boundaries. On Friday night, we make a legal declaration (*Kiddush*, i.e., "sanctification") over a cup of wine, stating that the Sabbath is holy and that holy time has begun. On Saturday night, after the sun has set and the day has concluded, we make a second legal declaration (*Havdalah*, "separation") over a cup of wine, stating that holy time has concluded. The two declarations clearly demarcate the holy from the normal, creating our sanctuary in time.

While it is true that the Sabbath was made for man, the Sabbath day is nonetheless holy to the LORD, a day set apart for God. We may spend the Sabbath in a variety of ways, fellowshiping in the company of family and friends, engaged in study, prayer, or the enjoyment of nature, but first and foremost, the Sabbath is LORD's day. It belongs to him.

DELIGHT AND HONOR

Keeping the Sabbath holy requires more than just a verbal declaration. Sabbath-keepers make the Sabbath holy by keeping it separate from normal days. Those things that define our normal time and fill the six normal days of the week must be held at bay on the Sabbath. Certain things do not contribute to the holiness of the Sabbath.

For example, your television has nothing to contribute to the holiness of the Sabbath. Neither do the radio, the internet, the smartphone, or the daily newspaper. A football game or sporting event likewise has no holiness to lend to the Sabbath. Media sources only waste precious holy time by filling a person's mind with the normal, mundane things of the day-to-day world. Using God's holy time for the profane is like stealing from God.

On the other hand, the Sabbath gives us time to attend to things that go neglected during the rest of the week. The Sabbath is a day for studying Torah and spending extra time in prayer. Time spent with one's spouse, children, family, and faith community is time well-spent on the Sabbath. Taking a walk, taking a nap, or taking time to sit around the table to sing hymns together are the kind of gentle things that compose the fabric of the Sabbath and make it feel holy and different.

The Prophet Isaiah speaks of the obligation to consider the Sabbath a delight and to honor it: "If you turn back your foot from the Sabbath, from doing your pleasure on my holy day, and call the Sabbath a delight and the holy day of the LORD honorable; if you honor it, not going your own ways, or seeking your own pleasure, or talking idly" (Isaiah 58:13). The Sabbath-keeper should consider the Sabbath a delight. He has the delightful duty to "sanctify the Sabbath with food and drink and clean clothing, all of which he enjoys, and God rewards him" (*Deuteronomy Rabbah* 3:1). Jewish tradition reserves the most elaborate meals of the week for the Sabbath in order to increase our delight on that day. The traditional Jewish Sabbath includes three festive meals: Friday night, Saturday after the morning prayers, and Saturday afternoon:

> And how does one delight in the Sabbath? Rav Yehudah ben Rabbi Shmu'el ben Shilath said in the name of Rav,

"With a large bowl of beets, a big fish, and a few heads of garlic." Rabbi Chiyya ben Ashi said in the name of Rav, "So long as it is prepared in honor of the Sabbath, even a small portion of food is a delight." What constitutes a small portion? Rabbi Papa said, "A gefilte-fish." (b.*Shabbat* 118b)

THE THREE MEALS OF THE SABBATH (AND ONE MEAL AFTER THE SABBATH)		
1	*Erev Shabbat* (Sabbath Eve Meal)	Friday Evening
2	*Kiddusha Rabba* (Great Sanctification Meal)	Saturday Lunch
3	*Se'udah Shlishit* (Third Meal)	Saturday Afternoon
	Melaveh Malkah (Escorting the Queen Meal)	Saturday Evening (after Sabbath)

To honor the Sabbath day, Jewish tradition requires the Sabbath-keeper to dress his best on the Sabbath. Sabbath-keepers consider the Sabbath to be no less a grand affair than a formal wedding or a function of royalty. We dress accordingly for the holy day.

The Sabbath-keeper does not seek his "own pleasure" on the Sabbath (Isaiah 58:13). The Talmud says, "A man should not pray for his material needs on the Sabbath." On the Sabbath, our prayers are not material requests and petitions for this or that or the other thing. Instead, our prayers are prayers of praise, thanksgiving, and worship.

A Sabbath-keeper should not speak "idly" on the Sabbath (Isaiah 58:13). This means avoiding conversations that pertain to mundane and profane matters. The Sabbath is not a day for discussing business, money, sports, entertainments, ambitions, or any of the mundane concerns of the common days. Talking about politics, world events, or one's occupation adds nothing to the Sabbath's holiness, nor does it help set it apart unto the LORD. Conversation should center on matters of faith, Bible, Torah, and godliness. The Talmud tells a story about a certain rabbi whose mother was prone to talk too much about idle matters on the

Sabbath. Whenever she did so, her son would gently remind her, "Mother, today is the Sabbath."

PHYSICAL AND SPIRITUAL SANCTITY

The Prophet Isaiah says, "Blessed is the man ... who keeps the Sabbath, not profaning it" (Isaiah 56:2). To "profane" something is to make it common and ordinary. The children of Israel are commanded to sanctify the Sabbath, i.e., to set the day apart as holy. This goes beyond just the prohibitions on work. Sanctifying the Sabbath requires an effort on the Sabbath-keeper's part to make the day different from other days of the week by elevating it in every way possible. The Sabbath-keeper tries to protect the Sabbath from intrusions by the outside world and mundane concerns and routines. In his comments on Isaiah 56:2, Rabbi David Kimchee (Radak) offers an explanation of what it means to keep from profaning the Sabbath in both the physical sense and the spiritual sense:

> This includes the sanctification of the Sabbath, i.e., the obligation to distinguish it from other days, for every expression of sanctification denotes elevation over something else ... Thus the Sabbath must be sanctified over all other days of the week with more elaborate food and drink, and with clean garments. This is its sanctification in the physical sense. In the spiritual sense, one must sanctify the Sabbath by freeing himself from thoughts of mundane matters and by engaging in words of Torah and wisdom and pondering God's wondrous deeds. (*Mikraoth Gedoloth*)

THE GOD OF DISTINCTIONS

The Sabbath teaches us to distinguish between the holy and the profane. That's important because the Bible calls us to live holy and godly lives. If we do not understand what holiness is, how can we live it out?

A popular modern theological sentiment claims that, for Christians, every day is a holy day and every place is a holy place. In Christ there are no longer any special days of sanctity. In Christ there is no longer any particular holy place. Those are things that belong to the Old Testament world. The New Testament world makes everything holy in Christ. True worshipers worship the Father in spirit and truth, not at a particular place and not at a particular time. The true worshiper esteems all days alike.

We will consider this argument in greater detail later in this book, but for now think about this. If every day is holy and every place is holy, then nothing is holy. Holiness implies separation from the profane, but if there is no profane (because everything is holy), there can be no sanctification to separate from it. The universal holiness of time and space eliminates holiness completely. If everything is holy, nothing is holy.

By observing the Sabbath, we learn to begin to make biblical distinctions between holy and profane, and this, in turn, teaches us about God. God is a God of distinctions. He separated between light and dark to form day and night. He separated between the waters above and the waters below to make heaven and earth. He separated between earth and sea to create the dry land and the oceans. He separated between male and female to create human beings. After six days of creating, he separated between the six days and the seventh day. When God gave the Torah through Moses, he further separated between the clean and the unclean, between Israel and the nations, and between the holy and profane. All these separations indicate that God is a God of distinctions. He teaches his people to distinguish between wrong and right, between wickedness and righteousness, between wisdom and folly, and so forth. It's difficult to imagine a religion more antithetical to the Bible than a religion that erases distinctions.

By sanctifying the Sabbath day, the Sabbath-keeper makes the Sabbath holy and also enters into the Sabbath's holiness. The observance of the Sabbath teaches the Sabbath-keeper to distinguish between the holy and the common, and those skills, in turn, teach the Sabbath-keeper about other important biblical distinctions.

CHURCH ON SATURDAY

You might suppose that I am suggesting that churches should move their worship services to Saturday morning instead of Sunday. That's not necessary, and it would not really help honor the Sabbath if they did.

Sabbath observance does not lend itself well to the seeker-sensitive trends in modern Evangelicalism. Today's seeker-sensitive churches do their best to imitate the popular culture. A good worship service seems like a rock concert. A good sermon sounds like a TED Talk. A good church service does not last longer than an average episode of our favorite television program. A person can be in and out and back to his own affairs in about an hour. You don't even need to dress up for a modern church service. Shorts and a T-shirt are fine. That's a good model for outreach, but it doesn't teach us about holiness.

The Sabbath day is not an hour-long worship service; it's a full twenty-four-hour day set aside for the Almighty. The liturgical tradition of the Sabbath day spans four worship services: Friday evening prayers, Saturday morning prayers, Saturday afternoon prayers, and Saturday evening prayers. The times of prayer correspond to the sacrificial services that took place in the Temple. It's not church on Saturday. It's a completely different kind of day, just as it's supposed to be. The Sabbath is supposed to be holy. That means it should not feel like the other days of the week.

SHABBAT UNPLUGGED

The modern world leaves no room for nurturing spirituality. The endless stream of information and entertainment flowing from our media-driven, plugged-in, online society constantly occupies our attention and numbs us to spirituality.

The Sabbath has us spending time in the presence of God rather than updating our Facebook pages. The Sabbath has us learning from the holy text rather than checking our text messages. Sabbath-keepers do not engage in commerce on the Sabbath day. The Sabbath is not a shopping day; it's not a day for going out to a restaurant. Sabbath-keepers learn about time set aside for God.

Without the Sabbath, there is no end to the interruptions posed by the secular world. Without the Sabbath, the urgency of the daily schedule, the demands from work, the pressures of business, the perpetual imminence of deadlines, the busyness of everyone's special events, the noise of the media, the internet, news, music, entertainment—our ceaseless absorption in secular life never abates.

By saying "no" to the world and all its demands and entertainments for twenty-four hours, we set the Sabbath apart from ordinary and normal time. We sanctify the Sabbath and enter the cathedral of God's holy day to worship him in his sanctuary of time.

FAVORITE DAY OF THE WEEK

When I was first considering becoming a Sabbatarian, I discussed the possibility with my father. He encouraged me to follow God's leading on the matter, but he warned me about making the experience unpleasant for my children.

When he was a boy, his church regarded Sunday as the Sabbath day. Sunday was the holy day. For my father and his brothers, this meant dressing in stiff, uncomfortable clothing and sitting quietly in church. Then they returned home and sat in the living room and listened while the adults talked. They were not allowed to play, read anything (except the Bible), or engage in any activities other than sitting still through that long and dreadful day of holiness.

In Jewish tradition the Sabbath is supposed to be a day of delight. There is still the formal clothing and the sitting through long synagogue services, but the atmosphere of the day is one of celebration and joy rather than austere and solemn piety. Three festive meals, treats and delicacies, special guests, surprise visits to friends' houses, story-telling, games, and delight in the Word of God combine to make the Sabbath an eagerly anticipated day of happiness. It is a day of song and good cheer.

My wife and I made efforts to make the Sabbath fun for our children when they were little. The best foods came out at Sabbath. My wife used to keep a bag of treats she called the Sabbath bag. The kids could choose a treat from the Sabbath bag while they sat at the table with us. I read stories, and my wife made sure the children had appropriate reading material for Sabbath days. We played games, went on family walks, and generally had a good time. None of our children ever dreaded the Sabbath. By unanimous consent, it was always their favorite day of the week.

Outsiders sometimes imagine that the Sabbath and its prohibitions are burdensome and restrictive. From a Messianic Jewish perspective, the Sabbath poses no burdens; we receive it as a precious gift. One never hears a Sabbath-keeper complain about the Sabbath. Our Master said, "Come to me, all who labor and are heavy laden, and I will give you rest" (Matthew 11:28). He said, "The Son of Man is lord of the Sabbath" (Matthew 12:8). The Sabbath is a gift; it is a blessing, not a burden. "The Sabbath was made for man, not man for the Sabbath" (Mark 2:27).

CHAPTER TWO

An Appointed Time

The story of the Sabbath begins at the beginning of time. It begins in the book of the Bible called "In the Beginning," that is, the book of Genesis. The Bible says that God created the heavens and the earth in six days. After its account of each day's work, the Bible says, "And there was evening and there was morning." We usually think of a day beginning either at dawn or at midnight. We think of nighttime following daytime. The Bible sees the daytime following nighttime. The new day begins when the sky darkens at night and it ends at sunset twenty-four hours later.

DAY FOLLOWS NIGHT

God arranged the daylight to follow darkness to teach us not to lose hope. Day and night are universal metaphors for light and dark, good and evil, life and death. From our point of view, it seems that night follows day; darkness swallows light; evil eclipses good; death ends life. God sees it differently. From the biblical perspective, day follows night, light dispels darkness, and life conquers death.

This explains why the Sabbath begins on Friday night and ends on Saturday night. It takes some getting used to, but if we want to be in tune with God's calendar, then it's important that we start thinking of time in biblical terms. Friday night is called *Erev Shabbat,* which means "Sabbath evening." The first Sabbath began on the very first Friday night.

To this day, Sabbath-keepers welcome the Sabbath on Friday nights. Before the sun sets on Friday night, we light special Sabbath candles to honor the Sabbath. By the time the candles are lit, we have already prepared the food we will eat on the Sabbath day, because we do not cook on the Sabbath. As the sun sets on Friday, we cross the threshold that divides the normal weekday world from the holy, sacred space called *Shabbat*. For the ensuing twenty-five hours, we bask in the Sabbath's holiness and blessing.

THE SEVENTH DAY

The Sabbath falls on the seventh day of the week, as the Bible says, "The seventh day is a Sabbath to the LORD your God" (Exodus 20:10). Jewish custom refers to each of the days of the week according to their relationship to the Sabbath. This reminds us that the Sabbath is the pinnacle of the entire week. The following chart demonstrates this relationship, but remember, the biblical day always begins at sunset of the previous day. That means that the Sabbath actually begins on Friday night, not Saturday morning:

SUNDAY	MONDAY	TUESDAY	WEDNESDAY	THURSDAY	FRIDAY	SATURDAY
First Day of the Sabbath	Second Day of the Sabbath	Third Day of the Sabbath	Fourth Day of the Sabbath	Fifth Day of the Sabbath	Sixth Day of the Sabbath *(Preparation Day/ Sabbath Eve)*	Sabbath

A person might suppose that it does not matter which day of the week he sets aside for the LORD, so long as he sets one day apart out of every seven. For example, Tuesday might be convenient. That type of sabbatarianism reflects the principle of Sabbath observance, but it does not actually fulfill the commandment of keeping the Sabbath. The Bible is clear about this. The Sabbath occurs on the seventh day. We do not get to choose which day is the seventh day. We do not have the luxury of picking which day will be the Sabbath.

People sometimes ask me how I know which day of the week the seventh day is. After all, God gave the Torah 3,400 years ago. Isn't it fairly likely that we have lost track of which day of the week the seventh day actually fell upon? Perhaps at one time, Tuesday was the seventh day of the week and Wednesday was the first day of the week. Who is to say?

If the Jewish people in the days of Moses had any doubt about which day of the week was the seventh day, the miracle of the manna made it obvious to them. The LORD made manna appear on the ground every morning for six days of the week. It was a miraculous food from heaven. Every morning the people went out to gather the manna, but the manna did not appear on the seventh day. The LORD said, "Six days you shall gather it, but on the seventh day, which is a Sabbath, there will be none" (Exodus 16:26). Therefore the people gathered an extra measure of manna on the sixth day.

The Jewish people today and the Jewish people that gathered manna in the wilderness thousands of years ago are all members of the same nation. This nation has existed continuously from the time the Jewish people left Egypt to the present day. Perhaps you or I might wake up one morning and not remember which day of the week it is. For example, I sometimes forget whether it is Wednesday or Thursday. It has never happened, however, that my entire family has simultaneously forgotten which day of the week it was. How much less likely it is that an entire nation of people could have simultaneously lost track of which day of the week it was. It's not possible.

For disciples of Yeshua, determining the Sabbath day requires even less of a reach back through history. We do not have to rely on a tradition carried all the way from Mount Sinai. We know that our teacher and Master honored the same seventh-day Sabbath that the rest of the Jewish people did in his day.

Judaism has certainly never taken a day off or lost track of the days of the week. A continuous chain of corporate testimony stretches from our day and our age all the way back to the days of Yeshua and even back to Mount Sinai. We know which day is the seventh day because, after all these years, the Jewish people are still keeping the Sabbath on it. The Jewish people are the wardens and guardians of God's holy day.

THE APPOINTED TIMES

The Bible calls the Sabbath day a *mo'ed*. A biblical *mo'ed* is an appointment with God. The Bible explains that the Sabbath is one of the LORD's appointed times (*mo'adim*) for meeting with his people.

Leviticus 23 presents a list of God's appointed times: "These are the appointed feasts of the LORD that you shall proclaim as holy convocations; they are my appointed feasts" (Leviticus 23:2). The appointed feasts are holy days that God has appointed, or planned in advance, to meet with his people Israel. The English Standard Version of the Bible translates the Hebrew word *mo'adim* as "appointed feasts," but the word actually indicates an appointed time or an appointed place—not necessarily a "feast." The chapter goes on to list off the biblical holy days: Sabbath, Passover, Pentecost, the Festival of Trumpets, the Day of Atonement, and the Festival of Booths. It lists the Sabbath first because the Sabbath is the first and most important of the LORD's appointed times.

The Bible also refers to the Tabernacle in which the LORD dwelt among his people in the wilderness as the *Ohel Mo'ed*, a term that our English Bibles translate as "Tent of Meeting." The Tabernacle was God's appointed place to meet with man at his appointed times. This hints toward a special relationship between the LORD's Sanctuary (his holy place) and the LORD's Sabbath (his holy day).

Our Master Yeshua once told a parable about how a certain king was giving a wedding feast for his son. He sent out his servants to call those who had been invited to the feast. The servants had two critical pieces of information. They were to declare the appointed time and the appointed place of the banquet. Likewise, as God summoned his people Israel to appear before him, he decreed an appointed place and appointed times. The appointed place was the Sanctuary. The appointed times were the Sabbath and the biblical festivals.

Since the destruction of the Temple in the days of the apostles, the appointed place has been removed, but the appointed times continue. God explains that the appointed times are to be a "statute forever throughout your generations in all your dwellings" (Leviticus 23:14). That means that they are never to be canceled. They will never be obsolete or done away with. They are to be celebrated and observed wherever we live.

HOLY CONVOCATIONS

The Torah says that God's appointed times are to be kept as "holy convocations." A convocation is a time of assembly. In the days of the apostles the people "convocated" by assembling in the Temple and in synagogues at the appointed times.

Unlike any other time of convocation or assembly, the appointed times have an intrinsic holiness. God set them apart with holiness, and by keeping them, we automatically participate in that holiness. They are like sanctuaries in time. Just as a person entering the Tabernacle entered into holy space, a person keeping the appointed times enters holy time.

Even though there is no Temple today, the Jewish people continue to hold "holy convocations" on the appointed times in the form of synagogue services, readings from the Torah, and special Sabbath and holiday prayers. Since ancient times, the Torah has been read in the synagogue every Sabbath. The Gospels tell us that it was Yeshua's custom to attend synagogue and read from the Torah on the Sabbath day.

GOD'S CALENDAR

The calendar of Leviticus 23 works differently than the one to which we are accustomed. The Gregorian calendar is based solely on the yearly cycle of solar activity; its months have no correlation with the movement of any heavenly body. In contrast, the biblical calendar incorporates the phases of the moon. The waxing and waning of the moon determine the day of the biblical month. The tiny sliver of the new moon is always the first day of the month, the full moon indicates the middle of the month, and the disappearance of the moon heralds the end of the month.

God declares certain days on this calendar to be his appointed times.

What does this mean? We can understand it if we think about our own busy schedules. Suppose you intend to meet your friend

Joe at a coffee shop. You and Joe might set a time—say, Tuesday, August 17, at 2:00 PM. You would flip open your day planner or open your Google Calendar to find the entry that shows your schedule for Tuesday, August 17. After you determine that the 2:00 slot is open, you write in, "Coffee shop with Joe."

Leviticus 23 works like God's day planner. He has made appointments on which to meet with his people. Unlike our day planners and easily-altered entries on electronic calendars, God's day planner does not change. His schedule is not flexible.

When we are uncertain about whether or not we will be able to keep an appointment, we might say, "I'll pencil it in." The implication is that if things change and we are unable to keep the appointment, we can change our plans. With God, there is no uncertainty about his schedule. You might say he doesn't even own a pencil. When he wrote out his day planner, he wrote in ink, and the ink has been dry for 3,400 years.

JEWISH HOLY DAYS

It is not uncommon to hear people refer to the appointed times as the Jewish festivals. That's not incorrect. God gave his appointed times to the people of Israel. He told the children of Israel, "These are the appointed feasts of the LORD that you shall proclaim as holy convocations; they are my appointed feasts" (Leviticus 23:2). He gave the Jewish people the responsibility to "proclaim" his appointed times "as holy convocations." In other words, the Jewish people are the wardens of God's calendar. The Jewish people have both the right and the responsibility to interpret, apply, and define the appointed times. God did not give any other people that right.

Think of it this way. A father owns a car. It's his car. But he gives it to his son to drive to school. That's what God did with his appointed times. He gave the keys to Israel. He entrusted his appointed times to the Jewish people. The Jewish people have the right to drive them.

Perhaps this is why many Christians and Jews think of the biblical Sabbath and the biblical festivals as the sole purview of the Jewish people. According to this line of thought, Gentile disciples of Yeshua are not supposed to celebrate the Sabbath or the other appointed times.

In reality, the LORD did not refer to the appointed times as Jewish festivals; he referred to them as "my appointed times." They are God's holy days. Paul asks, "Is God the God of Jews only? Is he not the God of Gentiles also? Yes, of Gentiles also" (Romans 3:29).

Think of it this way. A man owns a car, and he gives it to his son to drive to school. But he tells his son, "Give your brother a ride to school, too." The man is the father of both sons, and he wants both to get school, but both cannot drive. The two sons have different roles to play, but they are both in the same vehicle.

GENTILE HOLY DAYS

Here's another way to look at it. Open your Bible and try to find the appointed times that God has given to the Gentile believers. Did he give Gentile Christians new holidays? Here is a verse that you will not find in your Bible:

> You shall keep the first day of the week as the Lord's Day to remember the resurrection of my Son, and you shall keep a festival in the winter to remember his birth. (Gentiles 2:16)

Even if you search your whole Bible, you will never find this verse or anything remotely like it. The Bible never offered Gentile Christians any alternative festival days, nor did it grant them permission to make up their own.

If we say that Gentile believers are not expected to keep God's appointed times, then we are saying that Gentile believers are not supposed to have any holy days or days of worship at all. Neither the Gospels nor the Epistles grant the Gentile believers their own special festivals. The New Testament does not give Gentile Christians the authority to change God's holy days or to create new appointed times. After all, the holy days are the LORD's appointed times, not ours. He is the one who determines his appointed times, not us.

In the days of the apostles Jewish and Gentile believers observed God's appointed times together. They met in the synagogues and in the Temple on the Sabbath and festival days to celebrate and observe God's holy days. When Gentile Christianity left the cradle of Judaism, the Gentile Christians began to neglect the appointed times. They eventually replaced the Sabbath day with Sunday observance. They changed the celebration of Passover. Other festivals fell into disuse. Is this what God intended for believers?

The apostles never commanded the Gentile believers to keep the appointed times, but neither did they tell them not to observe them. They remained silent on the matter. In those days, the idea of not keeping the appointed times simply had not occurred to anyone.

ONE PLACE OF WORSHIP

Here's another way to think about it. In the previous chapter, we saw how the Sabbath and the festivals can be compared to the Temple. Just as the Temple is a holy place, a sanctuary in space, the Sabbath and the festivals are holy times, sanctuaries in time.

One might think that the Temple in Jerusalem was a Jewish Temple only for Jews, but Gentiles also prayed and worshiped at the Temple. When King Solomon built the Temple, he invited Gentiles from the nations to come and pray to the God of Israel in his Temple. In the days of the apostles, the "Court of the Gentiles" was the largest courtyard in the Temple.

God never chose some other location to place a Temple in which Gentiles could worship. He expected the Gentiles to worship him at his appointed place in Jerusalem. The prophets say that in the Messianic Era, all nations will go up to the house of God and worship him in his holy mountain. God is not going to make two different Temples, one for the Jews and one for the Gentiles. Instead, he says, "My house shall be called a house of prayer for all peoples" (Isaiah 56:7).

The Bible strongly warns the Jewish people not to create a Temple in any place other than the holy place that the LORD has chosen: Jerusalem. Just as we are not allowed to choose a new place to build a Temple, we are not allowed to create new holy days.

When the wicked Israelite king Jeroboam wanted to keep the people of Israel from casting their allegiance with the house of David, he changed the appointed holy place and he changed the appointed holy times. He made new sanctuaries in Dan and Bethel, and he made new festival dates: "Jeroboam appointed a feast on the fifteenth day of the eighth month ... in the month that he had devised from his own heart" (1 Kings 12:32–33). He did this in order to break their allegiance to Jerusalem and the throne of David. The prophets called this "the sin of Jeroboam," and they used it as a benchmark to measure the wickedness of subsequent kings.

Likewise, the prophecies in the book of Daniel predict that the antichrist "shall think to change the times and the law" (Daniel 7:25). Unlike wicked King Jeroboam and unlike the antichrist, our Master says, "Do not think that I have come to abolish the Law [that is, the Torah]... not an iota, not a dot, will pass from the Law until all is accomplished" (Matthew 5:17–18).

If the Temple is the appointed place at which the Bible expects both Jews and Gentiles to worship, then we should not be surprised that the Bible expects both Jews and Gentiles to worship on the biblical Sabbath and holy days, which are sanctuaries in time.

I am not suggesting that there is anything wrong with celebrating special occasions and observing special memorials. I do not believe it is wrong for Christians to worship on Sundays. (Jews worship every day of the week). I do not believe it is wrong for Christians to select dates to remember significant events in the life of the Master such as his birth. But at the same time, we do not have permission to replace God's appointed times with new holidays of our own making.

CHAPTER THREE

LESSONS FROM THE MANNA

God gave Israel the Sabbath as one of the Ten Commandments that he spoke directly to the people at Mount Sinai. The careful reader will have noticed, however, that the Sinai revelation was not Israel's first encounter with the seventh-day rest. A few days after crossing the Red Sea, the children of Israel received the heavenly gift of daily manna. Along with it, they received the gift of the Sabbath.

Exodus 16 assumes that the Israelites were already familiar with the institution of Sabbath, if not the particulars of Sabbath observance. As we have seen, the LORD ordained the Sabbath at the beginning of creation. Tradition says that Enoch and Noah passed it on to the patriarchs. Abraham, Isaac, and Jacob kept the Sabbath even though they were not Jewish and had not received the Torah at Sinai. While enslaved in Egypt, the children of Israel did not have the luxury of keeping the Sabbath, but they still must have known about the day of rest.

Like a man impatient to present his beloved with an engagement ring, the LORD was eager to give the Sabbath to his people. He began to give the laws of the Sabbath to Israel even before the giving of the Torah at Mount Sinai. He did not make them wait until they received the Torah to begin honoring his holy day. As soon as the LORD had liberated them from Egypt, he began to instruct them about the Sabbath. He introduced the laws of the Sabbath to the children of Israel in conjunction with the miracle of manna.

SPIRITUAL LESSONS FROM MANNA

The LORD led the children of Israel into the wilderness, a desolate place where there was no food. To sustain the nation during their sojourn in the wilderness, he provided bread from heaven, which appeared on the ground every morning. Moses explained, "It is the bread that the LORD has given you to eat" (Exodus 16:15).

Paul says that the stories about Israel in the wilderness, including the story of the manna, "happened to them as an example, but they were written down for our instruction, on whom the end of the ages has come" (1 Corinthians 10:11). What sorts of instructions can we derive from the story of the manna? It turns out that the story of the manna has a lot to teach us about God's provision, the difference between materialism and spirituality, and the rules of the Sabbath day.

The LORD supplied manna for the people every day and instructed the people to gather the manna every day. Each day they went out and gathered it in baskets. The LORD warned them not to attempt to gather excess for storage. Moses said, "Let no one leave any of it over till the morning" (Exodus 16:19). Those who did not heed the warning found maggots in the manna the next morning. It putrefied overnight: "It bred worms and stank" (Exodus 16:20).

The story of the manna teaches us about relying on God for our daily needs. It warns against the folly of storing up wealth for ourselves. The fool says in his heart, "[I] have ample goods laid up for many years; relax, eat, drink, be merry" (Luke 12:19). He forgets that he relies upon God for even the breath in his lungs. He stores up wealth for another.

The manna teaches us that God faithfully provides for the daily needs of his people. A person should not worry, saying, "What shall we eat?" or "What shall we drink?" or "What shall we wear?" Your heavenly Father knows that you need all these things (Matthew 6:31–32). God opens his hand and satisfies the desire of every living thing (Psalm 145:16). "He provides food for those who fear him" (Psalm 111:5). "A person cannot receive even one thing unless it is given him from heaven" (John 3:27). Everything we have comes directly from the hand of God, and we must rely upon him each day.

The excess manna, which putrefied overnight, symbolizes materialism. One should not cling to the things of this material world or try to heap them up, because those things are transient and impermanent. They are here today but gone tomorrow. They are the things that "moth and rust destroy and … thieves break in and steal" (Matthew 6:19). Like human life itself, which is destined for the grave, the things of this material world are doomed to decay and ultimately perish. Instead of investing in the things of this world and hoarding them up, a person should cleave to the eternal things. The putrefication of the manna symbolizes the ultimate end of the human being: "It bred worms and stank" (Exodus 16:20). Therefore a person should seek after the spiritual and eternal things, not the things of this perishing world.

ENDURING TREASURE

The prohibition on storing up manna has an exception. Moses told the children of Israel to gather two omers of manna on the sixth day—twice as much as usual—because the LORD would not provide the manna on the Sabbath. Extra manna gathered on the sixth day did not putrefy overnight. It stayed fresh through the Sabbath.

This teaches that when a person employs the material things of this world toward a spiritual end, he achieves an eternal result. In this way, we can transform the quickly fading things of the material world into things of permanence and eternal significance. Manna stored up for use on the holy Sabbath day did not turn rancid or breed worms. Likewise, we can redeem the things of this material world by utilizing them for the kingdom or in performance of a mitzvah. For example, we can exchange material wealth for spiritual wealth by donating money to the poor or using our resources to support the work of the kingdom. This is what Yeshua meant when he told us not to store up treasures on earth, where moth and rust destroy and thieves break in, but rather to store up treasures in heaven "where neither moth nor rust destroys and where thieves do not break in and steal. For where your treasure is, there your heart will be also" (Matthew 6:20–21). Likewise, money spent for the Sabbath is money saved in heaven. That's good news for Sabbath-keepers because keeping the Sabbath can be expensive. Serving a big meal every Friday night, hosting guests, and all the extras that make the Sabbath special—these expenses add up. The lesson of manna teaches us not to let that trouble us. The LORD provides us with extra specifically so that we can use it on the Sabbath. Money spent for the honor of the Sabbath takes on an enduring and spiritual value that does not perish.

PREPARING FOR THE SABBATH

The rule about gathering double the amount of manna on the sixth day teaches that one should gather and store up extra in preparation for the Sabbath. In our world, manna does not often fall from heaven or form on the ground; nevertheless, Sabbath observance still requires some conscious planning and preparation. Sabbath-keepers need to organize their workweek in such a way that they need not gather manna (so to speak) on the seventh day. They also need to set aside money for extra dishes and decorations; flourishes like these make the Sabbath special. The fact that the manna lasted the extra day through the Sabbath without spoiling teaches us that it is appropriate to lay up provisions for Shabbat.

The Talmud tells a story about how the great sage Shammai used to prepare for the Sabbath (b.*Beitzah* 16a). Whenever Shammai was in the marketplace, he always kept a lookout for exceptionally fine items that he might be able to purchase for the Sabbath. If he found a remarkably fine goat, an especially plump chicken, or unusually rare vintage of wine, he would purchase it and say, "This is for the Shabbat."

Another Talmudic story illustrates the idea of living simply during the week in order to save money for the sake of the Sabbath (b.*Shabbat* 119a):

> A certain Jewish slave named Joseph loved the Sabbath so much that he subsisted on a sparse diet of black bread and onions all week long in order to save money for the Sabbath. On the Sabbath, he hosted extravagant Sabbath meals for all his friends. His friends referred to him as "Joseph Who Loves the Sabbath." Some fortunetellers warned his Gentile owner, "Joseph will devour all your property." The Gentile took heed, sold all of his property, and used the proceeds to purchase one large precious

> stone which he concealed in his turban. Then he left for a distant land. While he was crossing a bridge, a wind blew the turban from his head and into the water. A fish swallowed the stone. The fish was caught and brought to market late on a Friday. The fish vendor asked, "Who will buy such a fine and expensive fish this late in the day?" They said, "Take it and show it to Joseph. He is accustomed to spend exorbitantly on his Sabbath dinners." They brought it to him. He bought the fish, opened it up; and found the jewel. He sold the jewel for thirteen vessels of gold coins. Then a certain old man met him and said, "He who spends on the Sabbath is repaid by the Sabbath."

BREAD FOR TWO DAYS

The LORD told the people to gather twice the amount of manna on the sixth day. He told them that he would not provide manna on the seventh day. Moses warned the people not to go out to gather manna on the seventh day. If any did go out to gather manna, they found none:

> "See! The LORD has given you the Sabbath; therefore on the sixth day he gives you bread for two days. Remain each of you in his place; let no one go out of his place on the seventh day." So the people rested on the seventh day. (Exodus 16:29–30)

This teaches us that if a person resolves to keep the Sabbath, the LORD will do his part to provide the means for him to do so: "He gives you bread for two days" (Exodus 16:29). People sometimes object to the idea of becoming Sabbatarian on the basis that they will lose income and will no longer be able to provide for their families. Before offering that argument, we should think about the lessons of the manna. Who is it that provides for us in the first place? Is he not able to meet our needs in six days?

A Sabbatarian couple living in Alaska once told me a true story that illustrates the idea. The year that they became Sabbatarian and started to honor the Sabbath, they had to decide what to do about the annual salmon run. Their yearly income relied on catching fish during the season when the salmon are running in the stream. The husband felt that he could not possibly keep the Sabbath during the salmon run. Despite his wife's protests, he went out to fish on the Sabbath. After the weekend, he returned home to his wife, dejected and nearly empty-handed. He had caught almost nothing all weekend. The next week, he resolved to keep the Sabbath. He stayed home on the Sabbath and went out fishing the following day. He returned home that night with twice the amount he ordinarily anticipated catching in an entire weekend.

It does not always work out that way. Many sacrifices made for the Sabbath day are not compensated in this world. Keeping the Sabbath often entails real financial loss and loss of worldly opportunities for profit. Nevertheless, the LORD exchanges all those losses for treasure in heaven.

DAY OF CONTENTMENT

Moses said to the people, "Six days you shall gather it, but on the seventh day, which is a Sabbath, there will be none" (Exodus 16:26). If the children of Israel had any doubt whatsoever about which day God meant when he referred to "the seventh day," the absence of manna on that day made it clear. God did not provide manna on the Sabbath.

Why did God withhold the manna on the seventh day? Was it because that was his day off too and he did not want to trouble with making manna on that day? Of course not. He withheld manna on the seventh day to teach us that we do not need to work and obtain seven days a week. He withheld manna on the seventh day because everyone already had enough. The prohibition against gathering manna on the Sabbath teaches that the Sabbath is a day to be content with what you already have.

The Sabbath is not a day to gather, harvest, work, acquire, or make money. Going out to gather manna corresponds to working for the acquisition of a livelihood, and it corresponds to shopping, purchasing, and acquiring. On the Sabbath, we rest from acquiring. Every other day of the week we spend our time making money so that we can make purchases. We spend most of our time working toward the gathering and acquiring of life's necessities.

Our materialistic, commercial society has brainwashed us to be constantly discontent. We always feel we need to buy something, whether a cup of coffee on the way to work, a snack from a snack machine, a meal at a restaurant, a few groceries on the way home, and so on and so forth. Modern society has brainwashed us to feel a gnawing discontent with what we already have.

The Sabbath is called a day of contentment. It teaches us the meaning of the words, "If we have food and clothing, with these we will be content" (1 Timothy 6:8):

> I have learned in whatever situation I am to be content. I know how to be brought low, and I know how to abound. In any and every circumstance, I have learned the secret of facing plenty and hunger, abundance and need. (Philippians 4:11–12)

The Sabbath teaches us to be content with whatever we already have when Friday night comes because on the seventh day we are not to be about the business of acquiring. The Sabbath prohibits popping into the grocery store, making a quick shopping trip, stopping off to rummage through a garage sale, swinging by a coffee shop for a coffee, and so forth. The spirit of the day even discourages paging through a catalog to consider purchases that we might make after the Sabbath. The Sabbath teaches us to cease from the constant need of consumerism. We learn the meaning of contentment.

IF WE HAVE FOOD AND CLOTHING

One old Chasidic story tells about a Jewish couple so impoverished that, one Friday, they had absolutely nothing left. They did not even have a handful of flour left to make some bread. The husband said, "We have already borrowed too much money from the neighbors. But let's do what we can to honor the Sabbath. I will go to the study hall and study Torah to honor the Sabbath." The wife said, "I will take my broom and clean our little cottage to honor the Sabbath." As she swept, she found a piece of jewelry that she had lost several years earlier. She quickly went and sold it and made enough money to buy flour, candles, wine, and a chicken. When her husband returned home after hours at the study hall, he caught the delicious scent of fresh hot bread and chicken soup. He saw candles burning on the table and a bottle of wine. He sat down with his wife, said the Sabbath blessings over the wine, and ate a hearty meal with her. Sighing contentedly, he said, "I only wish you had not gone to the neighbors to borrow more money." When she explained what had happened, he joyously leapt to his feet and caught her up into his arms, and together they danced the night away.

BUT IT'S FREE!

Perhaps we can understand why the Sabbath prohibits trips to the grocery store and shopping mall, but what if the thing I want to acquire on the Sabbath day is free? What if it does not involve any transaction of money whatsoever?

Remember that gathering manna on the Sabbath did not require any transaction either. It was free. Neither did gathering manna require any type of creative work, nor did it require working for an employer. The manna was free from heaven. It could not be construed as work in the sense of laboring for a wage nor even in the sense of working in a garden to harvest vegetables. A person only needed to pick the manna up off the ground and put it in a basket. Nevertheless, the LORD did not provide manna on the Sabbath, and he even forbade the people from going out to gather it on the Sabbath. Again, the Sabbath is simply not a day for gathering or acquiring.

COOKING ON SABBATH

Furthermore, the story about the manna teaches the prohibition of cooking food on the Sabbath. Moses told the children of Israel to prepare the manna for eating prior to the onset of the Sabbath. He commanded them, "Tomorrow is a day of solemn rest, a holy Sabbath to the LORD; bake what you will bake and boil what you will boil, and all that is left over lay aside to be kept till the morning" (Exodus 16:23). Baking and boiling are forms of work prohibited on the Sabbath. If baking and boiling were permissible on the Sabbath, Moses would not have needed to state that the manna should be baked and boiled on the day before the Sabbath.

This explains why Sabbath-keepers prepare their food in advance of the seventh day. Not only do we need to store up extra food for the seventh day, we also need to have all the cooking, baking, and boiling done in advance. Jewish law permits keeping already-cooked foods warm through the Sabbath, but they must be fully cooked and ready-to-eat before the Sabbath begins on Friday night.

STAY IN YOUR PLACE

There is one more principle about the Sabbath that we can learn from the story of the manna. Moses prohibited the Israelites from going out of their places on the Sabbath to gather manna. The prophecy of Isaiah refers to this prohibition when it says, "If you turn back your foot from the Sabbath, from doing your pleasure on my holy day ... then you shall take delight in the LORD, and I will make you ride on the heights of the earth" (Isaiah 58:13–14).

What does it mean to not go out from one's place on the Sabbath day? What exactly is one's place? In the context of the story, it seems clear that the Torah intended the prohibition to apply to gathering manna: "Let no one go out of his place on the seventh day" *to gather manna.*

Judaism did not understand it that way. Instead, Jewish tradition reads this passage to mean that a person should not go outside of certain boundaries on the Sabbath day. The conventional understanding of the passage interprets a person's "place" as the city in which he lives. Therefore, a person may walk any distance within his city limits.

What are the limits of a city? In Numbers 35:4–5 the Torah states that a city's limit extends for a distance of two thousand cubits beyond the city walls:

> The pasturelands of the cities, which you shall give to the Levites, shall reach from the wall of the city outward a thousand cubits all around. And you shall measure, out-

side the city, on the east side two thousand cubits, and on the south side two thousand cubits, and on the west side two thousand cubits, and on the north side two thousand cubits, the city being in the middle. This shall belong to them as pastureland for their cities. (Numbers 35:4–5)

Based on this text, Jewish tradition defined a "Sabbath-day's journey" as two thousand cubits (about two-thirds of a mile) beyond the edge of a city. If a person spent a Sabbath outside of a city or village, the Sabbath limit gave him two thousand cubits in a radius around the place in which he began the Sabbath:

> Come and hear: If a man spent the Shabbat in a town, even though it was as big as Antioch ... he may walk through the whole of it and two thousand cubits beyond. (b.*Eruvin* 61b)

A RABBINIC RULE

The law about the Sabbath-day's journey does not arise from a literal reading of the passage. Even the great Torah commentator Rashi says, "This law is not stated in the verse in explicit terms, for the laws of [a Sabbath-day's walk] are of rabbinic origin, and the essence of the verse was said with regard only to those who gathered manna." Despite that caveat, believing Sabbath-keepers should not dismiss the law of the Sabbath-day's walk. Luke refers to "a Sabbath-day's walk" as a point of reference for his readership in Acts 1:12. His use of this terminology shows us that his readership (Jewish and non-Jewish believers in the late decades of the first century) was Sabbath-observant and even keeping Jewish standards regarding a permissible Sabbath-day's walk. Had the early believers jettisoned Torah and Jewish tradition (as has been supposed by generations of Bible interpreters), Luke's reference would have been meaningless to his readers.

The commandment that a person should not go outside certain boundaries on the Sabbath day has historically fostered the creation of Jewish communities. This is especially unsurprising when we consider the laws that prohibit using transportation on the Sabbath. These prohibitions forced the Jewish people to cluster together into tight community groups which, in turn, protected Jewish identity and reinforced Jewish practice, faith, and Torah observance.

In the nineteenth century, Enlightenment-era Jews began to abandon the Sabbath prohibitions, including the one on staying within one's place. Jewish communities began to break up. Since then, Jewish identity and community integrity has eroded at an alarming rate.

THE SABBATH-DAY'S WALK IN MESSIANIC JUDAISM

If Messianic Jewish communities hope to establish themselves with intergenerational longevity, perhaps we will need to reconsider the importance of Sabbath prohibitions such as the commandment to stay within one's place on the Sabbath day. A commitment to these principles will foster the formation of localized communities where people live in close proximity to our places of worship and to one another.

Does the commandment to stay within one's place on the Sabbath also apply to Gentile believers? As we will see in later chapters, the apostles did not require God-fearing Gentile believers to observe the Sabbath prohibitions, but they seem to have assumed that the Gentile believers would at least honor the Sabbath day along with the rest of the Jewish community. Although Gentile believers are not prohibited from going outside of their "place" on the Sabbath day, they may want to keep the law in honor of the LORD's holy day and in concert with the practice of the Jewish people. If they want to do so, they need to measure that desire against other priorities that they might need to sacrifice for the sake of taking on an additional stringency. For example, staying in one's place might preclude attending a house of worship or visiting with brothers and sisters on the Sabbath. If so, the prohibition may force the God-fearing Gentile to break fellowship with other Sabbath-keeping believers, all for the sake of keeping a commandment that he is not commanded to keep. Despite this warning, Gentile Sabbath-keepers ought to at least consider whether they are able to stay in their place during the Sabbath. The holiness of the Sabbath is best maintained within its traditional boundaries.

CHAPTER FOUR

SIGN OF THE COVENANT

Nineteenth-century Messianic Jew Chaim Yedidiah Theophilus Lucky occasionally attended missionary conferences dedicated to the evangelization of the Jewish people. Despite the fact that he was both a Jew and a believer in Yeshua, Lucky never found a warm welcome at those types of events. Most of the other Jewish believers in attendance were converts who had left Judaism to be baptized into one church denomination or another. They had left the synagogue, Jewish practice, and the Jewish people behind. They certainly were not Sabbath-keepers. Lucky, on the other hand, believed that his calling as a disciple of Yeshua compelled him to be all the more faithful to the Torah. He taught against Jewish believers forsaking the Torah, and he himself remained devoutly observant. As a result, he often found himself criticized and even condemned by the missionaries.

On one occasion some Jewish Christians asked Lucky if he believed that they were sinning because they no longer observed the Sabbath. Lucky considered the question before replying. Then he said, "I do not say that you are sinning, and it is not for me to say … but I do feel sorry for you." Lucky felt sorry for his Jewish brothers who had found the Messiah but, in the process, had lost the Sabbath.

A SPECIAL JOB

The first few chapters of Genesis indicate that the Sabbath is, in some sense, universal. God instituted the Sabbath at creation. He sanctified and blessed the day of rest on the day after he created the first human beings. Yeshua said, "The Sabbath was made for man" (Mark 2:27). He did not say, "The Sabbath was made for Jews." His choice of words implies that the Sabbath day stands as a day of blessing, holiness, and rest for everyone, not just for the Jewish people.

At the same time, the Jewish people have a special connection to the Sabbath. Recall from the previous chapter that God gave the Sabbath and the appointed times to the Jewish people to "proclaim as holy convocations" (Leviticus 23:1). God did not command Adam and Eve to keep the Sabbath. He did not tell Noah and his sons to keep the Sabbath. He did not even ask Abraham, Isaac, and Jacob to keep the Sabbath. But he did say to the children of Israel, "Above all you shall keep my Sabbaths, for this is a sign between me and you throughout your generations, that you may know that I, the LORD, sanctify you" (Exodus 31:13). In this way he gave the Jewish people a special job, a unique obligation regarding the Sabbath. He expressed his desire that the Jewish people keep the Sabbath holy, "because it is holy for you" (Exodus 31:14). He commanded the Jewish people to observe the Sabbath as a solemn rest, abstaining from work on the seventh day.

By keeping the Sabbath day holy and observing the prohibitions against working on the Sabbath day, the Jewish people honor the sign of their special covenant relationship with God.

THE SABBATH KEEPS THE JEWISH PEOPLE

The famous Zionist writer Asher Zvi Hirsch Ginsberg (Ahad Ha'am) once said, "More than Jews have kept the Sabbath, the Sabbath has kept the Jews." The obligation of observing the seventh day as a day of rest has set the Jewish people apart from the rest of the world. As the Jewish people sanctify the Sabbath by setting it apart from the other days of the week, the Sabbath sanctifies them by setting them apart from the world.

The observance of the Sabbath has forced Jewish people to live and work together in communities. Since Jews who keep a traditional Sabbath do not drive on the holy day, the observance of the Sabbath forces them to live within walking distance of one another and their place of worship. These small, clustered communities foster and reinforce Jewish identity; in turn, a strong sense of identity safeguards against tendencies which might erode the Jewish people: assimilation, secularization, and intermarriage. In this way the Sabbath has kept the Jewish people intact as a holy people for thousands of years. When Jewish people do not observe a traditional Sabbath, they are quickly assimilated into the broader Gentile culture. It's almost as if the Sabbath is the glue that holds the people together.

Moreover, as the Torah says, the observance of the Sabbath is a sign that indicates the unique relationship between God and the Jewish people. So long as the Sabbath is observed, the Sabbath day reinforces that relationship every week. When the Sabbath is neglected, however, the entire covenant can more easily be forgotten.

As a sign of the covenant, the Sabbath can be compared to a wedding ring. The wedding band that a woman wears on her finger is a sign to others that she is a married woman. It is a sign of her covenant with her husband. Besides serving as a signal of her marital status to others, it also reminds the woman of her own promise to remain faithful to her husband. If (God forbid) she were ever tempted by another man, the presence of the ring on her finger should deter her. A woman who ceases to wear her wedding ring is headed for trouble. By neglecting the sign of her marriage, she conceals her obligations to her husband and signals other men that they are free to pursue her.

In this way the Sabbath can be compared to a wedding ring that the Almighty has placed upon Israel's finger. So long as the Jewish people observe the Sabbath, they declare their unbroken loyalty to the covenant and to their husband; however, when the Sabbath is neglected, the covenant falls into neglect and the nation becomes vulnerable.

Observing this principle at work, the rabbis mused that if the whole people of Israel would keep only two Sabbaths properly, the experience would so powerfully inspire them to repent that the Messiah would surely come.

HOLY PEOPLE AND THE HOLY DAY

When God brought the children of Israel to Mount Sinai, he made them an offer. He offered to set apart the whole nation of Israel from the rest of humanity and make them his holy people. He offered to make them a kingdom of priests. He said, "If you will indeed obey my voice and keep my covenant, you shall be my treasured possession among all peoples, for all the earth is mine; and you shall be to me a kingdom of priests and a holy nation" (Exodus 19:5–6).

What does it mean to be a kingdom of priests? Not just anyone can be a priest. Most Jews don't even qualify to be biblical priests. In the Bible only the men of the family of Aaron could serve in the priesthood. Other Levites did not qualify. The tribe of Judah did not qualify. Not even the exalted house of David could serve in the priesthood. God set apart Aaron's family as a holy household to serve him as priests. Only Aaron's direct male descendants qualify for the position.

God gave the priests special rules and laws that applied only to them. They had to observe strict prohibitions that the rest of the Jewish people did not have to observe. In their role as priests they served the rest of the nation. They were like servants to the other Jewish people. It was their job to offer the sacrifices on behalf of the people and to conduct the rites of worship in the Sanctuary. They had the responsibility of representing Israel before the LORD, and they had the responsibility of representing the LORD to the people of Israel.

As a "kingdom of priests and a holy nation," the Jewish people have a similar role to that of the Aaronic priests. God has categorically set the Jewish people apart from the nations. He has set them apart to be a holy nation with the responsibility and obligation of serving him. He gave the Jewish people special rules and laws that apply specifically to them. Many of these laws apply universally to all humanity, but a few of them were given specifically to underscore the setting-apart of the Jewish people. The Jewish people must observe certain prohibitions that do not apply to other nations. They must observe certain laws that other peoples are not required to observe.

In their role as a nation of priests the Jewish people are like servants to the rest of the nations. They have the responsibility of being a "light to the nations." The Apostle Paul explained how that works in the beginning of Romans chapter 9. Through the Jewish people has come the revelation of God's glory, the covenant promises, the revelation of the Scriptures, the giving of the Torah, the Levitical worship, and all that we know about God and how to serve him. Israel has inherited the promises of the forefathers, Abraham, Isaac, and Jacob; and through them has come the Messiah Yeshua. In these ways the Jewish people have been and continue to be a nation of priests on behalf of all nations.

This is what it means to be the chosen people. God chose the Jewish people out from all the nations to be his holy nation. He gave the Jewish people the Sabbath day as sign and a reminder that they are not like everybody else. They are the chosen people.

HOLY CALLING

The Friday night meal in Sabbatarian homes begins with a declaration of the holiness of the Sabbath day. This declaration is called *Kiddush*, a word that means "sanctification." The head of the table lifts a cup of wine, recites a passage from the Scriptures about the Sabbath, and pronounces a blessing over the wine. In Jewish homes, the *Kiddush* recitation continues with the following words:

> Blessed are you, O LORD, our God, King of the universe, who has sanctified us with his commandments and has shown us favor, and has lovingly and willingly let us inherit his holy Sabbath, a memorial of the work of creation. For it is the beginning day of the holy convocations, a remembrance of the exodus from Egypt. *For you chose us and sanctified us from all of the peoples and lovingly and willingly let us inherit your holy Sabbath.* Blessed are you, O LORD, who sanctifies the Sabbath.

These words join the holiness of the Sabbath day with the holiness of the Jewish people. The two are intertwined. God made the Sabbath day holy when he chose it from all the other days and made it a memorial of creation and a memorial of the exodus from Egypt. But he also chose the Jewish people and sanctified the Jewish people "from all of the peoples," and he gave the Sabbath to the Jewish people as an inheritance.

A PRECIOUS GIFT

Gentiles might think of the Sabbath as a heavy burden and a yoke, but the Jewish people see the Sabbath as a precious gift from God. The Sabbath existed from the beginning of the world, ever since God rested on the seventh day of creation. Yet the LORD did not give the Sabbath to the nations or command the peoples of the world to keep the Sabbath. He reserved it, so to speak, for his people Israel. Like a man who carefully guards a precious diamond ring, reserving it for the woman he intends to marry, the LORD reserved the commandment of Sabbath for Israel.

God did not make the observance of the Sabbath into a universal commandment that is binding upon all human beings or even into a commandment that is binding upon all believers. Instead he gave the privilege of being obligated to keep the Sabbath only to one people, his people Israel.

Jewish believers receive the same privilege. Just because they become believers in Yeshua does not mean that they cease from being Jewish, nor does their faith in Messiah cancel their obligation as Jews to keep the Sabbath.

SIGN OF THE COVENANT

Why does God call the Sabbath a "sign" between him and the people of Israel? What does it signify?

When two parties in the ancient Near East initiated a covenant with one another, they often chose some object or mark as a sign of their covenant relationship, a reminder of their covenant obligations to one another. For example, when Abraham made a covenant with the Philistine king Abimelech regarding water rights in the Negev, he gave him seven ewe lambs and said, "These seven ewe lambs you will take from my hand, that this may be a witness for me that I dug this well" (Genesis 21:30). Likewise, when Laban and Jacob made a covenant, they raised an altar as a sign of their treaty. Laban declared, "This heap is a witness between you and me today" (Genesis 31:48).

All God's covenants have associated signs. When he made a covenant with Noah and his sons, promising to never again flood the entire earth, he set his rainbow in the sky and said, "It shall be a sign of the covenant between me and the earth ... between me and you and every living creature" (Genesis 9:13–15). When God made a covenant with Abraham, he said, "You shall be circumcised in the flesh of your foreskins, and it shall be a sign of the covenant between me and you" (Genesis 17:11). When he made the covenant with Israel at Mount Sinai, he designated the Sabbath as a sign of his covenant relationship with the nation of Israel:

> Therefore the people of Israel shall keep the Sabbath, observing the Sabbath throughout their generations, as a covenant forever. It is a sign forever between me and the people of Israel. (Exodus 31:16–17)

A HOLY DAY FOR GENTILES

Exodus 31 says the Sabbath is a sign of God's relationship with the Jewish people "forever." The Jewish people are to observe the Sabbath day "throughout their generations, as a covenant sign forever." The same obligation does not apply to non-Jewish people.

Although the Sabbath is for everyone, and Gentile believers certainly should never be excluded from the Sabbath, only Jewish people are obligated to observe the Sabbath as a covenant sign. The Sabbath is a holy day for everyone, even for the Gentiles, but it is not a sign of the covenant for Gentiles.

In this way the Sabbath is like the sign of circumcision. God told Abraham that he and his children must be circumcised as "a sign of the covenant between me and you" (Genesis 17:11), but we learn from the apostles that Gentile believers are exempt from the requirement of circumcision. Paul says, "Was anyone at the time of his call uncircumcised? Let him not seek circumcision" (1 Corinthians 7:18). Likewise, he says, "I testify again to every man who accepts circumcision that he is obligated to keep the whole law" (Galatians 5:3). According to Paul's teaching, a Gentile believer is not obligated to receive circumcision and become Jewish. If he does become Jewish, however, then he will be obligated to keep the whole Torah, including the prohibition against work on the Sabbath.

This is one of the ways that the apostles made a distinction between Jewish people and Gentile believers. They did not require Gentile believers to take on the commandments that are signs: circumcision and Sabbath observance.

CONFUSION BETWEEN JEWS AND GENTILES

Church theology has historically missed the difference between Jews and Gentiles. This seemingly minor oversight has had catastrophic results. Follow the train of thought:

1. Church theology assumes that under the new covenant Christ has erased all the differences between Jews and Gentiles: "There is neither Jew nor Greek, there is neither slave nor free, there is no male and female, for you are all one in Christ Jesus" (Galatians 3:28).
2. Under the new covenant, Jews and Gentiles are "one new man" (Ephesians 2:15). Since there is no difference between Jews and Gentiles, and since Jews and Gentiles are one new man, the same laws and expectations should apply to both Jews and Gentile believers.
3. Since we know from the New Testament that Gentile believers are not obligated to be circumcised or to keep the Sabbath, neither are Jewish believers. After all, in Christ, we are all one.
4. Therefore the Sabbath, circumcision, and the whole Law for that matter, must have been canceled by Christ.

This is a tragic misunderstanding of the New Testament. The apostles never meant to imply that Messiah erases the distinctions between Jewish people and Gentile people. In Messiah, Jews and Gentiles have unity; they have equal access to salvation and the good promises of the new covenant; but that does not mean that they have exactly the same obligations. Jews and Gentiles are one in Messiah, co-heirs of the kingdom, co-religionists, and equal partakers in salvation. That does not mean that Jews and Gentiles are the same. Here is an important rule of biblical interpretation: "Oneness is not sameness. Unity is not uniformity."

For example, the New Testament also says that, in Christ, "there is no male and female," but no one would claim that Christ erased the distinctions between men and women. Likewise, God has not erased the distinctions between Jews and Gentiles.

As a result of confusing Jewish roles and Gentiles' roles, many New Testament teachers have taught Jewish believers that they are no longer obligated to observe the Sabbath. Since Jewish believers are now Christians, they no longer need to worry about observing the Sabbath day prohibitions or keeping the Sabbath holy. In fact, many Christian teachers actively discourage Jewish believers from keeping the Sabbath. Jewish believers are warned about slipping "back under the law" if they observe the Sabbath. They are encouraged to worship on Sunday with other Christians.

All this confusion has created a mess for the Jewish disciples of Yeshua. Most Jewish believers today do not observe the Sabbath, and they believe that they are under no obligation to do so. They have been misled by people who themselves have been misled.

YESHUA AND THE SABBATH

Another source of confusion about the Sabbath stems from the many stories in the Gospels in which our Master Yeshua clashes with religious leaders over questions of Sabbath observance. Yeshua often performed healings on the Sabbath, and those healings brought sharp criticisms from the sages of his day. To an outside observer unfamiliar with the issues of Jewish law involved in these stories, it might seem as if Yeshua were setting aside the Sabbath and encouraging his disciples to do so as well. This misunderstanding of the Sabbath-conflict stories in the Gospels has encouraged Jewish believers to abandon Sabbath observance or to adopt a lax and informal attitude toward Sabbath observance. When properly understood within their original Jewish context, however, the Gospels' Sabbath stories do not relax the obligation to observe the Sabbath.

I have previously explored the Sabbath-conflict stories in a companion book, titled *The Sabbath Breaker: Jesus of Nazareth and the Gospels' Sabbath Conflicts*. The same material also appears in later chapters of this book. For now, it is sufficient to state that Yeshua of Nazareth did not change or abolish the observance of the Sabbath.

Instead of depicting Yeshua as an abolisher of Sabbath observance, the Gospels depict him observing the Sabbath in the synagogues, celebrating Sabbath with meals among the Pharisees, and spending Sabbath among the disciples. To Yeshua, the Sabbath was the day of rest, the day of redemption and healing, and the day of his Father. The only work he did on the Sabbath was the work of redemption, the work of God his Father. He believed it was an auspicious day for healing human bodies and souls.

If there is any doubt about what Yeshua taught his disciples regarding the Sabbath, we need only look into the story of his burial. The Bible says, in the gospel of Luke, that the Sabbath was about to begin as the tomb was closed:

> It was the day of Preparation, and the Sabbath was beginning. The women who had come with him from Galilee followed and saw the tomb and how his body was laid. Then they returned and prepared spices and ointments. On the Sabbath they rested according to the commandment. (Luke 23:54–56)

To the disciples of Yeshua, the Sabbath was so holy that they would not violate it even for the sake of attending to his body. Had Yeshua taught them to disregard the Sabbath at all, they would not have been concerned with resting "according to the commandment." Nothing could have stood between the women and the body of their beloved teacher. But Yeshua had taught his Jewish disciples to revere the Sabbath. Even though it meant waiting an extra day before they could pay honor to the body of the Master, "on the Sabbath they rested according to the commandment." If Yeshua's Jewish disciples prioritized the Sabbath so highly that they would not even attend to his body on the Sabbath day, why do Messianic Jews today feel free to neglect the Sabbath?

NEGLECTING THE SABBATH

In many of today's Messianic Jewish congregations and communities, the Sabbath receives only nominal acknowledgment as a day of worship, similar to the way Christian churches observe Sunday as the Lord's Day. Jewish believers today typically come from secular or liberal households that did not keep the Sabbath. Sabbath observance is a new idea to them. Many Messianic Jewish believers, and even some Messianic Jewish leaders, have never experienced a traditional Sabbath. Fear, uncertainty, and misinformation about "traditions of men" and the "teachings of the rabbis" dissuade many Jewish believers from seriously considering traditional Sabbath observance.

At the same time, a surprising number of Messianic Jewish believers retain theological assumptions inherited from Christianity about the cancellation of the Sabbath. Moreover, some Messianic leaders are reluctant to become too traditional because they fear that a traditional Sabbath experience may hamper their efforts to reach out to liberal and secular Jews.

In addition, most Messianic congregations contain a large number of Gentiles who are unfamiliar with the traditional Jewish Sabbath. This Gentile presence further compounds the problem and distances the modern community from experiencing the Sabbath. Finally, as mentioned above, serious misunderstandings about the Master's own teachings regarding the Sabbath discourage Messianic Jews from keeping a traditional Sabbath.

LOST SHEEP

In the days of the Master many Jewish people were drawn to Hellenism and to the broader culture of the Roman world. They abandoned the particulars of Jewish life such as dietary laws and Sabbath observance. The Pharisees referred to assimilated Jews as "sinners and tax collectors." Our Master referred to them as "the lost sheep of Israel." He considered it his special mission to draw these lost sheep back to the flock. He said, "I was sent only to the lost sheep of the house of Israel" (Matthew 15:24).

In the modern world today most Jewish people could be defined as non-observant or secular. Although most Jewish people believe in God, many no longer observe the Torah's commandments as previous generations of Jewish people did. Likewise, Jewish people who identify with liberal branches of Judaism, such as Reform Judaism, are not apt to be Sabbath-observant—at least not in the traditional sense.

The reasons for the secularization of the Jewish people are complex. They constitute just some of a vast number of worldwide social changes that have led to the secularization of both Christians and Jews. Just as most people who identify themselves as Christian are only marginally religious, most people who identify themselves as Jewish do not feel compelled to keep the Sabbath. The observance of the Sabbath seems like something that was important in earlier generations but no longer is.

This secular attitude has had an unmistakable impact on Jewish believers. Most Jewish believers in the church and in Messianic Judaism today come from non-observant, secular Jewish homes. They did not grow up keeping the Sabbath, at least not very fastidiously. When secular Jews become believers, they sometimes unconsciously carry the values of secular and liberal forms of Judaism with them, including an unconscious disregard for the Sabbath. This makes it difficult for Jewish believers to take Sabbath observance seriously, despite what the Bible might say.

Our Master Yeshua seeks the lost sheep of Israel, beckoning his brothers and sisters to turn back to the Torah. He brings a message of repentance, restoration, and return. He says, "Come to me, all who labor and are heavy laden, and I will give you rest" (Matthew 11:28).

EARLY JEWISH BELIEVERS

It should go without saying that the early Jewish believers kept the Sabbath—even after the time of the New Testament. Just in case it does not go without saying, let me bring a few quotations from people who knew them.

Justin Martyr knew Jewish believers. Justin lived in the land of Israel, in Samaria, in the middle of the second century. In his *Dialogue with Trypho* he admits that there are Jewish believers who "wish to live in the observance of the institutions given by Moses, and yet believe in this Jesus who was crucified" (46:1). Justin Martyr states that some Christians condemn the Jewish believers for observing the Torah and the holy days, but he himself is more magnanimous and thinks that they might possibly still be saved.

The church writer Origen knew Jewish believers in the third century. He wrote, "Let it be admitted, moreover, that there are some who accept Jesus and who boast on that account of being Christians, and yet would regulate their lives, like the Jewish multitude, in accordance with the Jewish Law" (*Against Celsus* 5:61).

In the fourth century, Eusebius knew of Jewish believers. He said: "They observe the Sabbath and the whole Jewish system" (*Ecclesiastical History* 3:27).

In the fifth century, Jerome knew of Jewish believers. He said, "The Nazarenes accept Christ in such a way that they do not cease to observe the old Law." Likewise, the fifth-century writer Epiphanius considered the Jewish believers as heretics because they kept the Sabbath and the Torah; apart from their confession of Christ, they were in all ways like other Jews.

Jewish believers as a distinct sect disappeared from the historical record after the fifth century. But so long as they remained, they proudly kept the Sabbath, despite pressure from the Gentile church to abandon it.

ISRAEL'S ORNAMENT

The Sabbath is a gift for all the children of God. It bestows blessing and holiness on both Jews and Gentile believers. It is the LORD's appointed time and his holy day, a day for everyone to draw near to him.

At the same time, the Sabbath is the special inheritance of the Jewish people. Jewish believers should take pride in the Sabbath. The holy Sabbath day is a mark of Jewish identity, a sign of the unique covenant that God made with Israel. Like a wedding ring on the finger of the bride, the Sabbath is an ornament declaring Israel's relationship with the Almighty. It's a sign of the special, priestly status of the holy chosen people. This great treasure belongs to the Jewish people, and even more so, to Messianic Jews, who are heirs to the kingdom, heirs to that day which will be altogether Sabbath.

CHAPTER FIVE

SANCTUARY FOR ALL NATIONS

The Sabbath belongs to God. He instituted it when he rested on the seventh day of Creation. It is the LORD's day, the LORD's appointed time. In this respect the Sabbath is universal. Just as God is the God of the whole world, the Sabbath is the Sabbath of the whole world.

On the other hand, God specifically gave the Sabbath to the Jewish people and assigned Israel to observe the Sabbath. The Jewish people have a holy calling and special responsibility to keep the Sabbath. The Sabbath is a sign of the covenant between the Jewish people and the Almighty.

On that basis, Christians might admit that it makes sense for Messianic Jews to keep the Sabbath. Messianic Jews do not stop being Jewish just because they have become believers in Yeshua. Why should they quit observing the Sabbath? But that same reasoning might be used to exclude Gentiles from the Sabbath. Many argue that Gentile Christians should not observe the Sabbath day. If they do observe the Sabbath, they are accused of playing Jewish, and they might even be called "Judaizers."

Likewise, Messianic Jews themselves sometimes espouse a similar sentiment. A well-known Messianic Jewish leader once said to me, "I suppose a Gentile could observe the Sabbath if he wants, just so long as he understands that there is no reason for him to do so. There is no blessing in it for him, no reward for him, and no point to it." That particular rabbi's opinion does not speak for all or even a majority of Messianic Jews, but the sentiment is not uncommon in Messianic Jewish circles. Messianic Jews sometimes view Sabbath-keeping Messianic Gentiles as posers and wannabes misappropriating Jewish identity.

Similarly, traditional Judaism also discourages Gentiles from Sabbath observance. Since God did not give the commandment of the Sabbath to the nations, Judaism generally assumes that the Sabbath does not pertain to Gentiles. One infamous passage in the Talmud even goes so far as to say that a Gentile who keeps the Sabbath is worthy of the death penalty.

It's not very often that traditional Christians, traditional Jews, and Messianic Jews all find this kind of theological common ground—something that all three groups can mutually agree upon. It sounds like a unanimous decision: Gentile Christians should not keep the Sabbath.

A LITTLE ENCOURAGEMENT

That unanimity is discouraging for the would-be Gentile Sabbatarian.

A closer look at the New Testament, however, offers a little encouragement. The New Testament indicates that Gentile believers in the Apostolic Era celebrated the Sabbath along with the greater Messianic Jewish community to which they belonged. In the days of the stories that Luke tells us in the book of Acts, the Sabbath was an important part of the faith of every believer.

The early Gentile believers worshiped the God of Israel on the Sabbath and biblical holy days along with the apostles and Jewish believers. For the Gentile believers, the Sabbath was a day of worship, a day of holiness, and a day of blessing. They congregated together for prayer, study, and fellowship. They attended local synagogues where they could hear the Torah and the Prophets read aloud and explained. They used the Sabbath as a day to fellowship with other believers and to honor the LORD.

I believe that every Christian should consider the Apostolic-era church to be the model God intended all other churches to imitate. I believe that every Christian should look at the Apostolic-era Christians as models for living out faith and practice. Certainly I do not suggest that we start dressing in Roman-era sandals and tunics; however, we must take seriously all matters of faith and practice that the first communities of disciples modeled for us.

The first-century believers belonged to the generation that came immediately after the Master walked among us. They still had the living, abiding voice of Yeshua among them in the form of the teaching and guidance of his direct disciples. Taking on the Sabbath day represents a big step toward reconciling ourselves with the original, biblical model of Christianity.

THE GOD-FEARER AND THE SABBATH

In the days of the apostles there were Gentiles who celebrated and observed the Sabbath along with the Jewish community but did not become Jewish. They were called "God-fearers." The term "God-fearer" described a Gentile who, for some reason or another, felt attracted to Jewish monotheism and attached himself or herself to Judaism. Toby Janicki's book *God Fearers: Gentiles and the God of Israel* takes an in-depth look at the Roman-era subculture of Gentiles practicing Judaism.

Monotheism and Torah-observant Judaism attracted many Gentiles throughout the Roman world. Some of the Gentiles drawn to the God of Israel elected to undertake a legal conversion (including circumcision for males) and become Jewish. Others did not. They worshiped in the synagogue with Jews and proselytes, but chose not to undergo the ritual of conversion. They were not exactly idolatrous heathens anymore, but they certainly were not Jews. The Jewish communities generally tolerated their presence in the synagogue and appreciated their financial contributions. Nevertheless, God-fearers remained Gentiles unless they chose to undergo a formal, legal conversion to become Jewish. They did not enjoy all the rights, privileges, and responsibilities of the Jewish people.

F.F. Bruce provides a fair summary of the first-century God-fearer phenomenon:

> Many Gentiles of those days, while not prepared to become full converts to Judaism (the requirement of circumcision being a special stumbling block for men), were attracted by the simple monotheism of Jewish synagogue worship and by the ethical standards of the Jewish way

> of life. Some of them attended synagogue and became tolerably conversant with the prayers and Scripture lessons, which they heard read in the Greek version; some observed with more or less scrupulosity such distinctive Jewish practices as Sabbath observance and abstention from certain kinds of food (notably pork). Cornelius's attachment to the Jewish religion appeared particularly in his regular prayer to the God of Israel and acts of charity to the people of Israel. One may say, indeed, that he had every qualification, short of circumcision, which could satisfy Jewish requirements. (*The Book of Acts: New International Commentary on the New Testament*)

The first-century God-fearer can be compared to the *Ben-Noach* (Son of Noah) in Judaism today. God-fearers renounced idolatry and polytheism and attached themselves to the God of Israel and to the Jewish community. For whatever reason, however, they did not make a formal conversion to Judaism. They remained content to keep the laws that the Jewish community determined as incumbent upon Gentiles, and they voluntarily took on additional aspects of Torah observance, such as the Sabbath, to varying degrees.

The Jewish community did not hold the God-fearers responsible for observing all the prohibitions of the Sabbath. There does not seem to have been confusion about who was actually Jewish and who was not. The God-fearers were welcome to participate in the Sabbath along with the Jewish people, but they were not required to do so.

God-fearers commonly expressed their loyalty to God and to the Jewish people by becoming patrons of the local synagogue. Synagogue donor lists from the Roman Era often included the names of God-fearing Gentiles. In Capernaum a God-fearing centurion financed the construction of the synagogue. Cornelius, the God-fearing centurion of Caesarea, also donated to the Jewish community with generous alms. Other God-fearers in the New Testament include Lydia and her friends, who used to meet for prayer on the Sabbath day outside the gates of Philippi. Throughout the book of Acts, all the Gentiles whom Paul encountered in synagogues on the Sabbath day were God-fearers. (Why else would they have been in the synagogues?) Almost all of Paul's initial converts were God-fearers.

Through the ministry of Paul and the apostles, the God-fearing Gentiles accepted Yeshua as the promised Messiah, and they joined his school of disciples. Just because they became believers in Yeshua, however, does not imply that they quit honoring the Sabbath or attending the synagogue.

As more Gentiles became believers, the number of Sabbath-keeping Gentiles began to increase in the Roman world. First-century Roman writers sometimes complained about the number of Romans who had adopted the Jewish day of rest. The Roman writers considered Sabbath-keeping to be a sign of laziness. Near the end of the first century the Jewish historian Josephus observed that there was hardly a city in the inhabited world where the Sabbath was not being observed by Gentiles who had adopted Jewish laws. These cryptic references to early believers offer us a glimpse of the first-century Gentile disciples of Yeshua keeping the Sabbath.

The problem became so acute that the Emperor Domitian began to arrest Roman citizens who had slipped into Jewish ways. Sabbath-keeping was a dead giveaway. Christian history remembers this as the Domitian Persecution. It was the persecution during which the Apostle John was exiled to Patmos.

DECISION IN JERUSALEM

Despite all that, God-fearing Gentile believers were neither required nor expected to keep the Sabbath in the same way as the Jewish believers. God-fearing Gentiles understood that the Sabbath was a sign of the covenant between God and the Jewish people, just as circumcision was a sign of the covenant of Abraham. Gentile believers did not undergo circumcision or take on the Sabbath as an obligation.

Not all Jewish believers felt comfortable with this arrangement. They wanted the God-fearing Gentile believers to undergo conversion and become Jewish. They argued, "Unless you are circumcised according to the custom of Moses, you cannot be saved" (Acts 15:1). They lobbied the elders of the believing community to issue a ruling that would have required the Gentile believers to take on circumcision and Torah observance as Jews, which would have included the prohibitions against various forms of work on the Sabbath: "It is necessary to circumcise them and to order them to keep the law of Moses" (Acts 15:5).

James, the brother of the Master, met with the elders of the Jerusalem Assembly of believers to consider the question. Before making a decision, they heard testimony from Simon Peter, Paul, and Barnabas, and they considered the testimony of the Torah and the Prophets.

The elders knew what was at stake. If they decided in favor of requiring Gentile believers to become Jewish, this would place the Gentiles under the same Sabbath obligations as the rest of the Jewish people. Accordingly, Gentile believers would be liable to the death penalty for any intentional violations of the Sabbath, just as the Jewish people were. Similarly, Gentiles would be liable to flogging for minor violations of the Sabbath. Knowing this, James and the elders had to decide the legal status of the Gentile believers. Were they Jews and therefore liable to corporal punishment for neglect of Jewish obligations, or were they Gentiles and therefore exempt from those punishments?

James and the elders in Jerusalem decided against requiring Gentile believers to become Jewish. When they did so, they exempted the Gentile believers from the Jewish obligation to rest on the Sabbath and to abstain from all forms of work on the Sabbath. Their decision left the Gentile believers free to continue celebrating the Sabbath as God-fearers.

APOSTOLIC DECREE

James and the elders decided not to impose anything on the Gentile believers beyond the four laws of the apostolic decree: to abstain from meat contaminated by idolatry, from meats that are not slaughtered according to Jewish standards, from the consumption of blood, and from sexual immorality. The four laws applied to the Gentile believers over and above whatever laws of the Torah apply universally to all human beings. The four laws enabled Jews and Gentiles to congregate together more easily. Each law created an obstacle between the Gentile believer and social interaction with the pagan world. At the same time, the four laws removed obstacles to social interaction with Jewish people.

The four laws assured the Jewish community that Gentile believers no longer participated in the local idolatrous shrines, meals tainted by idolatry, sexual promiscuity, or any other pagan indecency. The laws brought Jewish and Gentile believers closer together in table fellowship by assuring the Jews that meat served by Gentiles was slaughtered in a kosher manner, consistent with Jewish law.

James explained, "For from ancient generations Moses has had in every city those who proclaim him, for he is read every Sabbath in the synagogues" (Acts 15:21). Jewish communities and synagogues existed in almost every major population center in the Roman world and Mesopotamia. In those days the Gentile believers still assembled within those synagogues. They considered the synagogues (both Messianic and non-Messianic) as their houses of worship. They considered the local Jewish community to be their larger spiritual family. Just as the Gentile believers had spiritually attached themselves to Israel, they literally moved among the people of Israel. James could depend on the Gentiles learning Torah—both the commandments that applied to them and those that were not incumbent upon them—as they attended the synagogue and heard the Torah read each Sabbath.

Notice that James took Gentile participation in Sabbath and synagogue Sabbath services as a foregone conclusion. Even though the apostles did not require Gentile believers to observe the Sabbath, they assumed that they would keep the LORD's holy day to some extent. They assumed that the Gentile believers would attend the prayer services and Scripture readings as they participated in Torah life along with the Jewish people, in accordance with the custom of the Master. As yet, no alternate, competing holy days existed. The God-fearing Gentile believers participated in almost every aspect of Torah life—whether or not they were obligated to do so.

The decision in Acts 15 must be interpreted within the broader context of Gentile believers participating in Torah, synagogue, Sabbath, and Jewish life. The apostles did not divorce the God-fearers from Judaism or Torah observance. They did not turn Gentile believers away from the Sabbath, the festivals, or any of the joys of Torah. They offered the Gentile believers an exemption, not an exclusion.

IS IT A SIN?

The decision in Jerusalem answers a question frequently posed about Gentiles and the Sabbath: "Is it a sin for a Gentile to break the Sabbath?"

This is a legal question, and it has to be answered from a legal perspective. According to James and the elders in Jerusalem, the answer is "No." If a Gentile Christian were sinning by violating the Sabbath, then Gentile Sabbath-breakers should have been liable to the death penalty just as Jews were. To take on this liability, they would have needed to undergo circumcision and become Jewish. Since the apostles and elders chose to exempt Gentile believers from circumcision and becoming Jewish, they also exempted them from the obligation of Sabbath-keeping. (Notice that this exemption applies only to Gentiles. They made no such exemption for Jewish believers.) The bottom line is this: The Bible does not require Gentile believers in Yeshua to keep the prohibitions of the Sabbath.

SABBATH OPTIONS

If we accept the authority of James, the elders in Jerusalem, and the apostles, then we cannot condemn Gentile Christians for neglecting the Sabbath. For Gentile believers, Sabbath observance is optional.

This means that Sabbath-observance for Gentile believers will look different from congregation to congregation, from family to family, and from person to person. Some Gentile believers will want to keep a completely traditional Sabbath in the manner prescribed by Jewish law. This person will observe the details of the Sabbath rules. He will keep the prohibitions on the thirty-nine forms of work that violate the Sabbath. He will refrain from driving on the Sabbath, from using electricity, and so forth. Other Gentile believers will honor the Sabbath by keeping the day to the LORD, making it a day off from their vocations, and refusing to work on the Sabbath. Others will find it is sufficient to merely treat the Sabbath as a day of worship. Still others might honor the Sabbath by simply welcoming it with a Friday night meal or spending extra time in prayer and study on Saturday.

In any case, the Gentile Christian should not feel required to keep the Sabbath according to all the stringencies and details of Jewish standards. In fact, I once asked an orthodox rabbi, "Am I in violation of Jewish law because I keep the Sabbath?" He replied, "So long as you are not keeping it according to all of the details of Jewish law, you have nothing to worry about." This means that, according to the opinion of traditional Judaism, Gentiles are permitted to keep the Sabbath as long as they do not do so under the supposition that they are obligated to do so according to the same standard as the Jewish people. This rule is intended to keep Gentiles from confusing themselves and others into thinking that they actually are Jewish.

Some God-fearing Gentiles find that they can honor the Sabbath by helping Jewish people keep a traditional Sabbath. A Gentile is free to do tasks and mundane services that the Sabbath prevents Jewish people from doing. For example, when I visit the homes of observant Jewish friends, I am able to shut off lights, turn up the heat, turn on the air conditioner, and a variety of other mundane tasks that are prohibited for Jews to do on the Sabbath by Jewish law. In this way I am actually honoring the Sabbath, enabling others to observe it.

The point is that Gentile believers enjoy a great deal of freedom and latitude when it comes to Sabbath observance. We can expect Gentile believers to engage in the Sabbath at a variety of different levels of observance, and we need to be okay with that. At the same time, a Gentile Sabbatarian should not criticize other Gentile Christians who feel no compulsion to observe the Sabbath at all.

OBSERVE AND REMEMBER IN A SINGLE WORD

Both Exodus and Deuteronomy record the Ten Commandments, including the giving of the Sabbath. Yet these accounts differ slightly. In the book of Exodus the commandment reads, "Remember the Sabbath day, to keep it holy." In Deuteronomy, however, we find, "Observe the Sabbath" instead of "Remember the Sabbath." Did the voice at Sinai say, "Remember the Sabbath," or did it say, "Observe the Sabbath"? The sages explained that God said "observe" and "remember" simultaneously.

EXODUS 20:8	DEUTERONOMY 5:12
Remember the Sabbath day, to keep it holy.	*Observe* the Sabbath day, to keep it holy.

In an article titled "Is the Sabbath Made for Man or Not?" the saintly Dwight Pryor pointed out that the two versions of the Sabbath commandment have another difference. In Exodus 20, God tells Israel to "remember" the Sabbath, and he gives a reason that could be said to apply to all humanity: "For in six days the LORD made heaven and earth, the sea, and all that is in them, and rested on the seventh day" (Exodus 20:11). In Deuteronomy 5, the LORD tells Israel to "observe" the Sabbath, and he gives a reason that can only be said to apply to the Jewish people:

> You shall *remember that you were a slave in the land of Egypt,* and the LORD your God brought you out of there by a mighty hand and by an outstretched arm; therefore the LORD your God commanded you to *observe* the sabbath day. (Deuteronomy 5:15 NASB)

Dwight Pryor suggests that the Torah is hinting toward two different types of Sabbatarians. The Jewish people "observe" the Sabbath as a memorial of the exodus from Egypt, and the God-fearing Gentiles "remember" the Sabbath as a memorial of the creation:

> Note that the reason given for "remembering" the Sabbath is the creation whereas the covenant obligation to "keep" or "observe" the Sabbath stems from the redemption from Egypt (Deuteronomy 5:15). Obviously both aspects are relevant to Israel, but perhaps at another level we see here a basis for humankind honoring the Sabbath as well. After all, long before the Mosaic covenant with Israel was struck at Sinai, God created *adam* (humankind) in the Garden and then ceased from His labors. Shabbat

> was a universal creation principle before it became a particular covenant precept. (Dwight Pryor)

Dwight Pryor suggests that the Torah draws a distinction between Jewish and Gentile Sabbath obligations. The Torah commands the Jewish people to observe the Sabbath; the Gentile is called, at a minimum, to remember the Sabbath, celebrate the Sabbath, and set the Sabbath apart as a holy day, without taking on all the prohibitions incumbent on the Jewish people.

Gentile Christians are often distressed because they want to keep the Sabbath but cannot do so in their current circumstances. Sometimes I meet a man or a woman who wants to keep the Sabbath at home but cannot convince a reluctant spouse to allow it. Other times a person has other obligations that make it impossible to keep the Sabbath. In such situations the Gentile believer should find consolation that God commands his people to both remember the Sabbath and observe the Sabbath. Even if a person cannot observe the Sabbath, he can at least remember the Sabbath. At a minimum, this requires being conscious of the Sabbath's presence. Remember it on Friday night when the sun goes down and the Sabbath begins. Remember it on Saturday morning when the sun rises on the day of rest. Remember it on Saturday night as the holy day comes to an end. By doing this much, a person can take at least a small share in the blessing of the Sabbath. The Sabbath is never all or nothing, and something is always better than nothing.

ABRAHAM THE GOD-FEARER

> Because Abraham obeyed my voice … (Genesis 26:5)

If Gentile believers are not required to keep the Sabbath, and if it is not a sin for them to neglect the Sabbath, then why would they bother with it? Why would anyone keep a commandment that is not incumbent upon him? One answer comes from Abraham, Isaac, and Jacob. The Torah says that Abraham kept all of God's commandments: "Abraham obeyed my voice and kept my charge, my commandments, my statutes, and my laws" (Genesis 26:5).

Traditional Jewish interpretation took this passage to mean that Abraham, Isaac, and Jacob kept the whole Torah, despite the fact that the Torah had not yet been given and despite the fact that they were Sons of Noah (i.e., Gentiles) and not obligated to the Torah as Israel was at Sinai. Jewish tradition firmly insists that Abraham, Isaac, and Jacob—who were all Gentile God-fearers—kept even those commandments of the Torah that did not apply to them as God-fearers:

> Rav said, "Our father Abraham kept the whole Torah, as it is written [in Genesis 26:5], "Because Abraham obeyed me ..." Rav Shimi bar Chiyya said to Rav, "Perhaps this refers only to the seven laws of Noah and circumcision." If that were so, why does the Scripture say, "My commandments and my laws"? ... Abraham our father kept even the obscure Sabbath laws. (b.*Yoma* 28b)

According to the talmudic interpretation above, Abraham kept the Sabbath, the calendar, the sacrificial laws, and other ceremonial concerns. Whether he actually did or not is beside the point. The very idea raises important questions that are pertinent to Messianic Gentile believers. Abraham's observance of Torah offers a precedent for Messianic Gentiles who want to keep the commandments that are traditionally considered specific to Jewish identity, such as circumcision, Sabbath, festivals, and other signs and identity markers. The Apostle Paul says that Gentile believers are "sons of Abraham" in the faith of Abraham (Galatians 3:7; Romans 4:9–18). Our Master Yeshua says, "If you were Abraham's children, you would be doing the works Abraham did" (John 8:39).

Rabbi Samuel ben Meir explains that Abraham, Isaac, and Jacob all observed the Sabbath, even though they were not required to do so, "because of the Sabbath's great importance as the testimony to God's creation of the world *ex nihilo*." Rabbi Judah Loew ben Bezalel explains, "The fulfillment of a positive commandment brings about a beneficial result in the universe. Therefore, even one who is not specifically instructed to do so is rewarded for its performance."

God-fearing Gentile believers who have taken on additional aspects of the Torah along with the Jewish people—these Messianic Gentiles may look to Abraham, Isaac, and Jacob as role models.

PROPERTY OF YESHUA

God gave the Sabbath as a special gift and a sign to the Jewish people. But the Sabbath can also be enjoyed by Gentile believers. The Torah specifically says that a Jewish person cannot make his male servant, his female servant, or the sojourner in his gates work on the Sabbath day. Even the "sojourner who stays with [Israel]" is allowed to rest on the Sabbath (Exodus 20:10 NASB). The Torah says that the Sabbath extends to livestock, servants, and even non-Jews, so that the Gentile may also be refreshed by the Sabbath day:

> Six days you shall do your work, but on the seventh day you shall rest; that your ox and your donkey may have rest, and the son of your servant woman, and the alien, may be refreshed. (Exodus 23:12)

According to this rule, it is incumbent upon a Jew to keep the Sabbath day. Not only that, he must not force his domestic animals, his slaves, or even the stranger (i.e., the non-Jew that works for him) to work on the Sabbath. This is not to say that the Sabbath's prohibitions are incumbent and binding on the ox, the donkey, or the stranger; but it does mean that a Jewish master must allow his servants to keep the Sabbath.

This has implications for Gentile Christians. Our Master, King Messiah, is Jewish. We are all his servants. Those of us who are not Jewish are "his Gentiles." We are the strangers in his gates and the aliens who belong to him. Since we belong to Messiah, he must grant the Sabbath rest to us, as the Torah indicates. This means that the Sabbath is for Jewish people, of course, but also for all believers. Not for all Gentiles, necessarily, but at least for all of the Messiah's Gentiles.

This teaching should not be misconstrued to mean that the Gentile believer is therefore under obligation to keep the Sabbath. If this were the case, the apostles would have said so when the question about circumcision and Torah was put to them. But even though Sabbath-keeping is not a requirement for the Gentile disciple, it is certainly a privilege that comes with the package of belonging to Messiah.

The Gentile Christian is not obligated to keep the Sabbath as a Jew, but in my opinion he should consider himself obligated to keep it as the servant of a Jew. The way we handle the Sabbath reflects on our Master's reputation.

All disciples of Yeshua are his male and female servants. The Messianic Gentile who wants to observe the Sabbath can justify doing so on the basis of discipleship. Discipleship consists of more than simply asking "What would Jesus do?" It also involves doing what Yeshua did. A disciple is not above his teacher, nor is a servant above his master. Yeshua says, "A disciple is not above his teacher, but everyone when he is fully trained will be like his teacher" (Luke 6:40). Even without a mandate to keep the Sabbath, the disciple of Yeshua may want to honor the holy day in imitation of Yeshua. We know that our Master kept the Sabbath and walked in obedience to all the Torah's commandments. He said, "Whoever does them and teaches them will be called great in the kingdom of heaven" (Matthew 5:19). He told his disciples to go out and "make disciples of all nations, baptizing them … teaching them to observe all that I have commanded you" (Matthew 28:19–20). This does not imply taking on all the obligations of the Sabbath as a Jew, but the Gentile disciple should still ask himself, "How would Yeshua observe the Sabbath if he were not Jewish? Would he ignore the LORD's holy day?"

FOREIGNERS AND EUNUCHS

Isaiah the prophet says that the Sabbath is also for "the foreigners who join themselves to the LORD, to minister to him, to love the name of the LORD, and to be his servants, everyone who keeps the Sabbath and does not profane it" (Isaiah 56:6). A Gentile who keeps God's Sabbath and holds fast to his covenant will be reckoned among the people of Israel:

> Let not the foreigner who has joined himself to the LORD say, "'The LORD will surely separate me from his people'; and let not the eunuch say, 'Behold, I am a dry tree.'" (Isaiah 56:3)

What do eunuchs and Gentiles have in common? Why did the prophet lump them together? They are both, in one sense or another, outside the community of Israel. The eunuchs might think that they have no place in Israel because of the law in Deuteronomy 23:1, which excludes them from the assembly. Furthermore, they will leave behind no heirs to carry on their name within the nation. The Gentile might think that he has no place in Israel because he is not Jewish. He is banned from the inner courts of the Temple. For example, Ezekiel 44:7 rebukes Israel for profaning the Temple by allowing foreigners to enter it.

Though the eunuch cannot have children to carry on his name or leave a legacy behind him within Israel, the LORD rewards him for keeping the Sabbath by giving him "a monument and a name better than sons and daughters" (Isaiah 56:5). Though the eunuch fears he will be barred from the Temple, the LORD promises that his memorial will be within the Temple's walls. The eunuch should certainly not think of himself as outside of the people. The LORD includes him because he honors the Sabbath and keeps the covenant.

Likewise, the LORD rewards the non-Jew who voluntarily holds fast to the Torah and the observance of the Sabbath. He gives that Gentile a status along with his people Israel, promising that, in the Messianic Era to come, he will even receive access into the Temple and a share in the Temple services. As a result, the Temple will be called a house of prayer for all nations:

> Everyone who keeps the Sabbath and does not profane it, and holds fast my covenant—these I will bring to my holy mountain, and make them joyful in my house of prayer; their burnt offerings and their sacrifices will be accepted on my altar; for my house shall be called a house of prayer for all peoples. (Isaiah 56:6–7)

Who is this Sabbath-keeping foreigner? Is he really a Gentile, or is he, as the rabbis assume, a Gentile who has already undergone some form of proselyte conversion to become Jewish? If the Gentiles discussed in Isaiah 56 are legal proselytes who have become Jewish, then there is nothing remarkable about their being gathered with Israel or given privileges in the Temple, nor could the Temple then be called a "house of prayer for all peoples." The proselyte leaves his identity in a foreign nation behind. If all Gentiles must become Jewish before entering the Messianic Temple, then it should be called "a house of prayer for one people." Therefore, the foreigners in Isaiah 56 must be real Gentiles who have maintained a distinct, non-Jewish identity, and yet have taken a place with the nation of Israel, observing the Sabbath and the Torah along with Israel. They are the God-fearing Gentile believers who have run to take shelter under the King of Israel.

CHAPTER SIX

DAY OF DELIGHT

The original disciples of our Master Yeshua had no need to learn about how to observe the Sabbath. They were all Jewish, and they grew up keeping the Sabbath. From early childhood, their lives revolved around the Sabbath. They had never experienced a period of life in which the Sabbath did not order their days. As adults, the Sabbath continued to conduct the routine and rhythm of their lives.

Yeshua did not need to say to them, "Keep the Sabbath on the seventh day. On the Sabbath day you shall have a day of rest. You shall do no work." He did not need to teach them about how to welcome the Sabbath, how to light Sabbath lamps, how to observe the special meals of the Sabbath, how to sanctify the Sabbath, how far it is permitted to walk on the Sabbath, how to worship on the Sabbath, how to properly rest on the Sabbath, or how to conclude the Sabbath. They were already Sabbath-keepers before they became disciples. They had been all their lives.

Neither did Yeshua need to teach his disciples about how to be Jews. Instead, he taught them about repentance, relationship with God, and the coming kingdom. His teachings deepened their devotion to the Torah and made them all the more zealous for the commandments: The Jewish believers were "all zealous for the Law" (Acts 21:20)—that is, the Torah. That is why the disciples of Yeshua were among the most devout Sabbath-keepers of all the Jewish people in those days.

THE IDEAL SABBATH

The Messianic Jewish experience of today is not like that. For reasons already explained, most Messianic Jewish congregations undertake only a nominal observance of the Sabbath, and most Gentile Christians have no familiarity with the Sabbath whatsoever.

This chapter attempts to compensate by offering a brief description and overview of the typical Sabbath as it might be lived out in an idealized Messianic Jewish community today. In reality, Sabbath observance differs from community to community and from family to family. Messianic Jewish communities contain members at various points on the continuum of observance, with some keeping the Sabbath more strictly than others, and some hardly observing it at all. Moreover, as explained in the previous chapters, there are differences between a Messianic Gentile's obligations and a Messianic Jew's obligations.

I have based the following idealized overview of the Sabbath day on my own experiences at the Messianic congregation Beth Immanuel, in Hudson, Wisconsin, but I do not mean to describe Beth Immanuel or any particular Messianic community. Instead, I have written about my personal experiences to provide an introduction to practical Sabbath observance according to the model we have inherited from the Jewish people.

PREPARING FOR THE SABBATH

Preparations for the Sabbath begin early in the week. Invitations for Friday night guests might be issued a week or more in advance. A Thursday grocery shopping trip is usually essential, especially in the winter months when the sun sets early on Friday evenings. The well-prepared Sabbath-keeper is already busy preparing food on Thursday, and a few women in the community bake their challah bread—the special braided loaves of Sabbath bread—on Thursday night. Others time the baking of the bread so that it will be fresh from the oven on Friday when the family comes around the table. The rest of us bring challah bread home from the bakery on Friday afternoon.

Friday is the busy day. The preparations that we make for the Sabbath day remind us of the preparations we make for the coming kingdom. This current age is the time for repentance and deeds. It corresponds to the six days of the week. In the age to come we will receive the reward for deeds committed in this current era. The Messianic Era and the World to Come correspond to the Sabbath day. In the kingdom and the World to Come, it will be too late to repent. We will then only be able to enjoy the preparations made in this age, in this world.

Ideally, we want to have the house clean and straightened up before the Sabbath begins. Jewish custom specifically makes reference to making up the beds. We wash all the dishes in anticipation of using practically every clean plate, bowl, fork, spoon, and knife over the next twenty-four hours. All the cooking needs to be completed before the Sabbath begins. We want to have enough food ready for three meals over the next twenty-five hours.

Before beginning the Sabbath, it is customary to make a contribution to charity. Even if it is only a few coins dropped into the charity box, we should give something in fulfillment of the verse that says, "None shall appear before me empty-handed" (Exodus 23:15).

Showers and bathing also start early on Friday, especially in larger households where everyone will need a turn before the Sabbath begins. It's important to get cleaned up and groomed before the Sabbath. We dress in our Sabbath finest. Formal wear demonstrates honor for the Sabbath.

In his booklet *The Talmud on Trial*, nineteenth-century Messianic Jewish pioneer Rabbi Isaac Lichtenstein writes, "As you change out of the soiled garments of the previous week, you will also remove at the same time the old man." We enter the Sabbath as new creations.

Lichtenstein also writes about the "wonderfully decked Sabbath table" on which we serve "not only earthly food but also manna from heaven, which refreshes both body and soul." We set the table with a nice tablecloth and our best dishes. The Sabbath meal is a formal affair, a weekly banquet. Fine china and a bottle of wine or grape juice stand ready for the *Kiddush* blessing that will initiate the meal. Two loaves of challah bread are concealed beneath a clean cloth, awaiting their turn to participate in the blessings. Two candles are prepared to cast their light at the Sabbath meal.

LIGHTING CANDLES

The light of the Sabbath candles reminds us of the light of the coming kingdom: "Arise, shine, for your light has come, and the glory of the LORD has risen upon you … and nations shall come to your light" (Isaiah 60:1–3). No one lights a lamp and hides it under a bowl. Instead, we light the lamps so that they may give light to everyone in the household. In the same way, we should let our light shine before men that they may see our good deeds and praise our Father in heaven (Matthew 5:15-16). Rabbi Isaac Lichtenstein writes, "The Sabbath lights do not only burn outwardly, but they also shine inwardly."

We light the Sabbath candles eighteen minutes before sunset. The eighteen minutes are a safety measure meant to ensure that we do not transgress the prohibition on lighting a fire on the Sabbath day: "You shall kindle no fire in all your dwelling places on the Sabbath day" (Exodus 35:3). The custom of lighting Sabbath lamps goes back to the days before electric lights. In a family context, the duty of lighting the Sabbath lights belongs to the women of the household. Jewish women recite a special blessing over the ceremony, praising God for commanding them regarding the lighting of the Sabbath lights. The sweet illumination of the Sabbath candles fills the room with an aura of holiness and signifies the onset of the Sabbath.

In a traditional Jewish home, as the Sabbath lights are kindled, the flipping on and off of electrical lights ceases, as according to Jewish law, the manipulation of electrical current violates the Sabbath. In my own home—a Messianic Gentile home—we never took on the prohibition on manipulating electricity, but if we had done so, we would have ensured that all the switches were flipped to the position we wanted them prior to the onset of the Sabbath. Some people use timers, set in advance, to turn lights on and off. Others go so far as to use masking tape to tape light switches into position, lest they inadvertently forget and reflexively flip the switch during the Sabbath day.

WELCOMING THE SABBATH BRIDE

To welcome the Sabbath, men of the community converge on the synagogue for a special prayer service. The women are also welcome to attend, and some do, but in many cases, the women remain at home to make last-minute preparations for receiving guests.

The prayer service is called *Kabbalat Shabbat*, which simply means "Welcoming the Sabbath." The prayer service can be found in any complete Jewish prayer book. (A prayer book is called a *Siddur*, which means "Order," short for "Order of Prayer.") *Kabbalat Shabbat* begins with a lively recitation of psalms, usually sung in happy and joyful melodies: Psalm 95–99, Psalm 29, Psalm 92–93. These psalms are all prophecies about the kingdom. They point to the future Messianic Era when the LORD will reign and the world will rejoice. They remind us that as we enter the Sabbath, we take a foretaste of the kingdom.

We also sing a special Sabbath song called *Lechah Dodi* (O Come, Beloved), which speaks of the Sabbath day as a beautiful, regal bride coming to meet her bridegroom under the wedding canopy. On the final verse of the song, we turn to the west, where the last light of the sunset is streaming through the windows, and we say, "Crown of her husband, come in peace, let joy and gladness now increase. With the treasured people, come, abide; to the faithful ones, come O bride!"

After the *Kabbalat Shabbat* prayers, the Sabbath begins. We conclude the service with the Sabbath evening prayers. Then we walk home to join our families.

Not everyone can attend the synagogue for the *Kabbalat Shabbat* prayers. I myself rarely have the opportunity because my family lives out of town. Anyone can take the time to pray through the Psalms and Friday evening prayers prior to sitting down to eat. It's a great way to welcome the Sabbath and to dedicate the day to the LORD.

BLESSING THE CHILDREN

After the Friday night prayers, we return to our families for the Friday night Sabbath meal, the biggest event of the week:

> Let the place at the Sabbath table beckon you, welcome you, wipe away the stress of your work week, cause you to forget the troubles and pains of life and the plagues that pursue you. Let it satisfy your soul's desires, the soul's joy, the soul's peace, untroubled and undisturbed. (Isaac Lichtenstein, *The Talmud on Trial*)

Before sitting down to eat, fathers in Sabbath-keeping families take a moment to administer blessings to their children. The father places his hands on the head of each of his sons and says, "May God make you like Ephraim and Manasseh." This blessing fulfills the prophecy of Jacob who said, "By you Israel will pronounce blessings, saying, 'God make you as Ephraim and as Manasseh'" (Genesis 48:20). We bless our daughters with the words, "May God make you like Sarah, Rebekah, Rachel, and Leah." The blessings continue with the words of the priestly benediction (Numbers 6:24–26) and the messianic prophecy of Isaiah 11:2:

> May the LORD bless you and protect you.
>
> May the LORD make his face shine toward you and be gracious to you.
>
> May the LORD lift his face toward you and establish peace for you.
>
> Let the Spirit of the LORD rest on him: a spirit of wisdom and discernment, a spirit of counsel and power, a spirit of knowledge and fear of the LORD.

In addition to these prescribed words, the Friday night blessing provides an opportunity for fathers to express some personal word of affirmation or affection on each child. All these blessings, and all the ensuing Sabbath-table blessings, songs, and prayers can be found in any complete Siddur. They also appear in the Vine of David book *The Sabbath Table: Prayers, Blessings, and Songs for the Sabbath.*

PEACE UNTO YOU

As the family and guests gather around the Sabbath table, we sing a customary song called *Shalom Aleichem*, which means "Peace unto you." Some families stand around the table and join hands for the song. Others sing while seated. Some sing through all four verses three times.

The traditional song invokes the Sabbath peace, beseeching God to send his angels to bless our households with peace for the Sabbath day. According to mystical folklore, the LORD dispatches two angels to each household—an angel of blessing and an angel of rebuke. If the angels find the household in order with the food prepared, the beds made, and the Sabbath lamps already lit, the angel of blessing says, "So may it be next week also," and the angel of rebuke replies, "Amen." However, if the angels find that the family has not completed their preparations for the Sabbath, the angel of rebuke says, "So may it be next week also," and the angel of blessing replies, "Amen." This legend reminds us of the eschatological meaning of the Sabbath as a portent of the coming kingdom. In that day, "The angels will come out and separate the evil from the righteous," and they will carry out judgments upon the earth (Matthew 13:49).

Messianic Jewish pioneer Rabbi Isaac Lichtenstein contrasts the experience of the Sabbath-keeping home (blessed by the angel of peace) against the experience of the non-observant home (rebuked by the angel of rebuke):

> As the man enters his home [on Friday night, returning from the synagogue], his family greets him with open arms, full of love. A holy shudder vibrates through the man's inner being as his wife and children transfigure before him. Crowned with halos of light, shining like the Sabbath lamps themselves, like adornments of the Temple, his family is radiant and delightful in his eyes. Forgotten is bickering and strife; forgotten is discord and quarrelling. The Angel of Peace, the angel of blessing, escorts the man over the threshold of his home, bringing a spirit of love, reconciliation, and unity with him. His family takes their places at the table. The evil angel of rebuke—which manifests in disinterest, jealousy, discontentment, contention—is disarmed and overcome by the consecration of the Sabbath, so that he must say, "Amen."

> To the man without any outward observance [of the Sabbath], each day is just like every other day. Covered with dust, he comes along with his walking stick and burden into his dark and bleak dwelling, though Sabbath eve beckons him. Dark is the dwelling, and even darker the moods: Defiance, disinterest, filthiness, and disgust allow no joyful feelings. Unfriendly is the greeting; nasty is the reception; a dark cloud of worry dominates the man; a sense of uneasiness dominates the wife and children; the evil angel of rebuke wields his scepter of discord, strife, dispute while the angel of blessing, the angel of peace, hangs his veiled head and sighs, and must answer with a groan, "Amen." (Isaac Lichtenstein, *The Talmud on Trial*)

AN EXCELLENT WIFE

After singing *Shalom Aleichem*, the father or head of household recites Proverbs 31:10–31, which begins with the words, "*Eshet chayil, mi yimtza*," that is, "An excellent wife who can find?" Like *Shalom Aleichem*, *Eshet Chayil* was instituted as part of the Friday evening meal by the mystics of the seventeenth century. They interpreted the "excellent wife" as a symbol for the Divine Presence of God. In the modern Sabbath custom, however, a husband sings the words of the *Eshet Chayil* as an ode to his wife, to the mother of the home, or to righteous women everywhere. Jewish tradition has a variety of melodies for the passage. The beautiful words of the proverb provide the children of the household an opportunity to bless their mother; the words provide the father of the household an opportunity to bless his wife. At the same time, the words of the song allude to the Messianic Era and the final redemption, when the Divine Presence of the LORD will be made manifest in Zion and in all the earth.

SANCTIFICATION

Immediately after reciting Proverbs 31, the head of the household leads the family in *Kiddush*. The *Kiddush* ("sanctification") marks the formal beginning of the Sabbath meal; it is a legal proclamation of the Sabbath's holiness over a cup of wine. This is the most important part of the Friday night meal. The custom of reciting the *Kiddush* over a cup of wine on Friday night began before the days of the Master. The *Kiddush* fulfills the commandment, "Remember the Sabbath day, to keep it holy" (Exodus 20:8). The formal proclamation of the Sabbath's holiness sets the day apart from the mundane workweek that precedes it. It reminds everyone at the table that the meal of which they are about to partake is meant for the honor of the Sabbath.

Everyone's glass is filled with wine or grape juice, and the head of the household lifts his cup and recites the traditional blessings. We begin the recitation with Genesis 1:31–2:3, describing the institution of the first Sabbath day. Then we pronounce a blessing over wine: "Blessed are you, O LORD, our God, King of the universe, who creates the fruit of the vine." In Messianic homes we might preface the blessing with these words from the *Didache*:

> We thank you, our Father, for the holy vine of your servant David that you made known to us through your servant Yeshua. Yours is the glory forever. (*Didache* 9.2)

The final blessing of the *Kiddush* contains language specifically appropriate to Jewish people. Some Messianic Gentiles leading *Kiddush* in their own homes prefer to offer a different version of the last blessing, derived from ancient Christian liturgy. Compare:

KIDDUSH FOR MESSIANIC JEWS	KIDDUSH FOR MESSIANIC GENTILES
Blessed are you, O LORD, our God, King of the universe, who has sanctified us with his commandments and has shown us favor, and has lovingly and willingly let us inherit his holy Sabbath, a memorial of the work of creation. For it is the beginning day of the holy convocations, a remembrance of the exodus from Egypt. For you chose us and sanctified us from all of the peoples and lovingly and willingly let us inherit your holy Sabbath. Blessed are you, O LORD, who sanctifies the Sabbath.	O LORD of Legions, God of Israel, you created the world by your word, and you separated a Sabbath as a memorial; for on it you ceased from your work in order to meditate on the words of your Torah. For the Sabbath is a rest from creation, a completion of the world, a seeking of the words of Torah, an expression of praise to God, to thank him for what he has given to mankind. Blessed are you, O LORD, who sanctifies the Sabbath.

At the conclusion of the last blessing, everyone at the table replies, "Amen" and drinks from the cup. The words of the Jewish version of the blessing connect the Sabbath day with both the creation and the redemption from Egypt, thereby alluding to the future redemption in the days of Messiah. The Gentile version reminds us that the Sabbath provides a foretaste of the peace and wholeness of the Messianic Era when all nations will ascend to Zion to learn the Torah. The *Kiddush* ritual also reminds us of the coming Messianic banquet when we will drink "this fruit of the vine" anew with our Master when he drinks it in his Father's kingdom (Matthew 26:29).

BLESSING FOR BREAD

In keeping with Jewish convention, the people around the Sabbath table undergo a ritual hand-washing to prepare for eating bread. The head of the household removes the covering from the two loaves of bread, salts them in memory of the sacrifices in the Temple, and then lifts the bread while pronouncing the usual blessing for bread: "Blessed are you, O LORD, our God, King of the universe, who brings bread out of the earth." In Messianic homes, we preface the blessing with the words from the *Didache*:

> We thank you, our Father, for the life and for the knowledge that you made known to us through your servant Yeshua. Yours is the glory forever. Just as this piece of bread was scattered over the mountains and gathered together, so may your assembly be gathered from the ends of the earth into your kingdom. For yours is the glory and the power through Yeshua forever. (*Didache* 9.3–4)

These words allude to the final redemption and the Messianic ingathering when the exiles of Israel and the disciples of Yeshua will be gathered to Zion "from the ends of the earth" into the Messianic Kingdom.

After the blessing, the head of household breaks or tears the bread and distributes it around the table. Then the meal commences.

A WORD OF TORAH

At the Sabbath meal, we serve the best food that we can afford. A good Friday night menu often includes a chicken soup, a side dish of pickled fish, a salad, a main dish of poultry, fish, or red meat, and a sweet dessert. The best part of the meal, however, is the teaching. Our Master called it "the good portion" (Luke 10:42). In other words, he considered the Torah to be the entrée of the meal.

The Friday night meal is not complete without a short teaching from the Torah. Every Sabbath comes with its own unique Torah portion—the section of the Torah scroll that will be read in the synagogue on Saturday morning. The weekly Torah portion is an important part of the Sabbath.

At the Sabbath table, we might read a few chapters from the weekly Torah portion, or we might simply discuss an idea or insight based on the weekly readings. When we come to the Sabbath table, we should already have completed the weekly readings from both the Torah and the Prophets, and we should be ready to discuss them. When my children were younger, I used to quiz them on the weekly Torah reading at the Sabbath table, and I asked them to bring a question of their own about the Torah portion to the table. We made a game out of it.

In addition to the word of Torah, the Friday night Sabbath table provides a good opportunity for reading inspiring stories. When my children were growing up, I read to them every Sabbath. We read tales from the Talmud, Chasidic stories, episodes from the Gospels, stories about the apostles, and biographies of great missionaries and men of God.

Disciples of Yeshua should not leave the Sabbath table before exchanging a few words of the Master. Toward this end, each member of my family used to take a turn reciting one of the sayings of Yeshua at the Sabbath table, or at the very least, recounting one of the stories from the Gospels. By speaking the words of Yeshua and telling the stories of Yeshua, we make him welcome at our Sabbath table.

SABBATH SONGS

In addition to words of Torah, stories, and teachings of the Master, a proper Sabbath meal requires a few songs. Traditional Sabbath songs are called *Zemirot Shabbat* (Sabbath Songs), and a collection of them appears in Vine of David's *The Sabbath Table.* Melodies for the *Zemirot* can be easily obtained online. It's great to get everyone at the table singing along. Worship songs are also appropriate for the Sabbath table. My family sometimes sings hymns around the table. In this way, the Sabbath table becomes an opportunity to fulfill the words, "be filled with the Spirit, addressing one another in psalms and hymns and spiritual songs, singing and making melody to the Lord with your heart, giving thanks always and for everything to God the Father in the name of our Lord Jesus Christ" (Ephesians 5:18–20):

> At the Sabbath table, the tears, the poverty, the distress, and the misery are all forgotten. Forgotten are all worries and cares, all burdens, all the bitterness of life. The higher level of sanctity which one feels on the Sabbath is a foretaste of greater holiness and a revelation of the secrets of hidden heavenly joys. (Isaac Lichtenstein, *The Talmud on Trial*)

GRACE AFTER MEALS

The Friday night Sabbath meal often continues late into the evening. In the summer months, when the Sabbath begins late at night, we are sometimes still at the table at midnight. In any case, when the evening has run its course and the time to conclude the meal has come, we pause to give thanks to God for the food. Many families sing through the traditional text of the Grace after Meals blessings. Others do so silently. Still others use the shorter apostolic prayers of thanksgiving from the *Didache* to thank God for the food. Whatever choice we make, it is important to conclude the meal with thanksgiving in order to fulfill the commandment, "You shall eat and be full, and you shall bless the LORD your God" (Deuteronomy 8:10).

THE SABBATH DAY WALK

The next morning, we attend synagogue for the Sabbath morning prayers and the reading of the Torah. Ideally, we walk to the synagogue. Starting an automobile violates the prohibition against creating a flame on the Sabbath as well as the prohibition on manipulating electricity on the Sabbath. Ideally, Sabbath-keepers live within walking distance of their place of worship. This forces us to live closely and in community, as the early believers did.

The early believers also observed the law of staying within a Sabbath day's walk, as the Bible says, "They returned to Jerusalem from the mount called Olivet, which is near Jerusalem, a Sabbath day's journey away" (Acts 1:12). The Sabbath day's journey extends less than a mile outside one's city limits.

As the time of prayer approaches, the streets around the synagogue fill with families dressed in their Sabbath finery. We converge on the synagogue in the quiet stillness of Saturday morning, and neighbors exchange greetings of "Shabbat Shalom."

In reality, most Sabbath-keepers in the Messianic world are still driving automobiles on the Sabbath. I myself drive some twenty-five miles from my home to my place of worship. Even though Messianic Gentiles are not under the constraints of the Sabbath's prohibitions on automobiles, this is certainly not an ideal arrangement. In an ideal Sabbath-keeping community, we would all live within walking distance of our place of worship.

SYNAGOGUE SERVICES

The Sabbath morning synagogue service is sparsely attended as the prayers begin, but as the service continues, more and more members of the community arrive. The traditional liturgical synagogue service lasts for several hours. Most attendees time their arrival to correspond to the reading of the Torah and the teaching.

The core of the Sabbath service consists of 1) a reading from the Torah, 2) a complementary reading from the Prophets, and 3) a teaching that expounds upon the two readings. The reading from the Torah follows a consecutive progression through the scroll from Sabbath to Sabbath. The reading from the Prophets is ordinarily a passage that in some way mirrors the language or the content of the reading from the Torah. The teaching is typically an expansion—though sometimes tangential—of that day's Scripture readings.

With great ceremony, the cantor takes the Torah out of the holy ark and carries it to the *bimah*—the raised platform at the center of the synagogue from which the Torah is read. Several members of the community assist in the honor of removing the scroll's decorations, unrolling it, and placing it on the *bimah*. A synagogue official called the *gabbai* takes charge, and he calls members of the congregation to come up to the *bimah* and receive the honor of reading from the Torah scroll. In actual fact, the honored reader only chants a blessing before and after the reading. A trained Hebrew reader steps in and reads from the Torah scroll on his behalf.

On the Sabbath day the *gabbai* calls up a total of seven readers to read through the Torah portion. The Torah portion is called the *parashah* (portion).

After the seven readers have completed their readings, the *gabbai* calls an eighth reader. The eighth reader rereads the last verses of the Torah portion (*maftir*), and then he reads a corresponding passage from the books of the Prophets. The Sabbath-day reading from the Prophets is called the *Haftarah*, which means "conclusion." In Messianic synagogues we add a reading from the New Testament to the conclusion of the *Haftarah*.

After the Torah has been returned to the ark, a teacher in the community offers a commentary on the day's Scripture readings.

The writings of the apostles provide the earliest evidence for the three-part synagogue service and the custom of reading from the Prophets on the Sabbath. Paul speaks of "the utterances of the prophets, which are read every Sabbath" (Acts 13:27). In Yeshua's Sabbath-day visit to the Nazareth synagogue, he participated in all three aspects of this service:

1. Torah: "He went to the synagogue on the Sabbath day, and he stood up to read [the Torah]" (Luke 4:16).

2. Haftarah: "The scroll of the prophet Isaiah was given to him. He unrolled the scroll and found the place where it was written ..." (Luke 4:17).
3. Teaching: "He rolled up the scroll and gave it back to the attendant and sat down. And the eyes of all in the synagogue were fixed on him. And he began to say to them ..." (Luke 4:20–21).

Paul's visit to the Galatian synagogue of Pisidian Antioch in Acts 13:15 demonstrates the same three-part order of service: "[1] After the reading of the Law and [2] the Prophets, [3] the rulers of the synagogue sent a message to them, saying, 'Brothers, if you have any word of encouragement for the people, say it'" (Acts 13:15).

Every time we attend synagogue and hear the Torah read aloud, it should remind us of the Master. We should remember how the Master used to read from the Torah every Sabbath. The Sabbath Torah service in the synagogue also reminds us that in the Messianic Era, the Torah will go forth from Zion and the word of the LORD from Jerusalem. All nations will gather to learn the Torah and hear the teaching of King Messiah.

Every time we attend the synagogue on the Sabbath, we receive a small foretaste of that day when Yeshua will teach all Israel (and all nations) the Torah. In that day, there will be a big Bible study in Jerusalem, and we are all invited. Everyone is going to be there. Yeshua himself will be our Torah teacher. In that day:

> Many peoples will come and say, "Come, let us go up to the mountain of the LORD, to the house of the God of Jacob; that He may teach us concerning His ways and that we may walk in His paths." For the Law [that is, the Torah] will go forth from Zion and the word of the LORD from Jerusalem. (Isaiah 2:3 NASB)

THE SABBATH DAY MEAL

After morning services, we are ready for the second meal of the Sabbath. It might take place in the synagogue, with the whole community, or it might take place back in our homes. In either case we begin the meal with a short declaration of the Sabbath's sanctity over wine and bread, just as we did on Friday night, in order to fulfill the verse, "Remember the Sabbath *day*, to keep it holy" (Exodus 20:8). The Torah says that we are to remember to make the Sabbath "day" holy, not just the Sabbath eve. This shorter version of the Friday night solemnities is called *Kiddush Rabba* (Great Kiddush). The ensuing meal involves teaching, singing songs, psalms, blessings, and prayers, much like the Friday night meal.

After the meal we spend the afternoon with family and friends, enjoying fellowship and the good things of the Sabbath.

AFTERNOON PRAYERS

As the Sabbath day comes toward its end, we might find our way back to the synagogue to participate in the short afternoon prayer service (*Minchah*). During afternoon prayers, we take the Torah out again to hear a brief preview of next Sabbath's Torah portion. Three readers are called up to read the first fifteen verses or so of the next chapter. This ceremony starts us on a new week of Torah study.

THE THIRD MEAL

In ancient times the daily meal schedule consisted of only two meals—an evening meal and an early afternoon meal. We set apart the Sabbath as a special day by adding an additional meal in the late afternoon—the mystical third meal (*Se'udah Shlishit*). The third meal of the Sabbath is a light meal—more of a ceremonial snack than a proper meal. It usually consists of not much more than bread and a few cold cuts, pickled fish, or boiled eggs. The point of adding an additional meal is to further set the Sabbath apart from a normal day. In this way we fulfill the words of the Torah that tell us to "eat it today," using the word "today" three times to hint that we should eat three meals on the Sabbath: "Eat it *today*, for *today* is a Sabbath to the LORD, *today*..." (Exodus 16:25). The third meal involves more teaching, singing songs, psalms, blessings, and prayers, concluding with the Grace after Meals.

HAVDALAH

By the time the Grace after Meals of the third meal has concluded, the Sabbath is practically over and the first day of the week is beginning. The sun has set and the first stars have appeared in the sky, signaling that the time has arrived for evening prayers. The evening prayer service follows the same synagogue liturgy as the weekday evening prayers, but it concludes with a sweet ceremony called *Havdalah*.

Havdalah means "separation." This ceremony marks a separation between the holy time of the Sabbath and the normal time of the weekday. For Messianic believers, the ceremony has special significance because our Master rose from the dead "after the Sabbath" on "the first day of the week," i.e., at Havdalah time on a Saturday night.

The person leading Havdalah begins by overfilling a cup of wine so that it runs over onto a saucer or plate, thereby fulfilling the verse that says, "My cup overflows" (Psalm 23:5). Just as we began the Sabbath by making a declaration of its holiness over a cup of the fruit of the vine, so too, we conclude the Sabbath over a cup of wine or grape juice.

The leader of the ceremony sets out fragrant spices. He lights a multi-wicked, braided candle. By the light of the candle he reads a compilation of short Scriptures and Bible verses and recites a series of blessings over the wine, the spices, and the flame. The text for Havdalah can be found in the Vine of David book *The Sabbath Table* or any standard Siddur. In our community we also read some teachings of the Master to bring us into the new week.

The flame of the candle reminds us that the Sabbath is over and that it is now permissible to ignite fire again. The prohibitions of the Sabbath are lifted. The light of the candle also symbolizes the spiritual light of the Sabbath shining into the new week and dispelling the darkness.

The spices symbolize resurrection. At the conclusion of the Sabbath a person's spirit feels sorrow over the departure of the holy day, and it desires to depart along with the Sabbath, leaving the body. If this were to happen, the person would die. The fragrance of the spices works like smelling salts, so to speak, to revivify a person and firmly reattach his spirit to his body for another week.

The person leading Havdalah pronounces a final blessing regarding the separation between the Sabbath and the weekday:

> Blessed are you, O LORD, our God, King of the universe, who makes a distinction between what is holy and what is common, between light and darkness, between Israel and the nations, between the seventh day and six days of creation. Blessed are you, O LORD, who makes a distinction between holy and common.

At the conclusion of the blessing he extinguishes the flame of the candle in the excess wine that was spilt over into the saucer, and he drinks from the cup. The first day of the week has begun. We say, "*Shavua Tov,*" which means, "Have a good week."

As the new week begins, a traditional song is sung to welcome Elijah the prophet, inviting him to come and herald the advent of Messiah. May he come speedily, soon, and in our lifetime.

CHAPTER SEVEN

Resting from Work

When my wife and I first became Sabbatarian, we wanted to set the day apart to the LORD by refraining from work on the Sabbath day as the Bible indicates. At the time, we were involved in a business venture that absolutely depended on working and making sales on Saturdays. I could not imagine how we would continue to make ends meet if we were to become Sabbath-keepers. I decided that we would have to do our best to honor the Sabbath while continuing to work on Saturdays. We welcomed the Sabbath on Friday night and went to Saturday services when we could, but at least for part of the year, I had to work on Saturdays.

This turned out to be a big mistake. A year later, other circumstances converged to force an end to the business venture, and it became clear to me that if we had simply stepped out of it twelve months earlier when we were first discussing the idea, we would have fared much better. Looking back on the situation with the benefit of hindsight, it's obvious to me that if we had been able to stay in business on Saturday, life would have gone in a different direction, and a wrong one at that.

On another occasion my employer began to schedule for me Saturday on-call shifts, even though I had made it completely clear that Saturday shifts were not an option for me. I decided to be courageous, and asked for a joint meeting with my employer and with the supervisor responsible for scheduling the shifts. I respectfully apologized for the inconvenience it might cause them, and I explained that the next time I was scheduled for a Saturday shift, they should consider that to be my termination notice. My employer and supervisor apologized and I was never asked to work on the Sabbath again.

SACRIFICES FOR THE SABBATH

Over the years I have heard plenty of stories about people who gave up incomes of one sort or another for the sake of keeping the Sabbath. In many cases these were Gentile believers who, strictly speaking, were not required to do so, but who nonetheless sacrificed jobs and career opportunities for the sake of keeping the Sabbath. In some stories the LORD returns a great financial blessing upon the people and they find that after setting aside the Sabbath, they are more prosperous than ever. In most stories, however, the observance of the Sabbath incurs real financial sacrifice, as opportunities are simply forfeit.

Keeping the Sabbath entails other sacrifices as well. Growing up in a Sabbatarian home, our children turned down opportunities to participate in sporting events, school activities, and countless events scheduled for Saturdays. The truth is that the Sabbath is expensive. It's a big commitment.

Despite the financial and social sacrifices, however, one never hears a Sabbath-keeper say, "I wish I did not have to observe the Sabbath." The Sabbath day compensates us with its own blessings. The reward for keeping the Sabbath is the Sabbath itself.

RESTING FROM WORK

Ironically, when my wife and I first considered becoming Sabbatarian and weighed the implication of resting from work on the Sabbath day, we scarcely understood what that really meant.

What does it mean to work on the Sabbath day? From what, exactly, are Sabbath-keepers supposed to rest? The answer might seem simple: A person should not go to work on Saturday, he should take the day off and relax. A closer look at the meaning of "work," however, reveals some big surprises. "Work" encompasses more than you might think. For example, on one occasion Yeshua's disciples broke the Sabbath simply by plucking heads of wheat and husking them in their hands.

SABBATH-BREAKERS

It happened that, after walking all day, Yeshua and his ever-growing entourage of disciples and followers were overtaken by the sunset and the onset of the Sabbath as they passed through a field. His disciples were hungry, and apparently they had no prospects of a big Friday night meal ahead of them. As they walked, some began to pluck the heads of grain from the stalks of wheat. Luke tells us that the disciples rubbed the heads of grain in their hands to husk them before eating them: "his disciples plucked and ate some heads of grain, rubbing them in their hands" (Luke 6:1).

Some disciples of the Pharisees were also traveling with the Master. They saw the disciples plucking and husking, and they said to Yeshua, "Look, your disciples are doing what is not lawful to do on the Sabbath" (Matthew 12:2); "Look, why are they doing what is not lawful on the Sabbath?" (Mark 2:24).

MELACHAH

The disciples' behavior astonished the Pharisees because it violated the prevailing interpretation of the Sabbath prohibition on work. Jewish law defines the biblical prohibition on work (*melachah*) as a prohibition on thirty-nine categories of creative and productive acts. The list of prohibited activities includes reaping, threshing, and winnowing. The Pharisees objected that the disciples, as they plucked the grain and husked it in their hands, violated all three:

> Six days shall work [*melachah*] be done, but the seventh day is a Sabbath of solemn rest, holy to the LORD. Whoever does any work [*melachah*] on the Sabbath day shall be put to death. (Exodus 31:15)

The English language contains no equivalent for the word *melachah*. "Work" is a poor translation. English readers mistakenly assume that the Sabbath's prohibition on "work" applies to the English-speaker's definitions of the word "work." People often think that the type of "work" prohibited on the Sabbath involves heavy physical labor. Others might suppose that the Sabbath prohibits only vocational work, i.e., one's job or career. However, the original Hebrew word, which our English Bibles translate as "work," does not necessarily mean one's vocation, nor does it mean heavy labor.

Although English has no equivalent for the word *melachah*, the creation narrative in Genesis provides the contextual meaning. The word first appears in Genesis: "And on the seventh day God finished his work [*melachah*] that he had done, and he rested on the seventh day from all his work [*melachah*] that he had done" (Genesis 2:2). This context defines *melachah* as creative acts of production, including the creation of light, the creation of substance, formation, separation, planting, and creative activities of making, mixing, shaping, and altering—even when those works are performed miraculously or *ex nihilo*. Any act that takes mastery of creation, therefore, might be considered to be a form of *melachah*.

The Torah offers additional clues by specifying forbidden forms of *melachah* such as cooking (Exodus 16:23), lighting a fire (Exodus 35:3), gathering (Exodus 16:29; Numbers 15:32–36), plowing and harvesting (Exodus 34:21), and carrying (Jeremiah 17:21–22), but it never provides what could be considered an exhaustive list of prohibited activities.

MASTERY OVER NATURE

Melachah involves taking mastery over nature to alter it in some fashion. The original *melachah* from which God rested when he first instituted the Sabbath involved shaping, creating, forming, making, ordering, structuring, organizing, separating, mixing, and molding things to produce results. He rested from imposing his will onto substance, and from creating order from disorder. He rested from producing.

This explains why Exodus 16:23 prohibits cooking, boiling, and baking on the Sabbath; these activities involve "making" food as part of a production process, changing one substance into another substance. Sabbath-observant people cook their meals prior to the Sabbath, not on Sabbath: "This is what the LORD has commanded: 'Tomorrow is a day of solemn rest, a holy Sabbath to the LORD; bake what you will bake and boil what you will boil, and all that is left over lay aside to be kept till the morning'" (Exodus 16:23).

On the Sabbath we are to rest from making things, but the distinctions between making and not making are not always self-evident. For example, pouring milk on cold cereal is not making the cereal, but cooking oatmeal in a pot is making the cereal and constitutes *melachah.* Therefore Jewish law deems it permissible to keep pre-cooked food warm on the Sabbath, but not to cook it.

On the Sabbath, we rest from imposing our will; we rest from restructuring, from reordering, and from making things. Even gathering is prohibited. It constitutes *melachah.* The LORD commanded Israel not to go out of their places to gather manna on the Sabbath. Moses had a man stoned for gathering wood on the Sabbath.

Obviously, *melachah* is not just physically intensive labor or vocational work. It involves the work of shaping, creating, and making things. It includes recreational and relaxing types of skills, hobbies, and crafts, like working in a garden or spending an afternoon doing needlework. Someone might object, "Why should I be prohibited from engaging in things that I enjoy on the Sabbath day?" This objection misses the point. God probably enjoyed creating the heavens and the earth. A religious Jew desists from *melachah* on the Sabbath day because God commands him to do so, not because he dislikes *melachah. Melachah* is not the opposite of play or leisure.

DEFINING "WORK"

As explained above, the Bible does not offer a definitive list of prohibited *melachah.* This is a problem if you are in danger of being put to death for breaking the Sabbath. The judges over the nation of Israel had to make hard decisions about what constituted *melachah* and what did not. People's lives hung in the balance. Correctly understanding the legal definition of the word *melachah* could be a matter of life and death. The judges of a court of Torah could not convict or absolve people accused of Sabbath violations unless they had a standardized definition, a definition upon which everyone agreed, which they could use to make the judgment. Unless the word had tight, specific, legal definition, such cases could be decided only arbitrarily and capriciously.

To develop that tight, specific legal definition, the rabbis pointed to Exodus 31 and 35, where the Torah indicates that the activities required to build the Tabernacle constitute *melachah*; the Torah prohibits Israel from performing those acts of *melachah* on Shabbat even for the sake of building the Tabernacle:

> Whoever does any work [*melachah*] on it shall be put to death. (Exodus 35:2)
>
> Bezalel and Oholiab and every craftsman in whom the LORD has put skill and intelligence to know how to do any work [*melachah*] in the construction of the sanctuary shall work [*melachah*] in accordance with all that the LORD has commanded. (Exodus 36:1)

THE THIRTY-NINE CATEGORIES

By studying the Torah's description of the construction of the Tabernacle, the sages determined that any type of work performed in the construction of the Tabernacle could be termed *melachah*. Employing this methodology, they derived thirty-nine specific categories (fathers) of *melachah*. Some of them arise directly from the biblical text; the rest must be derived logically. The official list reads as follows:

> "The principal fathers of *melachot* are forty lacking one: The one who plows, and the one who sows, and the one who reaps, and the one who binds sheaves, and the one who threshes, and the one who winnows, and the one who cleans [by sorting], and the one who grinds, and the one who sifts, and the one who kneads, and the one who bakes. The one who shears the wool, and the one who bleaches [or washes] it, and the one who combs it, and the one who dyes it, and the one who spins it, and the one who stretches the warp, and the one who makes two loops [across the warp], and the one who weaves two threads, and the one who separates two threads, and the one who ties, and the one who unties, and the one who sews two stitches, and the one who tears out a portion to

> sew two stitches. The one who snares the deer, and the one who slaughters it, and the one who skins it, and the one who salts it, and the one who prepares it, and the one who scrapes it, and the one who cuts it, and the one who writes two letters, and the one who erases a portion to write two letters. The one who builds, and the one who tears down. The one who extinguishes, and the one who burns, and the one who hammers with a *pettish,* and the one who transports from one domain to another. Indeed, these are the forty principal fathers of *melachot* lacking one." (m.*Shabbat* 7:2)

The big list of the thirty-nine categories of Sabbath violations describes bread-making, following the story of a loaf of bread from the field to the loaf. The list describes the story of wool production, following the wool from shearing to fabric. The list describes the story of creating parchment and written text, beginning with hunting, slaughtering, and leather production. The list concludes with some miscellaneous forms of production and destruction that constitute *melachah,* all of which violate the Sabbath.

A HEAVY BURDEN FOR JEWS

Jews who grew up in non-observant homes might feel overwhelmed by Sabbath law. From the outside, the details, stringencies, and enormous number of technicalities look difficult and burdensome. On the contrary, the Jewish people have been observing the Sabbath by these standards for many long centuries. Children raised in observant homes do not feel oppressed by the weight of legislation; most delight in the Sabbath and anticipate its arrival all week long. Far from burdensome legalism, the Sabbath is a day of delight and holiness for the religious family.

Reading through the list of the thirty-nine forms of prohibited work creates the false impression that the Sabbath must be enormously difficult to observe. Imagine if you had no previous experience driving a vehicle and had never seen one operated. You sit down to read a manual about how to drive an automobile. The numerous instructions are overwhelming. The choreography of litigious traffic rules seems baffling. On the other hand, when you watch a driver operate a vehicle and begin to learn to drive it yourself, you acquire the skills and necessary knowledge quickly and easily. The Sabbath is similar. It needs to be experienced, preferably with people already adept at observing it. Reading about it makes it sound complicated, confusing, and burdensome. Actually observing it, on the other hand, is a joy.

A HEAVY BURDEN FOR GENTILES

Christianity's negative assessment of the legislation defining the thirty-nine forms of labor is based on a misreading of the Sabbath-conflict stories in the Gospels, one that assumes that Yeshua challenged the conventional Sabbath law. In the next part of this book we will see that, contrary to popular opinion, our Master accepted the traditional Jewish laws governing Sabbath observance, arguing only that compassion for human beings should take priority over ceremonial prohibitions. He healed on the Sabbath because he prioritized alleviating human suffering above keeping the Sabbath.

Nevertheless, some will still complain that the Jewish observance of the Sabbath has been burdened with traditions of men and rules of rabbis. Before voicing those complaints, Gentile believers should keep in mind that neither the Torah nor the apostles nor even the rabbis require them to observe the Sabbath by abstaining from *melachah*. Although my wife and I have been Sabbatarian for more than two decades now, we do not consider ourselves obligated to observe the prohibitions on *melachah*, and in most cases, we do not. The Gentile Sabbatarian need not feel threatened by the thirty-nine prohibitions whatsoever. Strictly speaking, they do not apply to him, because a Gentile could not be convicted of violating the Sabbath by a court of law. The Gentile believer need not argue that the traditional Jewish interpretation of *melachah* is wrong in order to justify his own preferences or to defend his own Sabbath practices.

DON'T PANIC

The next chapter provides a brief overview and summary of the thirty-nine "fathers" of labor, hitting on major concepts and their origins as well as some of their extensions. Even in brief form, the legal material might make for tedious reading. If long legal discussions put you off, feel free to skip ahead to the subsequent chapter, which begins the next section of the book. You can always come back and read this material later if you like.

Some believers, both Jews and Gentiles, will want to begin observing the Sabbath according to these standards. A believer, and particularly a Jewish believer, should never be discouraged from better honoring the Sabbath. At the same time, it may be best to take on higher levels of Sabbath observance slowly and methodically. A person can quickly become overwhelmed by the prohibitions. Keeping the Sabbath is never all or nothing, and something is always better than nothing. Moreover, a person should not look down on others who do not follow the traditional prohibitions. The Sabbath is poorly understood among Christians and Jewish believers. Anti-Sabbatarian teachings in the church have left us without any anchor in Sabbath observance. Moreover, the long years of exile have eroded Sabbath observance for most Jewish people, and no single individual can be held responsible for rectifying that.

CHAPTER EIGHT

The Thirty-Nine Forms of Work

In the previous chapter we saw that the Biblical Hebrew word *melachah,* which we typically translate as "work," includes thirty-nine categories of production and creation. The rabbis derived these categories by comparing the Bible's Sabbath prohibitions with the story of the construction of the Tabernacle in Exodus 31 and 35, where the Torah indicates that the activities required to build the Tabernacle constitute forms of *melachah.* The Torah prohibited the children of Israel from performing those acts of work on the Sabbath:

> Whoever does any work [*melachah*] on it shall be put to death. (Exodus 35:2)
>
> Bezalel and Oholiab and every craftsman in whom the LORD has put skill and intelligence to know how to do any work [*melachah*] in the construction of the sanctuary shall work [*melachah*] in accordance with all that the LORD has commanded. (Exodus 36:1)

In this chapter, we will briefly explain and summarize each of the thirty-nine categories and consider the origin of each. If you feel yourself getting bogged down in all the details and legal minutia, feel free to skip ahead to the more interesting material in the subsequent chapters.

The following translation of the list attempts to clarify its internal logic by inserting topic divisions.

"The principal fathers of *melachot* are forty lacking one:"

1. FROM FIELD TO LOAF—TOTALING ELEVEN ACTS

Fieldwork—four acts

"The one who plows, and the one who sows, and the one who reaps, and the one who binds sheaves ..."

to Grain Processing—three acts

"And the one who threshes, and the one who winnows, and the one who cleans [by sorting] ..."

to Bread Production—four acts

"And the one who grinds, and the one who sifts, and the one who kneads, and the one who bakes ..."

2. FROM SHEEP TO FABRIC—TOTALING THIRTEEN ACTS

Wool Production—five acts

"The one who shears the wool, and the one who bleaches [or washes] it, and the one who combs it, and the one who dyes it, and the one who spins it ..."

to Weaving—four acts

"And the one who stretches the warp, and the one who makes two loops [across the warp], and the one who weaves two threads, and the one who separates two threads ..."

to Finished Product—four acts

"The one who ties, and the one who unties, and the one who sews two stitches, and the one who tears out a portion to sew two stitches ..."

3. FROM HUNTING TO LEATHER PRODUCTION AND WRITING—TOTALING NINE ACTS

From Securing the Hide—three acts

"The one who snares the deer, and the one who slaughters it, and the one who skins it ..."

to Producing Finished Leather—four acts

"And the one who salts it, and the one who prepares it, and the one who scrapes it, and the one who cuts it ..."

to Marking on Finished Parchment—two acts

"The one who writes two letters, and the one who erases a portion to write two letters ..."

4. VARIOUS ACTS OF PRODUCTION—TOTALING SIX ACTS

Building and Tearing Down—two acts

"The one who builds, and the one who tears down ..."

Fire for Blacksmithing—three acts

"The one who extinguishes, and the one who burns, and the one who hammers with a *pattish* ..."

Transporting—one act

"And the one who transports from one domain to another. Indeed, these are the forty principal fathers of *melachot* lacking one." (m.*Shabbat* 7:2)

The rest of this chapter provides a brief look at each category of prohibited labor, but it should not be considered a comprehensive guide or halachic (legal) standard. Those seeking to learn how to keep the Sabbath by traditional Jewish standards should consult a halachic guide dedicated to that subject. Our purpose is only to demonstrate that, contrary to popular belief, the thirty-nine forms of prohibited labor are not merely rabbinic hot air. The sages derived them reasonably, and when the prohibited forms of labor are understood within their original agricultural context, they do not seem nearly as capricious or oppressive as they are commonly reputed to be. Even the derivative laws and stringencies have their own internal logical consistency.

FROM FIELD TO LOAF

Ancient Israel was primarily an agricultural economy. The Mishnah follows the stages in agricultural production, from preparing the ground for planting all the way to making bread, counting eleven categories of *melachah*.

Plowing, planting, reaping, harvesting, threshing, and winnowing may not appear to be directly related to the construction of the Tabernacle, but the Tabernacle made heavy use of agricultural commodities. Its fabrics wove together linen (a fabric derived from flax), and the preparation of the Tabernacle required the loaves and bread offerings for the Tabernacle's inauguration.

1. PLOWING

The Torah specifically identifies plowing as a form of *melachah* when it says, "Six days you shall work, but on the seventh day you shall rest. In plowing time and in harvest you shall rest" (Exodus 34:21). Plowing (*choresh*) is clearly a form of *melachah*, but the traditional definition of plowing also includes any preparation or improvement of the ground, such as smoothing, leveling, and raking. The prohibition includes digging in the garden, fertilizing, and all manner of working the soil.

2. SOWING

Planting and sowing (*zorea*) qualifies as *melachah* because it is a component of agriculture, a creative and productive process. It involves manipulating and taking mastery of nature. The prohibition does not just forbid planting seeds; it includes any type of horticultural nurturing and care. Religious Jews will not even place cut flowers into water on the Sabbath day.

3. REAPING

Reaping and harvesting are also biblically identified as *melachah*, and are specifically included in the prohibition of Exodus 34:21: "In plowing time and harvest you shall rest." Reaping (*kotzer*) includes cutting, picking, or plucking any type of vegetation. This prohibition encompasses more than just plucking an apple or picking a strawberry on the Sabbath; religious Jews will not pluck even a single blade of grass on the Sabbath day.

Our Master's disciples did "what is not lawful to do on a Sabbath"; that is, "they began to pluck heads of grain and to eat" (Matthew 12:1–2). As we will see in the next chapter, Yeshua defended his disciples, but he did not at all deny that by picking grain his disciples were violating the Sabbath. On the contrary, he argued, according to his principle of prioritizing human need over ceremonial prohibitions, that their extreme hunger made it permissible for them to violate the Sabbath.

ANIMALS

Animals cannot be used as pack animals or steeds on the Sabbath day, as it says, "that your ox and your donkey may have rest" (Exodus 23:12). This prohibition also relates to the principle of not taking mastery over nature on the Sabbath day. Despite that, riding on a donkey does not really create anything. It is not formally a type of *melachah*, but the sages wanted to include the prohibition with the thirty-nine categories of forbidden labor. The prohibition on using animals is somewhat artificially connected to the prohibition on reaping on the basis of concern that one might forget and inadvertently pluck a branch for use as a switch while directing an animal.

4. BINDING SHEAVES

The Mishnah's term "binding sheaves" (*me'ammer*) refers to harvesting and gathering agricultural produce. This category includes other procedures and preparations necessary for harvesting. For example, when harvesting olives, the harvester places sheets beneath the tree prior to beating the branches. A person might assume that, so long as he waited until after the Sabbath to beat the branches, he could place the sheets beneath the trees on the Sabbath; however, the broad prohibition on harvesting disallows it. Harvesting also includes gathering in general. For example, the Israelites were not allowed to gather manna on the Sabbath day, even though it did not need to be reaped.

5. THRESHING

Like plowing, planting, reaping, and harvesting, threshing is a form of agricultural production that constitutes *melachah*. Threshing (*dash*) involves extracting grain from its husk; by extension, it refers to all processes of extracting a usable substance from an unusable substance. Squeezing fruits to make fruit juice and crushing grapes and olives to extract their juice are included in this category. Nehemiah specifically mentions treading winepresses as a Sabbath violation (13:15–18).

In Luke's version of the story of the grain fields he mentions that the disciples husked the grain in their hands, an activity that constitutes a form of threshing: "His disciples plucked and ate some heads of grain, rubbing them in their hands" (Luke 6:1).

6. WINNOWING

Winnowing (*zoreh*) is a form of agricultural mastery over nature. It involves separating threshed grain from its chaff and husks by means of wind.

7. SORTING

The construction of the Tabernacle involved the *melachah* of selecting and sorting good materials from bad. The Mishnah refers to it as "sorting" (*borer*). Sorting consists of separating unwanted portions from wanted portions by hand. The prohibition on selecting was originally drawn from its relevance to agriculture. It prevented a farmer from separating bad produce from good produce on the Sabbath day. The prohibition on selecting can equally apply to other trades. For example, the Master tells a parable about fishermen, which involves sorting: "They sat down and sorted the good into containers but threw away the bad" (Matthew 13:48).

Rabbinic tradition extended the prohibition to food preparation and meals. A person eating from a bowl of cherries cannot pick out the bad ones first. (He is permitted to eat only the good ones.) A person who uses a slotted spoon is sorting the solids and liquids in a soup. Similarly, this category forbids picking fish bones out of fish, which is why the boneless, ground *gefilte* fish is a favorite at the Sabbath table.

8. GRINDING

The construction of the Tabernacle involved various forms of grinding and milling (*tochen*), whether with a millstone or with pestle and mortar. For example, the ingredients in the holy incense needed to be finely ground together. Like the other agricultural *melachah*, grinding is a type of agricultural production, which involves taking mastery over nature. The prohibition on grinding disallows the use of mills, grinders, mortars, and other forms of crushing.

The religious Jew does not crush garlic or grind spices on the Sabbath. The prohibition on grinding also extends to grating things, such as cheeses.

In the days of the apostles medicines were prepared as needed by means of grinding. Therefore the sages forbade the use of non-vital medicines and medical treatments on the Sabbath day. This prohibition did not extend to life-threatening cases, but it may be the original source behind resistance to the Master's Sabbath-day healings.

9. SIFTING

The construction of the Tabernacle involved sifting (*merakked*). This is a form of *melachah* that also relates to agricultural production. In biblical times sifting was an important part of grain production: "As grain is shaken in a sieve, but not a kernel will fall to the ground" (Amos 9:9 NASB). Millers passed flour through sieves to separate the coarse from the fine. Tradition extends the prohibition on sifting into the kitchen by prohibiting the use of sieves, strainers, colanders, and other devices that might be used for sifting or straining during food preparation.

10. KNEADING

The construction of the Tabernacle involved kneading (*lash*), which is a process of combining a powder with a liquid to make paste or dough. This *melachah* includes making mud balls. When our Master spat on the ground, mixed his spittle with dirt, and applied the salve to the blind man's eyes, he seemed to violate the prohibition on kneading. Our Master's enemies declared, "This man is not from God, for he does not keep the Sabbath" (John 9:16).

11. COOKING (BOILING, BAKING, MELTING)

The construction of the Tabernacle entailed various forms of heating, boiling, baking, and melting—in other words, cooking with heat. The Torah explicitly identifies cooking food as a form of *melachah.* Exodus 16:23 prohibits cooking, baking, or boiling manna on the Sabbath, activities that the Mishnah refers to as "baking" (*ofeh*). This category includes boiling water and heating non-food items, even when the heating is accomplished without the use of flame. For example, baking in a microwave oven or a solar oven violates the Sabbath as much as using a conventional oven.

Does this mean that all Sabbath foods must be served cold? Not at all. Friday night meals are usually timed so that food for the Friday night Sabbath table is still hot. Also, precooked foods may be kept warm. Some homes place a tin sheet (called a *blech*) over the stovetop with the burners left on low to create a warm surface to maintain heat.

The laws pertaining to keeping food warm are complex to explain, but easy to carry out. The best way to learn how to manage a Shabbat kitchen is to learn from someone who is already familiar with the laws. Otherwise, a person should consult a pertinent guidebook.

The prohibition on cooking does not prevent other forms of food preparation, such as cutting fruit, preparing a salad, and so forth. Furthermore, the prohibition on melting things does not extend so far as melting a pat of butter over warm food or using ice cubes to cool a drink.

Believers in Yeshua in ancient times kept the Sabbath prohibition on cooking. According to the long version of his epistle to the Magnesians, the early second-century Christian bishop Ignatius criticized other second-century believers for keeping the Sabbath. He specifically mentioned food prepared in advance:

> Let every one of you keep the Sabbath after a spiritual manner ... not eating things prepared the day before, nor using lukewarm drinks, and walking within a prescribed

> space, nor finding delight in dancing and clapping which have no sense in them. (Ignatius, *Magnesians* 9:3, long version)

According to this piece of second-century evidence, early believers prepared their food the day before the Sabbath.

COOKING ON YOM TOV

In Jewish terminology, a festival on which work is restricted (that does not fall on the seventh day of the week) is referred to as a *Yom Tov*, that is, a "holiday." The Torah identifies seven such holidays: the first and seventh day of Pesach, the day of Shavu'ot, the day of Rosh HaShanah, the day of Yom Kippur, the first day of Sukkot, and the eighth day at the conclusion of Sukkot. The Torah forbids performing *melachah* on all the *Yamim Tovim*, but makes an exception for cooking (the exceptions to the exception being Yom Kippur, on which no *melachah* may be performed whatsoever, and any *Yamim Tovim* that happen to fall on the weekly Sabbath).

Exodus 12:16 also identifies cooking as a form of *melachah* when it says, "No [*melachah*] shall be done on those days [i.e., the *Yom Tov* of Passover]. But what everyone needs to eat, that alone may be prepared by you." The exception clause in the passage makes it clear that food preparation is not allowed on the weekly Sabbath. Since Sabbath observance ordinarily prohibits that type of food preparation, the Torah had to expressly state that it is permitted on the *Yom Tov*; otherwise we would assume that it was prohibited as it is on the weekly Sabbath.

The LORD permits food preparation on the *Yom Tov* to avoid hardship on Israel. A *Yom Tov* and the weekly Sabbath sometimes occur back-to-back. If the Torah prohibited food preparation on the *Yom Tov*, the prohibition would sometimes prevent a person from cooking or preparing food for more than forty-eight hours. Food cooked on *Yom Tov* must be cooked for consumption that same day (or on the ensuing day if it is also a Sabbath). According to Jewish tradition, cooking fires can be ignited on *Yom Tov* only from a pre-existing flame.

FROM SHEEP TO FABRIC

The agriculture of ancient Israel incorporated wool production. The Mishnah follows the stages in fabric making, from sheep shearing to final product, identifying thirteen categories of *melachah.*

12. SHEARING

The construction of the Tabernacle required fabrics obtained from "shearing (*gozez*) the wool" of sheep and goats. As an element of agricultural production and manufacturing, not to mention taking mastery over nature, shearing violates the Sabbath prohibition on *melachah*. Jewish interpretation includes shaving and haircuts. This includes all forms of removing hair or feathers from living creatures, including oneself. Religious Jews even avoid plucking eyebrows and using certain types of combs that might tear out hairs on the Sabbath.

13. WASHING

The construction of the Tabernacle required the preparation and washing of fabrics, specifically wool, a process the Mishnah refers to as "bleaching" (*melabben*). Therefore the sages categorize washing fabrics as a form of *melachah.* This includes immersing and wringing fabrics and removing spots or stains. It does not prevent washing of dishes except that a dishcloth or sponge, since it is a fabric, should not be wrung out. Use of hot water from the tap is another issue that might fall under the prohibition on burning or cooking. Although it is not a form of *melachah,* Jewish tradition also prohibits bathing and showering on the Sabbath except under certain conditions.

14. COMBING

The construction of the Tabernacle required woolen threads. The process of rendering wool into fabric involves combing (*menappetz*) the wool, a form of *melachah* that prepares wool (and cotton) for use as thread. Obviously, combing of wool or cotton is a component of production, manufacturing, and taking mastery over nature.

15. DYEING

The construction of the Tabernacle involved dyes to make "blue and purple and scarlet material," so the sages determined that the process of "dyeing" (*tzovea*) constitutes *melachah.* This includes all processes that change something's color: dyeing, painting, adding a colored liquid to a clear liquid, mixing paints, and mixing cosmetics.

16. SPINNING

After the yarn-maker has thoroughly combed the wool, he may spin it into thread. The Mishnah refers to this process as "spinning" (*toveh*). The category of spinning includes associated forms of production such as making thread, rope, felt, and fabric: "And every skillful woman spun with her hands, and they all brought what they had spun in blue and purple and scarlet yarns and fine twined linen. All the women whose hearts stirred them to use their skill spun the goats' hair" (Exodus 35:25–26).

17. STRETCHING THE WARP

The construction of the Tabernacle involved setting up the warp of the loom in preparation for weaving. The Mishnah calls it "stretching (*meisech*) the warp on the loom." Even though the warp without the weave was not a complete fabric, warping a loom is part of the process of *melachah* and therefore is not permitted on the Sabbath.

18. MAKING TWO LOOPS

The construction of the Tabernacle involved the weaving process of setting up the woof of the loom. The Mishnah refers to it as "making two loops" (*oseh shnei vatei nirin*), the beginning of a woven web with two meshes, attaching them to the crosspieces or to the slips, i.e., preparing the loom to pass the spool with the woof across the warp. The broad application of this prohibition includes all types of needlecraft, knitting, crochet, braiding, basket-making, and net-making.

19. WEAVING

The construction of the Tabernacle and the priestly garments required weaving, which the Torah explicitly identifies as *melachah*. The curtains, screens, and priestly vestments were the work of a weaver: "a weaver, as performers of every work [*melachah*]" (Exodus 35:35 NASB). The Mishnah calls it "weaving (*oreg*) two threads." Weaving includes needlework such as embroidery, needlepoint, basket-making, and rug-making. In legal terms, these restful hobbies, activities, and handicrafts are no less violations of the Sabbath than carpentry and stonework.

20. SEPARATING TWO THREADS

If chain stitching, warping, and weaving are forms of *melachah*, the sages deemed that the opposite action of removing the woven product from the loom must be *melachah* as well. The Mishnah refers to it as "separating (*potzea*) two threads." It includes a general prohibition on unraveling fabrics.

21. TYING

The construction of the Tabernacle involved tying knots to attach fabrics and curtains and to fasten tent cords. The sages inferred that some forms of knots can constitute *melachah*. The Mishnah refers to "tying" (*kosher*) any type of permanent knot, such as a sail knot, as *melachah*. The prohibition does not apply to temporary knots, such as those found on one's shoes or necktie.

22. UNTYING

The sages reasoned that if knotting was part of the construction of the Tabernacle and therefore constitutes a form of *melachah*, then the inverse must also. The Mishnah calls it "untying" (*mattir*). Jewish tradition permits the untying of temporary knots, leaving one free to remove his shoes or necktie, but knots intended to be permanent should not be untied on the Sabbath.

The sages, however, specifically permitted the tying and untying of knots for the purpose of leashing animals and drawing water. Yeshua took it for granted that tying and untying knots violates the Sabbath. He also took it for granted that an exception must be made for the sake of watering one's animal:

> Does not each of you on the Sabbath untie his ox or his donkey from the manger and lead it away to water it? And ought not this woman, a daughter of Abraham whom Satan bound for eighteen years, be loosed from this bond on the Sabbath day? (Luke 13:15–16)

23. SEWING

The construction of the Tabernacle involved stitching and sewing fabrics, an activity the Mishnah calls "sewing (*tofer*) two stitches." Sewing certainly constitutes *melachah*. The prohibition on sewing includes all forms of stitchery, needlework, knitting, and the like. Jewish law includes pasting, gluing, taping, and stapling under the same category. Applying adhesive stamps, stickers, or sealing an envelope are also forms of *melachah*. However, fastening objects with temporary fasteners, such as safety pins, is permitted.

24. TEARING

The construction of the Tabernacle involved tearing, a category of *melachah* that includes rending fabrics. The Mishnah calls it "tearing (*korea*) in order to sew two stitches." By extension, the law prohibits separating glued papers or other objects affixed by adhesives or permanent fastenings. For example, opening the lid on a new box of cereal involves separating the adhesive and is not permitted.

FROM HUNTING TO LEATHER PRODUCTION AND WRITING

The exterior of the Tabernacle was protected by a covering of tanned skins. Several classes of labor relate to the process of preparing hides, beginning with hunting or trapping an animal. Ancient Israel depended on the tanning industry for the production of leather and parchments. The Mishnah follows the stages of document production from tanning, to parchment-making, to writing, identifying nine categories of *melachah*.

25. TRAPPING

The Mishnah refers to trapping an animal as "snaring (*tzad*) a deer." Trapping an animal takes mastery over nature. The sages regard setting traps, hunting, and capturing wild animals as a form of *melachah*. This stands to reason. If gathering manna was forbidden on the Sabbath, how much more so is the pursuit of wild game contrary to the Sabbath. This category includes fishing. However, one may trap a dangerous animal in order to protect people from harm.

Sportsmen might protest that hunting and fishing are legitimate Sabbath activities because they are a means of relaxation and a way to enjoy the outdoors, but many other prohibited forms of labor are also sources of relaxation and enjoyment. Pursuing, trapping, hunting, and gathering game certainly violates the Sabbath. Sportsmen should consider who it is that provides fish for their hooks and draws game into their sights. Will he not bless the sportsman who honors his Sabbath?

26. SLAUGHTERING

The construction of the Tabernacle required the slaughter of animals to procure their hides for the covering of the Tent of Meeting. The Mishnah considers "slaughtering (*shochet*) an animal" to be a form of *melachah*. Religious Jews try to avoid all types of slaughtering on the Sabbath, even to the point of sparing the lives of insects on the holy day. The prohibition extends to all forms of killing or injuring. The Sabbath is a day for life, not death. Killing imposes the killer's will and takes mastery over nature. Of course, one may kill to save a life or protect people from harm. The sacrificial services in the Temple represent another important exception to the rule. The priests in the Temple have a commandment to carry out the Sabbath-day sacrifices. Yeshua observed that according to the Torah, the priests in the Temple broke the Sabbath to carry out the sacred service, yet they were guiltless (Matthew 12:5).

27. SKINNING

Procuring skins for the Tabernacle involved flaying and skinning animals. The Mishnah refers to this form of *melachah* as "skinning" (*mafshit*), the first step in the tanning process. This prohibition includes all forms of gutting animals, such as cleaning fish, as well as processing meat.

28. TANNING

Tanning is a process by which hides are made into leather. The Mishnah refers to it as "salting" (*moleach*) and "preparing (*me'abbed*) a hide," the early stages in the tanning process. Tanners also rub oil and saddle soap into the hides.

29. SCRAPING

The tanning process involves scraping the hair from the hides and smoothing the surface of the skin. The Mishnah refers to it as "scraping" (*memachek*). This category includes all types of smoothing and polishing. Traditional Jews do not polish shoes, silver, or even the lenses of eyeglasses on the Sabbath day.

On that basis, Jewish interpretation bans the application of lotions, salves, and medications that must be smeared onto the skin, such as lipstick. Our Master smeared mud and spittle onto the blind man's eyes to demonstrate that the alleviation of human suffering takes priority over the Sabbath.

30. CUTTING

The construction of the Tabernacle involved cutting objects. The Mishnah calls it "cutting" (*mechattech*). The prohibition on cutting applies to changing the size or shape of an object to make it more useful, such as chopping a piece of wood or tearing a piece of paper into a certain shape, hence the proverbial pre-torn toilet paper. Foods for the Sabbath day, however, are exempt from the prohibition, since they are not permanent and will be shortly consumed.

The category of cutting also includes shaping and forming. It takes no great leap of logic to see that shaping and reshaping are a type of *melachah*. The *melachah* of creation from which God rested on the seventh day includes the act of shaping. He shaped the first man from clay. Obviously, acts of shaping like spinning pots on a wheel or carving wood are forms of prohibited work. Unfortunately, shaping includes making snowmen. Even snowballs are problematic, not so much because they involve shaping, but because they involve crushing and compacting in order to create.

31. WRITING

The construction of the Tabernacle required marking and writing. A person might not think of writing notes as a form of *melachah*, but writing something down on paper or on any other type of permanent medium creates a document. The Mishnah refers to it as "writing (*kotev*) two letters." The prohibition on writing includes handwriting, typing, printing, photocopying, stamping, and record-keeping. Drawing, sketching, etching, scribbling, doodling, highlighting, and underlining all fall into the same category. A rabbinic stringency forbids games of chance since they ordinarily involve notations and record keeping. *Pictionary* and tic-tac-toe are definitely off-limits.

The prohibition on writing also precludes all activities that require the creation of a written document such as conducting a marriage (which requires the signing of a *ketubbah*), issuing a divorce (which requires writing a divorce certificate), and business arrangements (which require creating and signing contracts).

32. ERASING

The construction of the Tabernacle may or may not have involved erasing, but if writing is a form of *melachah*, it stands to reason that the inverse is also. The Mishnah refers to it as "erasing (*mochek*) a portion to write two letters."

The Mishnah was only concerned with erasing for the purpose of rewriting, but rabbinic stringencies extended the prohibition to forbid any form of destroying written letters on the Sabbath. That means no erasing letters, tearing through letters, smudging out letters, or any other form of deleting text. Chalkboards and dry erase boards are not Sabbath-friendly.

VARIOUS ACTS OF PRODUCTION

The remaining six categories of *melachah* are a miscellaneous assortment of prohibited forms of work. The Mishnah derived some, such as igniting a fire and carrying a load, directly from the biblical text; others are logically inferred from the construction of the Tabernacle.

33. BUILDING

The construction of the Tabernacle involved "building" (*boneh*). This broad category includes all types of construction and repair. Jewish law includes pitching a tent as a form of building, and rabbinic opinions extend this idea even to small acts such as opening an umbrella (which is the same as pitching a very small tent). The general category of building includes all types of assembly projects. Sabbath is not the day for building an addition onto your house, tearing down an old wall, or even assembling a doghouse. Nails, hammers, pry-bars, and other tools have nothing to contribute to the Sabbath. Even the holy Tabernacle was not to be built on the Sabbath day; how much less the mundane projects of home improvement.

34. DEMOLISHING

The opposite of assembling is disassembly, and the Mishnah refers to it as "demolishing" (*soter*). It includes all forms of dismantling anything that cannot be built on the Sabbath. Even taking down a tent on the Sabbath is a form of *melachah*. On the other hand, tearing down a tower of toy blocks is permitted, because building a tower of toy blocks is permitted.

35. EXTINGUISHING

The building of the Tabernacle required the extinguishing of flames for various reasons. For example, a fire used to heat a material to a certain temperature must be extinguished to prevent overheating. According to one opinion, the prohibition pertains to extinguishing a fire to produce charcoal.

The sages reasoned that if igniting and feeding a fire constitutes *melachah* (see below), it makes sense that extinguishing a fire does so as well. The Mishnah refers to it as "extinguishing flame" (*mechabbeh*). This interpretation does not arise directly from the biblical text. The reasoning is not clear, but it seems to be in keeping with the idea of taking mastery over nature and imposing our will onto something. Extinguishing fire is as much a part of the production process as igniting fire. For example, a man who makes maple syrup might say, "It is not permissible to make a fire on Sabbath; therefore I will make the fire before Sabbath begins. Then I need only put out the fire when the syrup has been rendered." The *melachah* of extinguishing closes this loophole and others like it.

In Jewish homes, Sabbath candles are left to burn down; thermostats and stoves are not adjusted. Lights are not turned off. As always, however, the Sabbath must be violated when it is necessary to do so in order to save a life. Thus, traditional Jewish law requires one to put out a fire if it constitutes a threat to life.

36. BURNING

The building of the Tabernacle required the people of Israel to make fire for a variety of stages in production. Fire is a key component in smithing and many other forms of manufacturing, and is one of the primary means by which man takes mastery over nature to alter it.

The Torah defines making a fire as *melachah*. It explicitly states, "You shall kindle no fire in any of your dwelling places on the Sabbath day" (Exodus 35:3 NASB). Making a fire (*mav'ir*) includes both igniting and feeding a fire.

This law is the reason why we light candles before the Sabbath begins. The Sabbath candles are a remembrance of the days when candles and lamps provided the only source of illumination. If a person wanted light on the Sabbath, he had to ensure that lamps were lit before the Sabbath began.

Non-Jewish readers sometimes argue that the Torah prohibited making a fire on the Sabbath only because making a fire was a lot of work in those days. One needed kindling, wood, and a source of flame. In modern times, simply turning on the stove or flicking a cigarette lighter produces effortless flame—it does not take much work at all.

This is faulty thinking. The Torah does not prohibit making a fire on the Sabbath day because it required a lot of work. It did not. The ancient Israelites were not cavemen rubbing sticks together. The amount of effort involved in the process has no relevance. The Torah simply says not to make a fire, with no indication of whether it was easily lit or not.

Burning something constitutes a form of *melachah* because it involves intentionally transforming one substance into another. When we burn something, whether it is a log in the fire or the butane in a cigarette lighter, we engage in a process of manipulating the elements of the creation (oxidation) to pass from matter (solid or gas) to energy. We are shaping, forming, making, and creating. *Melachah* involves making things, and fire makes heat, light, smoke, and ash.

The prohibition on burning means that smoking a cigarette or pipe is forbidden on the Sabbath. A gasoline engine burns gasoline; therefore, one cannot drive a car on the Sabbath. (Electric cars are a different matter. See below.) Observant Jews take note of even less obvious forms of burning. For example, drawing hot water from a gas-burning water heater causes the water heater to burn more gas to heat the water.

How do Sabbath-keepers survive in cold climates? Would not a Sabbath-keeping family freeze to death? Saving life always takes precedence over the Sabbath. In a desperate situation, the Sabbath-keeper would light a fire. In most cases, however, such emergency measures would be unnecessary. Stoves can be heated in advance and set up with fuel-feeders, and heat can be stored in water and stone. Even more useful, friendly Gentile neighbors can help by firing up stoves on cold mornings because the Torah does not prohibit non-Jews from voluntarily performing *melachah* on the Sabbath (even though it does prohibit non-Jews from doing so as the servant or agent of a Jew).

ELECTRICITY AND BURNING

According to some opinions, heating a metal filament to the point where it glows is also a form of burning; therefore, flipping a light switch to turn on the lights violates the Sabbath. According to many opinions, electricity has the same legal status as fire. (The uncertainty in the area of electricity and Shabbat has mostly to do with the fact that the technology of electricity developed at such a late time. There are no authoritative courts or precedents or early commentators on which to base the decision.) The Torah sometimes refers to lightning as "fire." Observant Jews do not turn appliances or electrical devices off or on during the Sabbath, nor do they operate any devices that use electricity.

Some opinions prohibit the use of electricity on other grounds, such as the idea that completing a circuit constitutes "finishing."

Imagine a world without smartphones, tablets, computers, music players, video games, and other electronic devices. That world is called the Sabbath. All traditional opinions agree that using electrical devices at least violates the spirit of the Sabbath. Lights turned on before the Sabbath are left on. Telephones and mobile devices are used only in a life-and-death emergency.

37. FINISHING

The construction of the Tabernacle entailed a variety of tasks categorized as "finishing" or "completing." The Mishnah refers to this category as "striking with a hammer" (*makkeh bepattish*), an idiom for completing a job. The biblical text does not specifically prohibit this general category, but the creation narrative certainly implies it: "God *finished* his work that he had done, and he rested on the seventh day from all his work that he had done" (Genesis 2:2).

The general category of "finishing" includes all forms of repairs or completions of projects. Examples include sanding, planing, carving, painting, shaping, sharpening, and assembling. Any finishing touch on a project falls under this category.

Traditional interpretation includes adjustments to mechanical devices such as winding a clock, setting a watch, or tuning a musical instrument. The rabbis forbade the use of all musical instruments on the Sabbath lest the musician feel compelled to tune the instrument. (Levitical musicians were permitted to use instruments on the Sabbath in the Temple, much as the priests were permitted to carry out their Temple duties on the Sabbath.)

The prohibition on finishing prevents making an unusable object usable on the Sabbath. Light repairs, like changing a bulb, fall under this prohibition. Finishing includes reaffixing a bicycle chain; for that reason, religious Jews do not ride bicycles on the Sabbath. Even something as mundane as threading new laces into a pair of shoes can be considered finishing.

SAILING AND SWIMMING

The construction of the Tabernacle involved neither sailing nor swimming, but the rabbis considered making adjustments to a sail in order to catch the wind to be a type of finishing; therefore they banned sailing on the Sabbath. Harnessing the wind involves taking mastery over nature. Jewish law allows a Jewish person to ride as a passenger on sailing vessels operated by non-Jews on the Sabbath, so long as the Sabbath-keeper does not embark or disembark on the Sabbath day. Although swimming has nothing to do with finishing or any of the other categories of *melachah,* a special rabbinic enactment forbids swimming on the Sabbath. Religious Jews do not go to the beach on Saturday afternoons.

38. CARRYING

Building the Tabernacle entailed carrying objects from one place to another. Carrying a load constitutes *melachah* and is forbidden on the Sabbath. The Mishnah refers to it as "transferring an object from one domain to another" (*hamotzi mereshut lirshut*). Contrary to popular belief, the prohibition on carrying a load is not a rabbinic innovation. It is one of the few categories specifically mentioned in the Bible. Rabbinic legislation has interpreted and extended this prohibition in ways we might not find to be intuitive, but the law against carrying arises indirectly from the Torah (Exodus 16:29; Numbers 15:32–36) and directly from the Prophet Jeremiah:

> Take care for the sake of your lives, and do not bear a burden on the Sabbath day or bring it in by the gates of Jerusalem. And do not carry a burden out of your houses on the Sabbath or do any work, but keep the Sabbath day holy, as I commanded your fathers. (Jeremiah 17:21–22)

A person might argue that the "burden" or "load" referred to in Jeremiah 17 must be a load of merchandise. That may be the case, but traditional Jewish interpretation has defined the idea of "load" more broadly to include moving any object carried from a private domain into a public domain, or carried in a public domain four cubits or more. Jewish law extends that definition even to trivial objects like a house key or gloves in the pockets.

In any case, the prohibition on carrying a load applies only outside of one's home. Carrying within one's home or within a private domain is permissible. The Bible says, "Do not carry a burden out of your houses on the Sabbath day," but it does not prohibit carrying a load within one's home.

The terms "public domain" and "private domain" used in Jewish law can be somewhat misleading, because they do not refer to whether a space is publicly or privately owned. A public domain is a large, open space with a substantial amount of traffic, such as the main thoroughfare of a town. A private domain is an area that is enclosed by walls or certain kinds of natural borders.

Some places are neither completely private nor completely public, such as a courtyard shared with a neighboring house. Jewish law determines that carrying in this type of area is not technically prohibited on a biblical level. However, since it is not always easy to tell whether or not an area is truly "public," as a rabbinic safeguard it is forbidden to carry in this semi-public area. To clarify the status of any disputed area, a carefully defined border can be used to include the semi-public domain within the private domain, thereby allowing carrying within the combined space (*eruv*). The Talmud discusses these complicated laws in tractates *Eruvin* and *Shabbat*; generally speaking, though, once an *eruv* is erected an adjacent area can be declared to be part of one's private home.

Disciples of Yeshua will be familiar with a certain miracle story in which the Master told a crippled man to "pick up his mat and carry it" on the Sabbath day. Does this mean that Yeshua disregarded the Sabbath or that he made the law forbidding carrying a load obsolete? On the contrary, as we will see in the next chapters, he taught that compassion for human suffering and the dignity of his fellow Jew should take priority over the uncertainties of carrying or not carrying in a semi-public domain.

BUYING AND SELLING

Carrying is allowed within one's home, but Jewish tradition also forbids even handling things which may not be used on the Sabbath, such as tools, pencils, candles, money, wallets, weapons, and the like. This rabbinic safeguard can be compared to telling your children, "Don't play with matches."

The prohibition on carrying a load also forbids all types of financial transactions on the Sabbath day, including transfer of property, transfer of ownership, buying, selling, trading, and all other types of commerce. These extensions are not rabbinic stringencies; they are explicit in the Bible (Amos 8:5; Nehemiah 10:31, 13:15–21). Sabbath-observant people do not use money, neither cash nor credit, on the Sabbath day. Religious Jews will not even handle money on the Sabbath. All business transactions stop, including electronic purchases and exchanges. Perhaps Paul instructed the Corinthian believers to set aside a portion of their money on the first day of the week because of the taboo around handling money and finances on the Sabbath (1 Corinthians 16:2).

If this seems counterintuitive, consider that money represents work. Every society uses currency as a token of a person's labor, efforts, and time. If a person works for a wage of $10 an hour, then a $5 bill represents one-half hour of work.

The prohibition on financial transactions also excludes hiring services on the Sabbath. Going to a restaurant entails paying for the hire of someone else's *melachah* and the purchase of food. Nehemiah saw buying and selling, even the buying and selling of food, as an "evil thing" and a "profaning" of the Sabbath. According to Nehemiah, buying and selling constitute as much a desecration of the Sabbath as treading winepresses or loading donkeys (13:15–18).

39. MARKING

The construction of the Tabernacle required various forms of marking and scoring. The sages designated marking and cutting the hides of animals as a category of *melachah*; this category includes marking any kind of line or scoring any surface in preparation for cutting or working on a piece. Hence one should not take measurements and make markings on the Sabbath day, even if the actual cutting or fitting is not done on the Sabbath. Marking and measuring in anticipation of a project violates the spirit of the Sabbath.

YESHUA AND THE TRADITIONS OF MEN

New Testament readers ordinarily object to the traditional definition of *melachah* on the basis that Yeshua rejected rabbinic stringencies, traditions of men, and traditional Jewish laws for keeping the Sabbath. Yeshua healed on the Sabbath, he allowed his disciples to pluck grain on the Sabbath, he told a man to carry his mat home on the Sabbath, and so forth. On the surface these stories seem to indicate that Yeshua rejected traditional Jewish interpretation of the Sabbath. The next section of this book will consider the merits of this position and investigate a possible alternative.

PART TWO

Yeshua and the Sabbath Conflicts

CHAPTER NINE

In the Grain Fields on the Sabbath

Christians often raise an objection against Sabbath observance on the basis of an accusation that Jesus broke the Sabbath. Why would his disciples want to keep the Sabbath if Jesus broke the Sabbath? That's a fair question. Did Yeshua break the Sabbath?

Consider one quick example.

Once, it happened that the Master and his disciples were walking through the holy city of Jerusalem on the Sabbath day when they encountered a man blind from birth. Our Master spat on the ground, made clay of the spittle, and applied the clay to the man's eyes. Then he told the man, "Go, wash in the pool of Siloam." The man went and immersed, and, miraculously, he could see.

To heal the man, Yeshua spat on the ground and made clay of the spittle. Mixing two substances to form a third is a form of work that Jewish law prohibits on the Sabbath day. Yeshua smeared the mud on the man's eyes. Applying a salve or medicine by means of smearing is also considered a form of work prohibited on the Sabbath day. It is a violation of the Sabbath. He sent the man to immerse himself. At least by conventional definition in traditional Jewish interpretation, immersions are not done on the Sabbath. This single healing incident from the Gospels potentially involves three Sabbath violations.

The Pharisees claimed, "This man is not from God, for he does not keep the Sabbath" (John 9:16). Vocal critics of the Master insisted, "He is a Sabbath-breaker."

Do we appreciate the gravity of this allegation?

The Master's enemies wanted to prove that he was a Sabbath-breaker because according to the Torah, breaking the Sabbath is a serious sin for a Jew. God requires the Jewish people to keep the seventh day holy, and to cease from any labor on it. This is one of the Ten Commandments; it ranks with the prohibitions on idolatry, adultery, and murder. The LORD declared the Sabbath as an eternal sign between himself and the children of Israel—a statute to be observed by Israel throughout all generations. He made it a sign of his covenant with Israel, and he commanded it as an everlasting obligation. According to the strictest interpretation of the Torah, a Jew who violated the Sabbath might incur the death penalty:

> Everyone who profanes it shall be put to death. Whoever does any work on it, that soul shall be cut off from among his people. Six days shall work be done, but the seventh day is a Sabbath of solemn rest, holy to the LORD. Whoever does any work on the Sabbath day shall be put to death. Therefore the people of Israel shall keep the Sabbath, observing the Sabbath throughout their generations, as a covenant forever. (Exodus 31:14–16)

Today, in the absence of an official Sanhedrin with real civil authority in the land of Israel, all death penalties are suspended; in Yeshua's day, however, a death penalty for Sabbath-breaking was a real possibility. If Yeshua's critics and opponents could prove in a court of law that he broke the Sabbath, they had legal grounds for his execution. At the very least, they knew that if they could prove that he was a sinner and condoned the sin of violating the Sabbath, they could prove that he was not the Messiah.

BREAKING THE SABBATH

The same allegation is still being lodged against Yeshua nearly two thousand years later. "Jesus broke the Sabbath!" But this time it is his followers, not his enemies, who accuse him of Sabbath-breaking. Why are we so eager to affirm the Pharisees' allegations against our Master?

From a simple reading of the Gospels, it does seem that Yeshua must have been a Sabbath-breaker. His disciples plucked grain on the Sabbath; he defended them. He healed people on the Sabbath. He told a man to carry his mat home on the Sabbath. He healed a man with a withered arm on the Sabbath; he healed a man with dropsy right at the Sabbath table of prominent sages; he healed a woman with a bent back, straightening the bent, on the Sabbath. All of these are obvious violations of the Sabbath. So what's going on here?

Ordinarily these incidents are cited to prove that Yeshua was all about abolishing the Sabbath. Traditional Christian interpretation supposes that he did these things to send an implicit message that the Sabbath (along with the rest of the "Old Covenant") is no longer binding. Every Christian Bible-reader should think about this carefully and realize the danger of this proposition. A Messiah who breaks the Sabbath and advocates breaking the Sabbath is no Messiah at all. He is a false-Christ and a deceiver. God himself commands the Jewish people to reject such a Messiah.

THE SABBATARIAN EXPLANATION

Christian Sabbatarians (Sabbath-keepers) rightly reject the notion that the Master abrogated the Sabbath. Most Sabbatarians, however, still interpret the gospel stories about Yeshua and the Sabbath to mean that he did not care about the particulars of Sabbath law. That is to say, he broke the "rabbinic" and "man-made" traditions about Sabbath in order to show everyone that Jewish interpretation of the Law is illegitimate. He let his disciples husk grain on the Sabbath, he healed on the Sabbath, and he made mud and smeared it on a blind man's eyes on the Sabbath all to demonstrate that Judaism had misinterpreted the Sabbath. He did these things to show his followers that the thirty-nine types of labor that Jewish law prohibits on the Sabbath may be safely disregarded.

On this basis, the Sabbath-conflict passages seem to provide believers—even Jewish believers— a license to disregard the particulars of the Sabbath. Christian Sabbatarians make a sharp distinction between the biblical Sabbath and traditional Jewish interpretation of the Sabbath. They teach that Yeshua kept the former but disregarded the latter. Because of this, Jewish believers who choose to be scrupulous about the particulars of traditional

Sabbath observance might find themselves accused of legalism by both Gentile Sabbatarians and assimilated Jewish Christians: "Don't you get it? Don't you understand that Yeshua overturned the hypocritical legalism of the Pharisees?"

THE MESSIANIC JEWISH EXPLANATION

Neither the traditional Christian explanation (Jesus canceled the Sabbath) nor the Christian Sabbatarian explanation (Yeshua canceled Judaism) adequately answers the questions raised by the Sabbath-conflict stories. Does a third option exist?

The Messianic Jewish movement maintains that Yeshua canceled neither the Sabbath nor Judaism. Therefore, Messianic Judaism needs to re-examine the Sabbath-conflict stories. The following three chapters of this book will attempt to demonstrate that a halachic (legal) consistency runs through all of the Sabbath-conflict stories that appear in the Gospels. We will discover an underlying legal principle that, rather than abrogating the traditional Jewish Sabbath legislation, actually defends traditional observance of the Sabbath. The rest of this chapter and the next will examine the Sabbath-conflict stories appearing in the Synoptic Gospels. The subsequent chapter examines the Sabbath stories from the Gospel of John.

IN THE GRAIN FIELDS WITH YESHUA

"At that time Jesus went through the grainfields on the Sabbath. His disciples were hungry, and they began to pluck heads of grain and to eat" (Matthew 12:1). The Pharisees saw the disciples of Yeshua plucking and husking, and they said to him, "Look, your disciples are doing what is not lawful to do on the Sabbath." (Matthew 12:2); "Look, why are they doing what is not lawful on the Sabbath?" (Mark 2:24). Though Yeshua himself did not pluck, husk, or eat the grain, the Pharisees lodged their complaint and posed their question against him. As the rabbi over his school of disciples, he had responsibility for their behavior. By allowing the disciples to perpetrate the alleged Sabbath violation, he endorsed their behavior.

THE MASTER'S DEFENSE

Yeshua defended his disciples, arguing that they were "guiltless" (Matthew 12:7). For most Christian interpreters, the incident and the Master's justification present no difficulties. In traditional Christian interpretation, Jesus allowed his disciples to violate the Sabbath because he had the authority to override the Sabbath. Indeed, he came to cancel the ceremonial aspects of the Torah. Therefore, the grain field incident is a token of his disregard for the Sabbath, and the end of the Torah's jurisdiction. In the new economy of Grace, Jesus sets the Law aside.

This explanation does not work for Messianic Judaism. From a Messianic Jewish point of view, Yeshua neither cancels the Torah nor violates the Sabbath. For him to do so would constitute sin and disqualification from his Messianic claims. The apostolic community could not have reckoned him as sinless if he violated the Sabbath or endorsed its violation. This tension has led Sabbatarian apologists (along with some Messianic Jewish interpreters) to explain that the disciples were not breaking the written Torah's Sabbath prohibitions but only the "rabbinic fences" and "man-made traditions" around Sabbath-keeping. According to this view, Yeshua and the disciples held to a literal, *sola scriptura* view of Sabbath observance, which does not prohibit reaping by hand, husking by hand, and eating.

If that were the case, one should expect the Master to reply to his critics along these lines: "Hypocrites! Foolish Pharisees who lay your rules and traditions of men upon men's shoulders. Where is it written that picking grain and rubbing it in one's hands violates the Sabbath day? The Torah neither forbids picking grain nor husking it on the Sabbath day!"

Note that he does not say any of that.

In reality, the Torah does forbid harvesting on the Sabbath. Exodus 34:21 specifically prohibits harvesting. What is harvesting? Picking grain. Yeshua did not challenge or criticize the Pharisees' interpretation of Sabbath violations. Instead of saying, "No, you are in error. My disciples are not breaking the Sabbath," Yeshua admitted that they were breaking the Sabbath, but he defended their right to do so by citing two legal precedents from Scripture: the incident of David with the bread of the Presence and the Sabbath-day work of the priesthood in the Temple.

DAVID AND THE PRIESTHOOD

The Master retold the story of how David, while on the run from King Saul, came to the sanctuary set up at Nob and asked Ahimelech the priest for bread to supply him and his men (1 Samuel 21:2–7[1–6]). Ahimelech replied that he had no ordinary bread; he only had the twelve loaves of the bread of the Presence, the holy bread placed on the table inside the Tabernacle and changed out with fresh loaves every Sabbath. The Torah says that only the priesthood may eat the bread of the Presence, and that it may be eaten only within the sanctuary (Leviticus 24:9). Nevertheless, Ahimelech gave David the bread. David took the bread, ate, and left with the rest of it. The Master briefly retold the story of David and the holy bread as he defended the disciples:

> Have you not read what David did when he was hungry, he and those who were with him: how he entered the house of God and took and ate the bread of the Presence, which is not lawful for any but the priests to eat, and also gave it to those with him? (Luke 6:3–4)

The story of David and the holy Sabbath bread may have been a common illustration used by the rabbis to discuss the laws of Sabbath observance. The midrashic collection *Yalkut Shimoni* uses the story to prove that the preservation of life takes precedence over the Sabbath:

> It was Shabbat, and David saw that they were baking the Bread of the Presence on Shabbat … Since he had not found anything there except the Bread of the Presence, David said to him, "Give it to me so that we do not die of hunger, since when there is a case of doubt regarding life, it supersedes Shabbat." How much did David eat on that particular Shabbat? Rabbi Chuna said, "David ate almost seven se'ahs due to his hunger, since ravenous hunger had gripped him." (*Yalkut Shimoni* 2:130 on 1 Samuel 21:5)

The rabbinic version of the story places the episode on the Sabbath day. The narrative of 1 Samuel 21 also indicates that this story about David may have happened on the Sabbath day—the day the bread was changed out.

The Master admitted that David and his companions did something "which is not lawful" when they took and ate the holy bread. In saying this, he conceded, by way of comparison, that his disciples also did something "which is not lawful" on the Sabbath. In the analogy David and his men correspond to the disciples. Both parties were hungry and without food. Both parties acquired food by forbidden means. David violated the ritual sanctity of the Temple service by taking and eating the bread of the Presence. The disciples violated the sanctity of the Sabbath by plucking, husking, and eating grain on the Sabbath day.

David violated the sanctity of the Temple service because "he was hungry" as were "those who were with him." Yeshua justified David on the basis that "he was in need and was hungry, he and those who were with him" (Mark 2:25). Yeshua reasoned that the "need" and "hunger" of David and his men provided them with adequate reason for violating the ritual sanctity of the Temple service by eating the bread of the Presence.

THE PRIESTHOOD AND THE TEMPLE

The Master then took his argument a step further, pointing out that the priesthood serving in the Temple must necessarily violate the Sabbath prohibitions. Slaughtering animals, tending the altar pyre, igniting incense, lighting the menorah, baking bread, and so forth all constitute explicit Sabbath violations, and yet the Torah commands the priests to do all of these things on the Sabbath day. The Master said, "Have you not read in the Law how on the Sabbath the priests in the temple profane the Sabbath and are guiltless?" (Matthew 12:5).

Jewish law also points out similar contradictions between the Torah's positive and negative commandments. To reconcile such moral dilemmas, the Talmudic-era sages derived the following axiom:

> Wherever you find a positive commandment and a negative commandment contradicting, if you can fulfill both of them, it is preferable; but if not, let the positive command come and supersede the negative command. (b.*Shabbat* 133a)

The priests violated the Sabbath when serving in the Temple, but they were "innocent" because the Torah commanded them to do so. The positive commandment to conduct the Temple service superseded the negative commandment of the Sabbath prohibitions. In the words of the sages, "The Temple service takes precedence over the Sabbath" (*Mechilta*).

How does this argument fit the situation in the grain fields? The priesthood's violation of Sabbath prohibitions for the sake of the Temple service seems to have only tangential relevance to David taking and eating the forbidden bread of the Presence, and neither example seems relevant to the disciples plucking and husking grain on the Sabbath day. What is the connection between the three episodes? Yeshua tied them all together when he said, "I tell you, something greater than the temple is here" (Matthew 12:6).

SOMETHING GREATER THAN THE TEMPLE

> I tell you, something greater than the temple is here. (Matthew 12:6)

On the basis of the two case precedents he cited, Yeshua declared the need and hunger of his disciples to be a greater priority than the Sabbath. His argument follows: 1) if the hunger and need of human beings takes precedence over the sanctity of the Temple service (demonstrated by David taking the forbidden, holy bread when he was hungry and in need), and 2) if the Temple service takes precedence over the sanctity of the Sabbath prohibitions (demonstrated by the priesthood violating the Sabbath to carry out the Temple services), then 3) human need must take precedence over the Sabbath. The logic is simple: The Temple service trumps the Sabbath, and human need trumps the Temple service. "Something greater than the temple is here," namely human need.

If

Human Need > Temple Service

And

Temple Service > The Sabbath

Then

Human Need > The Sabbath

In the Talmud the sages employ the same pattern of argumentation to defend the use of life-saving medical treatments on the Sabbath: "If the service in the Temple supersedes the Sabbath, how much more should the saving of human life supersede the Sabbath laws!" (b.*Yoma* 85b).

Christian interpretations generally prefer to teach that Jesus himself is "something greater than the temple." Accordingly, the reasoning would stutter along as follows: David violated the sanctity of the Temple because he was greater than the Temple service. The Temple service is greater than the Sabbath, and Jesus is greater than all of them. Therefore, his disciples may violate the Sabbath with impunity because Jesus, who is greater than the Sabbath, allows them to do so.

This conclusion, which amounts to a divine "You're-not-the-boss-of-me" argument, does not arise naturally from the flow of the Master's argument, nor is it logical. If Yeshua was arguing that his Messianic or divine status granted him the authority to set aside the Sabbath at will, then we have returned full circle to the standard Christian interpretation, which teaches that Yeshua did not keep the Sabbath or require his followers to do so. That same reasoning could be applied to the prohibition on adultery. After all, Yeshua is greater than the laws of marriage, isn't he? Why should his disciples be required to observe them?

Neither does the argument make sense as a halachic (legal) defense. When he said, "Something greater than the temple is here," he could not have been referring to himself or his divine status. Would the Pharisees have accepted that defense? Instead, the thing "greater than the temple" must be the need and hunger of the disciples.

Rabbi Akiva made a similar argument based upon the Temple service:

> Did the Torah impose greater stringency on the Temple service or on the Sabbath? It was more stringent in regard to the Temple service than the Sabbath, for the Temple service overrides the prohibitions of the Sabbath, but the Sabbath does not override the Temple service. Now argue the matter from the light to the heavy. If the Temple service supersedes the prohibitions of the Sabbath and a matter of potentially saving a life overrides it [i.e., the Temple service], how much more so should the potential of saving a life supersede the Sabbath, which is superseded by the Temple service. Thus you have learned that the potential of saving a life overrides the Sabbath. (t.*Shabbat* 15:17)

PRESERVATION OF LIFE

As cited above, a strong parallel to the Master's argument occurs in the midrashic collection *Yalkut Shimoni* where David demands his right to the bread of the Presence on the basis that he and his men are in danger of starving and the preservation of life takes precedence over the Sabbath's prohibitions:

> David said to him, "Give it to me so that we do not die of hunger, since when there is a case of doubt regarding life, it supersedes Shabbat." (*Yalkut Shimoni* 2:130 on 1 Samuel 21:5)

That the preservation of life (*pikuach nefesh*) overrides the Sabbath laws is a true and well-attested law in rabbinic literature. Jewish law sets aside most of the commandments, even the Sabbath prohibitions, for the sake of saving a human life. The Torah says, "You shall therefore keep my statutes and my rules; if a person does them, he shall live by them" (Leviticus 18:5). The sages interpreted this to mean that a commandment may be set aside to save a life. Life takes precedence over the commandments because it says "you shall live by them," not "you shall die by them." Therefore, the sages derived that it is permissible to violate the Sabbath to save a life:

> A man may profane one Sabbath so that he may live to keep many Sabbaths … [because it says] "He shall live by them." (b.*Yoma* 85b)

In the early second century, after the failed Bar Kochba Revolt and in the midst of Roman persecutions, the surviving sages of that generation met in Lydda to discuss what commandments a man might justifiably break in order to save his life. The Romans frequently outlawed the observance of Torah. At times, keeping the commandments constituted grounds for arrest, punishment, and possibly execution. The sages decided that, in order to save his life, a man was justified in breaking any commandment except the prohibitions on murder, idolatry, and sexual immorality:

> If a man is commanded, "Break the commandment and you will not suffer death," he may transgress and not suffer death, excepting idolatry, sexual immorality and murder." (b.*Sanhedrin* 74a)

After all, the Torah says, "live by the commandments," not "die by them."

MERCY AND NOT SACRIFICE

If Yeshua's disciples were literally starving to death, and they needed to harvest, husk, and eat the grain or drop dead on the spot, then Pharisaic law teaches that the threat to their lives justified violating the Sabbath. But the narrative does not indicate that they were near to starvation—only that they were hungry. The Bible does not tell us how hungry the disciples were, but it is safe to assume that their hunger was sufficient to warrant distress. We may assume that sunset and the onset of the Sabbath had overtaken them as they returned from a distant village. They may have walked without food all day, and the Sabbath began as they neared their destination. They may have been faint with hunger. Fasting on the Sabbath is always discouraged. Despite all of this, the passage gives us no grounds to imagine that, if not for the heads of grain in the grain fields, the disciples would have starved to death that Sabbath. Threat to life cannot be reasonably inferred.

Nevertheless, Yeshua declared that his disciples were "guiltless." According to his argument, their hunger alone justified the transgression. He rebuked the Pharisees with a quote from Hosea 6:6, saying, "And if you had known what this means, 'I desire mercy, and not sacrifice,' you would not have condemned the guiltless" (Matthew 12:7):

> For I desire [mercy] and not sacrifice, the knowledge of God rather than burnt offerings. (Hosea 6:6)

Yeshua often used Hosea 6:6 to teach that compassion for human beings, specifically the alleviation of human suffering, should come before ceremonial and ritual concerns. For example, when the same Pharisees criticized him for eating and drinking with sinners and tax collectors, he quoted Hosea 6:6 to justify his choice of table-fellowship. He explained that he chose to associate with sinners because, like a physician caring for a sick patient, he sought to alleviate their spiritual sickness:

> But when he heard it, he said, "Those who are well have no need of a physician, but those who are sick. Go and learn what this means, 'I desire mercy, and not sacrifice.' For I came not to call the righteous, but sinners." (Matthew 9:12–13)

In the parable of the Good Samaritan, the Samaritan fulfilled the commandment to love his neighbor as himself by showing the wounded man mercy, while the priest and the Levite failed to do so on the grounds of ceremonial concerns:

> Which of these three, do you think, proved to be a neighbor to the man who fell among the robbers?" He said, "The one who showed him mercy." And Jesus said to him, "You go, and do likewise." (Luke 10:36–37)

Messianic Jewish scholar Rabbi Yechiel Tzvi Lichtenstein clarified this point as follows:

> It is not his intention (Heaven forbid!) to permit desecration of the Sabbath (as confused people suppose); rather, the meaning is that mercy is more important to the Holy One, blessed be he, than the Sabbath. Mercy takes precedence over the ceremony. Likewise, the Prophet Hosea in this verse did not intend to nullify the sacrifices, but instead he meant to teach that the internal service of the heart is more important, as he says there, "And the knowledge of God rather than burnt offerings." (*Commentary on the New Testament*)

Mark 12:33 invokes the same passage (Hosea 6:6) when it says that "to love him [God] with all the heart and with all the understanding and with all the strength, and to love one's neighbor as oneself, is much more than all whole burnt offerings and sacrifices."

Yeshua used Hosea 6:6 to teach a principle of placing compassion for human beings and the alleviation of human suffering ahead of ceremonial concerns. In that regard, the alleviation of human suffering is greater than the Temple. Why was it permissible for David and his men to violate the sanctity of the Temple service by taking the bread of the Presence? Was King David greater than the Temple? No, he was not, but his human need and desperate circumstance were greater than the Temple service. Yeshua applied this ethic to the situation with his disciples. Their need was greater than the Temple service because, like David, they were hungry. Compassion for human suffering is a higher priority than even the Temple service, and since the Temple service is already a higher priority than Shabbat, the disciples were "guiltless" in violating the Sabbath.

THE SABBATH WAS MADE FOR MAN

According to the Master's reasoning, the urgent human need of his disciples was of greater importance than ceremonial concern for the Sabbath. God desires mercy more than sacrifice. In Mark's version of the story, Yeshua punctuated his argument by explaining, "The Sabbath was made for man, not man for the Sabbath" (Mark 2:27). In other words, compassion for human beings should take priority over the Sabbath. The same sentiment was echoed by Talmudic-era sages. For example, the Talmud justifies the administering of life-saving medical treatment on the Sabbath by saying, "The Sabbath has been given over to you, but you have not been given over to the Sabbath" (b.*Yoma* 85b).

When Yeshua said, "The Sabbath was made for man, and not man for the Sabbath," he alluded to the creation narrative, where the creation of Adam precedes the sanctification of the Sabbath day, just as the creation of Adam precedes the creation of Eve. God made man before he set apart the seventh day; likewise, he made man before he made Eve. Paul's letters also stress the order of creation: "For Adam was formed first, then Eve" (1 Timothy 2:13). "Man was not made from woman, but woman from man. Neither was man created for woman, but woman for man" (1 Corinthians 11:8–9). Compare:

MARK 2:27	1 CORINTHIANS 11:8–9
The Sabbath was made for man, not man for the Sabbath.	Neither was man created for woman, but woman for man.

Perhaps the parallel between Eve and the Sabbath (both of which were created after Adam and for Adam) explains why Jewish tradition speaks of the Sabbath as a regal queen, and depicts the Sabbath as the bride of Israel. It also helps explain what the Master means when he says that the Son of Man is "lord of the Sabbath." The Hebrew equivalent *ba'al HaShabbat* might also be translated as "husband of the Sabbath."

THE SABBATH WAS MADE FOR HUMANS

In Yeshua's teaching, the human being is likened to the groom. The Sabbath is likened to the bride. The union of man and the Sabbath is likened to a marriage.

When Yeshua said, "The Sabbath was made for man," his statement includes all human beings, not just Jews. This is not the same as saying that all human beings are obligated to keep the Sabbath in the same manner as the Jewish people. It only means that the Sabbath is God's gift to human beings. It is his blessed and holy day. He did not institute the Sabbath at Mount Sinai; he instituted it immediately after the sixth day of creation, which is to say, immediately after the creation of the first human beings.

A non-Jewish disciple of Yeshua does not have the same covenantal obligation to keep the Sabbath that a Jewish person has. Nevertheless, he has the privilege of enjoying the Sabbath, celebrating the Sabbath, and even keeping the Sabbath to whatever extent he is able. According to our teacher, the Sabbath was made for everyone.

THE SON OF MAN IS MASTER OF THE SABBATH

According to all three versions of the story about the grain field, the Master concluded his exoneration of his disciples by stating, "The Son of Man is lord of the Sabbath" (Mark 2:28; Matthew 12:8; Luke 6:5). What did he mean?

One might suppose that he referred to himself. Yeshua is certainly lord over the Sabbath and over all things that the Father has set beneath his feet. Moreover, he often applied the title "Son of Man" to himself. In Hebrew the term "son of man" is *ben adam*, a common biblical idiom for "a human being." *Ben Adam* corresponds to the Aramaic form *bar enosh* which is also a common way to say "a human being." Ordinarily, the Master used the term—whether in Hebrew or Aramaic we are not certain—in the definite sense ("the Son of Man") as if he were calling himself "the Human Being." As a messianic title, it alluded to texts such as Psalm 8:5[4], 80:18[17]; Daniel 7:13; and passages from the apocryphal book of *Enoch* where the divine messiah-figure is called the Son of Man.

In this instance, however, Yeshua must have used the term in the general sense of "human being" and not as a messianic title to indicate himself. If Yeshua closed his argument with the Pharisees by declaring that he himself is the lord of the Sabbath, it seems to imply that he invoked his divine prerogative to set aside and even break the Sabbath. That interpretation fits well with the traditional

Christian reading. It argues that Jesus had abolished the Sabbath for his disciples, a power vested in him to do so, because he is, after all, lord of the Sabbath.

That interpretation is not satisfactory for Messianic Jewish theology. If we accept that line of reasoning, we must also reject Yeshua as a prophet and as the Messiah. A prophet who performs signs and wonders and teaches his followers to violate the commandments of Torah is a false prophet. This interpretation falls into the hands of the anti-missionaries and the critics who say, "This man is not from God, for he does not keep the Sabbath" (John 9:16).

In addition, if Yeshua meant to declare to the Pharisees that he himself is lord of the Sabbath, then the statement was disconnected from the argument leading up to it. The hunger of David and his men, the work of the priesthood on the Sabbath, the call for mercy and compassion instead of sacrifice, and the notion that Sabbath is made for man and not man for the Sabbath all become irrelevant—swept aside—when he suddenly switched to a new line of argument: "Besides, since I am lord of the Sabbath, my disciples don't need to keep the Sabbath or your silly rules."

THE HUMAN BEING IS LORD OF THE SABBATH

Of course the Messiah is lord of all, including the Sabbath. This, too, is a sentiment consistent with Jewish theology. Rabbinic literature commonly refers to the anticipated Messianic Era as the ultimate Sabbath of creation. The sages compare the Sabbath to the Messianic Kingdom and refer to it as a foretaste of the World to Come. They compare the waiting for redemption during this present age to the other six days of the week. As King of the Messianic Era, the Messiah is lord of the ultimate Sabbath, so to speak. This line of reflection, however, is far afield from the conversation Yeshua had with the Pharisees that day in the wheat fields of Galilee.

The Pharisees did not know that Yeshua was the Messiah, nor was he trying to convince them that he was during this particular conversation. Instead, he was attempting to argue on solid legal grounds that his disciples were innocent of the charges leveled against them. He was attempting to legally justify picking grain on the Sabbath; he was not trying to establish his reputation as Messiah.

All these things considered, it is most likely that Yeshua used the term "son of man" in this instance in its more general and common Hebrew sense: a human being. In that case, he concluded his argument by saying to the Pharisees, "A human being is lord of the Sabbath." If so, his conclusion remains completely consistent with his preceding argument:

1. Compassion for human need and suffering takes priority over the Temple service.
2. The Temple service takes priority over the Sabbath.
3. Therefore compassion for human need takes priority over the Sabbath.
4. After all, the Sabbath was made for human beings, not human beings for the Sabbath.
5. Human beings are lord of the Sabbath, and take priority over it.

By saying that a human being is lord of the Sabbath, Yeshua uses a biblical Hebrew idiom to say that human beings rank above the Sabbath on the scale of priority, not below it—much as a husband is the head over his wife. In Hebrew, the term "lord" can refer to ownership, stewardship, mastery, and, as noted above, a husband. Just as Adam was the steward over his wife who was created after him and for him, human beings are lord of the Sabbath, which was created after them and for them. This reading of the passage seems obvious in Mark's telling of the incident:

> He said to them, "The Sabbath was made for man, not man for the Sabbath. So the Son of Man [human being] is lord even of the Sabbath." (Mark 2:27–28)

A strong rabbinic parallel to the saying also supports reading "son of man" as "human being" in this instance instead of as a messianic title:

> The Sabbath was given to you [i.e., human beings], you were not given to the Sabbath. (*Mechilta* on Exodus 31:14)

THE RULE OF THE MASTER

The incident in the grain fields provides an ethical and legal framework for understanding all the Master's conflicts over the Sabbath with the religious authorities of his day. All of the ensuing conflicts about whether or not it is permissible to heal on the Sabbath center on this one point of contention: Yeshua believed that compassion for human beings and the alleviation of human suffering takes priority over ceremonial concern. God desires compassion for human beings above sacrifice and burnt offering.

The Gospels tell numerous stories of the Master's healing work on the Sabbath, demonstrating that Sabbath-related issues remained completely relevant to the early believers for whom the Gospels were written.

Contrary to popular opinion, the Master does not mean to trivialize the Sabbath or even to reduce the fences that had traditionally been placed around Sabbath observance. On the contrary, he was concerned with restoring a balanced perspective regarding Sabbath observance, a perspective that prioritizes human need. His conflict with the Pharisees over the particulars of how one ought to observe the Sabbath proves that the Sabbath was an important institution to him, one that he did not lightly dismiss or teach his disciples to disregard.

CHAPTER TEN

The Man with the Withered Hand and Other Sabbath Stories

After telling the story of the incident in the grain fields, all three Synoptic Gospels report another Sabbath conflict with religious authorities: "On another Sabbath, he entered the synagogue and was teaching" (Luke 6:6). According to his custom, Yeshua went to the synagogue on Sabbath morning to join the congregation for the prayers, to participate in the Torah reading, and to offer teaching about the kingdom of heaven. On this particular Sabbath, "a man was there whose right hand was withered" (Luke 6:6).

The now-lost Hebrew *Gospel of the Nazarenes* had a longer version of the story, which explained that the man was a stone mason and that he begged the Master for healing. In his commentary on Matthew, Jerome reports the passage as follows:

> In the Gospel which the Nazarenes and the Ebionites use, which we recently translated from Hebrew to Greek, and which is called by many the authentic text of Matthew, it is written that the man with the withered hand was a mason, praying for help with words of this kind: "I was a mason, seeking a livelihood with my hands. I beseech you, Yeshua, that you restore health to me, lest I must beg shamefully for my food." (Jerome, *On Matthew*)

The Master's opponents among the sages watched him carefully to see whether or not he would respond to the man's need and, in doing so, heal on the Sabbath day.

HEALING ON THE SABBATH

Arguments in the Talmud demonstrate that the legality of preparation, application, and ingestion of medicines on the Sabbath day for the purpose of healing remained under debate centuries after the ministry of Yeshua. The variety of opinions and legal maneuvers offered in the Talmud suggest that there might not have been complete consensus on this issue in the days of the Master. Nevertheless, the Gospels make it clear that Yeshua's opinion on the matter was at best a minority opinion. In the gospel narratives, the sages and Pharisees seem to share a unanimous opinion that healing constitutes a violation of the Sabbath.

As students of the Gospels read the Sabbath-healing controversies, they might assume that Yeshua argued only with the Jewish interpretation of the Sabbath, not with the Sabbath law itself. In other words, Yeshua believed that healing did not constitute *melachah* (prohibited work) and that, biblically speaking, healing did not violate the Sabbath. That is to say, he argued against the sages in order to correct their mistaken ban on healing. He was attempting to reconcile them with a more *sola scriptura* interpretation of Sabbath law that never explicitly prohibits healing.

Tempting as that explanation may be, it has a few critical weaknesses. According to a *sola scriptura* reading of the Torah, the sages over Israel possessed the God-given right to interpret the application of God's laws. Scripture vested them with the legal authority to offer definitive rulings on ambiguities concerning Torah observance (Deuteronomy 17:8–13). Yeshua himself endorsed that authority:

> The scribes and the Pharisees sit on Moses' seat, so do and observe whatever they tell you, but not the works they do. For they preach, but do not practice. (Matthew 23:2–3)

For that reason, he did not dismiss the Sabbath halachah (Jewish legal interpretation) to justify healing on the Sabbath;

instead, he argued within the halachah. That is, he argued within the parameters of rabbinic legal discourse.

He never told the Pharisees, "It is permissible to heal on the Sabbath because healing does not constitute a prohibited form of work." Instead, his arguments with the Pharisees all assume that healing does constitute a prohibited form of work. He argued that even though healing violates the Sabbath, the alleviation of human suffering is a weightier matter than the observance of the Sabbath prohibitions. If he meant to tell the Pharisees that healing should not be considered a form of *melachah* (prohibited work), then his arguments failed to make logical sense.

One might object that the miraculous types of healing that Yeshua performed cannot be construed to be a type of "work" that violates the Sabbath in any sense. On the contrary, miraculous or not, such healings constitute *melachah* as defined by rabbinic law in that they deliberately change and transform something from one state to another state. Just as repairing a leaky faucet on the Sabbath violates the Sabbath, so too, repairing a human body violates the Sabbath.

Another example: Suppose a man had magic powers with which he could light fires. He did not even need a match or cigarette lighter to start the fire; he could simply ignite a flame by the power of thought. Nevertheless, he would still be in violation of the prohibition on igniting a fire on the Sabbath even if he did so magically. The Torah does not prohibit any particular method of igniting a fire; it simply prohibits igniting a fire on the Sabbath. From this perspective, breaking the Sabbath is not about *how* the work is accomplished but simply *that* it is accomplished. If healing is a form of prohibited *melachah*, it does not actually matter how Yeshua accomplished it; he still violated the prohibition on work.

TO DO GOOD ON THE SABBATH?

Yeshua knew that his opponents were watching him, hoping that he would heal the man with the withered hand so that they would have a basis for denouncing him as a Sabbath-breaker and disregarding his teaching. He summoned the man to stand before him. Turning to his opponents, Yeshua answered their question by returning it to them. He said, "I ask you, is it lawful on the Sabbath to do good or to do harm, to save life or to destroy it?" (Luke 6:9).

The answer to his first question is "Yes." It is lawful to do good on the Sabbath. To "do good" refers to the performance of a positive commandment. When there is a command to do good, the performance of that commandment supersedes a prohibition that would impede it. As noted in the previous chapter, the Talmud says that if a positive commandment and a negative commandment contradict, the positive commandment supersedes the negative commandment. Based upon this principle, Yeshua could argue that the positive command of showing mercy by alleviating suffering overrides the prohibition against work on the Sabbath.

Is there a positive commandment to heal? "Is it permissible to save life or to destroy it?" Yeshua asked. According to Jewish law, the Sabbath can be set aside when a medical condition constitutes a threat to life. The Sabbath laws may be breached in any situation where one's life is at risk, even if the risk is uncertain. The Mishnah cites the principle of danger to life overriding the Sabbath as a general rule of thumb. The Talmud makes various arguments to justify this principle:

> He who has a sore throat—they administer medicine to him even on the Sabbath because it is uncertain if [the sore throat] might be a danger to life, and any case in which life might be endangered overrides the prohibitions of the Sabbath. (m.*Yoma* 8:6)

> Rabbi Yehudah said in the name of Shmu'el, "If I had been in on the argument, I would have proven (that medical attention is permissible) with a better proof-text than the one they used. It is written [in Leviticus 18:5], 'The man who obeys [my laws] will live by them.' It says 'he will live by them'; it doesn't say 'he shall die because of them.'" (b.*Yoma* 85b)

Had Yeshua's clients been in any distress that constituted a danger to life, he had license to heal them with impunity. The rabbinic principle of *pikuach nefesh* (saving a life) ensures that much. It is lawful on the Sabbath to save life, not to destroy it. The principle of *pikuach nefesh*, however, applies only to life-threatening conditions. The Talmud, for example, forbids the splinting of a broken bone on the Sabbath because a broken bone does not constitute a threat to life.

Neither does a shriveled hand constitute a danger to life. As one synagogue official said, "There are six days in which work ought to be done. Come on those days and be healed, and not on the Sabbath day" (Luke 13:14). Had Yeshua been concerned with honoring the prohibition against healing on the Sabbath, he certainly could have waited a few hours until sunset and the Sabbath's conclusion to heal the man's hand.

The Master did not invoke the "threat-to-life" argument as his legal justification for healing. Strictly speaking, his healings were never a matter of *pikuach nefesh*. Another principle is at work. According to the opinion of the Pharisees, healing was permitted only in the case of saving a life that was in mortal danger; in the teaching of Yeshua, on the other hand, it is permitted to do good even when there is no mortal danger. The sages taught that *pikuach nefesh* (saving a life) takes precedence over the Sabbath, but in the opinion of Yeshua, even when life is not in danger it is permitted to desecrate the Sabbath for the sake of mercy.

On what legal basis, then, did Yeshua justify his decision to heal on the Sabbath?

MERCY ON ANIMALS

As the man with the withered hand stood expectantly in front of him, Yeshua posed another question to the sages present in the synagogue: "Which one of you who has a sheep, if it falls into a pit on the Sabbath, will not take hold of it and lift it out?" (Matthew 12:11). One might wonder why this question would even raise a concern, but according to Sabbath law, one may not lift or carry an object (or an animal) outside of an established boundary. Lifting an animal constituted "carrying" on the Sabbath day.

Yeshua's hypothetical question was a standard rhetorical scenario for discussing Sabbath prohibitions. The Essene community that produced the *Damascus Document* forbade lifting an animal out of a pit on the Sabbath day; apparently, though, in first-century

Pharisaic-Galilean practice the priority of rescuing an animal from a pit was assumed, even on the Sabbath.

Later arguments in the Talmud take up the same question. For example, one passage discusses options for removing an animal from a pit on the Sabbath, expressing concern for the welfare of the beast:

> Rabbi Yehudah said in Rab's name, "If an animal falls into a pit, one may bring cushions and blankets to put under the animal, and if it climbs out, it climbs out." Another opinion objects, "If an animal falls into a pit, provisions may be made for it in the pit to keep it alive" ... Preventing the suffering of animals is a biblical law. The biblical law comes and supersedes the authority of the rabbis. (b.*Shabbat* 128b)

According to the Talmud then, it may be necessary to violate some prohibitions in order to alleviate or prevent the suffering of animals. The Talmud says that showing kindness to animals "is a biblical law" and biblical law (in theory at least) trumps rabbinic mandates. For that reason, the sages deemed it permissible to carry provisions to an animal to feed it or to enable it to climb out of a pit on the Sabbath day. All of these fall into the category of "doing good" on the Sabbath, because showing mercy to animals is a positive biblical commandment.

The Master appealed to what must then have been a standard practice, at least in the Galilee. Saving one's animal's life supersedes the Sabbath prohibition on carrying and lifting. No one in the synagogue raised any objection to that premise. If his example had not referred to an accepted standard of that time and place, Yeshua's argument would have lost its rhetorical force. Several men in the synagogue could have simply raised their hands and said, "We would not take hold of it or lift it out."

The Master declared, "Of how much more value is a man than a sheep! So it is lawful to do good on the Sabbath" (Matthew 12:12). Thus the logic proceeds from the light matter to the more serious matter: If it is permissible to violate Shabbat in order to do good to animals and alleviate their suffering, how much more so is it permissible to do good for human beings by alleviating their suffering?

GOOD OR EVIL?

The sages did not answer the Master's rhetorical questions, but if they had, they could have simply said, "It is lawful to save a life on the Sabbath, but if one's life is not in danger, let the matter wait until the Sabbath concludes." Anticipating such an answer, Yeshua framed his question in black and white, yes-or-no terms. He literally asked, "Is it lawful on the Sabbath to do good or to do harm?" (Luke 6:9). He left no room for a "wait until later" answer.

From Yeshua's perspective, the question had only two possible answers. One could do good, which was the equivalent of saving life and alleviating suffering, or one could do evil by refusing to alleviate suffering. He categorized the latter option as destroying life. From where did Yeshua derive such urgent absolutes? Why must the answer be "yes" or "no," "do good" or "do harm"? He might have been alluding to a prominent passage in the book of Proverbs, which condemns withholding good as a sin of omission:

> Do not withhold good from those to whom it is due, when it is in your power to do it. Do not say to your neighbor, "Go, and come again, tomorrow I will give it"—when you have it with you. (Proverbs 3:27–28)

James, the brother of the Master, summarizes the Master's dichotomous, good-versus-evil teachings, saying, "Whoever knows the right thing to do and fails to do it, for him it is sin" (James 4:17).

No one ventured to engage the rabbi from Nazareth in the legal argument. The sages and teachers present simply sat in stoic silence, neither affirming his reasoning nor objecting to it. Their silence irritated Yeshua. He would have invited further discourse on the subject. "And he looked around at them with anger, grieved at their hardness of heart, and said to the man, 'Stretch out your hand.' He stretched it out, and his hand was restored" (Mark 3:5). "It was restored, healthy like the other" (Matthew 12:13).

THE MAN WORKING ON THE SABBATH

One Greek manuscript of Luke contains an extra verse following the grain field incident described in the previous chapter of this book:

> On the same day he saw a man working on the Sabbath and said to him, "O man, if you know what you are doing, you are blessed; but if you do not know, you are accursed and a transgressor of the Torah." (Luke 6:5, *Codex Bezae*)

Scholars agree that this saying does not belong in Luke 6:5. It is a floating piece of tradition that happened to come to rest there. A disconnected saying of the Master from outside of the Canonical Gospels is called an *agraphon*. Scholars tend to dismiss the authenticity of this Sabbath agraphon. Just for the sake of argument, let's pretend that it is an authentic incident from the life of the Master that was passed on orally in the apostolic community until it finally came to rest in the *Codex Bezae* version of Luke. If so, how might we understand the story and the Master's words?

Traditional Christian interpretation would be quick to use the Master's words as evidence that—for those in the know—the Sabbath was no longer binding. Yeshua tells them, "If you know what you are doing—that is, if you are breaking the Sabbath because you know that the new covenant has canceled it—then you are blessed; but if you are not aware that I have canceled the Sabbath and you are breaking it belligerently, then you are accursed and a transgressor of the Torah." This interpretation does not work because it assumes that Yeshua cancels the Sabbath and encourages his followers to do so as well. It also assumes two separate standards of righteousness: one for Jewish Christians, and the other for Jewish non-Christians.

A better interpretation can be discerned from the Master's perspective on compassion for human need taking priority over the Sabbath. In that context he says to the man, "If you know what you are doing—that is, if you are breaking the Sabbath because you have some justifiable reason for doing so, such as alleviating human suffering—then you are blessed; but if you do not have a justifiable reason for violating the Sabbath and you are simply breaking it belligerently, then you are accursed and a transgressor of the Torah."

This interpretation fits the context of the Master's own work on the Sabbath. He knows what he is doing. He has a justifiable, legal reason for the work he does on the Sabbath. Therefore he is blessed and not a transgressor of the Torah.

THE WOMAN WITH THE BENT BACK

The Synoptic Gospels tell another Sabbath-healing story that took place in a synagogue: the story of the woman who could not straighten herself. "As was his custom, he went to the synagogue on the Sabbath" (Luke 4:16). Whenever Yeshua visited a synagogue, he packed it out to standing-room only. The local synagogue leaders could scarcely object to allowing him the honor of addressing the crowds that flocked in to hear him speak.

On one Sabbath, while he sat teaching in a certain Galilean synagogue, the Master saw a woman bent and crippled by a spirit of infirmity. For eighteen years she had suffered with a condition that might have been *spondylitis ankylopoietica* (a fusion of the spinal bones). She walked stooped over, unable to stand straight:

> And behold, there was a woman who had had a disabling spirit for eighteen years. She was bent over and could not fully straighten herself. When Yeshua saw her, he called her over and said to her, "Woman, you are freed from your disability." And he laid his hands on her, and immediately she was made straight, and she glorified God. (Luke 13:11–13)

When he saw her, he stopped in the middle of his teaching, perhaps mid-sentence. He called her forward. As she shuffled awkwardly through the congregation, Yeshua stood to receive her and said, "Woman, you are freed from your disability." He laid his hands on her. She immediately stood straight, completely healed. Luke tells us, she began "glorifying God," a phrase the gospel writers use to indicate the pronouncement of blessings and praise. An appropriate blessing from the Jewish prayer book declares, "Blessed are You, LORD our God, King of the Universe, who straightens the bent."

SIX DAYS TO WORK

By that time, the controversy around Yeshua's healing ministry was well known, and opinions varied as to whether or not he should be allowed to continue healing on Sabbaths. The Pharisees continued to believe that it was permitted to heal on the Sabbath only when life was in danger, and here there was no mortal danger.

The dramatic and public healing that day placed the synagogue official in an awkward position. If he simply ignored the matter, he might appear to be tacitly endorsing Yeshua's Sabbath activities and thereby incite the ire of several of his conservative congregants. On the other hand, if he condemned the healing outright, he would incite the disapproval of the crowds and the many disciples of Yeshua present that day. He did not venture to offer the Master a direct rebuke. Instead, he tactfully turned the rebuke toward the people in attendance, saying, "There are six days in which work should be done; so come during them and get healed, and not on the Sabbath day."

If the Master believed that healing did not constitute a violation of the Sabbath, he would have said so at that point. Instead, his ensuing argument assumed that healing does violate the Sabbath, but he argued that mercy for a human being should take precedence over Sabbath prohibitions:

> Then the Lord answered him, "You hypocrites! Does not each of you on the Sabbath untie his ox or his donkey from the manger and lead it away to water it? And ought not this woman, a daughter of Abraham whom Satan bound for eighteen years, be loosed from this bond on the Sabbath day?" (Luke 13:15–16)

Jewish Sabbath laws prohibit the tying and untying of certain types of knots on the Sabbath day. Both tying and untying can constitute *melachah,* prohibited forms of work on the Sabbath day. The sages, however, specifically permitted the tying and untying of knots for the purpose of leashing animals and drawing water.

The Talmud also teaches that one can lead a horse to water, but he cannot make it drink:

> Is it not taught that a man must not fill a bucket with water and hold it in front of his beast on the Sabbath? Instead he fills his bucket and pours it into a trough and the cow drinks on his own accord. (b.*Eruvin* 20b)

Yeshua took it for granted that tying and untying knots violates the Sabbath. He also took it for granted than an exception must be made for the sake of watering one's animal. In this case, the owner of the animal violates the Sabbath prohibitions merely for the sake of alleviating the animal's discomfort—so that it does not suffer from thirst. Immediate threat to life is not necessarily in view. Surely the animal's thirst could be slaked after the Sabbath's conclusion.

Having established that the accepted *halachah* (legal interpretation) permitted violating some Sabbath prohibitions in order to prevent suffering to animals, Yeshua reasoned from the light to the heavy: How much more so then is it permissible to violate the Sabbath in order to alleviate the suffering of a human being.

Most gospel readers probably would not consider the mere tying or untying of a knot to constitute *melachah,* a form of work forbidden on the Sabbath, but apparently Yeshua did. If he considered tying or untying as actually permissible on Sabbath, his argument loses all its force.

Our Master established that quenching the thirst of an animal justified temporarily violating the Sabbath by loosing the knot with which the animal was bound. If so, surely a daughter of Abraham, whom Satan bound for eighteen years, should be "loosed" from her bond on the Sabbath day rather than having to wait until the conclusion of the Sabbath. By loosing Satan's captive, the Master fulfilled the prophecy that says, "He has sent me to proclaim liberty to the captives" (Luke 4:18).

His critics did not have any answer, but the common people rejoiced in the miracle.

SABBATH DINNER WITH THE SAGES

Our Master Yeshua loved the Sabbath. His teaching and healing ministry seemed to revolve around the Sabbath day. The Sabbath typically found him as the guest speaker in a synagogue teaching about the kingdom or as a dinner guest in someone's home.

Once, it happened that one of the prominent Pharisees invited our Master in for one of the meals of the Sabbath. The prominent Pharisee had disciples of his own:

> One Sabbath, when he went to dine at the house of a ruler of the Pharisees, they were watching him carefully. (Luke 14:1)

The Pharisees harbored contradictory opinions regarding Yeshua. Some reviled him and sought his demise, but many found him intriguing. They followed him, studied him, criticized him, and very often invited him home for a Sabbath meal.

A PROMINENT PHARISEE

A Sabbath meal in the home of a Torah sage was a splendid affair. The rabbis placed before their guests the best that the marketplace had to offer. They served the best meats, breads, and wines they could afford in honor of the Sabbath. The disciples of the sage became guests in his home, where they crowded about their teacher's table to enjoy the Sabbath peace together. The conversation always turned to matters of Torah.

In this case, the prominent Pharisee invited Yeshua to his table specifically to engage him in discussion about a certain matter of Torah. Perhaps the disciples of that particular sage had participated in the argument over whether or not healing justifies violating the Sabbath. The argument may well have ensued after hearing reports of the controversy around Yeshua of Nazareth. The theological conundrum created by Yeshua's seemingly divine Sabbath-day healings must have piqued their acute interest in the question. If such healings did indeed constitute a violation of the Sabbath, why did God validate them through this man? One can imagine the argument that initiated the dinner invitation. "How can he be a real prophet if he heals on the Sabbath?" "But is it really a sin to heal on the Sabbath?" "Let's invite the man and see what he will say," they might have suggested.

A HEALING AT THE TABLE

When our Master Yeshua came to recline in their midst, they seated him across from a man who suffered from a dropsy, perhaps a type of swelling like edema. Would the healer perform one of his controversial healings? "They were watching him carefully" (Luke 14:1).

Yeshua took the bait, but first he deferred to his host. The Pharisees considered offering a legal decision in the presence of one's teacher without his consent a serious social taboo and an act of impertinence. Even if the teacher was not one's own teacher, the sages refrained from offering a legal opinion in the presence of an older teacher or an esteemed rabbi. Those who ignored the convention received chastisement. Yeshua decorously navigated the situation by offering his host the opportunity to render a legal opinion first. He asked them, "Is it lawful to heal on the Sabbath, or not?" (Luke 14:3). Only after his host and his host's disciples all declined to comment did Yeshua offer his opinion.

Torah sages and rabbis were accustomed to answering legal questions pertaining to the Sabbath. The Master's question was not as straightforward as it sounds. He was not asking for advice; he invited them to engage him in argument. None of them ventured to offer an answer or spar with the Master. They themselves felt a measure of uncertainty about the question. Yeshua took their reticence as tacit approval. He healed the man, and then offered his legal justification for doing so.

One might consider the miraculous hand of God to be justification enough. Why argue further? If God frowned upon healing on the Sabbath, why would he have endorsed it by enabling Yeshua to accomplish it? Such simple reasoning, however, would not satisfy the minds of men trained in the logic of Jewish law. The rabbis did not accept signs and miracles as proofs in legal arguments over Torah. To satisfy his hosts, Yeshua launched into a legal discourse defending healing on the Sabbath day.

He asked them, "Which of you, having a son or an ox that has fallen into a well on a Sabbath day, will not immediately pull him out?" (Luke 14:5). As in Matthew 12, the question is rhetorical:

> Which one of you who has a sheep, if it falls into a pit on the Sabbath, will not take hold of it and lift it out? Of how much more value is a man than a sheep! So it is lawful to do good on the Sabbath. (Matthew 12:11–12)

None of them would hesitate to violate the Sabbath in order to rescue one of their animals or children from a well on the Sabbath day. In this instance the argument asks: If it is permissible to violate Shabbat in order to rescue a life or alleviate an animal's suffering, why should they postpone the infirm man's healing?

Apparently, the prominent Pharisee and his disciples accepted the Master's reasoning.

CONCLUSION TO THE SYNOPTIC SABBATH CONFLICTS

In the end, Jewish law came to similar conclusions as those of our Master, albeit by different lines of justification. Today, Jewish doctors are required to work over the Sabbath (when their duty shift dictates) without raising questions of Sabbath prohibitions. Theoretically, the potential for saving a life is always present when a doctor is on duty, but Jewish law now allows the Jewish doctor to conduct all medical procedures whether life is threatened or not—so long as he is on duty with the potential to save a life.

In the Synoptic Gospels Yeshua based his argument for healing on the Sabbath primarily upon the rabbinic principle of arguing from the light to the heavy: "If it is permissible to violate Sabbath in order to do good to animals and alleviate their suffering, how much more so is it permissible to do the same for human beings?" These acts, though justifiable, still breach the Sabbath. Likewise, he justified the disciples' act of picking grain to alleviate their hunger on the same basis.

Yeshua prioritized the alleviation of human suffering above the prohibitions of the Sabbath on the basis of Hosea 6:6, "For I desire [mercy] and not sacrifice, the knowledge of God rather than burnt offerings." If picking and husking grain, healing a withered arm, lifting an ox out of a pit, and tethering and un-tethering an ox or donkey to lead it to water did not actually constitute legal violations of the Sabbath, Yeshua could have simply said so. He would not have needed to bother with a legal justification that attempted to demonstrate why it should be permissible to violate the Sabbath in these instances.

For many Bible readers, this distinction may be too obscure, but if missed, the reader also misses the essential message of all the Sabbath stories in the Gospels. The point of these stories is not that Yeshua has canceled the Sabbath or that the rabbinic interpretation of Sabbath is illegitimate. The Sabbath-conflict stories are designed to teach that acts of compassion and mercy performed to alleviate human suffering are more important than ceremonial and ritual taboos. The miraculous power by which Yeshua performs the healings only serves to imply God's endorsement to his legal rationale.

Did Yeshua's disciples break the Sabbath in the grain fields? Yes. But they were justified in so doing because their need took precedence, just as the hunger of David and his men took precedence over the Temple service, and the Temple service took precedence over the Sabbath. Therefore Yeshua declared them guiltless and told the Pharisees, "If you had known what this means, 'I desire mercy, and not sacrifice,' you would not have condemned the guiltless" (Matthew 12:7).

Did the Master break the Sabbath when he healed on the Sabbath day? Yes. Would fixing a car break the Sabbath? Of course it would, and by the same standard so does fixing a human body. Nevertheless, the Master justified doing so because compassion for his fellow man overrides the Sabbath.

Outside of this exception of doing good and offering compassion to alleviate human suffering, Yeshua did not deem the aforementioned violations justifiable. If the disciples picked and husked the grain and carried it away in their pockets or threw it on the ground, they would have broken the Sabbath without justification. If Yeshua decided to apply his healing power to cracked pottery, and if instead of healing human beings, he began to miraculously heal cracks in pottery on the Sabbath just for the sake of repairing pottery, he would have been breaking the Sabbath without justification, because pots are not lord of the Sabbath and the Sabbath was not made for pots.

The Son of Man, who took such great delight in healing the afflictions of his fellow Jews on the holy Sabbath day, thereby revealed the true nature of that day of redemption. He also revealed the true heart of the Father, who made the Sabbath for man and not man for the Sabbath, and who made the human to be the lord of the Sabbath, that man should "call the Sabbath a delight and the holy day of the LORD honorable" (Isaiah 58:13).

A CHASIDIC STORY

A popular Chasidic story illustrates the point. This story takes place on Yom Kippur, the holiest festival of the year. The Torah calls it a *Shabbat Shabbaton*, the "Sabbath of all Sabbaths," and the Torah strictly warns the Jewish people not to do any work at all on that holy Sabbath of all Sabbaths:

> Whoever does any work on that very day, that person I will destroy from among his people. You shall not do any work. It is a statute forever throughout your generations in all your dwelling places. It shall be to you a Sabbath of solemn rest. (Leviticus 23:30–32)

That explains why the disciples of Reb Schneur Zalman, the founder of Chabad Chasidism, were so shocked to see their holy rebbe break the prohibition against working on Yom Kippur. During morning prayers, they saw him remove his *tallit* and his *kittel* and leave the synagogue. A few of his disciples followed at a distance to see where he was going. They followed him to a small cottage on the outskirts of town where he picked up an axe and chopped some wood. They watched through the window as he used the wood to light a fire in the stove. They blinked in disbelief as they saw him bring water to a boil and prepare a pot of soup. Then they saw him feeding the soup, spoon by spoon, to a bedridden woman, a new mother.

Word had come to the rebbe that the woman had just given birth, but had no one to help her. He knew that her life was in danger, and he prioritized saving her life above keeping the prohibitions of Yom Kippur. When later asked why he did not send one of his disciples as a *shaliach* (an emissary) to perform these tasks, he replied that the opportunity to save a life is a privilege, a mitzvah that he wanted to fulfill with his own hands.

Did Reb Schneur Zalman violate the prohibitions of Yom Kippur? Of course he did. He did it to save a life. Something greater than Yom Kippur was present—compassion for a fellow human being.

CHAPTER ELEVEN

The Healing at Bethesda and the Man Born Blind

Once, it happened that our Master was on his way to the Temple courts, passing through the colonnades that surround the pools of Bethesda. Here and there, the sick and disabled lay beside the pool, waiting for the miraculous stirring of the waters.

PICK UP YOUR MAT

Yeshua stopped at the mat of one particular man, a paralytic who had not walked for thirty-eight years. In the race to reach the water first, he had an obvious disadvantage. The Master knew the man had waited a long time. Perhaps more than anyone else at the pool that day, he was a man without hope. The Master asked him, "Do you want to be healed?" (John 5:6). The man had never seen Yeshua before; he knew nothing about him. He did not realize that Yeshua offered him healing. He explained, "Sir, I have no one to put me into the pool when the water is stirred up, and while I am going another steps down before me" (John 5:7).

The Master said, "Get up, take up your bed, and walk" (John 5:8). Before the man had time to consider whether or not he believed or had enough faith in the mysterious healer, he felt life and revivification pour into his limbs. He obeyed the stranger, stood up, and picked up the bedroll on which he had been lying. "Now that day was the Sabbath" (John 5:9).

CARRYING ON THE SABBATH

Yeshua told the man to pick up his bedroll and carry it. Several other people protested when they saw the healed man carrying his bedroll over his shoulder. Traditional Sabbath law prohibits a Jewish person from carrying an object in a public domain. Objects can be moved about and carried within a private home, courtyard, or pre-determined domain, but they cannot be carried from a private domain into a public space, nor may they be carried in public space. Practically speaking, this means that on the Sabbath day a Jewish person is not to carry an object more than four cubits if he is outside his home.

Ordinarily, Christian readers dismiss the law against carrying an object on the Sabbath day as a rabbinic fiction. But while the interpretation of the law is part of Jewish tradition, the law itself is based squarely upon biblical text. The rule is derived principally from two passages of Scripture:

> Remain each of you in his place; let no one go out of his place on the seventh day. (Exodus 16:29)

> Thus says the LORD: Take care for the sake of your lives, and do not bear a burden [carried thing] on the Sabbath day or bring it in by the gates of Jerusalem. And do not carry a burden [carried thing] out of your houses on the Sabbath or do any work, but keep the Sabbath day holy, as I commanded your fathers. (Jeremiah 17:21–22)

In addition, the Torah tells a story about a man who was found gathering and carrying sticks on the Sabbath day. Moses did not know what to do with the man. The LORD instructed the community to stone him to death for violating the Sabbath (Numbers 15).

The sages determined that transferring an object from one domain to another constitutes a violation of the Sabbath. The rule allows a Jewish person carrying an object outside of a private domain to walk no more than four cubits on the Sabbath. Knowing this, the carrying of the bedroll seems to violate the Sabbath.

The laws of carrying are extremely complex; moreover, they underwent significant development during the first century. It is difficult to know with much certainty exactly how they might have applied at the time of the story of the healing at Bethesda. The sages admit that "The laws of the Sabbath ... are like mountains hanging by a single hair, with few scriptures but many laws" (t.*Eruvin* 8:23). We do not know exactly how they were understood or practiced in the days of the Master.

An early opinion in the Mishnah states, "One who carries a living person on a litter is not liable for carrying the litter because the litter is dependent upon the person being carried" (m.*Shabbat* 10:5). This law seems to imply that some opinions allowed for carrying another person on the Sabbath, even if the person was carried upon a bed. The same opinion, however, implies that if a person was not in the bed, the bed should not be carried.

As the man walked through the porticoes of Bethesda with his bedroll over his shoulder, several religious leaders challenged him: "It is the Sabbath, and it is not lawful for you to take up your bed" (John 5:10). The man quickly explained that he had been miraculously healed only moments earlier, and that the man who healed him was the one who told him to pick up his mat and carry it. The man's explanation raised another concern. Who was going about and healing people on the Sabbath day?

The religious leaders asked him, "Who is the man who said to you, 'Take up your bed and walk'?" (John 5:12). The man did not know.

AN UNANSWERED QUESTION

The Gospel of John uses the bedroll incident only to explain why the Judean religious authorities took notice of the man at Bethesda. If they had not seen him carrying his bedroll, the entire healing miracle might have escaped their notice. The writer of John pays no further attention to the question of carrying on the Sabbath, and the matter is not raised again. That leaves the reader wondering, "Why did Yeshua tell the man to pick up his bedroll and carry it?"

Surely our Master could have healed the man simply by telling him, "Stand up and walk." Was it necessary to also tell him to carry his mat?

We might suppose that he told him to carry his bedroll in order to make a public statement. Christian interpretation ordinarily assumes that Jesus wanted to prove to everyone that the Sabbath has been abolished. Even Sabbatarian interpretations often assume that, while upholding the biblical Sabbath, Yeshua demonstrated that the prohibition on carrying an object on the Sabbath is an unjustified rabbinic fiction. Perhaps by telling the man to carry his mat, Yeshua demonstrated that carrying an object in a public space does not violate the Sabbath. If so, he was thereby encouraging people to throw off the rules of traditional Judaism and to begin carrying objects around on the Sabbath.

This interpretation does not work. Yeshua never made any statements about carrying on the Sabbath. In John 5 he did not stay behind to defend the man, nor did he argue about the Sabbath with the sages. Instead, Yeshua slipped away from sight, fading into the crowd. He did not attempt to correct their interpretation, and he offered no legal justification for carrying on the Sabbath.

He himself did not carry, nor did his prosecutors ever accuse him or any of his followers of carrying on the Sabbath. So why does he tell the man to carry his bedroll on the Sabbath?

Unfortunately, the Gospel of John omits any explanation and shifts its focus to the question of whether or not Yeshua is justified in healing on the Sabbath. John leaves the entire bedroll incident unexplained and unresolved. Nevertheless, we may still indulge in some speculation on this topic.

WITHIN THE ERUV

In his *Jewish New Testament Commentary*, Messianic teacher David Stern suggests that the problem was simply a disagreement over what constituted a proper *eruv*. As mentioned earlier, Sabbath law allows a Jewish person to carry an object within his own domain, but he must not carry an object more than four cubits in a public domain. In order to alleviate this restriction, the sages devised a way for members of a community to join their homes, courtyards, and neighborhood into one large common legal domain.

Several requirements had to be met in order for this joining to have legal force. Prior to the Sabbath, the community needed to agree on the borders (*eruv*) of their shared domain and mark them off. Then, the residents needed to make a communal declaration of shared property within that circumference for the duration of the Sabbath. If the *eruv* was erected properly, the community could legally declare a whole village or city as one common domain. So long as one was within the limits of the *eruv*-border, he was free to carry certain objects as if he were in his own home.

The laws of *eruv* are complex. We have already discussed the distinction between public and private domains, but the establishment of an *eruv* involves a third category of domain, a *karmelit*, which is not quite public and not quite private. Most communal spaces belong in this category. Jewish law considers it biblically permissible to carry within a *karmelit*, to carry from one private domain to another, and to carry between a *karmelit* and a private domain. However, the features that distinguish between a *karmelit* and a public domain are complex and subtle. The sages felt that they were too easy to take for granted, so they made a rabbinic prohibition against carrying in a *karmelit*, carrying between a *karmelit* and a private domain, and carrying from one private domain to another. These more stringent prohibitions are regarded as a rabbinic fence around the biblical commandment. A public domain is a public domain *de facto* and cannot be declared a private domain *de jure*. An *eruv* cannot ever be declared within a public domain. Therefore, the tradition of *eruv* alleviates the rabbinic prohibition, not a Torah prohibition. The *eruv* allows for leniency in the rabbinic law under a certain set of specific conditions, which can be met only within a community whose members fully understand the laws of *eruv* and intentionally create an *eruv* according to these laws.

David Stern argues that, as a walled city, all of Jerusalem was within the Sabbath *eruv*, and that by Pharisaic law, carrying should have been permitted within the city. He assumes that the pool of Bethesda lay within the walls of Jerusalem and therefore within the *eruv*. Stern suggests that the Pharisees suspected the man was about to leave the *eruv* while carrying his mat.

Unfortunately, Stern's suggestion does not solve the problem. Why did Yeshua not simply explain to his critics, "We were within the *eruv* when I told him to carry his mat"? Stern is also making an assumption about the layout of Jerusalem's walls in the days of the Master. According to most archaeologists—and as can be seen in most reconstructions of the walls of Jerusalem—the pool of Bethesda was still outside the city walls in those days, being right outside the Sheep Gate. A few decades later, King Herod Agrippa expanded the city and brought Bethesda inside the walls, but in the days of the Master, the pool remained outside the walls and hence outside the *eruv*. The pool of Bethesda may have been considered *karmelit,* but it was certainly not within Jerusalem's walls in the days of the Master.

MERCY, NOT SACRIFICE

Many believers assume that the story of the man carrying the mat on the Sabbath is evidence that Yeshua disagreed with the interpretation of the laws that forbid carrying on Sabbath. Even if that were the case, it does not adequately explain why the Master told the man to pick up his mat and walk. Why make the unfortunate paralytic into a pawn in a legal debate?

Arguing about the laws of carrying or what constitutes a proper *eruv* seems out of character for our Master. We never see him intentionally overturning Jewish tradition unless he has a sound reason for doing so, and when he does, he always states the reason. Entering an argument about whether or not a man is permitted to carry a particular object on the Sabbath seems beneath his dignity and outside the scope of his concern. It seems like an argument that Yeshua would avoid because it fails to address "the weightier matters of the law: justice and mercy and faithfulness" (Matthew 23:23).

As mentioned above, other stories about Yeshua healing on the Sabbath always point toward the weightier provisions of Torah. In those stories the Master justifies violating the Sabbath for the sake of alleviating human suffering on the basis of a passage from Hosea 6:6: "If you had known what this means, 'I desire mercy, and not sacrifice,' you would not have condemned the guiltless" (Matthew 12:7). He used the passage to teach that compassion for human beings, specifically the alleviation of human suffering, takes precedence over ceremonial concern. Is there some way in which allowing the paralytic to carry his bedroll could be understood as an act of mercy?

RIGHTEOUSNESS BEFORE THE LORD

We may assume that after thirty-eight years of paralysis, the man at Bethesda had no other possession to his name other than the bedroll upon which he slept. The Torah shows special concern for just such a situation.

A passage in Deuteronomy creates a hypothetical scenario in which a poor man must secure a loan from a creditor. The poor man has nothing to offer for collateral except his cloak, which also doubles as his bedroll. The Torah warns the creditor not to keep the collateral overnight. The creditor must return the man's cloak before sunset so that he will be able to sleep in it. If the creditor will do so, the LORD will reckon his act of mercy on the man as righteousness:

> When you make your neighbor a loan of any sort … If he is a poor man, you shall not sleep in his pledge. You shall restore to him the pledge as the sun sets, that he may sleep in his cloak and bless you. And it will be righteousness for you before the LORD your God. (Deuteronomy 24:10–13)

In John 5, the sick man's bed is equivalent to the poor man's cloak. Would our Master have told the man, "Get up and walk, but abandon your mat here because today is the Sabbath"? Would that not have violated the spirit of Deuteronomy 24:10–13?

Yeshua, prioritizing mercy above ceremonial concern, told the man to get up, go, and take his mat with him. In so doing, Yeshua did not abrogate the prohibition on carrying on the Sabbath or declare that prohibition illegitimate. Neither did he criticize traditional Jewish observance of the Sabbath. Instead, he acted according to a higher ethical standard: mercy on a human being overrides ceremonial prohibitions when necessary. Even according to strict rabbinic law, human dignity should take precedence. Yeshua summarizes this ethical override with the words, "The Sabbath was made for man, not man for the Sabbath" (Mark 2:27).

This is especially so in the case of rabbinic prohibitions (stringencies, fences). Judaism teaches that any rabbinic decree can be justifiably violated for the sake of human dignity (*kevod haBeri'ot*). Some of the laws of carrying on the Sabbath apply on the level of Torah prohibition, whereas others apply only on the aforementioned level of rabbinic decree (*de'rabbanan*). According to traditional Jewish law, the types of carrying that are merely rabbinic fences can be violated, when necessary, for the sake of human dignity. In this case, even though it was outside the *eruv* boundary demarcated by the city walls, the area of the pool of Bethesda should have been considered *karmelit* (neither completely public nor completely private domain), an area in which carrying on the Sabbath could be permitted.

Evidently, the authorities chose not to allow carrying in that area, perhaps because they could not agree on the exact legal parameters of an *eruv* outside the walls, or perhaps in order to prevent people from taking the prohibitions on carrying lightly. If this is so, carrying within the area of the pool of Bethesda was a rabbinic prohibition that should have been lifted in a case of preserving human dignity. The Talmud contains many other examples where human dignity is at issue, sometimes even arguably overriding blatant Torah law, let alone rabbinic stringencies.

JEWISH BELIEVERS AND THE LAWS OF CARRYING

Yeshua showed mercy to the sick man with the bedroll by making an exception to the prohibition against carrying. He did not intend to set a new, lower standard by which he allowed his followers to disregard Sabbath law. Aside from the story in John 5, his opponents never accused him, his disciples, or his followers of ever carrying an object on the Sabbath. If the Master and his followers routinely broke that law, their opponents would have had ammunition for criticism and legal grounds to prosecute them as Sabbath-breakers.

Neither the Gospels nor the rest of the New Testament indicate that Yeshua or his followers began to carry objects in public domains on the Sabbath. On the contrary, our Master told his disciples, "Pray that your flight may not be ... on a Sabbath" (Matthew 24:20). Why? Sabbath law allows a person to break the Sabbath to save his life. Accordingly, flight from enemies is permissible on the Sabbath. However, the immediate threat to life does not justify carrying one's personal possessions. Compare Matthew 24:17–18, where Yeshua warns his disciples to flee in haste, not returning home to pack their possessions before their flight. This implies that the question of baggage is in view when he tells them to pray that their flight will not take place on the Sabbath. A direct threat to life justifies fleeing on the Sabbath, but a man's life is not at stake if he leaves his bedroll and money belt behind him on the Sabbath day. Perhaps the Master told his disciples to pray that they will not have to flee on the Sabbath so that they will not have to leave their possessions behind. He assumed that they would not carry on the Sabbath outside of a private domain.

TWO JUSTIFICATIONS

Sometime later that same day, Yeshua saw the man in the Temple. Apparently he had deposited his bedroll someplace and then gone up to the Temple to offer thanks to God.

The Master congratulated him on his healing and offered him a word of repentance: "Sin no more, that nothing worse may happen to you" (John 5:14). The man left and told the religious authorities the name of the one who had healed him: Yeshua of Nazareth. The healed man intended no malice. He was not informing on the Master; Yeshua never told him to keep his identity private. The man may have felt that he was honoring Yeshua by reporting his name. The religious leaders who had rebuked the man for carrying the bedroll came to challenge Yeshua about the matter of healing on the Sabbath day. Notably, their inquiry ignites the Master's first confrontation with the religious establishment of his day.

As soon as the Judean leadership was able to verify that Yeshua was healing on the Sabbath, they harried him over the issue. They cornered him in the Temple courts and asked for some explanations.

As explained in earlier chapters, most of the rabbis of that day believed that healing constituted a form of "work" forbidden on the Sabbath. Yeshua did not disagree with this opinion. Instead, he justified the work he did on the Sabbath with two different arguments. His first argument employs a philosophical and mystical justification which appears in his dissertation in John 5. The second argument employs a legal justification for healing on the Sabbath, and it appears in his dissertation in John 7.

THE MYSTICAL JUSTIFICATION

Yeshua explained why he felt justified performing acts of healing on the Sabbath: "My Father is working until now, and I am working" (John 5:17).

Though God rested on the seventh day from the work of creating the universe, he did not rest from all forms of work. A similar teaching in the *Midrash Rabbah* depicts God working on the Sabbath to punish the wicked and reward the righteous:

> Rabbi Pinchas said in Rabbi Oshaya's name, "In the Torah it says, 'By the seventh day God completed his work which he had done, and he rested on the seventh day from all his work.' He rested only from the work of creating his world, but not from the work of punishing the wicked and the work of rewarding the righteous, for he works with the former and with the latter. He shows the wicked their true nature, and the righteous their true nature ... the punishment of the wicked is called work ... bestowing the reward of the righteous is called work. (*Genesis Rabbah* 11:10)

The *Midrash Rabbah* (11:15) also mentions that God causes wind to blow and rain to fall even on the Sabbath. Though he rests from the work of creation, God continues with all other forms of "God-work" even on the Sabbath day.

Our Master argues that God continued to do the work of redemption even after the sixth day of creation. Until the ultimate and final Sabbath when redemption is complete, God will not rest from that labor. Until that day when there is no more sickness, suffering, or sin, the Father continues to work among men. In the same way, Yeshua does the work of redemption even on the Sabbath.

Whether he is ordering the universe, stirring the winds, punishing the wicked, rewarding the righteous, or healing the sick, God receives an exemption from ceasing on the Sabbath. Yeshua claims that since he is doing the work of his Father (i.e., redemption and healing), he enjoys the same exemption.

EQUAL WITH GOD

Our Master justified healing on the Sabbath by saying, "My Father is working until now, and I am working" (John 5:17). The religious leaders misunderstood. They thought he was claiming to be on par with God. They reduced his argument to mean, "If God can break the Sabbath, then I can break the Sabbath because I have the same privileges as God." They thought that because he claimed the same rights as God, he claimed to be equal with God.

Was Yeshua claiming divine exemption from the Sabbath on the basis that he was equal with God? Or did the religious leaders misunderstand him? Would the Gospel of John present Yeshua as God's equal? Christian theology teaches that the Son is equal to the Father in regard to his divinity, but subordinate to the Father in regard to his humanity. The New Testament narrative tells the story of Yeshua primarily from the viewpoint of his humanity. Paul teaches that Yeshua "did not count equality with God a thing to be grasped" (Philippians 2:6), and John 14:28 reports Yeshua saying, "The Father is greater than I."

John presents Yeshua as the *Logos* made flesh in whom the fullness of God dwells in bodily form, but that was not the Master's point as he tried to explain why he felt free to heal on the Sabbath. He never justified his actions with the argument, "I'm God in the flesh, therefore, I can do whatever I want." He never invoked divine privilege to exempt himself from rules incumbent upon "normal" human beings. Instead, "God sent forth his Son, born of a woman, born under the law" (Galatians 4:4). "Although he was a son, he learned obedience" (Hebrews 5:8). He "did not count equality with God a thing to be grasped" (Philippians 2:6).

Instead of arguing that he was exempt from observing the Sabbath because of his divine status, the Master argued that God performs certain labors on the Sabbath day because they take priority over the Sabbath. For example, God causes the wind to blow and the rain to fall on the Sabbath because sustaining the natural order takes precedence over the Sabbath. So too, God heals and saves on the Sabbath because human lives hold priority over the Sabbath. Yeshua justified healing the man on the Sabbath because it is the kind of work that the Father has been doing since the six days of creation.

THE PARABLE OF THE APPRENTICE

The Judeans who hassled the Master about healing on the Sabbath misunderstood his explanation. They thought that by referring to himself as the Son and God as his Father, Yeshua claimed that he had the right to work on the Sabbath because he was equal to God.

He attempted to clarify his words by comparing himself to a boy apprenticed in a trade by his father:

> So Jesus said to them, "Truly, truly, I say to you, the Son can do nothing of his own accord, but only what he sees the Father doing. For whatever the Father does, that the Son does likewise. For the Father loves the Son and shows him all that he himself is doing. And greater works than these will he show him, so that you may marvel." (John 5:19–20)

The teaching evokes scenes from the carpenter's shop in Nazareth. Just as Yeshua learned the carpentry trade from watching his father Joseph, so he learned his healing trade from observing his Father in heaven. Since God heals and saves on the Sabbath, his apprentice does so as well. A more developed version of this teaching might have sounded like this:

To what can it be compared? It can be compared to a man who wanted his son to take up a trade, but the son did not know how to do anything by himself. The man said, "I love my son and want him to be able to provide for himself. I will bring him to work with me and show him how to do everything I do." The son watched his father at work, and he learned to do all that his father could do. Soon the son could do whatever he saw his father doing. Whatever the man did the son also learned to do. "Truly, truly, I say to you, the Son can do nothing of himself, unless it is something he sees the Father doing."

Yeshua argued that he heals on the Sabbath primarily as a matter of imitating God. The principle of imitating God is at the core of all Jewish ethics:

> Just as the Holy One, blessed be he, is called Merciful, so should you be merciful; just as he is called Gracious, so should you be gracious; just as he is called Righteous, so should you be righteous; just as he is called devout, so should you be a devout one. (*Sifrei* on Deuteronomy 10:12)

Yeshua performed works of healing that he learned to do from observing his Father in heaven. He told his critics that he anticipated learning even greater works from his Father in the future. He said, "The Father will show [me] greater works than these, so that you will marvel," which is to say, "You have not seen anything yet." Yeshua promises that his detractors will marvel at the works God gives his Son to accomplish.

THE LEGAL JUSTIFICATION

Yeshua's mystical justification for healing on the Sabbath did not satisfy his critics. Years later, the religious authorities in Jerusalem were still complaining about the healing at Bethesda. "I did one work, and you all marvel," Yeshua said (John 7:21). That "one work" had garnered the resentment of some prominent sages. "And this was why the Jews [religious authorities] were persecuting Jesus, because he was doing these things on the Sabbath" (John 5:16).

In John 7, we find the Master once again caught up in a debate about the healing that took place at Bethesda and the topic of healing on the Sabbath day. This time he tried a new approach. Rather than arguing from a mystical perspective, he argued from a *halachic* perspective. The Hebrew word *halachah* refers to the specific legal application of a commandment of the Torah. The sages routinely engaged in *halachic* arguments and discussions about Sabbath observance. Yeshua's argument in John 7 falls into the same genre of legal wrangling:

> Moses gave you circumcision (not that it is from Moses, but from the fathers), and you circumcise a man on the Sabbath. If on the Sabbath a man receives circumcision, so that the law of Moses may not be broken, are you angry with me because on the Sabbath I made a man's whole body well? Do not judge by appearances, but judge with right judgment. (John 7:22–24)

CIRCUMCISION ON THE SABBATH

Circumcision is a surgical procedure; as such, it falls into the category of medical treatment. It therefore constitutes a form of work (*melachah*) forbidden on the Shabbat. The Torah, however, mandates that a baby boy be circumcised on the eighth day. When a woman gives birth to a son on the Sabbath day, a contradiction arises. The eighth day will also be a Sabbath. On the one hand, the Torah commands the family to "do no work," but on the other hand, the Torah commands the family to perform an act of *melachah* by circumcising the infant on that specific day. Which commandment holds more sway? According to the sages, a positive commandment takes precedence over a prohibition:

> Wherever you find a positive commandment and a negative commandment contradicting, if you can fulfill both of them, it is preferable, but if not, let the positive command come and supersede the negative command. (b.*Shabbat* 133a)

The sages agreed that the positive commandment to circumcise on the eighth day supersedes the prohibition against *melachah* on the Sabbath. Whenever the eighth day falls on a Sabbath, the family of the child must set aside the Sabbath prohibition and perform the circumcision. Rabbi Yosi said, "Great is circumcision, since it overrides the prohibition of the Sabbath, which is subject to strict regulations" (m.*Nedarim* 3:11).

The Mishnah describes how the Sabbath can be broken in order to deliver a baby. This falls into the category of *pikuach nefesh*: breaking the Sabbath to save a life. Then the Mishnah derives the permission to circumcise on Shabbat. If it is permissible to break the Sabbath to deliver a child, it must be permissible to break the Sabbath to circumcise that same child eight days later:

> They deliver a woman's baby on the Sabbath [even if it requires violating the Sabbath]. They will summon a midwife from a distant place, and they violate the Sabbath on account of the mother. They [also violate the Sabbath when they] tie the umbilical cord. Rabbi Yosi said, "They also cut it." Likewise, they perform everything necessary for a circumcision on the Sabbath. (m.*Shabbat* 18:3)

The Mishnah provides a vivid description of how many ways the Sabbath must be broken in order to carry out the circumcision: "They perform everything necessary for a circumcision on the Sabbath. They cut, tear, suction, dress with poultice and cumin" (m.*Shabbat* 19:2).

The rabbis considered the surgical procedure of circumcision as a medical correction, an improvement to the body. Rabbi Yehudah observed, "Despite all the commandments which Abraham our father observed, he was called complete and whole only when he had circumcised himself, as it says [in Genesis 17:1], 'Walk before me, and be blameless.'"

Yeshua reasoned, "If it is then permissible to make a medical adjustment to one small part of the body to correct it, how much more so should it be permissible to make a medical adjustment to correct the rest of the body." The Master's logic follows a simple line of legal reasoning:

1. A surgical procedure constitutes *melachah* forbidden on Sabbath.
2. Circumcision is a surgical procedure and should, therefore, not occur on Sabbath.
3. Yet, the commandment to circumcise supersedes the Sabbath prohibition.
4. Circumcision is a surgical procedure performed for the sake of only one body part.
5. Therefore the healing of man's whole body should supersede the Sabbath even more so.

Yeshua employs the same line of reasoning when he asks the Pharisees, "Have you not read in the Law how on the Sabbath the priests in the temple profane the Sabbath and are guiltless?" (Matthew 12:5). In other words, there are situations where the Torah requires us to violate the Sabbath:

> Lest one suppose that circumcision or the Temple service or a potential loss of life [are subject to the prohibitions of the Sabbath], the Scriptures make a distinction ... There are times that you must rest on the Sabbath, and times that you must not rest on the Sabbath. Rabbi Eliezer says, "As to circumcision, why do they allow it to supersede the prohibitions on the Sabbath? It is because they are liable to being cut off [from Israel] if it is not accomplished at the proper time. Now behold, this can be argued from the light to the heavy. If they override the Sabbath on account of a single member of the body, how much more should they override the prohibitions of the Sabbath to save the whole body?" (t.*Shabbat* 15:16)

THE MASTER'S ARGUMENT

The sages agreed with Yeshua's reasoning up to a point. Rabbi Eliezer, a disciple of Yochanan ben Zakkai, may have heard the Master's conversation that day with the sages and derived his argument from Yeshua. Note the similarities in their arguments. As Rabbi Eliezer articulates in the argument above, the Sabbath should certainly be set aside for the sake of saving a life, even if the threat to life is uncertain. However, Eliezer did not go so far as to say that the Sabbath should be set aside to heal a person even when no threat to life is present.

The rabbis used principles drawn from the practice of circumcision on the Sabbath to justify breaking the Sabbath only in cases where life is in immediate danger. The man at the pool of Bethesda was in no immediate danger to life. He had waited thirty-eight years. He could have waited a few more hours until the conclusion of the Sabbath. The same is true in all the Sabbath healing stories. Yeshua believed that it is permitted to heal on the Sabbath even when the malady posed no immediate threat to life.

Notice that Yeshua's argument regarding circumcision and healing on the Sabbath falls apart if he did not believe that healing constitutes a legitimate violation of the Sabbath prohibitions. If he believed that healing did not fall into the category of "work" (*melachah*) forbidden on the Sabbath, he should have framed the argument completely differently. Instead, his argument assumes that circumcision is a legitimate violation of Sabbath, and yet the Torah requires it to take place on the Sabbath. Likewise, his argument assumes that healing—even miraculous healing—breaks the Sabbath prohibitions, yet that the priority of compassion for human beings requires it.

As noted above from Eliezer's argument in the Tosefta, Yeshua's legal argument was so cogent and well-reasoned that the sages themselves seem to have adopted it for application in cases that involved a potential threat to life:

> Rabbi Eleazar [ben Azariah] answered, "If circumcision, which involves a remedy for only one of the 248 parts of the human body, supersedes the Sabbath, how much more does saving the whole body supersede the Sabbath!" (b.*Yoma* 85b)

Yeshua concluded his legal argument with an allusion to Deuteronomy 16:18, "Do not judge by appearances, but judge with right judgment" (John 7:24).

MUD AND SPITTLE

Shortly after the discussion about circumcision and the Sabbath, the Master and his disciples encountered a man blind from birth. Yeshua spat on the ground, made mud of the spittle, and applied the mud to the man's eyes. Then he told the man, "Go, wash in the pool of Siloam." The man went and immersed, and miraculously, he could see. "Now it was a Sabbath day when Jesus made the mud and opened his eyes" (John 9:14).

The Master's other healings demonstrate that none of this was necessary. He could have just touched the man, or even just spoken a single word to open the man's unseeing eyes. Yeshua ordinarily healed men and women in a purely supernatural manner. Why the elaborate concoction this time?

This single healing incident from the Gospels potentially involves three Sabbath violations. To heal the man, Yeshua spat on the ground and made mud out of the spittle and the earth. Mixing two substances to form a third falls under the prohibition of kneading. It is *melachah*. It is making. Therefore, it is prohibited on the Sabbath day.

First-century Jewish folk medicine considered spittle, particularly the spittle of a firstborn son, a remedy for eye trouble. Yeshua mixed his spittle with the dirt of the ground to make mud. He then applied the mud/saliva mixture to the man's eyes as a salve. Applying a salve or medicine by means of smearing is also considered a form of work prohibited on the Sabbath day. It is a form of *melachah*, a violation of the Sabbath. The application of spittle to the eyes on Shabbat is expressly forbidden in the Jerusalem Talmud.

He sent the man to immerse himself. At least by convention, Jews do not immerse on the Sabbath.

Our Master's enemies declared, "This man is not from God, for he does not keep the Sabbath" (John 9:16). They wanted to prove that Yeshua of Nazareth broke the Sabbath and taught others to do so as well. According to the Torah, breaking the Sabbath is a sin for a Jew. If they could prove that he was a sinner and that he condoned sin, they could prove that he was not the Messiah.

A TALMUDIC DEBATE

A discussion from the Talmud illustrates the issues at hand in the story of the blind man of John 9. The rabbis argue about whether or not an eye condition is serious enough to warrant setting aside the Sabbath prohibition in order to apply a medical salve. According to one opinion, the salve could be applied only if one had already brought and prepared the herbal medicines prior to the Sabbath:

> Rabbi Zutra bar Toviah said in the name of Rav: "An eye that is irritated, it is permissible to apply salve to the eye on the Sabbath. Rav was understood to be of the opinion that it is only permissible when the medicine for the salve

> had been ground the previous day, but if it is necessary to grind them on the Sabbath and carry them in public, it would not be permissible." (b.*Avodah Zarah* 28b)

A second opinion states that grinding the medicines and carrying them on the Sabbath is also permissible for the sake of treating an inflamed eye:

> But one of the rabbis, Rabbi Yaakov, contradicted him saying, "It was taught to me according to Rav Yehudah that even grinding on the Sabbath and the carrying through the public street are permissible." Rav Yehudah declared it as permissible to apply salve to the eye on the Sabbath. (b.*Avodah Zarah* 28b)

Not everyone agreed with this second opinion. Rabbi Shmu'el bar Yehudah said, "Anyone who acts according to Yehudah's opinion breaks the Sabbath!" Ironically, sometime later, Shmu'el suffered from an inflamed eye on the Sabbath. He asked Rav Yehudah if treating his eye on the Sabbath was permissible or forbidden. Rav Yehudah replied, "For everyone else it is permitted— but for you it is forbidden."

Rav Yehudah told a story to explain why preparing and administering medicine for a sore eye should be permitted even on the Sabbath:

> It once happened to a maidservant in Mar Shmu'el's house that her eye became inflamed on a Sabbath. She cried, but no one attended her [because of the Sabbath prohibitions] and her eye burst. The very next day, Mar Shmu'el went out and taught that if one's eye gets out of order it is permissible to apply salve even on the Sabbath." (b.*Avodah Zarah* 28b)

The Talmud goes on to justify eye treatments on the basis that an inflamed eye might further develop to cause a threat to one's life. "What is the reason it is permitted?" the sages asked. "Because the eyesight is connected with the muscles of the heart." In other words, the eye condition might develop into a more serious matter that constitutes a threat to life, and therefore its treatment takes precedence over the Sabbath as a matter of saving a life. Nevertheless, all agreed that this exception to the rule did not apply to a preexisting condition, nor could medicine be prepared and applied to an eye on the Sabbath simply to improve one's vision.

HALACHAH OF YESHUA

Had Yeshua been party to the above conversation, he would have disagreed with the final ruling. As we saw in the synoptic Sabbath conflicts, Rabbi Yeshua believed that compassion for human beings overrides Sabbath prohibitions, even when a man's malady or disability poses no immediate threat to life. He taught that the Sabbath is made for man and not man for the Sabbath.

Citing Hosea 6:6, "I desire [mercy] and not sacrifice," Yeshua reminded the rabbis of his day that the Temple service, with its sacrifices and burnt offerings, takes priority over the Sabbath. Since mercy takes priority over the Temple sacrifices, and the Temple sacrifices take priority over the Sabbath, then mercy must also take priority over the Sabbath.

Likewise, he taught that if it is permissible to violate the Sabbath in order to show mercy to animals and alleviate their suffering, the same allowance applies much more so to human beings.

The essential message is not that Yeshua has canceled the Sabbath, or that the rabbinic interpretation of Sabbath is illegitimate. The message is that acts of compassion and mercy performed to alleviate human suffering take precedence over the Sabbath's prohibitions. The miraculous power by which Yeshua performs healings only serves to add God's endorsement to Yeshua's legal rationale.

PRACTICING MEDICINE ON THE SABBATH

This explains why the Master used the spittle, the mud, and the immersion to heal the blind man on the Sabbath. As mentioned above, he could have dispensed with all of that and simply touched the man's eyes, or spoken a word to heal him. Instead, he chose to apply a medical treatment, just as a first-century doctor might have done. He chose deliberately to step over the boundaries of

Sabbath law for the sake of healing the man, and he chose to do so in a manner that any disciple of his might emulate.

In so doing, Yeshua provided a model for his disciples. If he had never used conventional medical means to heal on the Sabbath, we might have supposed that Sabbath-day healings are permissible only so long as they are of a completely miraculous nature. By making the mud, smearing it on the man's eyes, and telling him to wash it out of his eyes, the Master demonstrated that one may prepare and administer medical treatments on the Sabbath even if they are not miraculous.

Christian Sabbatarians object; they ask, "Where in the Bible does it say that mixing mud and applying salve violate the Sabbath?" They contend, "Yeshua did these things to demonstrate that such actions are not a violation of the Sabbath."

This logic falls apart when the healing of the blind man is compared with similar Sabbath conflict stories in the Synoptic Gospels. In every instance, Yeshua offered a legal justification for why the healing overrides the prohibitions of the Sabbath. He never said, "Do you not realize that healing is not a violation of the Sabbath?" Instead, he always assumed that the miraculous healing he had performed had broken the Sabbath, but he justified breaking the Sabbath because compassion for human beings supersedes ritual concern. If Yeshua admitted that a miraculous healing constituted an act of *melachah* ordinarily prohibited on Sabbath, how much more so does an act of conventional healing?

JUDGE WITH RIGHT JUDGMENT

When viewed as Jewish literature, the gospel stories about Yeshua's conflicts with the sages of his day look like typical Jewish legal disputations, such as those that fill the volumes of the Mishnah and Talmud. His arguments about whether or not healing and acts of compassion override the Sabbath are of the same type as those in which the sages and rabbis routinely engaged. They did so to keep the sacred charge Moses issued to the judges and legislators: "Judge the people with righteous judgment" (Deuteronomy 16:18). The Great Assembly of Ezra's generation reiterated the charge: "Be deliberate in judgment" (m.*Avot* 1:2). In the Gospel of John,

Yeshua reminded his colleagues of that responsibility when he concluded his legal argument for healing on the Sabbath. With a clear reference to Deuteronomy 16:18, he said, "Do not judge by appearances, but judge with right judgment" (John 7:24).

The same admonition applies to us.

Traditional Christian interpretation has judged by mere appearances. From a simple, cursory reading of the Gospels, it does *appear* that Jesus must have been a Sabbath-breaker. His disciples broke the Sabbath when they plucked grain on the Sabbath; he defended them. That makes him *appear* to have no regard for the sanctity of the Sabbath.

He broke the Sabbath by healing people on the Sabbath. He healed a man with a withered arm on the Sabbath; he healed a man with dropsy right at the Sabbath table of prominent sages; he healed a woman with a bent back, straightening the bent, on the Sabbath. All of these are obvious violations of the Sabbath. These stories make him *appear* to disregard God's laws against performing acts of work (*melachah*) on the Sabbath.

He told a man to carry his mat home on the Sabbath. This makes it *appear* that he disagreed with the traditional laws of honoring the Sabbath by not carrying objects outside a private domain.

Judging by *mere appearances,* it looks like Yeshua was all about abolishing the Sabbath. Traditional Christian interpretation assumes that Jesus did these things to send an implicit message that the Sabbath is no longer binding.

We have failed to judge with right judgment.

Likewise, anti-missionaries in the Jewish community judge by mere appearances. They point out, somewhat gleefully, that Yeshua cannot be the Messiah of Israel, nor can he be considered a sinless or righteous man, because he flagrantly broke the Sabbath and taught others to do so as well. These critics of our Master make the same allegations against him that his enemies among the religious leaders made two thousand years ago. Ironically, we, his disciples, have affirmed those allegations because we, too, have judged his teachings about the Sabbath by mere appearances.

As we have seen, even Christian Sabbatarians and Messianic believers who reject the notion that Yeshua abrogated the Sabbath usually interpret these incidents to mean that Yeshua did not accept the particulars of Sabbath law. It is popular to explain that he broke the "rabbinic" and "man-made" traditions about Sabbath in order to show everyone that Jewish interpretation of the law is illegitimate. Therefore, he let his disciples husk grain on the Sabbath; he healed on the Sabbath; he made mud on the Sabbath to demonstrate that the thirty-nine types of labor (*melachah*) prohibited by Jewish law on the Sabbath may be safely disregarded. Again, we have judged by mere appearances and failed to judge with right judgment.

If picking and husking grain, healing a withered arm, lifting an ox out of a pit, tethering and un-tethering an ox or donkey to lead it to water, mixing mud and spittle, applying salve, and carrying a mat did not actually constitute legal violations of Shabbat, Yeshua would have simply said so. He would not have bothered with legal justifications that attempted to demonstrate why such acts should be permissible under certain circumstances. For example, if he believed healing on the Sabbath was not an actual violation of the Sabbath, he would not have compared healing with circumcision.

Yeshua taught that under certain compelling circumstances, a man must break the Sabbath in order to keep another, weightier commandment. This halachic (legal) principle connects and unites all of the Gospels' Sabbath stories. It reveals a legal consistency that, rather than abrogating traditional Jewish Sabbath legislation, actually upholds a halachic approach to Sabbath and Jewish law.

If we judge Yeshua with right judgment, the evidence compels us to admit that he upheld the Sabbath and practiced it according to the norms of Jewish practice in his day. Only when a weightier matter arose, such as demonstrating mercy for another human being, did he feel justified in setting aside the prohibitions of the holy day—be they biblical or traditional rabbinic prohibitions.

By logical extension, the same principle may be applied to other ceremonial concerns. Compassion for one's fellow human being takes priority. Alleviating human suffering should be sufficient cause to set aside ceremonial prohibitions. This principle illustrates our Master's greatest teachings about the precedence of love:

For the commandments, "You shall not commit adultery, you shall not murder, you shall not steal, you shall not covet," and any other commandment, are summed up in this word: "You shall love your neighbor as yourself." Love does no wrong to a neighbor; therefore love is the fulfilling of the [Torah]. (Romans 13:9–10)

PART THREE

Other New Testament Objections

CHAPTER TWELVE

Shadow-Keeping

Sometimes when Christians discover that I am a Sabbatarian, they react with dismay, as if Sabbath observance is incongruous with devotion to Jesus. For example, upon learning that I observe the seventh-day Sabbath, one Christian woman began to refer to me and other Sabbatarians as "shadow-keepers." She argued that the Sabbath was just "a shadow of the things to come, but the substance belongs to Christ" (Colossians 2:17). In her opinion, by holding on to the shadow, we were missing the substance. She felt that the other shadow-keepers and I had exchanged Christ for a mere phantom—the Sabbath day. She said, "If you want to have the shadow, go ahead; I'll take the real thing: Jesus."

She was right about one thing. The Sabbath is a shadow of things to come and the substance of Messiah. So are the other holy days and appointed times:

> Let no man therefore judge you in meat, or in drink, or in respect of an holy day, or of the new moon, or of the sabbath days: Which are a shadow of things to come; but the body is of Christ. (Colossians 2:16–17 KJV)

ASCETICISM AND SABBATH-KEEPING

Bible interpreters often cite Colossians 2:16–17 as evidence that the early believers did not observe the Sabbath or the biblical calendar. According to that interpretation, the proper context of this passage involves Jewish legalists condemning the early Christians for failing to keep the Jewish holy days and other matters of the Torah. Paul's words encourage the Colossians not to take those criticisms seriously. Paul says, "Don't let those Jewish legalists judge you about not keeping the holy days. The holy days are only shadows of things to come. The real substance is in Christ."

That's the conventional interpretation of this passage, but I believe it's completely wrong. The Colossian believers were not criticized for failure to keep the festivals; they were criticized because they were observing the festivals. Paul encouraged them to ignore the criticism and to press on with their celebration of the holy days.

Who was judging them for keeping the festivals?

In the first few centuries after the resurrection of the Master, several sects of Gnostic heretics emerged. The Gnostics rejected the physical world and clung instead to arcane knowledge, spiritual ideas, and theological formulations as the way to salvation. They believed that the attainment of correct knowledge could set the spiritual being free from the prison of the physical body and material world. The Gnostics taught that everything in the physical world is corrupt. They also taught against observing the Torah because they regarded the Torah and its laws to be part of the corrupt system of this physical world—to be beneath true spirituality. They looked for a more intangible form of religion, one less tied to the material and physical observances of Judaism. In an epistle to Timothy, Paul refers to their teachings as "teachings of demons" (1 Timothy 4:1) and "the irreverent babble and contradictions of what is falsely called 'knowledge'" (1 Timothy 6:20).

Because they believed that the material and physical world of the flesh is corrupt, the early Gnostics advocated fasting and abstaining from all worldly pleasures, "insisting on asceticism" (Colossians 2:18). They taught celibacy, "asceticism and severity to the body" (Colossians 2:23), and they warned against enjoying any of the delights in this world: "Do not handle, do not taste, do not touch!" (Colossians 2:21). Paul warned:

> See to it that no one takes you captive by philosophy and empty deceit, according to human tradition, according to the elemental spirits of the world, and not according to Christ. (Colossians 2:8)

Apparently, they also taught against observing the Torah's holy days, and they condemned eating and drinking on the Sabbath and the festivals.

Eating and drinking on the Sabbath and holy days is what Judaism is all about. We eat three meals on the Sabbath because the Bible tells us to "call the Sabbath a delight" (Isaiah 58:13). The Sabbath meals are the best meals of the week. The same goes for the other festivals. Messianic Judaism is not the optimum religion for people trying to lose weight. The calorie-conscious person might have better success as a Gnostic.

Apparently, proto-Gnostic ascetics in Colossae criticized the believers there for indulging in food and drink on the holy days. They saw it as a shameful concession to the physical world, and urged the believers to distance themselves from the celebration of the Jewish holy days.

In Colossians 2:16–17 the Apostle Paul dismissed their criticisms. He pointed out that the Sabbath and the biblical festivals foreshadow the work of Messiah and the redemption.

Paul told his readers, "Do not let anyone judge you about eating and drinking on the holy days. After all, the holy days are a shadow of the things to come and their substance is of Messiah."

BAD TRANSLATIONS

Our English translations betray a theological bias by intentionally altering the reading of Colossians 2:17. For example, the New International Version paraphrases the verse: "These are a shadow of the things that *were* to come; the reality, *however,* is found in Christ." In other words, the holy days are not reality, and they are only shadows of things that *were* to come, implying they no longer have any relevance for Christians. The New American Standard Bible inserts the dismissive word "mere" into the verse: "Things which are a *mere* shadow of what is to come." The implication is that these things are not for Christians because they are nothing more than a *mere* shadow, ultimately insubstantial and without value. The New Living Translation departs even further from the text: "For these rules are only shadows of the reality." All these translations intentionally or unintentionally change the meaning of the passage to imply that Paul advocated a disregard for the holy days, as if he was saying, "Let no one pass judgment on you for abstaining from the celebration of a festival or a new moon or a Sabbath."

On the contrary, Paul says, "Let no one pass judgment on you because you are keeping the festivals, the new moons, and the Sabbath by celebrating them with food and drink. After all, they are shadows of things to come. They are the substance of Messiah."

The literal reading of this verse in its original Greek does not set Messiah and holy days in antithesis, nor does it dismiss the holy days as irrelevant relics of the past. Paul is attempting to tell the Colossian believers that the true relevance of the biblical calendar and the biblical Sabbaths and festivals is that they are shadows of coming things and the substance (literally "body") of Messiah.

SHADOW OF THINGS TO COME

What does Paul mean when he says that the holy days, new moons, and Sabbath days are shadows of things to come? What coming things do they foreshadow?

The Sabbath and the holy days foreshadow the redemption, the Messianic Era, the kingdom on earth, and the World to Come. In the same regard, the apostles taught that the whole Torah is "a shadow of the good things to come" (Hebrews 10:1).

Every appointed time on God's calendar teaches about the end times and the coming of the Messiah. For example, Passover, the festival of redemption, points toward the final redemption. Just as God redeemed Israel from Egypt at the first Passover, he will redeem his people from the nations in the future. Pentecost, the festival of the giving of the Torah, points to the Messianic Era, when the Torah will go forth from Zion and the whole world will be filled with the knowledge of the LORD. The Festival of Trumpets points to the day when the trumpet of Messiah will sound. The Day of Atonement is a picture of the final judgment. The Festival of Booths foreshadows the kingdom, when each man will sit in the shade of the Almighty under his own vine and fig tree, and there will be peace on earth. In this way the holy days are shadows of things yet to come; specifically, they foreshadow the Messianic Era.

In the Messianic Era everyone will observe the new moons and the Sabbath: "From new moon to new moon, and from Sabbath to Sabbath, all flesh shall come to worship before me, declares the LORD" (Isaiah 66:23).

The Sabbath also foreshadows things to come. According to the author of Hebrews, the Sabbath symbolizes the kingdom of heaven: "There remains a Sabbath rest for the people of God, for whoever has entered God's rest has also rested from his works as God did from his" (Hebrews 4:9–10). God's rest is the Sabbath; God created the heavens and the earth in six days, and on the seventh day he rested. Early rabbis viewed the seven days of creation as a prophetic outline of history, with each day of the week representing an era of one thousand years: "For a thousand years in your sight are but as yesterday when it is past" (Psalm 90:4). They considered the Sabbath rest day as a symbol for the thousand-year era of Messiah.

The Apostle Peter reminds us:

> With the Lord one day is like a thousand years, and a thousand years like one day. The Lord is not slow about His promise, as some count slowness, but is patient toward you, not wishing for any to perish but for all to come to repentance. But the day of the Lord will come like a thief. (2 Peter 3:8–10 NASB)

The apocryphal *Epistle of Barnabas* ensconces some early Apostolic-era traditions and teachings, including one about the Sabbath and the thousand years of the Messianic Era:

> My children, attend to the meaning of this expression: "He finished in six days." This implies that the LORD will finish all things in six thousand years, for a day with Him is a thousand years. And He Himself testifies, saying, "Behold, 'today' will be as a thousand years." Therefore, my children, in six days, that is, in six thousand years, all things will be finished. "And He rested on the seventh day." This means that when His Son, coming again, shall destroy the time of the wicked, and judge the ungodly, and change the sun, and the moon, and the stars, then He shall truly rest on the seventh day. (*Barnabas* 15:4–5)

In view of these teachings, the weekly Sabbath can be seen to celebrate the coming of the Messiah. The Sabbath offers a weekly foretaste of the era of peace and rest when Messiah will rule the earth. By keeping the Sabbath, we participate in the kingdom of heaven on earth even now. Each Sabbath may be likened unto a down payment on the Messianic Era. We rest on the Sabbath to symbolize the peace that we will have in the days of the Messiah.

The meals of the Sabbath symbolize the banquet of the Messianic Era. Yeshua teaches that in the kingdom, the righteous will enjoy a great banquet, reclining at the table of Abraham, Isaac, and Jacob. They will drink wine with the Messiah as he drinks it again with his disciples in his Father's kingdom. The three meals of the Sabbath allude to the banquet of the kingdom, when we will eat and drink in the presence of the Messiah.

Paul had that Messianic banquet in mind when he spoke of eating and drinking on the Sabbath and holy days as a "shadow of things to come," a foretaste of the great messianic banquet of the future. According to Paul's view, when we keep the Sabbath, the new moons, and the biblical festivals, it's as if we are eating from the table of the Master in the Messianic Era, and drinking from the wine that will be served at that very banquet.

THE SHADOW-CASTER

Paul says that the Sabbath and holy days are shadows of things to come, and that "the body is of Christ." What does it mean that the body of the Sabbath is of Messiah?

Every shadow needs a shadow-caster—a solid body that casts the shadow. Messiah is the body; the Sabbath and the holy days are the shadow that he casts. Paul told the Colossians not to allow people to judge them in regard to things that are substantially about Messiah.

The classical Christian reading of Colossians 2:16–17 supposed that Paul dismissed the value of keeping the Sabbath and the festivals. On the contrary, Paul tells us that they are a shadow of things to come and the substance of Messiah. If anything, his words encouraged his original readers to see the Messiah as the true meaning of the festivals. When we realize that the substance of the appointed times is Messiah, we are more inclined to keep them. It becomes a matter of discipleship.

A shadow shows the shape of an object that casts the shadow. How ironic it is, then, to argue from Colossians 2:16–17 that Sabbath-keeping is not for Christians because "the substance is Christ." Why would Christians want to ignore something that shows them the shape and substance of Messiah? That seems backward.

Every time we keep the Sabbath, eat one of the three meals of the Sabbath, rest on the Sabbath, attend the services of the Sabbath, or hear the Torah on the Sabbath, we partake in the kingdom and in the Messianic Era, and participate in the body of Messiah.

FINDING THE SPIRITUAL IN THE MATERIAL

The Gnostics taught that everything in the physical world is corrupt. They believed that to achieve spiritual perfection, a person must divorce himself completely from the physical world. The Gnostics taught their followers to "forbid marriage and require abstinence from foods that God created to be received with thanksgiving by those who believe and know the truth" (1 Timothy 4:3).

The apostles taught a completely different worldview: "For everything created by God is good, and nothing is to be rejected if it is received with thanksgiving" (1 Timothy 4:4). The apostles taught that the spiritual world animates and vivifies the material world. They believed that true spirituality can be experienced in the physical world because the physical world is actually a reflection of the spiritual, a shadow cast by spiritual realities. For example, the Temple on earth is "a copy and shadow of the heavenly things" (Hebrews 8:5). The worship that takes place in the Temple in Jerusalem reflects the heavenly worship that takes place in the Temple above. This does not negate the Temple worship on Earth; it makes it all the more precious because it offers the worshiper a glimpse of the heavenly.

This mystical idea helps explain how the apostles intended us to experience the spiritual in this material world. Unlike the Gnostics, the apostles taught that we can experience spiritual realities by engaging in their reflections and shadows in the material world. In other words, we do not need to divorce ourselves from the physical world to attain the intangible; instead, we should be seeking the spiritual qualities inherent in the tangible physical world, especially those things ordained by the Torah.

Paul says that the substance of the Sabbath and the holy days is Messiah. By participating in the Sabbath and the holy days, we participate in the substance of Messiah. A person can sit down to eat a meal on Friday night and treat it like any other meal of the week, or he can sit down to eat a Sabbath meal and realize that the food he eats in honor of the Sabbath and the wine he drinks in honor of the Sabbath is infused with the holiness of the Sabbath. Then he is, in a sense, eating from the table of the Master. He finds the spiritual reality behind the physical shadow. Likewise, a person can take a day off from work and rest and relax for his own sake, or he can enjoy the Sabbath rest as a foretaste of that perfect spiritual rest he will enjoy through Messiah in the kingdom and the World to Come.

THE SHADOW-KEEPERS

I don't mind being a "shadow-keeper" so long as the shadow is cast by the coming kingdom of Messiah. I am happy to keep the shadow when the shadow-caster is Messiah. I feel sorry for my brothers and sisters in Messiah who do not have the weekly Sabbath or the observance of the holy days to offer them tangible, physical tokens of the kingdom and to usher them into the presence of holiness and blessing. Like the Gnostics before them, they cling to ideas, doctrines, theologies, and the attainment of correct spiritual knowledge. From my perspective, they are the ones grasping at the insubstantial phantoms of man's ideas. I prefer to find the Master in two loaves of Sabbath bread, a cup of red wine, the fellowship of family and friends around the Sabbath table, and all the sweet and humble rituals of the Sabbath day.

CHAPTER THIRTEEN

ENTER MY REST

I once had a meeting with a pastor of a large evangelical megachurch where I was a teacher in the adult education program. The subject of this particular meeting had to do with some classes that were coming up; I was scheduled to teach about the biblical Sabbath and the festivals. He had recently attended *Jars of Clay*, a First Fruits of Zion conference. The pastor had concerns that I might try to start a Sabbatarian movement in his church. This was several years before I worked with First Fruits of Zion, but I was already guilty by association with Messianic Judaism.

The pastor spoke frankly with me and said, "I think it's fine if people want to keep the Sabbath as a spiritual discipline, so long as they do not become legalistic about it. They need to understand that they do not have to keep the Sabbath because, as it says in Hebrews 4, Christ is our Sabbath rest now. There remains a Sabbath rest for God's people, and that's Christ."

> So then, there remains a Sabbath rest for the people of God, for whoever has entered God's rest has also rested from his works as God did from his. Let us therefore strive to enter that rest. (Hebrews 4:9–11)

According to the pastor's interpretation of Hebrews 4:9, Christ has replaced the Sabbath. In Old Testament times, people observed a Sabbath day, but now, in New Testament times, Christ is our Sabbath. When it comes to defending the theology of the abolishment of the Sabbath, Hebrews 4 tends to be one of the first places that a pastor will turn. Christian teachers like to use Hebrews 3–4 as evidence that the literal seventh-day Sabbath rest has been replaced by a spiritual Sabbath for the people of God.

I did not bother trying to argue with the pastor. Theological arguments rarely bear good fruit. However, since this is one of the main passages used to teach against Sabbatarians, it's important for us to have a solid understanding of Hebrews 3–4. In order to understand Hebrews 3–4, we will need to understand Psalm 95. In order to understand Psalm 95, we will need to understand the story of Israel entering the land of Canaan.

TASTE OF THE KINGDOM

Before the children of Israel entered the land of Canaan, they sent twelve spies to explore the land. The twelve spies went out in midsummer, during the season of the grape harvest. They cut a cluster of grapes so large that they had to carry it on a pole between two men. They brought the giant grapes, some pomegranates, and some figs back to Moses and the children of Israel so that they could sample the land.

Ten spies returned with a bad report. They told about military fortifications, walled cities, and giant Canaanites. They advised the people to return to Egypt. Two spies, Joshua and Caleb, offered good reports. They said that the land was very good. They encouraged the people to trust God, and to obey him and enter the land.

Ultimately the people listened to the ten spies and ignored the advice of Joshua and Caleb. The LORD punished that generation by forcing them to remain in the wilderness for forty years. He did not let them enter into the promised land until the entire generation had died.

The good report of Joshua and Caleb corresponds to the good news of Yeshua and his apostles. Just as Joshua and Caleb urged their generation to obey and enter the land, Yeshua and the apostles urged their generation to repent and enter the kingdom.

The story of the spies carrying a cluster of giant grapes back to Moses and the children of Israel foreshadows the days of the apostles. Our Master Yeshua and his twelve disciples brought the first fruits of the kingdom to their generation. Those who saw the miracles of Yeshua and experienced the work of the Spirit through his hands—these fortunate souls tasted the fruit of the age to come.

Although the children of Israel saw the evidence of the goodness of the land of Canaan, they nevertheless refused to listen to the counsel of Joshua and Caleb. They misinterpreted the enormous fruit as nothing more than evidence of the presence of giants. They hardened their hearts and refused to accept the good report.

Likewise, in the days of the Master, his generation rejected his call to repentance. Though they saw his works, they hardened their hearts and refused to heed him:

> Therefore I was provoked with that generation, and said, "They always go astray in their heart; they have not known my ways." As I swore in my wrath, "They shall not enter my rest." (Hebrews 3:10–11, quoting Psalm 95:10–11)

PSALM 95

Traditional Jews recite Psalm 95 as a Sabbath Psalm. The synagogue liturgy includes the recitation of this psalm every Friday night as part of the prayers for welcoming the Sabbath (*Kabbalat Shabbat*). Appropriately enough, Psalm 95 alludes to entering the Messianic Era. The psalm warns us not to forfeit the opportunity to enter the kingdom, as the generation of Moses forfeited entering the promised land:

> Today, if you hear his voice,
> Do not harden your hearts, as at Meribah,
> As on the day at Massah in the wilderness,
> When your fathers put me to the test and
> put me to the proof,
> Though they had seen my work.
> For forty years I loathed that generation and said,
> "They are a people who go astray in their heart,
> And they have not known my ways."
> Therefore I swore in my wrath,
> "They shall not enter my rest."
> (Psalm 95:7–11)

MY SABBATH REST

The psalm concludes with the words, "They shall not enter my rest." What is God's rest?

The Hebrew verb *shavat* means to cease, or to rest. The Torah says, "And on the seventh day God finished his work that he had done, and he rested (*shavat*)" (Genesis 2:2). That's why the Shabbat is called "Shabbat": because it's a day of *shavat*, a day of resting.

But there is another word closely associated with the Shabbat that can also be translated as "rest." That's the Hebrew word *menuchah*. When Psalm 95 says, "They shall not enter my rest," the psalmist uses the word *menuchah*: "They shall not enter my *menuchah*."

The verb form, *nu'ach*, means "to rest." It is closely tied to the concept of Sabbath rest because the Torah says, "In six days the LORD made heaven and earth, the sea, and all that is in them, and rested (*nu'ach*) on the seventh day" (Exodus 20:11).

We could translate Psalm 95:11 to read, "They shall not enter my Sabbath rest." This might explain why Jewish liturgy considers Psalm 95 to be a Sabbath psalm and uses it as one of the psalms for welcoming the Sabbath day.

MY RESTING PLACE

According to this interpretation of "my *menuchah*" as "my Sabbath rest," the generation of Moses that perished in the wilderness forfeited entering God's Sabbath rest: "Therefore I swore in my wrath, 'They shall not enter my *menuchah* (i.e., my Sabbath rest).'"

That interpretation does not make a lot of sense. Psalm 95 refers to the generation that forfeited the land of Canaan and perished in the wilderness over the course of forty years. Neither that story nor Psalm 95 has anything to do with the literal Sabbath day.

The Hebrew word *menuchah* means "rest," but it can also mean "resting place." For example, Psalm 132:8 says, "Arise, O LORD, and go to your resting place (*menuchah*)." Likewise, Isaiah 66:1 says, "Heaven is my throne ... what is the place of my rest (*menuchah*)." Therefore Psalm 95:11 could be translated to say, "I swore in my wrath, 'They shall not enter my *resting place*,'" i.e., they shall not enter the promised land. According to this interpretation, the "rest" that the generation failed to enter was the promised land, the land of Canaan.

THE KINGDOM AND WORLD TO COME

The sages, however, had a different interpretation of the LORD's *menuchah* in Psalm 95:11. Rabbi Akiva taught that the *menuchah* refers to the Messianic Era and the World to Come:

> The generation of the wilderness has no portion in the World to Come, as it is written: "For forty years I loathed that generation and said, 'They are a people who go astray in their heart, and they have not known my ways.' Therefore I swore in my wrath, 'They shall not enter my rest.'" (b.*Sanhedrin* 110b)

According to this interpretation, the psalm declares that the generation that perished in the wilderness will not enter the kingdom.

Does that mean that the generation in the wilderness is damned? Not necessarily. Rabbi Akiva is not the judge of that. The Talmud presents Akiva's view as just one opinion. Other rabbis disagreed with his interpretation. In any case, the important thing to realize is that we can understand the LORD's *menuchah* to refer to the Messianic Era and the World to Come.

So far we have seen three possible interpretations of Psalm 95:11:

1. They shall not enter my Sabbath rest.
2. They shall not enter the promised land.
3. They shall not enter the kingdom or the World to Come.

Which one of these three possible interpretations do you suppose the writer of the book of Hebrews had in mind when he quoted the psalm? Did he see the *menuchah* of the LORD as the Sabbath rest, the promised land, or eternal life?

A SABBATH PSALM

In reality, I have proposed a false trichotomy. We don't have to assume that the writer of Hebrews had just one interpretation in mind. In fact, Hebrews 3–4 employs all three associations listed above, because both the weekly Sabbath and the land of Israel can symbolize the kingdom.

The writer of the book of Hebrews compared his own generation with the generation of Moses. Both generations stood poised on the edge of attaining the final redemption. The generation of Moses stood at the border of the promised land. If Moses had brought them into Canaan, they would have enjoyed the kingdom immediately. The generation of the Master also stood at the edge of the kingdom. If they had heeded Yeshua's message of the gospel and repented, they would have entered the kingdom of heaven. The Messianic Era hung within their grasp.

Both the generation in the wilderness and the generation of the Master forfeited their opportunity to enter the kingdom. On the other hand, some people from the generation of Moses did enter the promised land. Those who had faith (Joshua and Caleb) received their inheritance. The writer of the book of Hebrews compares the believers in his generation to Joshua and Caleb. Those who have faith (the believers) will yet enter the kingdom. He warns them not to let go of their confidence. He quotes Psalm 95:7: "Today, if you hear his voice, do not harden your hearts."

The weekly Sabbath celebrates the coming of the Messiah. The Sabbath offers a weekly foretaste of the coming era of peace and rest, the era when Messiah will rule the earth. By keeping the Sabbath, we participate in the kingdom of heaven on earth even now. The Sabbath may be likened unto a down payment on the age of Messiah yet to come.

In a similar way, the land of Israel represents the kingdom. It is the place where the promises of the kingdom will be fulfilled; really, all the prophecies about the kingdom are actually prophecies about the land of Israel. Israel will be chief over the nations, and Jerusalem the capital of all people. Even in the World to Come, the holy land is not forgotten; the great city that comes down from Heaven is called New Jerusalem. So both the land and the Sabbath symbolize the kingdom of heaven and the World to Come.

TODAY, IF YOU WILL HEAR

"Today, if you hear his voice, do not harden your hearts," the psalm says. To "hear God's voice" means to obey him. To translate the idiom, this passage can be understood to say "Today, if you will obey me." The Talmud interprets these words to refer to the time of repentance that will accompany Messiah's coming:

> If all Israel would repent even for one day, the son of David would immediately arrive, as this verse attests: "Even today, if we but heed his voice" ... Scripture refers to the Sabbath as "Today" ... and the Psalmist assures Israel, "Even today the Messiah will come, if we but heed his voice." (y.*Ta'anit* 1:1)

The writer of Hebrews derived a similar lesson:

> Take care, brethren, that there not be in any one of you an evil, unbelieving heart that falls away from the living God. But encourage one another day after day, as long as it is still called 'Today,' so that none of you will be hardened by the deceitfulness of sin. (Hebrews 3:12–13 NASB)

He warned the believers in his generation not to have "an evil, unbelieving heart" like the generation in the wilderness. He said, "For good news came to us just as to them, but the message they heard did not benefit them, because they were not united by faith with those who listened" (Hebrews 4:2). This refers to the good news that Joshua and Caleb brought concerning the land of Israel. Just as the generation in the wilderness rejected the good news about the land of Israel, the generation of the apostles rejected the good news about the Master and the kingdom of heaven. The writer of the book of Hebrews warned that just as God did not spare the generation of the wilderness, neither would he spare the current generation. He compared entering the land to entering the kingdom. Both required faith and obedience. "Those who were disobedient ... were not able to enter because of unbelief" (Hebrews 3:18–19).

The epistle goes on to point out that the promised "rest" from which God barred the generation in the wilderness cannot be understood merely as the weekly Sabbath day of rest, because God's "works were finished from the foundation of the world" (Hebrews 4:3). Likewise, it cannot refer merely to the promised land, because David wrote Psalm 95 long after Joshua settled the nation in the promised land:

> If Joshua had given them rest, God would not have spoken of another day later on. So then, there remains a Sabbath rest for the people of God. (Hebrews 4:8–9)

A SABBATH REST REMAINS

What is the Sabbath rest that remains for the people of God? The Messianic Kingdom and the World to Come "remain" for those who cling to Yeshua and do not turn away from the living God. Contrary to common Christian interpretation, this does not in any way imply a cessation of the biblical Sabbath or its replacement by a spiritual Sabbath. Instead, the author of Hebrews invoked the Sabbath to symbolize the kingdom and the World to Come, just as the sages of the Talmud did in the passages cited above.

The writer of the book of Hebrews encouraged his readers to "be diligent," striving hard to enter that rest. He warned them not to follow the example of the generation in the wilderness:

> For whoever has entered God's rest has also rested from his works as God did from his. Let us therefore strive to enter that rest, so that no one may fall by the same sort of disobedience. (Hebrews 4:10–11)

The generation in the wilderness did not perish in its entirety, but only Caleb and Joshua, the two men who expressed their faith, entered the land of Canaan; the rest of the generation did not. So too, those who believe and repent today will enter the Sabbath rest of the Messianic Era in the future. In Messiah, we take hold of the future kingdom today.

STRIVE TO ENTER THAT REST

The writer of the book of Hebrews says that we must "strive to enter that rest." This sounds like a contradiction. Striving and resting are opposites.

If you keep a traditional Sabbath, you will understand the picture. When the Sabbath is coming, we strive to get ready for it. We hurry, hustle, scurry, clean, prepare, cook, wash, and work. When the Sabbath finally arrives, the work stops. It is finished. We cease from the labor, even if the labor isn't really finished. Quiet, calm, and peace enter. Whether your work is done or not, whether you finished everything that needed to be done or not, the Sabbath arrives. Of course, one never accomplishes everything he intended to accomplish before the Sabbath arrives, but this only reminds us that, ultimately, the Sabbath rest does not depend upon our merit. The success of our preparations does not make the Sabbath rest happen. It's his rest, not ours.

If we think we can take a Sabbath rest only after we finish all our work, we will rarely, if ever, enjoy a Sabbath rest. So too, if we believe that we will inherit the kingdom only if we have earned it, we will never qualify to enter it. Nonetheless, we work hard now to enter, and when Sabbath comes, then we rest.

Even though a person can have full confidence in God's grace and mercy, he should nevertheless live his life on earth as if entering salvation depended upon his good works. When we finally cross over the threshold, we will look back and realize that we accomplished very little, certainly not enough to merit salvation. At that point, however, it will not matter, because the Sabbath rest will already have begun, and we will already have entered it.

Just as the work of creating the heavens and the earth have been finished since creation, the work of salvation was finished on the cross. A Sabbath rest remains for the people of God because of the finished work of Messiah. Therefore, we work hard to enter into it. We work hard to rest.

WHAT WILL YOU EAT ON THE SABBATH?

The writer of the book of Hebrews warned his readers to repent now in order to prepare for the kingdom. He warned them not to be like the unbelieving generation in the wilderness that turned away from the good news that Joshua and Caleb brought. Like Hebrews 3–4, the following rabbinic parable uses Sabbath symbolism to demonstrate the efficacy of repentance in preparing for the hereafter:

> Consider the case of two wicked men who associated with one another in this world. One of them repented before his death while the other did not repent. It was found that the one stands in the company of the righteous while his fellow stands in the company of the wicked. When the latter saw the former he said, "Woe is me! Is there then favor shown here? I and he, both of us were robbers, both of us were murders together, yet he stands in the company of the righteous and I stand in the company of the wicked!"
>
> The angels said (to the man in Gehenna), "You fool ... you also had the opportunity of repenting and you did not take it." When he heard this, he said to them, "Permit me to go and repent now!" And they answered him and said, "You fool! Do you not know that this world is like the Sabbath and the world from which you have just come is like the eve of the Sabbath? If a man does not prepare his meal on the eve of the Sabbath, what shall he eat on the Sabbath?" (*Ruth Rabbah* 3:3)

A SPIRITUAL SABBATH IN CHRIST

The explanations above reveal that the book of Hebrews used the Sabbath day and the land of Israel as symbols for the kingdom of heaven and the World to Come. In other words, entering the Sabbath rest and entering the land of Israel are two different metaphors for entering the kingdom and attaining eternal life. The metaphors are not, however, intended to supplant the literal observance of the Sabbath or the significance of the literal, physical land of Israel.

Perhaps, as mine did, your pastor will one day call on you to defend your interest in Sabbath observance in light of Hebrews 3–4. This long explanation, which brings Hebrew terminology and rabbinic parallels to support it, might be more involved than you should expect your pastor to wade through. I did not bother trying to work through it with my pastor either. Nevertheless, it's important for us to have at least a cursory understanding of this passage so that we will not be shaken by arguments invoking Hebrews 3–4. If nothing else, it's important to understand that these chapters do not replace Sabbath observance with a spiritual Sabbath in Christ or something on that order. Instead, the author of Hebrews used the Sabbath day as a metaphor to teach about the kingdom. Why? Because the Sabbath day was familiar territory for the original readers of the epistle, who were all Sabbath-keepers.

CHAPTER FOURTEEN

ENSLAVED BY THE LAW

If you are a Christian thinking about becoming a Sabbatarian and keeping the seventh-day biblical Sabbath, you will experience resistance from concerned Christian friends. Those who are well-versed in the Scriptures might ask you, "Have you read Galatians?"

This question implies that if you had only read Paul's epistle to the Galatians, you would not be talking nonsense about observing the Sabbath and Jewish holy days. Apparently, the book of Galatians puts the kibosh on any tendency toward following Old Testament laws. According to Galatians 4:9–11, observing the holy days and the biblical calendar enslaves a person to the weak and worthless elementary principles of the world:

> But now that you have come to know God, or rather to be known by God, how can you turn back again to the weak and worthless elementary principles of the world, whose slaves you want to be once more? You observe days and months and seasons and years! I am afraid I may have labored over you in vain. (Galatians 4:9–11)

On the surface it sounds like Paul rebuked his readers for observing "days and months and seasons and years" and warned them not to become "enslaved" again (Galatians 4:10). This leads us to believe that Paul viewed the celebration of the Sabbath and festivals as a step backward for Gentile believers—a form of enslavement.

According to this view, when he wrote, "You observe days," he meant the Sabbath and festivals. He said "You observe months," meaning the new moons and the biblical calendar. He said, "You observe seasons," meaning festival seasons like the counting of the days until Pentecost, the days of repentance, and the Days of Awe. He said, "you observe years," meaning the Sabbatical Year of release.

Traditional interpretation of Galatians 4:9–11 teaches that it is un-Christian to keep the biblical calendar or honor the Bible's holy days such as the Sabbath. At the same time, Christian tradition sees no conflict between Galatians 4:10 and the celebration of "days," so long as they are Sundays; "months," so long as they are not the biblical months; "seasons," so long as they are Lent, Advent, Christmas, or Easter; and so forth.

The traditional Christian interpretation of Galatians 4:10 reads it as a rebuke for Sabbatarians. In fact, that very interpretation of Galatians 4:10 can easily be turned on its head to mean that Gentile believers are not allowed to have any holy days whatsoever.

Is that really what Paul meant?

HOLY EPISTLE TO THE GALATIANS

The conventional interpretation of Galatians places God's grace in antithesis to the Law. Most New Testament teachers suppose that the epistle of Galatians does away with observance of the Torah, the Sabbath, the festivals, and other ceremonial laws, such as circumcision. In my book, *The Holy Epistle to the Galatians,* I have offered an alternative interpretation of Galatians based upon its historical context in first-century Judaism and the insights that can be gained from a Messianic Jewish reading of the epistle.

I suggest that the epistle of Galatians poses no conflict between Judaism and faith in Messiah. Instead, the epistle argues that Gentile believers do not need to become Jewish in order to be disciples of Yeshua and heirs of kingdom. Paul has no argument with Judaism or Torah observance; his arguments belong within Judaism and are directed against those who believe that Gentiles must undergo a conversion and become Jewish in order to be saved.

Paul addressed the epistle to God-fearing Gentile believers who were under extreme pressure to accept circumcision and become full converts—that is, to become Jewish. The entire epistle argues for the inclusion of Gentiles without requiring them to undergo circumcision and become Jews.

If you find Paul's arguments in Galatians vexing or seemingly contradictory, I recommend studying through *The Holy Epistle to the Galatians*. For our purposes here, we will concern ourselves only with Galatians 4:1–11.

GENTILES IN THE SYNAGOGUE

Paul's epistle to the Galatians addresses God-fearing Gentile believers in the Roman territory of Galatia. Paul first encountered the Gentile believers of Galatia in the synagogue of Pisidian-Antioch on the Sabbath day:

> They ... came to Antioch in Pisidia. And on the Sabbath day they went into the synagogue and sat down" (Acts 13:14).

After the reading from the Torah and the *Haftarah* reading from the Prophets, the elders of the Galatian synagogue encouraged the visitors to offer a few words of teaching, "Brothers," they said, "If you have any word of encouragement for the people, say it" (Acts 13:15).

As Paul began his presentation of the gospel, he said, "Brothers, sons of the family of Abraham, and those among you who fear God, to us has been sent the message of this salvation" (Acts 13:26). The threefold address refers to the three types of people one might find in any Diaspora synagogue of the first century. To make any sense at all out of Paul's epistle to the Galatians, one must differentiate between these three groups.

1. "BROTHERS" ARE JEWS: In the context of the Pisidian-Antioch synagogue, Paul's brothers are his fellow Jews. He means to refer to those who are legally Jewish from birth, those who are physical descendants of Abraham, Isaac, and Jacob through a Jewish mother.
2. "SONS OF ABRAHAM" ARE PROSELYTES: The second type of congregant Paul found in the

Pisidian-Antioch synagogue was the proselyte. Proselytes were those non-Jews who had made a formal conversion to Judaism, thus becoming legally Jewish. According to Jewish law, they were no longer regarded as Gentiles. Through the rituals of circumcision and immersion (and sacrifice when possible), they had taken on the religious and legal status of Israelites. The Jewish community referred to them as "sons and daughters of Abraham." This conversion process was based upon biblical texts that speak about the stranger who undergoes circumcision as a member of Abraham's household (Genesis 17) or as a sojourner who desires to eat of the Passover sacrifice (Exodus 12). In the days of the apostles the biblical "stranger who dwells among you" was understood by the Jewish world to refer primarily (though not exclusively) to the formal, legal proselyte to Judaism.

3. "GOD-FEARING GENTILES" ARE NON-JEWS: The third type of congregant Paul addressed that day in the Pisidian-Antioch synagogue was the God-fearing Gentile. The term "God-fearing Gentiles" describes non-Jews who were attracted to Judaism. They worshiped in the synagogue with Jewish people and proselytes, but chose not to undertake the ritual of conversion. They were not exactly pagans anymore, but they were not Jews either. While the synagogue community may have tolerated them and even appreciated their financial contributions to the community (as with the centurions in Luke 7 and Acts 10), they did not regard God-fearers as Jewish. They did not enjoy the rights and privileges of the Jewish people, nor did they have responsibilities within Judaism.

As Paul discoursed on the gospel, he included all three groups of people in his address. The synagogue received his message enthusiastically and asked Paul and Barnabas to return and speak again the following Sabbath. "Many Jews (*Group One*) and devout converts to Judaism (*Group Two*) followed Paul and Barnabas, who, as they spoke with them, urged them to continue in the grace of God" (Acts 13:43). The next Sabbath, however, things did not go as well. "Almost the whole city gathered to hear the word of the Lord" (Acts 13:44). Apparently, the God-fearing Gentiles (*Group Three*) had invited their relatives, friends, and neighbors to attend. The large crowd of Gentiles in the synagogue irritated the Jewish community—so much so that they tossed Paul and Barnabas out.

That's our introduction to the Gentiles of Galatia. They were not Jewish, yet they could be found gathering in the synagogue along with the Jewish community on the Sabbath day. In other words, they were already drawn to the observance of the Sabbath. Paul encountered them in the synagogue on the Sabbath because they were already worshiping the God of Israel on the Sabbath.

PRINCIPLES OF THE WORLD

At first glance, Galatians 4:10 seems to warn the God-fearing Gentile believers against observing the Sabbath and the festivals and thereby becoming enslaved to Jewish law. The interpretation of the passage hinges on one cryptic phrase: "The elementary principles of the world."

Paul explained that, just as the Jewish people were once enslaved to "the elementary principles of the world" (Galatians 4:3), likewise, his Gentile readers were once slaves to "the weak and worthless elementary principles of the world" (Galatians 4:9). What does that mean? What are the elementary principles of the world, and how is it that both the Jewish people and Gentile idolaters were once enslaved to them?

No one is sure what Paul meant when he used the term "elementary principles (*stoicheia*) of the world." Scholars bring a variety of opinions, but no one knows exactly what he meant. The Greek word *stoicheion* has to do with elements that comprise a series, essential parts, or members of a row. The term originally denoted a row, rank, or line in military formations. In Paul's day, the term was used of the degrees on a sundial; of letters, syllables, or words in a sentence; of the basic elements of the cosmos (fire, earth, air, and water); or even simply of the rudimentary fundamentals of a subject of study, like the three "R"s: reading, writing, and arithmetic. No one is sure exactly what sense Paul intended. The analogy is notoriously cryptic.

Two explanations seem possible for Paul's use of the term in Galatians 4: The elementary principles refer to Torah and Judaism or the elementary principles refer to paganism and idolatry.

ELEMENTARY PRINCIPLES = TORAH

Let's begin by supposing that the term "elementary principles" refers to the Torah and Judaism in general. In that case, when Paul criticized the God-fearing Galatian Gentiles for observing "days and months and seasons and years," he meant Sabbath days, new moon observances, festival seasons, and Sabbatical Years—all components of the Torah's calendar. The thought seemed to distress him. He wondered if he had labored in vain for the Gentiles of Galatia. He did not understand why they would want "turn back again to the weak and worthless elementary principles of the world" and become enslaved by them again (Galatians 4:9).

If this interpretation is correct, then the elementary principles of the world must be Paul's way of referring to Torah observance. If so, however, then Galatians 4:3–5 must also be read to mean that the Messiah came to redeem the Jewish people from the keeping the Torah:

> In the same way we [Jews] also, when we were children, we were enslaved to the elementary principles of the world [i.e., the observance of the Torah]. But when the fullness of time had come, God sent forth his Son, born of woman, born under the law, to redeem those who were under the law, so that we might receive adoption as sons. (Galatians 4:3–5)

According to this interpretation, Messiah was born under the Torah to rescue "those who were under the law" from further obligation to the Torah. The Jewish believer need no longer keep the Torah, because the Messiah redeemed him from its jurisdiction. This is why Paul speaks of the Jewish people as those "who were under the law," using the past tense to imply that they are no longer under the law.

This interpretation has several problems. First, the Gospels do not support the idea that Yeshua removed the Jewish people from under the law. It is unwarranted to bring that assumption into this passage. Additionally, an examination of the original Greek behind Galatians 4:5 reveals that Paul did not use the past tense to refer to the Jewish people's relationship with the Law. A more literal translation might read, "that those under Law he may redeem." To Paul, Jewish believers are still under the law simply because they are still Jewish. To be "under the law" is just Paul's way of saying "legally Jewish and therefore obligated to observe the Torah." The Messiah did not redeem the Jewish people from the Torah; he redeemed them from sin and exile. He rescues from condemnation, but not from obligation to obedience. He does not make Jewish people into non-Jews.

Moreover, this interpretation has Paul speaking of the Torah as something "weak and worthless" (Galatians 4:9), something he considers equivalent to "those that by nature are not gods" (Galatians 4:8). If we believe that Paul was indeed speaking about the Sabbath, the festivals, and the Torah's ceremonies, then we are saying that Paul placed God's holy commandments into a category that he considered no different than idolatry. If Paul uses the term "elementary principles" to refer to the Torah and the Sabbath, then Paul considered Judaism to be the same as idol worship.

This explanation does not work unless Paul is a blasphemer. It contradicts the Bible, the teachings of all the other apostles, the Master's clear teaching about the Torah, and even Paul's own life and testimony as an observant Jew.

ELEMENTARY PRINCIPLES = IDOLATRY

In my book *The Holy Epistle to the Galatians* I cite scholars who suggest that the "elementary principles" of which Paul spoke refer to idolatry, and not to Torah or Judaism at all. This definition can be derived from Galatians 4:8:

> Formerly, when you [Gentile believers] did not know God, you were enslaved to those that by nature are not gods. (Galatians 4:8)

In this verse Paul obviously speaks about idolatry, which he calls the worship of "those that by nature are not gods." Gentiles in the Roman world were polytheistic idolaters, required by law to participate in the Roman cult and the worship of the emperor. They needed to be part of an approved religious affiliation, all of which were idolatrous and polytheistic except for Judaism. Paul contrasted the Gentile believers' former state with their current state. In their former state, they were enslaved to the idols they worshiped. In their current state, they know the one true God:

> But now that you have come to know God, or rather to be known by God, how can you turn back again to the weak and worthless elementary principles of the world, whose slaves you want to be once more? You observe days and months and seasons and years! (Galatians 4:9–10)

The "weak and worthless elementary principles of the world" are the idolatrous rituals and religion that the God-fearing Gentiles had recently left behind when they began to worship the God of Israel. The "days and months and seasons and years," which the Gentiles once observed, and by which they were in danger of becoming enslaved once more, can only be pagan holidays and celebrations.

From this perspective, Paul was not speaking about the Jewish calendar at all, but rather about the pagan calendar. Paul's God-fearing Galatian converts were, of course, ex-pagans who previously participated in the imperial cult, worshiping the gods and the emperors as required by Roman law. As Gentiles in the Roman world, they had observed idolatrous ceremonies on certain days dedicated to certain gods. They had celebrated festivals to certain deities at certain propitious times and seasons.

YOUR CIVIC DUTY

Religion was a critically important part of the Gentile believer's previous life. One's religious obligations were as central to Roman society as getting a Social Security number, acquiring a driver's license, and registering for the draft are to ours. A person's loyalty to the state and his civic duty demanded his observance of the calendar of the imperial cult. To abstain from participation in these civic religious functions disrupted relationships with family, friends, business associates, and civil authorities. It also placed a person in jeopardy of persecution, arrest, and possibly execution for the crime of atheism. Roman law exempted only Jews from participation in those ceremonies. Roman law considered Judaism to be a legal religion. Jews did not need to worship the Roman gods or the emperors.

Unfortunately for Paul's Galatian converts, they did not have that status. They were not legally recognized as converts to Judaism. The Jewish community did not claim them. They were merely God-fearers; they were guests in the synagogue, so to speak, and not members. Though the Jewish community might have granted them some sort of honorary guest status in the synagogue, that honorary status did not grant them any legal exemptions from their civic and religious duties as subjects of Rome. Claiming "I'm a believer" did not exempt them from the duty of participating in the imperial cult and observing its sacred days. This left the God-fearing believers in a state of social limbo—not fully accepted by Judaism and, at the same time, in conflict with the Roman authorities, their extended families, and the rest of society.

The obvious solution was to go the full distance and convert to Judaism. As Jews, they would be free from social and civic pressure to conform to paganism or to observe the imperial cult's calendar. It seems that the Gentile believers in Galatia felt as if they had no other choice than to convert to Judaism and become legally Jewish, and until then to at least nominally observe the calendar of the imperial cult.

Apparently, Paul's readers were pursuing conversion. Until they could obtain the legal exemption that full conversion would grant them, they had gone back to observing the imperial cult and its calendar of days, months, seasons, and years. They relapsed into these idolatrous observances, even as they continued to proclaim their faith in Messiah. They were effectively trying to live in both worlds. One can see how it would be easy for a born-and-bred polytheist to rationalize this state of affairs: Worship the old gods one day, and worship the new God another day.

Paul's epistle to the Galatians argued against both conversion to Judaism and participation in idolatry. In lieu of either choice, he presented a third option: an identity in Messiah that completely broke with "those that by nature are not gods" to which they were formerly enslaved, but still maintained a distinct Gentile identity by not becoming Jewish.

Paul warned the Galatian Gentiles not to return to observing the days of the imperial cult—not even temporarily. This, he argued, would be a return to enslavement under those who are by nature not gods (i.e., the emperor-seen-as-a-deity). "Do you want to be their slaves all over again?" he asked.

THE FULLNESS OF TIME

In that case, Galatians 4:3 speaks of Israel's enslavement to the same elementary principles of the world—not as a reference to Torah at all, but rather as a reference to the nation's own history of enslavement in Egypt, and to those times when it fell into apostasy and idolatry. Might Paul even be speaking of the exile, of which it says in the Torah, "And the LORD will scatter you among all peoples, from one end of the earth to the other, and there you shall serve other gods of wood and stone, which neither you nor your fathers have known" (Deuteronomy 28:64)?

The Messianic redemption brings the end of the exile. Paul says, "But when the fullness of time had come, God sent forth his Son, born of woman, born under the law, to redeem those who were under the law, so that we might receive adoption as sons" (Galatians 4:4–5). In other words, "God sent forth his Son, born of a woman, born Jewish, to redeem those who were Jewish, so that we might receive adoption as sons." Likewise, the Gentile believers also receive adoption as sons of God through Yeshua. Therefore, they should not revert to serving the false gods of the world.

YES, I'VE READ GALATIANS

When you are challenged with the book of Galatians, just remember that all the Galatian Gentiles were also Sabbatarians. They attended synagogue on the Sabbath. If they had not, they would never have heard the message of the gospel that Paul presented there.

Those Gentiles believers were under enormous pressure. On one hand they felt pressure to undergo conversion and become Jewish so that they would be accepted in the Jewish community. On the other hand, so long as they did not become Jewish, they felt pressure to participate in Gentile religion, which was categorically idolatrous.

When Paul warned these Gentiles against becoming circumcised or coming "under the law," he was simply trying to deter them from undergoing a legal conversion to become Jewish. When Paul warned them about observing "days and months and seasons and years," he was trying to deter them from slipping back into idolatry.

CHAPTER FIFTEEN

THE WEAK AND THE STRONG

When my church friends and acquaintances find out that I am a Sabbatarian, a few might raise objections, but most do not. In fact, most of the time, it doesn't bother them at all. We live in a day when people's personal religious convictions are considered to be nobody's business but their own. Accordingly, if someone wants to keep the Sabbath day, that's his personal business. That's between him and God.

One passage from the New Testament is frequently called on to support that idea. Romans 14:5–6 seems to allow for a person to live out his convictions regarding Sabbath observance, whatever those convictions might be—just so long as he does not attempt to impose those convictions on other believers:

> One person esteems one day as better than another, while another esteems all days alike. Each one should be fully convinced in his own mind. The one who observes the day, observes it in honor of the Lord. (Romans 14:5–6)

This sounds like Paul is saying that if you think the Sabbath is important, you should go ahead and observe the Sabbath day. On the other hand, if you think the Sabbath is the same as any other day of the week, that's fine too. The important thing is that you live out your own convictions on the matter without trying to impose those convictions on anyone else.

WHATEVER YOU BELIEVE IS TRUE

This interpretation sounds attractive to the modern reader who has become accustomed to Western social messages, which preach tolerance, diversity, and moral subjectivity. It fits hand-in-glove with the sentiment, "Whatever you believe is true for you." Paul seems to say, "If you think you should keep the Sabbath, then you should keep it. If you think the Sabbath is just like any ordinary day, then don't worry about it. Whatever you believe about the Sabbath day is true for you."

Moreover, this conversation comes in the middle of a discussion about dietary concerns. The chapter begins with a warning against quarrelling over opinions about permissible foods:

> As for the one who is weak in faith, welcome him, but not to quarrel over opinions. One person believes he may eat anything, while the weak person eats only vegetables. Let not the one who eats despise the one who abstains, and let not the one who abstains pass judgment on the one who eats, for God has welcomed him. (Romans 14:1–3)

This sounds like Paul is saying that someone who eats kosher is weak in faith, but the person who eats everything is strong in faith, and that, actually, it's all a matter of opinion. Since it's just a matter of opinion, we should not judge one another.

Further on in the chapter, Paul even says that, in his opinion, no food is unclean:

> I know and am persuaded in the Lord Jesus that nothing is unclean in itself, but it is unclean for anyone who thinks it unclean. (Romans 14:14)

Paul's wording makes it easy for us to believe that it's all a matter of personal opinion. But while that sentiment has a lot of traction in today's world, it makes no sense in the world of the Bible. Do we really believe that Paul considered the Bible's laws to be a matter of opinion? The Torah clearly forbids Jewish people from eating certain animals, and it clearly forbids Jewish people from profaning the Sabbath day. The Bible goes so far as to say that when a Jew breaks the Sabbath, he becomes liable to the death penalty. Our Master warns, "Whoever relaxes one of the least of these commandments and teaches others to do the same will be called least in the kingdom of heaven" (Matthew 5:19). How can Paul suggest that Sabbath-keeping is only a debatable matter of personal conviction?

If Paul is saying what it sounds like he is saying, that is a real problem. If he is saying that a person who keeps the Bible's dietary laws is weak in faith, that nothing is actually unclean, and that keeping the Sabbath and the dietary laws is simply a matter of opinion, then he is clearly contradicting the Torah.

A TERRIBLE WRITER

I once had the opportunity to discuss the issues raised by Romans 14 with a Messianic Jewish rabbi who was writing a book about the Jewishness of Paul. He wanted to hear what I thought of his interpretations on several difficult Pauline passages, including Romans 14.

According to the rabbi's opinion, the issue in Romans 14 was simply a question of distinguishing Jews from Gentiles. The Jews, who were continuing to keep the Torah, ate only vegetables and observed the Sabbath. The Gentile believers, however, were not required to keep the Bible's dietary laws or the prohibitions of the Sabbath. Therefore the Gentiles could eat anything and regarded each day as the same, while the Jewish people continued to observe the dietary laws and the Sabbath day.

I pointed out a few problems with his explanation. First of all, Paul does not frame it as a distinction between Jews and Gentiles, he frames it as a distinction between "the weak" and "the strong." Would Paul characterize Jewish believers as "weak in faith" and Gentile believers as "strong"?

Furthermore, the dietary laws do not require Jews to take on a vegetarian diet, but the "weak" in Romans 14 are eating only vegetables. Finally, I pointed out that Romans 14 actually makes no reference to the Sabbath day at all. It only refers to a person observing a particular day, but it does not call that day the Sabbath.

Then I explained my own interpretation of the passage.

My explanation of Romans 14 did not convince the Messianic rabbi. He insisted that Paul must have had the Sabbath day in mind. He exclaimed, "If Paul wasn't referring to the Sabbath when he said, 'the one who observes the day, observes it in honor of the Lord,' then Paul was a terrible writer!" In other words, Paul should have anticipated that his words would be read in regard to the Sabbath, and he should have clarified that he was not speaking about the Sabbath.

I disagree. Why would Paul feel compelled to clarify that he was not speaking about the Sabbath? It would have never entered Paul's mind, nor the minds of his readers, that he could possibly have been referring to the Sabbath as "a debatable matter," a matter of opinion, and something observed only by those "weak in faith." Paul was not a terrible writer, but "there are some things in [Paul's epistles] that are hard to understand" (2 Peter 3:16). The discussion in Romans 14 is one of them.

THE VEGETABLE DIET

To get to the bottom of this, we will need to take a closer look at Romans 14. Let's start with the specific dietary standards described in this passage. Paul contrasts two different types of eaters. One man eats only vegetables. Paul considers him to be weak in faith, but he respects the man's convictions. Another man believes he can eat everything. Paul apparently considers him to be strong in faith. Nevertheless, Paul advocates mutual respect of both opinions.

Contrary to popular interpretation, this passage does not have the Torah's dietary laws regarding the meat of clean and unclean animals in view. Instead, it contrasts two opinions that split the believing community. The weak in faith eat only vegetables—a standard of dietary observance totally absent from the Torah. The strong in faith eat "everything"; however, as it is used specifically in contrast with a vegetarian diet, the term "everything" does not necessarily imply that the strong eat things that the Bible forbids; given the immediate context, a more obvious interpretation would take Paul to mean that the strong do not feel constrained to eat only vegetables, like the weak in faith do.

If the Torah doesn't prescribe a vegetarian diet, then why do the weak in faith eat only vegetables?

The only place the Bible mentions a vegetable-only diet is the book of Daniel. When the Babylonians took Daniel and his Jewish friends captive, they tried to feed them Babylonian wine and meat, but "Daniel resolved that he would not defile himself with the king's food, or with the wine that he drank" (Daniel 1:8). Daniel was not concerned about avoiding pork. He could have simply instructed the king's steward to feed them plenty of beef, sheep, goat, and poultry. So why did Daniel ask to be fed only vegetables?

Daniel and his friends knew that all of the Babylonian food was defiled by contact with idolatry. Since it was prepared by Gentile idolaters, it was offered in part to idols, and Daniel and his friends did not want to eat anything tainted by idolatry. They wanted to keep the prohibition against eating food offered to idols. Therefore, Daniel said, "Let us be given vegetables to eat and water to drink" (Daniel 1:12).

According to Jewish custom of the Apostolic Era, an observant Jew could not eat any meat or wine prepared by Gentiles because the Gentiles might have contaminated the food and drink with idolatry. To get around this problem, an observant Jew among Gentiles could eat only uncooked vegetables and drink only water, just as Daniel and his friends had done.

DEALING WITH IDOLATRY

It was difficult to be a Jew in the Roman world. Idolatry was everywhere in the Diaspora. Foods for sale in the marketplace had almost certainly been sacrificed to an idol or otherwise tainted by idolatry. Whenever the city celebrated a festival or special occasion, it had something to do with the pagan gods.

To survive in the midst of idolatry, the Jewish communities formulated legal rulings designed to keep them separate from the contaminations of the idolatrous world around them.

Jews survived in the midst of paganism by avoiding food that might have been sacrificed to an idol. Food bought from an idolater was almost certainly prepared with prayers to false gods and offered in part to those gods. The same was true with wine. Gentiles almost always poured out the first drawing of the wine vat to the god of wine, thereby rendering the whole vat polluted by idols. The only food prepared by Gentiles that the sages declared safe to eat was vegetables.

The solution to this problem, from the Jewish perspective, was simply to declare food prepared by a Gentile as defiled.

This solution worked until Gentiles started abandoning idolatry to follow Yeshua. If the Gentile was now a believer and had renounced idolatry, was his food to be considered defiled or not? Could a Jew eat a Gentile's food if the Gentile was not an idolater? While the answer might seem obvious to us today, a halachic standard or custom was not easily set aside.

EATING WITH GENTILES

The book of Acts tells us that the apostles wrestled seriously with this issue. It contains a famous account in which Peter had a vision of a sheet descending from heaven, on which stood many clean and unclean animals. A voice told him to eat. We won't enter into a full discussion of this passage here, but the narrative does not support the commonly held idea that Peter's vision was intended to do away with the distinctions imposed by the biblical dietary laws. Rather, it showed Peter that he could, in good conscience, eat in the house of Cornelius the God-fearing Gentile without worrying that the food had been defiled by Gentiles. He explained to Cornelius, "God has shown me that I should not call any person common or unclean" (Acts 10:28). The other apostles scolded him: "You went to uncircumcised men and ate with them" (Acts 11:3), but Peter explained the vision of the sheet and that "the Spirit told me to go with them [and eat with them], making no distinction" (Acts 11:12).

After the Cornelius incident, Jewish believers began to eat with Gentile believers. Paul referred to these Jewish believers who set aside their objections to eating food prepared by Gentile believers, and to eating at the table with Gentile believers, as the strong in faith.

Some Jews in Rome disagreed with Paul's assessment. Not all the Jewish people attending the Roman synagogues were believers, and even the Jews who were believers did not always feel like they should be eating food prepared by a Gentile, even if that Gentile was a believer. The same issue once caused trouble in the believing community at Antioch (Galatians 2:12–13). Paul referred to the Jewish believers who still harbored objections to eating with Gentiles and eating food prepared by Gentiles as "weak in faith."

COMMON AND UNCLEAN

In Jewish estimation, any food that had been offered in part to an idol or as part of an idolatrous feast was defiled, and was therefore no longer fit to be used as holy food. It was regarded as "common." The Greek word is *koinos*. It means "common," "vulgar," or "profane." It does not, however, necessarily refer to food that is ritually unclean or even forbidden. The Greek word for something that is biblically, ritually unclean is *akathartos*. The Septuagint (the Greek version of the Old Testament) translates ritual uncleanness as *akathartos*.

KOINOS: Common. When used in reference to Jewish dietary law, it refers to otherwise permitted food rendered unfit for consumption by contact with idolatry, non-Jews, or some other source of defilement.

AKATHARTOS: Unclean. When used in reference to Jewish dietary law, it refers either to foods that have become ritually unclean, or to the meat of unclean animals.

Though both words refer to food that was considered prohibited, it is important to keep in mind the difference between *koinos* (common) and *akathartos* (unclean). The meat of unclean animals, for example, is always *akathartos*. Wine poured out to an idol might not be *akathartos*, but it is rendered *koinos* because of its association with the idol.

Some Jewish believers in Rome considered foods prepared by Gentile believers as *koinos* (common) because they were potentially defiled by idolatry. Rather than eat meat or drink wine that might have been associated with idolatry and Gentile defilement and thereby rendered *koinos*, these conservatives chose to refrain from meat and wine when in a mixed Jewish-Gentile setting. Instead, they ate only vegetables, just as Daniel did in Babylon. Paul regarded this as a debatable matter, and he left it to the conscience of the individual.

When Paul said, "I know and am persuaded in the Lord Jesus that nothing is unclean in itself, but it is unclean for anyone who thinks it unclean" (Romans 14:14), he did not use the Greek word *akathartos*; he used the word *koinos*, which means "common":

> I know and am persuaded in the Lord Jesus that nothing is [common] in itself, but it is [common] for anyone who thinks it [common]. (Romans 14:14)

This passage is almost universally misapplied as if it pertained to the Torah's prohibitions against eating the meat of unclean animals—as if Paul said that "nothing is *akathartos* in itself." His statement that "nothing is unclean in itself" is completely unrelated to the laws of clean and unclean animals. It is a question of whether or not food is permissible when it might potentially have been offered to an idol or prepared by a Gentile.

Therefore, the one who was "weak in faith" was the person who regarded food to be *koinos* solely on the basis that it had been prepared by, or come in contact with, Gentile hands. As a result, the "weak in faith" ate only vegetables when eating with Gentiles.

AVOIDING DAYS OF IDOLATRY

A similar matter of Jewish law informs Paul's words about "days" in this chapter: "One person esteems one day as better than another, while another esteems all days alike. Each one should be fully convinced in his own mind" (Romans 14:5).

Judaism developed another survival strategy to insulate its communities from the idolatrous Gentile context of the Roman world. Strictly observant Jews refused to do business with Gentiles on or around the pagan festival days. The Talmud warns against conducting business with Gentiles on their festival days because any money paid to a Gentile was likely to go toward idol worship, and any products purchased on or around the pagan festival days were likely tainted by idolatry. The extremely pious refused to do business with Gentiles for a three-day period before and after an idolatrous festival. The complicated laws of avoiding pagan festival days are discussed in the Mishnah's tractate titled *Avodah Zarah* ("Idol Worship"). For example:

> For a period of three days before idolatrous festivals, it is forbidden to engage in business transactions with Gentiles, to ask them for something or to be asked for something by them, to lend or to borrow from them ... Rabbi Yishma'el says, "It is forbidden for three days before the festivals and three days after the festivals." The Sages say, "It is forbidden before the festivals, but it is permitted after the festivals." According to Rabbi Meir, these are the primary days of idolatrous festivals: Kalendis, Saturnalia, Kratesis, the emperor's day of accession, the emperor's birthday, and the emperor's day of death. (m.*Avodah Zarah* 1:1–3)

Jewish law also forbade Jews traveling to a Gentile city from entering it on the day of a pagan festival:

> When an idolatrous festival is celebrated within a city, it is permissible to transact business outside the city. If it takes place outside the city, it is permitted to conduct business inside the city. What is the rule in regard to going to a city in which an idolatrous festival is taking place? If the road leads solely to that place, it is forbidden, but if the road leads also to other destinations, it is permitted. (m.*Avodah Zarah* 1:3)

These laws pertained to the Jewish community in Rome, and raised questions for dealing with the God-fearing Gentile believers. Was a Jewish believer allowed to conduct business with a God-fearing Gentile believer on an idolatrous day, or should he abstain from contact with all Gentiles on those days? Were the Gentile believers to abstain from conducting business on idolatrous days, as the Jewish community did, or were they free to engage in business as usual? Differing opinions on the matter created tensions among the Roman believers.

Apparently, some Jewish believers were careful not to engage with Gentiles or even go into a Gentile city on a pagan festival day. Perhaps they even avoided contact with God-fearing Gentile believers on the days of idolatrous festivals. Others, like Paul, ignored those types of stringencies. Paul believed they were unnecessary impediments to his gospel to the Gentiles, but he was not interested in arguing with people who held those convictions. He said, "As for the one who is weak in faith, welcome him, but not to quarrel over opinions" (Romans 14:1). Paul may have regarded those who harbored such scruples as "weak in faith," but he nevertheless advocated respecting their convictions. Consider my translation of Romans 14:5–6:

> One man judges one day from another, while another judges every day alike. Each one should be fully convinced in his own mind. He who regards the day [as forbidden to transact with Gentiles], regards it so for the sake of the Lord; and he who does not regard the day [as forbidden to transact with Gentiles], for the sake of the Lord he does not regard it. Likewise, the one who eats [with Gentiles], eats for the sake of the Lord, since he gives thanks to God, while the one who does not eat [with Gentiles] abstains for the sake of the Lord and gives thanks to God. (Romans 14:5–6, my translation)

Paul did urge believers to demonstrate sensitivity and tolerance for differing opinions regarding the status of Gentile believers in the midst of the Jewish community in Rome. He knew that his readers did not always agree on the proper way to handle these debatable questions, but he expected them to be gracious to one another as they sorted out the relationship:

> For none of us lives to himself, and none of us dies to himself. For if we live, we live to the Lord, and if we die, we die to the Lord. So then, whether we live or whether we die, we are the Lord's. For to this end Christ died and lived again, that he might be Lord both of the dead and of the living. Why do you pass judgment on your brother?

> Or you, why do you despise your brother? For we will all stand before the judgment seat of God. (Romans 14:7–10)

SUMMARY OF ROMANS 14

Paul may be difficult to understand, but he was not an apostate from Judaism, advocating some type of relativistic "whatever you believe is true, is true for you" religious observance. It turns out that Romans 14 has nothing to say about whether or not we should keep the biblical dietary laws, and it has nothing at all to say about the Sabbath day. Paul was talking about completely different issues.

Paul did not view Sabbath observance or the Torah's dietary laws as a subjective matter of personal opinion. He never suggested that Jewish believers should consider themselves as exempt from observing the Sabbath day or the Torah's dietary standards. Nor did he consider Jewish believers to be "weak in faith" for keeping the Sabbath or for keeping kosher. Instead, the discussion in Romans 14 centers on the contentious question of Jewish-Gentile interactions in first-century Rome.

Nevertheless, we can still learn an important principle from the discussion in Romans 14. We should not quarrel over contentious issues or matters of opinion. When people express their opinions about the Sabbath day, it will not profit us to engage them in an argument—we would be arguing against their own personal opinions, and those types of arguments are fruitless. They fall into the category of "foolish controversies ... dissensions, and quarrels about the law," and "they are unprofitable and worthless" (Titus 3:9). Rather, "Each one should be fully convinced in his own mind" (Romans 14:5). I am fully convinced that the seventh day is the holy Sabbath.

CHAPTER SIXTEEN

THE FIRST DAY OF THE WEEK

Messianic Judaism claims that the Apostolic-era believers honored the biblical Sabbath along with the rest of the Jewish community. Even God-fearing Gentile believers worshiped on the seventh day. If the New Testament-era believers were Sabbatarian and continued to honor the seventh-day Sabbath, why does the New Testament seem to indicate that the believers met on the first day of the week? For example, Acts 20 depicts an assembly of believers gathered to hear Paul's teaching "on the first day of the week, when we were gathered together to break bread" (Acts 20:7). Paul instructed his communities to set aside money for a special collection on the first day of the week: "Now concerning the collection for the saints: as I directed the churches of Galatia, so you also are to do. On the first day of every week, each of you is to put something aside and store it up" (1 Corinthians 16:1–2). Do these passages indicate that the early believers of the Apostolic Era had transitioned from Sabbath observance to Sunday observance?

We will briefly look at both instances.

THE FIRST DAY OF EVERY WEEK: 1 CORINTHIANS 16:1–2

At a certain point during his ministry, Paul saw the need to begin conducting fundraising efforts for the beleaguered believing community in Jerusalem. He wanted the Diaspora congregations of believers "to make some contribution for the poor among the saints in Jerusalem" (Romans 15:26). Paul reasoned, "If the Gentiles have come to share in their spiritual blessings, they ought also to be of service to them in material blessings" (Romans 15:27).

The apostle to the Gentiles directed each community to begin preparing a collection. He told each person to set aside a small amount according to his means "on the first day of every week." After they had collected a large sum, they were to designate a courier to carry the collection to Jerusalem along with official letters from Paul or, if necessary, accompanied by Paul himself:

> Now concerning the collection for the saints: as I directed the churches of Galatia, so you also are to do. *On the first day of every week*, each of you is to put something aside and store it up, as he may prosper, so that there will be no collecting when I come. And when I arrive, I will send those whom you accredit by letter to carry your gift to Jerusalem. If it seems advisable that I should go also, they will accompany me. (1 Corinthians 16:1–4)

Why did Paul tell the Corinthians to set aside money on the first day of the week? Does this not imply that the early believers had already begun to observe the first day of the week as their day of assembly and worship?

It does not imply Sunday observance at all. Sabbath-keepers do not handle money or engage in any type of financial transaction on the Sabbath. Synagogues take no collections on the Sabbath. Paul would not have told the believers to set aside a sum of money on the Sabbath. The first day of the week is the first possible opportunity to handle money after the Sabbath ends.

Paul chose the first day of the week as an appropriate time for setting aside a sum of money because he envisioned the contribution as a type of first fruits or tithe that must be separated from the main sum—something that should be done at the outset rather than the end of the week.

The instructions in 1 Corinthians 16:1–4 do not necessarily imply a public assembly at all. Paul instructed each individual to set aside and save his sum of money privately. He did not direct the believers to contribute the money into a public coffer. The passage does not indicate that the believers gathered together to make a public contribution.

Even if Paul did instruct the believers to gather the contribution into a public fund on the first day of every week, that does not imply a Sunday morning gathering.

HAVDALAH IN TROAS

Others cite Acts 20:7 as evidence that the early believers met on Sundays: "On the first day of the week, when we were gathered together to break bread." This verse is conventionally interpreted to mean that the believers gathered together on the first day of the week to conduct the Eucharist.

The narrative does not support that interpretation. If Paul met with the Troasian believers on Sunday morning, they had a very long church service. Paul spoke until midnight: "Paul talked with them, intending to depart on the next day, and he prolonged his speech until midnight" (Acts 20:7).

The Greek text of Acts does not indicate that they met on Sunday morning at all. Instead it literally says, "On the first of the Sabbath," that is, the first day of the count until the next Sabbath. The word "day" does not appear in the Greek. According to the Jewish reckoning of time, the first of the week begins Saturday after sunset. (The biblical day begins at sunset.)

Luke records events in the book of Acts only in reference to Sabbaths and festivals. In Luke's writings, things happen from one Sabbath to another and from one festival to another. That is to say, he records his narrative with reference to the Jewish way of reckoning time. Therefore, when he speaks of the believers meeting on the first day of the week, the reader should resist the temptation to interpret that statement as a Sunday morning. By the Jewish way of reckoning time, Saturday night is in view. Apparently, the early believers were accustomed to assembling on Saturday nights, after the Sabbath.

It is completely possible that the early believers customarily gathered together on the first day of the week. They probably gathered on Saturday night after dark, after the Sabbath, when the "first day of the week" began. This day begins at the appearance of three stars on Saturday night, at which time it is traditional to greet one another with the words, "*Shavua Tov!* May you have a good week."

SATURDAY NIGHT MEAL

On the Sabbath, the early believers seem to have attended the local synagogue to hear the Torah and join in the prayer services. Afterward, they gathered together privately in a home. There was precedent for this sort of gathering; from ancient times, Jews have concluded the weekly Sabbath with a special ceremony called *havdalah*, which means "separation." The ceremony includes wine, spices, and the reintroduction of flame.

The lighting of a candle is an appropriate way to mark the end of the Sabbath, for the Torah forbids the kindling of a fire on the Sabbath day. That is why Sabbath-keepers light candles on Friday before sunset. In the days before electric lights, if one did not light lamps before Sabbath began, he would be sitting in the dark that night. The Sabbath-keeper is careful not to light lamps or candles after the sun has set on Friday because by then Sabbath has already begun: "You shall kindle no fire in all your dwelling places on the Sabbath day" (Exodus 35:3).

By Saturday night, most of the lamps had burned out, and only coals remained in the hearth. After sunset on Saturday, the Sabbath-keeper relit lamps and stoked up the fire. The book of Acts says, "There were many lamps in the upper room where we were gathered" (Acts 20:8). Sabbath-keepers still practice the *havdalah* ritual of lighting a flame to mark the separation between the Sabbath and the first of the week, and pronouncing a blessing over the reintroduction of flame.

If the believers in Troas followed this custom, they would have lit their Sabbath lamps Friday night as they prepared for Sabbath. On Saturday morning they attended a local synagogue, heard the Torah, and met up with other believers. After service, they might have gathered together in someone's house, talking about the things of the kingdom and learning about the Master. Saturday evening, as the Sabbath came to a close, they assembled together and broke bread in memory of the Master's rising.

Gathering on Saturday night rather than on the Sabbath enabled the disciples to travel, prepare food, carry provisions, light lamps, handle money, distribute charity, and discuss community concerns unencumbered by Sabbath restrictions. In places where the believers still attended and participated in local synagogue services, the smaller after-Sabbath gatherings gave them an opportunity to fellowship, pray, and learn in a private environment with other disciples.

MELAVEH MALKAH

As mentioned above, Luke says, "There were many lamps in the upper room where we were gathered" (Luke 20:8). This seemingly superfluous detail might indicate that the community had gathered to celebrate a special Saturday night meal called *Melaveh Malkah*. The *Mishnah Berurah*, a code of Jewish law penned at the beginning of the twentieth century, mentions the custom of lighting "many lamps" for this special meal after *havdalah*:

> A person should always set his table on the evening following the Sabbath in order to escort the Sabbath, even if he does not need more than an olive-sized piece. For this reason there are some who have the custom to have many lamps on the evening following the Sabbath, more so than on weekdays. (*Mishnah Berurah*, Sabbath Laws 300:3)

At least as early as the Talmudic Era, Jews gathered on Saturday night, after the Sabbath, for this special meal to bid farewell to the Sabbath (b.*Shabbat* 119b). The Saturday night meal is called *Melaveh Malkah*, "Escorting the Queen," because it is a formal farewell to the Sabbath day. Just as we welcome the Sabbath like a royal bride on Friday night, we escort her like a departing queen on Saturday night. Think of *Melaveh Malkah* as a prolonging of the holiness of the day and as a farewell party for the Sabbath.

Even though by the time of *Melaveh Malkah* the Sabbath is already over and the first day of the week has already begun, the Saturday night meal actually helps sanctify the Sabbath. The Saturday night meal sets the earlier third meal of the Sabbath apart as a special meal intended just for the honor of the Sabbath, so that it cannot be considered simply an early dinner.

The *Melaveh Malkah* meal appears to be in view when Luke says, "On the first day of the week, when we were gathered together to break bread …"

The Saturday night *Melaveh Malkah* meal and the beginning of the first day of the week have messianic associations in Judaism. Jewish tradition teaches that the Messiah will not come on a Sabbath day. Therefore we anticipate his arrival at the conclusion of the Sabbath. It is traditional to sing a song welcoming Elijah the prophet at the conclusion of the Sabbath because we hope that Elijah will come at that time and announce the arrival of King Messiah.

According to tradition, the meal after the Shabbat is also called "The Meal of David, King Messiah." A Jewish legend about King David says that David asked God to reveal to him the day of his death. God revealed to him that he would die on a Sabbath. From that time on, David made a special meal for the members of his household at the conclusion of each Sabbath to thank God that he was still alive.

Melaveh Malkah is supposed to be eaten after the Sabbath concludes. Some rabbis prolong the meal as long as possible to preserve the spirit of the Sabbath. Jewish law says it should be eaten by midnight at the latest. This accords with Acts 20, where it says, "On the first of the week they were gathered together to break bread … and Paul prolonged his message until midnight." Then it says a few verses later, "When he had broken bread and eaten, he talked with them a long while until day break."

When we understand the custom of *Melaveh Malkah,* it makes sense to see the disciples of Yeshua gathering together on Saturday night. They gathered on "the first of the week" in concert with Jewish tradition and in honor of the departing Sabbath.

COMMEMORATING THE RESURRECTION

Jewish tradition also associates the end of the Sabbath with the idea of resurrection. According to Jewish tradition, the Sabbath-keeper receives an extra portion of soul on the Sabbath day. This

"Sabbath soul" represents a special measure of Sabbath peace—*shabbat shalom*. At the end of the Sabbath, as the daylight fades away, the Sabbath soul leaves the body. A small death occurs because when the soul leaves the body, the body is dead. For that reason, we distribute spices at *havdalah* to revivify the body, much the same as smelling salts are used to rouse an unconscious person.

Gospel readers ordinarily imagine the resurrection of Yeshua occurring at dawn on the first day of the week, because the women discovered the empty tomb at dawn. According to the tradition Matthew records in his gospel, however, the resurrection seems to have occurred at *havdalah* time, just after the Sabbath ended on Saturday night: "After the Sabbath, as it began to dawn toward the first day of the week" (Matthew 28:1 NASB). This translation makes it sound as if Matthew is describing something that occurred at dawn on Sunday morning. The Greek text, however, can mean "as the first day of the week began," that is, as the Sabbath ended on Saturday night. It's a Semitic idiom for the conclusion of the day.

The early believers seem to have gathered together at the conclusion of the Sabbath in order to commemorate the resurrection with a weekly *Melaveh Malkah* meal. New Testament scholar Raymond Brown explains:

> The association of Sunday and the resurrection was a secondary development ... Originally, on Saturday evening after the close of the Sabbath (ca. 6 PM) and thus, by Jewish reckoning, on what was already Sunday, Jewish Christians who had observed the Sabbath now met at their homes to break the Eucharistic bread (cf. Acts 2:46), as a prolongation of the Sabbath. Thus it would seem that the earliest Christian celebrations on "the first day of the week" were not on the day of Sunday but late in the evening on the vigil of Sunday. (Raymond Brown, *The Gospel According to John XIII–XXI*)

SUNDAY

When the Greek Gospel of Matthew began to circulate, Gentile Christians unfamiliar with Jewish idiom misunderstood Matthew

28:1 to refer to Sunday morning. As Christians began to abandon Sabbath observance, they substituted the first day of the week as a day of worship. They referred to the first day of the week as "the Lord's Day." Initially, they did not treat it as a Sabbath. Early second-century Christians met on Sunday mornings for prayers before dawn, and then went off to their respective occupations. After the workday, they gathered again for a shared meal (Pliny, *Epistle* 10.96).

By the middle of the second century, assemblies of Christians hosted Sunday morning services that followed the basic conventions of a synagogue service—a reading of the Scriptures, a teaching, a prayer service, and a shared meal. Justin Martyr explained, "Sunday is the day on which we conduct our assembly because it is the first day, the day on which God transformed darkness and created the world, and on which Jesus Christ our Savior rose from the dead" (*First Apology* 67:3–7).

In the next chapter we will discover that the transformation from Sabbath to Sunday observance took place slowly over more than two generations. Paul and the apostles knew nothing about it, nor could they have foreseen it. When Paul met with the believers in Troas for a meal on Saturday night, and when he told the Corinthian believers to set aside a small sum of money on the first day of the week, he had no notion that, one day, the first day would become the *de facto* Christian day of worship.

PART FOUR

From Sabbath to Sabbath

CHAPTER SEVENTEEN

How We Lost the Sabbath

The Sabbath is one of the most frequently repeated commandments in the Bible. It's obviously something important to God. He mentions the Sabbath more than he mentions the prohibition on adultery. All things considered, it seems surprising that most Christians today neither observe, nor celebrate, nor even remember the Sabbath. The celebration of Sunday has completely supplanted the Sabbath. Have you ever wondered how that happened?

It's a complicated story that involves war, persecution, social stigmatization, cultural movements, and theological errors. These numerous factors came together so quickly that within a century of the Master's resurrection, the Gentile Christian church had largely adopted Sunday as the preferred day of worship.

We have early textual evidence of this rapid change. In the early second century, the Christian bishop of Antioch sent out several epistles to congregations in Asia Minor condemning their ongoing observance of the Sabbath and other aspects of Judaism. These epistles from Ignatius indicate that less than a century after the Master's resurrection, his followers had created something that looked very different from the sect of Judaism he originally planted.

The transition from Yeshua to Ignatius, a process spanning less than eight decades, seems startlingly abrupt. How did things come to such a state so quickly? If the Yeshua movement started out as a sect of Judaism, how can it be explained that a representative of the same movement, not more than eighty years later, considered Judaism to be the opposite of faith in Yeshua? The following chapter briefly summarizes the factors that led to the separation between Judaism and Gentile Christianity. This is the story of how we lost the Sabbath.

APOSTOLIC-ERA SABBATARIANS

There is really no question, historically speaking, that Jewish believers continued to keep the Sabbath. Early church writers frequently referred to the persistent presence of Jewish believers who kept the Sabbath like other Jews. Even as late as the fifth century, the church writer Epiphanius complained about Jewish believers who kept the Torah, practiced circumcision, observed the Sabbath, and kept Jewish customs. He complained that the Jewish believers were no different than other Jews except in their confession of Yeshua. They congregated together in sects called the Nazarenes and the Ebionites, and do not seem to have mixed with the Gentile Christians—at least, not during the third and fourth centuries.

One cannot reasonably deny that Jewish believers remained Sabbath-observant even after the end of the Apostolic Era; the textual evidence for this is overwhelming. But do we have any reason to believe that Gentile believers also kept the Sabbath?

The Jewish historian Josephus offers evidence that they did. Near the end of the first century, he described a growing movement of Gentile Sabbath-keepers in cities all throughout the Roman Empire:

> There is not any city of the Greeks, nor any of the barbarians, nor any nation whatever, where our custom of resting on the seventh day has not come, and by which our fasts and lighting lamps, and many of our prohibitions as to our food, are not observed. (Josephus, *Against Apion* 2:282)

Josephus provides an extraordinary snapshot from the late Apostolic Era. He gives us a tantalizing glimpse of the practices of God-fearing Gentiles, a category that includes the early Gentile believers. Josephus says that they were resting on the seventh day, observing the fast days of the Jewish calendar, lighting the

Sabbath lamps, observing the dietary laws, and emulating Jewish community values.

The first-century Roman writer Juvenal also wrote about the problem of Romans becoming Sabbatarian, which he saw as the first step to becoming Jewish:

> Some who have had a father who reveres the Sabbath, worship nothing but the clouds, and the divinity of the heavens, and see no difference between eating swine's flesh, from which their father abstained, and that of man; and in time they take to circumcision. Having been wont to flout the laws of Rome, they learn and practice and revere the Jewish law, and all that Moses committed to his secret tome ...For all which the father was to blame, who gave up every seventh day to idleness, keeping it apart from all the concerns of life. (*Satire* 14)

THE FIRST DAY

In the previous chapter, we learned that the disciples of Yeshua originally revered the first day of the week as a conclusion to the Sabbath, which they celebrated with a special meal in memory of the Master's resurrection. According to some opinions, the early believers referred to the first day of the week as "the Lord's day" in reference to it as the day of the resurrection. An early apostolic document called the *Didache* offers evidence of the believers keeping a commemorative meal "on the day of the Lord":

> On the day of the Lord, being gathered together, break bread and give thanks after having confessed your transgressions, so that your sacrifice may be pure. (*Didache* 14.1)

The Talmud contains a hint about this practice, indicating that the Nazarenes in the Apostolic Era revered the first day of the week as a day on which fasting is prohibited (b.*Ta'anit* 27b). The Jewish people commemorated the days on which miracles, great deliverances, and good things happened by forbidding fasting on the anniversary of those occasions. Perhaps the disciples of Yeshua avoided fasting on the first day of the week every week. Beyond that, there is no indication that they engaged in any special Sunday observances.

A BIG CHANGE

A century later, Christian observance of the Sabbath was in a process of transition. Naturally, most Jewish believers remained fully Sabbath-observant. Gentile believers, however, had developed an ambivalent relationship with the Sabbath. In some places Gentile believers continued to assemble on the Sabbath and cease from work on that day. In other places Christians no longer rested on the Sabbath or used it as their principal day of assembly. They continued to regard it as the holy Sabbath, but they believed that the death of the Messiah had canceled the obligations associated with it.

One famous second-century Gentile Christian bishop, Ignatius of Antioch, is known for holding this latter opinion. Ignatius argued that to keep the Sabbath was to live apart from Christ. Ignatius did not believe that the Sabbath had changed from the seventh day to the first day; he did not consider the Lord's Day to be a new Sabbath. He believed instead that it was inappropriate for Christians to keep the Sabbath at all. He taught that Christians should make the Lord's Day their day of assembly because it represented the resurrection of Christ, but he did not advocate observing it as a day of ceasing from labor.

IN ACCORDANCE WITH CHRISTIANITY

Ignatius was the bishop of Antioch. "The disciples were first called Christians in Antioch" (Acts 11:26 NASB). Originally, the term "Christians" referred to the particular sect of Judaism that identified with Yeshua of Nazareth. By the time of Ignatius, it no longer signified a sect of Judaism; it signified a competing religion.

Ignatius understood Judaism as the religion of the Torah. He understood Christianity as the religion of Christ, and as the religion that supplanted the Torah. Ignatius was troubled by disciples of Yeshua who lived according to the principles of Judaism. His theology had no room for Jewish believers or God-fearing

Gentile believers who practiced Judaism. To him, anyone who did not "live according to the principles of Christianity" was not a Christian, and "whosoever is called by any other name besides Christianity is not of God":

> Since we have become His disciples, let us learn to live according to the principles of Christianity. For whosoever is called by any other name besides this is not of God. (Ignatius, *Magnesians* 10:1)

What were the principles of Christianity that he had in mind? In this context, the principles of Christianity included a repudiation of the Torah's ceremonial laws along with all other practices considered characteristically Jewish. His language implies transition from one state to another; as he saw it, the previous state was Judaism. Ignatius pushed his readers to disassociate from Jewish practice and Judaism.

THE OLD LEAVEN

Ignatius compared Judaism to the old leaven, which must be cast out at Passover. Jesus Christ is the new leaven. The old leaven of Jewish ways spiritually putrefied the believer. To Ignatius, then, just as a little leaven leavens the whole lump, a little Judaism spoils the whole church:

> Cast out, therefore, the evil leaven, the old, sour leaven, and be transformed into the new leaven, which is Jesus Christ. Be salted with Him, lest any one of you become putrefied, for by your odor you will be tested. (Ignatius, *Magnesians* 10:2)

Ignatius drew his inspiration from Paul's first epistle to the Corinthians: "Clean out the old leaven so that you may be a new lump, just as you are in fact unleavened. For Christ our Passover also has been sacrificed" (1 Corinthians 5:7 NASB). In this case, Ignatius hijacked the language of the passage and repackaged it into a condemnation of Judaism and Torah. Paul applied the leaven metaphor completely differently. In Paul's epistle, the leaven was not Judaism; it was sexual immorality, malice, and wickedness. The new leaven was not Christ; it was "sincerity and truth" (1 Corinthians 5:8). Ironically, outside a Jewish context in which Passover is both understood and practiced, Paul's leaven metaphor falls flat.

UTTERLY ABSURD

Ignatius had no patience for Jewish believers and God-fearing Gentiles who continued to keep the Sabbath and other ceremonial aspects of Torah. He considered it "utterly absurd" for a believer in Christ to practice Judaism. Contrary to all historical evidence, he even argued that Christianity did not grow out of Judaism:

> It is utterly absurd to profess Christ Jesus and to practice Judaism. For Christianity did not base its faith on Judaism, but Judaism on Christianity, and every tongue believing on God was brought together in it. (Ignatius, *Magnesians* 10:3)

According to Ignatius, Judaism grew out of Christianity. In other words, the true Old Testament religion of Israel was Christianity, but the Jews, in their spiritual blindness to Christ, perverted their observance of the Scriptures into the manmade religion of Judaism. Ignatius' influence has still not run its course; these bigoted assumptions about Jews and Judaism are still prevalent among Christians today.

JEWISH HOSTILITY

From the outset, normative forms of Judaism resisted the small sectarian Yeshua-movement. All the apostolic writings testify to an acrimonious relationship between Yeshua (or his followers) and the religious authorities who defined the broader Jewish community. The believers experienced conflict with the Pharisees, Sadducees, Herodians, and Zealots. The betrayal and death of Yeshua left a psychological scar on his followers that tended to color their relationship with the religious authorities thereafter. Resulting tensions and conflicts left their mark on apostolic literature.

Gentiles reading that literature outside of its Jewish context, which portrays these conflicts as an internal dispute within Judaism, tended to understand the larger Jewish world only as antagonists. Their own personal interactions with that larger Jewish world often reinforced the stereotype. The insular Jewish community had no affection for the influx of Pauline Gentiles. As the book of Acts demonstrates, the synagogue environment reacted negatively to the arrival of large numbers of God-fearing Gentile believers. That reaction further fed the Gentile believers' sense of alienation from the Jewish community. A natural human reflex for those excluded from a group or closed society is to form their own competing society. By excluding God-fearing Gentile believers from fellowship within the larger Jewish community, Judaism created the social dynamic from which Christianity emerged.

Jewish hostility toward believers continued under the Roman persecutions. The Jewish community often found it necessary to disown the believers in order to escape the danger they represented. From the perspective of the believers, it looked as if the Jews were betraying them to the pagans.

TENSION BETWEEN JEWISH AND GENTILE BELIEVERS

The writings of the apostles indicate that significant friction existed between Jewish and Gentile believers. The tension centered itself in Antioch, where Gentile believers first began to press into the faith, where Paul and Barnabas introduced the Pauline gospel of Gentile inclusion, and where the largest community of Gentile believers existed. That tension manifested itself openly in Paul's conflict with men from James and in a conflict between Peter and Paul. Paul's frequent appeal for Jewish and Gentile believers to live harmoniously in Messiah testifies to the presence of a significant amount of disharmony in the relationship.

Long before Ignatius was born, the believers in Antioch had undergone many trials and tribulations. During the ministry of Paul of Tarsus, the Antiochian community repeatedly experienced internal tensions between Jewish and Gentile members of the community. The tense situation in Antioch forced the Jerusalem Council of Acts 15 to intervene and offer a definitive ruling on the status of God-fearing Gentiles within the believing community.

The ruling brought peace temporarily, but tensions between Jewish and Gentile believers must have continued to smolder. As the Gentile side of the community grew to eclipse the Jewish side of the community, it created a precarious imbalance in the Antiochian Synagogue of the Christians.

Paul envisioned communities in which Jews and Gentiles freely fellowshiped together and respected one another's unique roles. Unfortunately, Paul's idealism did not work sociologically. Gentile believers always felt like second-class citizens next to their Jewish co-religionists. How could it be otherwise? That inferiority complex led many Gentiles, such as the Galatian influencers, to abandon their Gentile identity and undergo circumcision. Those who did not do so had to find some other way to overcome their religious-social insecurities and legitimize themselves. Turning against Judaism and declaring Jewish identity to be invalid helped to satisfy that need. Gentile believers could find self-affirmation and clear identity by priding themselves as superior to Jews and Judaism.

PERVASIVE ANTI-SEMITISM

The Roman world had a pervasive anti-Semitism that colored every interaction between Jews and Gentiles. God-fearing Gentile believers were not immune to its effects. On one hand, they unconsciously internalized some of larger society's anti-Jewish attitudes; on the other hand, they suffered under that same anti-Semitism because of their own close association with Jews and Judaism. To alleviate the discomfort of that association, they needed to distance themselves from the Jewish world and Jewish identity as much as possible.

The First Jewish Revolt against Rome exacerbated anti-Jewish sentiments. By the time of Ignatius, a second Jewish revolt was brewing in many places in the empire. The revolts gave the believing Gentiles political and social motivations to define themselves against Jews and Jewish practice. As the number of Yeshua's Gentile disciples continued to increase, they soon disproportionately outnumbered the Jewish believers in most Diaspora communities. That Gentile-heavy ratio allowed the believers to eclipse and diminish the strong Jewish basis of the original apostolic faith.

MISUNDERSTANDING PAUL

Paul, the apostle to the Gentiles, left behind a significant body of literature addressed primarily to Gentile believers. Paul's epistles argued that Gentile believers did not need to become Jewish in order to attain salvation. Outside of the context of the apostolic argument about Gentile inclusion, Paul's epistles create the impression that he argued against the legitimacy of Torah and Judaism.

Moreover, readers misunderstood his statements about the unity of Jewish and Gentile believers. They misunderstood his declarations about the two groups being joined into one new man, in which there is no difference between Jew and Gentile. Paul meant that Gentile believers were just as eligible for salvation as Jews, but his readers have generally misconstrued him to mean that Christ eliminates all distinctions between Jews and Gentiles. If one assumes that Christian Jews and Gentiles are homogenized in Christ and then reads Paul's argument against requiring Gentiles to undergo circumcision and keep the distinctively Jewish aspects of Torah observance, one must conclude that Paul taught the cancellation of the Torah: "Teaching all the Jews who are among the Gentiles to forsake Moses, telling them not to circumcise their children nor to walk according to the customs" (Acts 21:21 NASB). That interpretation of Paul became the predominant reading of his epistles even before the apostle's death. Despite concerted effort, Paul and the apostles failed to correct that misinterpretation.

With such a reading of Paul as the guiding principle to define Gentile Christian identity, a complete break from Judaism was inevitable. By the time of Ignatius, Jewish believers who still practiced Judaism were considered less than full Christians. Ignatius, who seemed to fancy himself as the second coming of the Apostle Paul, had no respect for Messianic Jews. He dismissed them as "utterly absurd" for professing Christ Jesus while practicing Judaism.

THE JEWISH WAR

The First Jewish War against Rome (66–73 CE) brought murderous repercussions against Jews and God-fearing Gentiles in cities throughout the empire. Thousands died in the pogroms, and whole Jewish communities vanished. As a matter of self-preservation, Gentiles needed to convince their fellow citizens that they were not Jewish sympathizers.

The unique situation in Antioch made that city a particularly fertile environment for the cultivation of anti-Jewish Christianity. The third largest city in the empire, Antioch had the second largest Jewish population in the Diaspora. That Jewish population faced extreme peril, especially during the turbulent years of the Jewish War.

When the Jewish War broke out, disaster struck. The people of Antioch wanted to kill all the Jewish residents, just as the other cities in Syria did at the outbreak of the war. The presence of Roman legions in the city prevented them from carrying out their murderous intentions. However, an apostate Jew named Antiochus then accused the God-fearing Gentiles of plotting with the Jews to burn down the city of Antioch. The people of the city launched a pogrom against the Gentile believers. They tested any Gentiles suspected of collusion with Jews by forcing them to worship idols. They put to death all those who would not consent to worship the idols.

Moreover, they introduced a new law forbidding Gentiles from observing the Sabbath. The law spread to other cities in Syria. Josephus says, "The rest of the seventh day was abolished, not only at Antioch, but the same thing which first began there was also done in other cities, in like manner." At that point, Sabbath-keeping became a sign of civic and imperial disloyalty. The new law disrupted Sabbath assemblies. Attendance at Sabbath synagogue services marked the God-fearing Gentiles for persecution. Believing God-fearers who did not show up to work or open their shops on Saturdays risked their lives (*Jewish War* 7:42–53/iii.3). Ignatius was probably born during those turbulent years.

Meanwhile, other Jewish communities in the Gentile cities of Syria were massacred. People considered the God-fearers loyal to the Jewish people and Jewish practice as traitors and enemies, and in many cases the God-fearers met the same fate as the Jewish populations. Henceforth, their allegiance to Yeshua, the Jewish King, indicated enmity with Rome. The ruthless massacres motivated the God-fearing believers to quickly distance themselves from the telltale signs of Jewish practice. The threat of death pressured them to demonstrate that they were not Jews and that their religion was not the religion of the Jews.

THE JEWISH TAX

After the Jewish War the Romans imposed a punishing tax called *Fiscus Judaicus* on Jewish households. In an attempt to increase the tax base and general revenues, the Emperor Domitian investigated claims of Gentiles who had adopted Jewish ways. He discovered the ubiquitous presence of Gentile believers and launched a bitter persecution against them.

After the death of Domitian, Nerva instituted a tax reform that required official Roman identification of who was Jewish and who was not. Believers who were not Jewish were categorized as atheistic Christians and part of an illegal superstition.

The *Fiscus Judaicus* tax policy and its reform under Nerva forced Christians to identify as not Jewish, and thereby created a watershed moment that left Gentile believers searching for self-identification outside of Judaism. When both the Jewish community and the Roman authorities placed the Gentile believers under the category of "Christian" and "not Jewish," the Christian community began to self-identify in contrast to Judaism.

EXPULSION FROM THE SYNAGOGUE

At the same time, synagogues began to introduce a liturgical curse against heretics into the daily prayers. The curse was designed to push sectarians, including believers in Yeshua, out of the synagogue. This liturgical innovation officially declared faith in Yeshua to be outside the acceptable boundaries of Judaism. Henceforth, Judaism necessarily adopted an anti-Yeshua and anti-Christian posture and rhetoric that further inflamed Gentile Christianity's distaste for Jews and all things Jewish. The synagogues of Antioch may have been among the first to adopt the imprecation against believers.

As Gentile Christianity hurried to come to a sense of self-identification, it necessarily looked to those areas where its practice was distinct from Judaism. Since Gentile Christianity was, of course, primarily Gentile, the most obvious distinctions involved matters of Torah that were not incumbent upon Gentiles. As a result, Christianity's self-identity became primarily defined by the rejection and invalidation of the ceremonial aspects of the Torah of Moses that were incumbent upon Jews but not upon Gentile believers.

ATTRITION

Prior to the expulsion from the synagogue and the introduction of the malediction against believers, attrition had not been a serious concern for believers. Gentile believers who wanted to become Jewish could simply choose to ignore Paul's warnings and undergo circumcision and conversion. They did not need to renounce their faith in the Master to do so. They effectively became Jewish believers through conversion.

Presumably, after the believers' expulsion, the Jewish community no longer accepted converts unless they renounced their messianic beliefs in Yeshua. Yet this did not stop Gentile Christians from making the transition to become Jewish.

Judaism and the prospect of being Jewish was attractive to many first-century Gentile Christians, just as it is attractive to many Gentiles in the Messianic Jewish movement today. The large, well-established, venerable religion had many advantages: a strong sense of stability and antiquity, a fully developed tradition, wide social and community networks, strong central leadership, and the psychological perks that can only be obtained by admission into an exclusive, members-only club. Best of all, becoming Jewish eliminated the problem with persecution under Roman authorities. Christianity was still an illegal superstition; Judaism was legal and respected.

For all these reasons, Gentile Christians were sometimes willing to deny their allegiance to Yeshua of Nazareth in order to find acceptance within the synagogue and the larger Jewish world.

Justin Martyr complained that proselytes to Judaism were more vitriolic in their criticism of Christianity than native-born Jews, and that these apostates often led the persecutions against Christians. He said to Trypho the Jew, "The proselytes not only do not believe [in Christ], but they blaspheme His name twice as much as you do and wish to torture and put to death those who believe in Him. In all things they strive to be like you" (*Dialogue with Trypho* 112). The same psychology can be observed among apostates today. The most aggressive anti-missionaries are often former Christians and Messianic believers.

To protect the flock from straying too close to Judaism and the Jewish people, to keep them from being snared and absorbed, Christian leaders like Ignatius demonized the whole religion. The synagogue remained attractive to members of the church for many centuries, presenting such a problem that church leaders often felt compelled to deliver sermons filled with hateful, anti-Semitic diatribes warning against association with the synagogue. For example, in the late fourth century, John Chrysostom delivered a vicious series of sermons in Antioch against the Jews and against Christians participating in Judaism.

DAWN OF A NEW ERA

By the time Ignatius took his position as bishop in Antioch, the above factors had combined to create a new religious identity. Ignatius did not invent this new religious movement; he was simply a product of it. Nevertheless, the case should not be overstated. The Christianity of Ignatius was a recent development and it had not yet taken root everywhere. As demonstrated by the contents of his epistles, Ignatius seems to have been troubled to find a great deal of Jewish practice, including Sabbatarianism, in the assemblies of Asia Minor.

The cosmopolitan Ignatius may have been a little bit ahead of his time, but it did not take long for the rest of Gentile Christianity to catch up with him in disassociating from Torah and Jewish practice. The popular epistles of Ignatius actually contributed to the process and accelerated it. So did a forgery called the *Epistle of Barnabas* that began to circulate shortly after the time of Ignatius.

EPISTLE OF BARNABAS

Sometime near the middle of the second century, a new epistle began to circulate among the believing communities. The letter is anonymous, but tradition attaches the name of Barnabas to it. Some scholars speculate that it might have originally been written by an otherwise unknown Christian teacher named Barnabas (commonly called Barnabas of Alexandria), and that it was only mistakenly attributed to Paul's traveling companion. On the other hand, deliberate forgery cannot be ruled out. A writer seeking to influence emerging Christian identity and theology might have found it attractive to write an epistle in the name of a well-known apostle. The writer certainly assumes the tone and authority of an apostle writing to his congregations.

The *Epistle of Barnabas* is another strong indication of the rising anti-Jewish and anti-Torah sentiment among the Gentile believers in the early second century. The writer of the epistle explains to his readers that the followers of Jesus, and not the Jews, are now the true covenant people. The Jews are deluded by an evil angel who taught them to literally apply those things that had been intended only figuratively, allegorically, and spiritually. The author of the epistle interpreted the ceremonial commandments of the Torah as figurative allegory. He derided the Jewish people for literally obeying the Sabbath and the rituals prescribed by the Torah. He explained that observance of the calendar, the dietary laws, the law of circumcision, and the entire sacrificial system was based on a misunderstanding.

The writer of the epistle warned his readers not to commit the grave sin of saying, "The covenant is both theirs (the Jews) and ours (the followers of Jesus)." He explained that God's covenant with the Jewish people has been null and void since Moses broke the two tablets after the sin of the golden calf. Only the Christians are the people of God. For *Pseudo-Barnabas*, Christianity does not replace Judaism. Judaism never had any validity. The Scriptures have always been only about Christianity.

The *Epistle of Barnabas* is certainly not an authentic apostolic document, but to capture an authentic-sounding apostolic voice, the writer of the epistle seems to have incorporated and adapted earlier sources, which may originally have been apostolic in origin. For example, the closing chapters of the epistle utilize the same source behind the opening chapters of the *Didache* ("The Two Ways"). Other passages in the epistle betray sources that must have also originated with Jewish believers. Therefore, the *Epistle of Barnabas* ensconces some traditions and teachings of the early Jewish believers, like prehistoric bugs preserved in amber, despite its overriding agenda against the ceremonial laws of Judaism.

The *Epistle of Barnabas* creatively uses Jewish eschatology about the Sabbath day to de-emphasize the importance of literally observing the Sabbath. *Barnabas* does not imply that Christians were not resting on the seventh day, nor does it attempt to identify Sunday as the new Sabbath, but it does encourage believers to regard Sunday as "the eighth day." It recommends that Christians should "keep the eighth day" as a remembrance of the resurrection of the Master: "Keep the eighth day with joy, the day on which Jesus rose again from the dead" (15:9). The implication is clear: The Sabbath need not be observed as a Sabbath, but the first day should be celebrated as the day of Christ's resurrection.

Regrettably, much of the Christian world mistook the *Epistle of Barnabas* as an authentic writing of the Apostle Barnabas. For several centuries, congregations read it in the church along with the Gospels and other New Testament writings. For example, both Origen and Clement of Alexandria accepted it as authentic. The anti-Torah and anti-Jewish agenda of the epistle became part of the Bible that defined the shape of emerging Christianity.

MARCION THE HERETIC

The break from Sabbath observance was helped along by Marcion the heretic and the teachings of the second-century Gnostics. Marcion and the Gnostics taught a radical dichotomy between the Jewish Scriptures and the Gospels. They believed that the Old Testament God of the Jews was a corrupt and inferior being who had marred his creation with his own imperfections. The physical matter of the universe, which he created, possessed intrinsically evil qualities. Marcion taught that the Jewish God's own Scriptures revealed his complete ignorance and incompetence. As the creator of Adam, he brought evil into the world. Marcion believed that the Jewish God revealed his vengeful, spite-filled nature with laws such as "eye-for-eye and tooth-for-tooth."

Marcion and the Gnostics taught that the true and unrevealed most-high God sent Christ into the world to appear in the guise of a human being, yet without a real physical body, because all physical matter is corrupt. Marcion believed that the divine Christ opposed Judaism and taught against the Torah and the God of the Jews. Christ came to reveal the way to the true God.

According to Marcion, all the apostles failed to understand the true teaching of Jesus except for the Apostle Paul. Marcion rejected the twelve disciples and other apostles as Judaizers. He claimed that because of their thick-headedness, they taught a modified form of Judaism that was still repugnant to the true God. Only Paul had truly apprehended the meaning of the gospel.

To support his views, Marcion had to create his own version of the apostolic texts. Marcion compiled the first official collection of Apostolic Scriptures into a new Bible—the first New Testament. Marcion's New Testament canon consisted of one gospel and ten of Paul's epistles. He edited down the epistles by removing all quotations from the Old Testament and stripping out all the passages that he considered to be Jewish interpolations. He claimed that anything in Paul's writings that sounded Jewish must have been inserted by Jews and could not have been written by Paul. Marcion also rejected all the Gospels except for a heavily edited version of the Gospel of Luke. He stripped out the Master's genealogy, birth narrative, and all of his Jewish-sounding teachings. He even published a book called *Antithesis*, which explained how his New Testament collection supplanted the Jewish Scriptures.

Marcion forged this new form of Christianity during the turbulent Bar Kochba years and the ensuing Hadrianic persecutions—a time during which the Roman Empire treated Judaism as an illegal religion. During those years, anti-Jewish sentiment ran at its height among pagans and Christians alike. At the end of this process, Marcion accomplished what other Christian theologians had been unable to accomplish: a complete and total separation from Judaism. Marcion's Christianity did not grow out of Judaism or the Old Testament; it completely opposed both.

For the remainder of the century and well into the next century, Marcion's popular, Gnostic form of Christianity posed a serious threat to the true faith. In the end, Marcionite Christianity failed to survive, but the ideas that Marcion propagated—particularly his emphasis on contrast between Old Testament and New Testament and Judaism and Christianity—have been woven into the warp and woof of Christian teaching. By publishing and circulating his New Testament, Marcion successfully planted the idea of antithesis between the Jewish Scriptures and the Apostolic Writings, an idea that is still with us today. Marcion's corrupted versions of Paul's epistles and the Gospel of Luke forced Christian leaders to compile a competing collection of Apostolic Writings, a process that eventually resulted in the formation of our New Testament canon.

TRANSITION TO SUNDAY

The events, social circumstances, and theological developments explained above were more than adequate to initiate a separation between Judaism and Christianity. Since the observance of the Sabbath day is the most obvious and externally visible cultural marker of Jewish identity and Torah observance, Gentile Christians eager to disassociate themselves from the Jewish people needed to disassociate themselves from the Sabbath. The celebration of the first day of the week as the Lord's Day offered a natural substitution for Sabbath observance.

This explains why Ignatius was able to say to the believers in Magnesia:

> Let us therefore no longer keep the Sabbath after the Jewish manner, and rejoice in days of idleness ... Let every one of you keep the Sabbath after a spiritual manner, rejoicing in meditation on the law, not in relaxation of the body, admiring the workmanship of God, and not eating things prepared the day before, nor using lukewarm drinks, and walking within a prescribed space, nor finding delight in dancing and clapping which have no sense in them. And after the observance of the Sabbath, let every friend of Christ keep the Lord's Day as a festival,

the resurrection-day, the queen and chief of all the days of the week. (Ignatius, *Magnesians* 9:3, long version)

These words are astonishing because even though Ignatius was theologically anti-Torah and anti-Judaism, he did not try to convince the Magnesians to completely abandon the biblical Sabbath. He only wanted to put an end to *literal* Sabbath observance. He told them instead to keep the Sabbath in a *spiritual* manner. He wanted them to use it for a time to meditate on the Scriptures and to admire the workmanship of creation, both of which are right and proper things to do on the Sabbath.

He did not attempt to completely uproot the Sabbath, but said instead, "After the observance of the Sabbath, let every friend of Christ keep the Lord's Day as a festival." He hoped to diminish the Sabbath by convincing believers to step back from literally observing it. At the same time, he advocated observance of the first day.

So it's not as if the Gentile Christians one day suddenly switched from Saturday to Sunday. It happened slowly. It started with Christians keeping the Sabbath, then honoring Sunday with a commemoration of the resurrection.

CHURCH COUNCILS

Many early Christians continued to keep the Sabbath. Many honored both the Sabbath and Sunday. They considered the Sabbath to be the day of rest, and the first day to be a commemoration of the resurrection. For example, the third-century *Apostolic Constitutions* commands Christians to observe both Sabbath and Sunday:

> Keep the Sabbath, and the Lord's day festival; because the former is the memorial of the creation, and the latter of the resurrection … Let the slaves work five days; but on the Sabbath day and on the Lord's day let them have leisure to go to church for instruction in piety. We have said that the Sabbath is observed on account of the creation, and the Lord's Day is observed on account of the resurrection. (*Apostolic Constitutions*)

We know that some Gentile believers still observed the Sabbath in the fourth century. The Council of Laodicea concedes that the Sabbath day was still the day on which the Scriptures were read in the churches, and the council imposed a ruling to mandate that readings from the Gospels should be included in the Sabbath-day Scripture readings:

> The Gospels are to be read on the Sabbath [i.e., Saturday], with the other Scriptures. (Canon 16)

Other church rules also make reference to the Sabbath and differentiate between the Sabbath and the Lord's Day:

> During Lent the bread must not be offered except on the Sabbath Day and on the Lord's Day only. (Canon 19)

> The nativities of martyrs are not to be celebrated in Lent, but commemorations of the holy Martyrs are to be made on the Sabbaths and Lord's Days. (Canon 51)

The Council of Laodicea's Canon 29 forbids Gentile Christians from observing the Sabbath day as a day of rest. The council encouraged the Christian community to rest on the Lord's Day instead. This legislation indicates that in the fourth century, when the Council of Laodicea issued these rules, many Christians were still observing the Sabbath:

> Christians must not Judaize by resting on the Sabbath, but must work on that day, rather honoring the Lord's Day; and, if they can, resting then as Christians. But if any shall be found to be Judaizers, let them be anathema from Christ. (Canon 29)

Similar admonishments against observing the Sabbath can be found elsewhere in Christian literature. For example, John Chrysostom's sermons in Antioch against the Jews and against the Judaizers among the Christians singled out the observance of Torah as a disease in Christianity. Chrysostom denounced Christians who participated in the festivals, the Sabbath, and the dietary laws. He rebuked them for attending the synagogue. In total, he delivered eight consecutive sermons on the subject, ample testimony that even in fourth-century Antioch, the hometown of Ignatius, many believers were still observing the Sabbath and the holy days. In the end, however, the will of the church prevailed, and the divorce between Christianity and Judaism was completed.

CHAPTER EIGHTEEN

The New Sabbatarians

The previous chapter told the story of how Christianity lost track of the Sabbath and eventually switched to a different holy day. This chapter will attempt to briefly tell the story of how Messianic Judaism is getting the Sabbath back and how the return of the Sabbath provides us with a token of the coming kingdom.

THE RADICAL REFORMATION

Since the Protestant Reformation began five hundred years ago, various groups of Protestant Christians have attempted to reinstate Sabbath observance. The dissemination of the Bible, which fueled the Protestant Reformation, also raised the question of Sabbath observance. When people began to read the Bible for themselves in their own languages, they noted incongruities between biblical prescriptions and church practice. One of the most conspicuous incongruities was the Sabbath day.

Reformation-era groups of Christian Sabbatarians sprang up throughout the Christian world. Christian historians refer to them as part of the Radical Reformation. When people began to read the Bible for themselves outside of the church's predefined interpretive grid, they realized that authentic and original Christianity was both Jewish and Sabbatarian.

As early as 1538, just twenty-one years after the Wittenberg door incident that set off the Reformation, Oswald Glaidt and Andreas Fischer attempted to reintroduce Christians within the Anabaptist church of Moravia to Sabbath observance. Fisher translated Jewish liturgy out of the Hebrew for use in services and even went so far as to write a Christian Siddur, essentially a translation of the Jewish prayer book. For a short time, a few believers were observing the Sabbath, praying the ancient blessings, and offering the basic prayers of Jewish expression. Other reformers began to incorporate Jewish observances and interpretations.

Luther and his associates labeled them as Judaizers. Luther saw the Reformation spinning out of control and, in some places, rapidly returning to Jewish form and practice. Refuting the Radical Reformation became synonymous with rejecting Judaizers.

To put a stop to the problem, Luther wrote a treatise titled *Against the Sabbath Keepers*. He condemned Sabbath observance as un-Christian. Due to stiff resistance from Luther and direct persecution from the larger Protestant world, much of the nascent Sabbatarian movement quickly died out; however, the tendency toward Sabbatarianism continued in remote corners of Protestantism. In 1543, Luther published *On the Jews and Their Lies* in which he advocated burning down synagogues in every town and forcing Jews to convert to Christianity or die. Some scholars believe his vitriolic attacks on Judaism were meant to curb the Judaization of the Reformation.

In the late sixteenth century, András Eössi launched a Sabbatarian movement among the Unitarians of Transylvania. Despite great persecution from the church, the Transylvanian Sabbatarian communities kept the Sabbath and the holy days for more than three centuries until the Nazis extinguished the last remnants of their communities in the Holocaust. The tendency toward Sabbatarianism occurred even outside the confines of Protestantism. The Russian Orthodox Church spawned groups of so-called *Subbotniks* who left the official church and took on the observance of the seventh day. Some groups of *Subbotniks* survive to the present day.

So long as Christians read their Bibles, Sabbatarianism continues to spring up. The Seventh Day Baptists trace their origin to seventeenth-century London. The Seventh Day Adventists have roots in the nineteenth-century Millerite movement. Numerous other groups could be mentioned.

Sabbatarian Christians have carried the banner of Sabbath observance for centuries. They have sometimes been subjected to persecution for their convictions. Mainstream churches often consider them to be dangerous cults. In some places, such as Transylvania, Sabbatarians died for their convictions.

SABBATH AND THE KINGDOM

Sabbatarian groups typically share a strong emphasis on eschatology, the second coming of Messiah, and the kingdom of heaven on earth. Christians who practice the Sabbath tend to be *chiliast*, a word that indicates belief in a literal thousand-year kingdom on earth. They see a relationship between the seventh day and the seventh millennium, and they take the relevant Bible prophecies literally. They are looking for a literal second coming of the Messiah and the establishment of the throne of David in Jerusalem.

Traditional church theology de-emphasizes the belief in a literal thousand-year kingdom on earth, preferring to find a spiritual fulfillment of the kingdom prophecies in the expansion and triumph of the church. Instead of a restoration of Zion, mainstream theology looks for spiritual Zion in heaven. Instead of a literal resurrection of the dead, the mainstream places its emphasis on an afterlife in heaven.

Christian Sabbatarians reject that type of allegorization. Likewise, they reject the allegorizing away of the Sabbath day. They consider the literal observance of the Sabbath to be closely tied to the expectation of a literal kingdom on earth.

THE SABBATH IN EARLY MESSIANIC JUDAISM

Christian Sabbatarianism is a large step in the right direction, but the Christian Sabbatarians sometimes misunderstand the holy day that they so ardently defend. Christian Sabbatarians have often combined their love for the Sabbath with anti-Semitic notions inherited from replacement theology. They miss the vital connection between the Sabbath and the Jewish people, and they often fail to acknowledge that the apostles exempted Gentile believers from observing the Sabbath's prohibitions. Messianic Judaism offers a different perspective on the Sabbath, one that is more thoroughly rooted in the New Testament and the teachings of the apostles.

The modern Messianic Jewish movement came to the Sabbath by a different route than that taken by Christian Sabbatarians. Messianic Judaism as we know it today grew out of missionary efforts to evangelize Jews. Prior to the emergence of modern Messianic Judaism, the majority of Jewish Christians saw Sabbath observance as a step backward and in the wrong direction—a return to the religion they had recently forsaken. Churches involved in Jewish missions often discouraged Jewish Christians from observing the Sabbath. A small minority of early Messianic Jewish pioneers, however, advocated Sabbath observance for Messianic Jews.

In nineteenth-century Ukrainian Kishenev, Joseph Rabinowitz began the first Messianic Jewish congregation. They met on the Sabbath day and used Hebrew liturgy. At the same time, his brother-in-law, Yechiel Tzvi Lichtenstein-Herschenson, wrote Hebrew commentaries on the New Testament defending Yeshua and the apostles as Sabbath-keepers and arguing that the Sabbath has never been abolished. Likewise, around the same time, Rabbi Isaac Lichtenstein, a district rabbi in Hungary, confessed his faith in Yeshua and became a celebrated personality in missionary circles, yet he refused to renounce Sabbath observance. He insisted on remaining within Judaism and the Jewish people.

Nineteenth-century Galician Jew Chaim Yedidiah Theophilus Lucky strongly argued for Sabbath observance and for a Jewish reading of the New Testament. His followers were strictly Sabbatarian, and he found strong allies among Sabbatarian Christians such as the Seventh Day Baptists. After the turn of the century, the Belarussian Jewish believer Paul Philip Levertoff pioneered a Messianic Jewish congregation in pre-war London with Sabbath synagogue services in an Anglican Church. A Russian-German Jew, Abram Poljak, dedicated his life to trying to establish Sabbatarian Messianic Jewish colonies that could absorb displaced refugees from Europe. Poljak's efforts saw the advent of Sabbath synagogue services in London, Haifa, and Jerusalem. None of these men worked alone. All of them represented communities of Sabbath-keeping Jewish believers.

For all their efforts, however, the Sabbath did not take hold among Jewish believers until after the formation of the State of Israel and, even more significantly, after the euphoric success of Israel's Six-Day War. In the wake of that conflict, a swell of pride surged through the Jewish world. Not coincidentally, Messianic Judaism began to take shape in America at that time. Messianic congregations formed and adopted Saturday as their day of worship, primarily as a missionary tactic, but also as a way of establishing continuity with the broader Jewish community.

Sabbath-keeping Messianic Jewish congregations formed primarily as venues for Jewish outreach. In this way, Sabbatarian Messianic congregations began as something of a façade conceived with the intent of luring Jews into the faith. In some ways, much of the façade still remains. From its very inception, such an enterprise flirts with disingenuousness and invites pretense and pretending. However, in its attempt to create a veneer of Judaism, the Jewish missionary movement hit upon something authentic: the Sabbath. When Messianic congregations decided to meet on Sabbath so that Jewish people might feel more comfortable in a Christian context, someone must have raised the obvious question: "Hey, isn't this the real biblical holy day anyway?"

By returning to Sabbath observance, Messianic Judaism inadvertently returned the gospel and the New Testament to its natural habitat. Once believers were released back into that natural habitat, the New Testament and the whole Bible suddenly made much more sense. Messianic Judaism accidentally restored the New Testament context from which our faith originally sprang.

Today, the new Sabbatarians of the Messianic Jewish movement are keeping the Sabbath in concert with the rest of the Jewish world, not in antithesis to Jewish tradition. Messianic Jews are lighting candles on Friday night, saying the blessings over the wine and the bread, and resting on the Sabbath according to Jewish tradition. They are gathering in Messianic communities to pray together and to learn the Torah on the Sabbath day. Others are attending non-Messianic synagogues to participate in the Sabbath with other Jews. For today's Messianic Jews, Sabbath observance is not an innovation or the next big step in the Radical Reformation; the

Sabbath is simply a normal part of what it means to be a disciple of Yeshua the Jew.

THE RESTORATION AS A SIGN OF THE KINGDOM

Many of us view the restoration of Sabbath observance among the disciples of Yeshua as a harbinger of the coming kingdom. As explained earlier in this book, the Sabbath and the kingdom are closely tied together. The Sabbath day symbolizes and, in some sense, spiritually taps into the Messianic Era. Today, there are more disciples of Yeshua honoring and keeping the Sabbath than there have been at any other time in history since the first century and the Apostolic Era. That has to be spiritually significant. I believe it's an indication that we are drawing closer to the kingdom.

The restoration of the Sabbath among the disciples of Yeshua can be compared to the restoration of the Jewish people in the land of Israel and the formation of the State of Israel. Numerous prophecies predicted that the Jewish people would be gathered back to the land of Israel. Hardly anyone in the church expected these prophecies to be fulfilled in any kind of literal sense. Then Zionism happened. World War II happened. The State of Israel happened. Suddenly people began to pay more attention to biblical prophecy and to the role of Israel in the end times. The old prophecies were coming true.

Just as God has resurrected the Jewish people within the land of Israel, he is resurrecting the observance of the Sabbath among the disciples of Yeshua. I believe this resurrection is a necessary preparation for the last days and the advent of the kingdom of heaven. Many things that have been lost during the long years of exile are being rediscovered. It's an exciting time to be a believer.

DIFFERENT POINTS OF ORIGIN

The growth of Sabbatarianism today is closely connected to the formation of the State of Israel and the development of Messianic Judaism. Ironically, the founders of modern Messianic Judaism never intended to start a reformation movement to restore the Sabbath.

Most Messianic Jews did not start to keep the Sabbath out of any desire to reform the church or bring it back to its first-century origins. Rather, Jewish believers observed the Sabbath simply because it's a Jewish thing to do—Sabbath observance is an expression and reinforcement of Jewish identity. Others might observe the Sabbath because they truly believe that it is an effective way of doing Jewish evangelism. They suppose that, as Jewish believers observing the Sabbath, they might draw Jewish people to think twice about Yeshua.

In more recent years, Messianic Judaism has arguably entered a post-missionary phase, a position advocated in Rabbi Dr. Mark Kinzer's book *Post-Missionary Messianic Judaism.* Kinzer argues that Messianic Judaism has its own integrity as a viable and biblical expression of Yeshua-faith, independent of any missionary purposes. One step on that journey will be for Messianic Judaism to recognize the Sabbath as something more than a component of Jewish culture, and as something more than a tool for Jewish outreach.

Messianic Gentiles like myself come to the Sabbath from a completely different direction. For us, Sabbath observance is not about reinforcing our Jewish identity (we have none) or about reaching Jewish people for the gospel. For us, the celebration of the seventh-day biblical Sabbath is a component of restoring our faith to its biblical, Jewish roots. It's about conforming our lives and our families to the biblical model of faith and practice. For us, the Sabbath is a beacon of the old faith, drawing us closer to the LORD, closer to Yeshua, and closer to the Jewish people.

Even though Messianic Jews and Messianic Gentiles may be coming to the Sabbath from different points of origin, we are all arriving at the same destination. That destination is the restoration of the Sabbath among the disciples of Yeshua. Ultimately, that destination will be the day that is completely Sabbath—the kingdom of heaven and the World to Come.

GLIMPSE OF THE FUTURE

For many Messianic Jewish believers, the abundant number of Sabbatarian Gentiles in their midst is probably a nuisance. I can understand that. It's difficult to establish a Messianic Jewish congregation when the Jewish members are eclipsed by a majority of non-Jews. That's a real problem. It's easy for Jewish believers to feel like the token Jew even in an ostensibly Messianic "Jewish" congregation.

Eventually, Messianic Judaism will have to come to terms with this problem. The Messianic Jewish movement should probably start thinking about creating viable multi-national venues to handle the influx of Gentile Sabbatarians because, according to the prophets, the problem is not going to get better; it's going to get a lot worse. It's going to be a global problem.

According to the prophets, when the Messianic Era comes, all flesh will worship the LORD "from Sabbath to Sabbath" (Isaiah 66:23). "All flesh" means "all human beings." All of humanity will be worshiping God, not from Sunday to Sunday, but from Sabbath to Sabbath. This should not be surprising to anyone. Yeshua already taught us that the Sabbath is made for mankind. The Sabbath is from the beginning. It's universal.

The prophets predict that, in the coming kingdom, ten Gentiles from each of the nations will cling to each of the four corners of a single Jew's garment, saying, "Let us go with you" (Zechariah 8:23). Rashi explains this passage with some quick math. The Torah lists seventy nations comprising the sons of Noah. Ten men from each of the seventy nations would make seven hundred people. There are four corners on a garment. Multiplying the number of men by the four corners of the garment, he arrives at 2,800 Gentiles for every Jew. We should not expect the influx of Gentile Sabbatarians to abate just yet.

In the kingdom, "all the foreigners who join themselves to the LORD … everyone who keeps the Sabbath and does not profane it," will be flooding into Jewish space. Not only will they be spilling into the synagogues; the Temple itself will be called "a house of prayer for all peoples" (Isaiah 56:7). At that time, Messianic Judaism will no longer be a religion exclusively for Jewish believers and a few odd-duck Gentiles like myself; it will be the religion of the whole world, and the whole world will be keeping the Sabbath.

Many peoples and nations will say, "Come, let us go up to the mountain of the LORD, to the house of the God of Jacob, that he may teach us his ways and that we may walk in his paths" (Isaiah 2:3). Those ways and paths include the observance of the Sabbath. Then the Torah will go out from Zion, and all nations will find Sabbath rest and Sabbath peace. "There will be neither hunger nor war, neither jealousy nor competition, but goodness will spread over everything. And all the delights will be as common as dust. And the whole world will have no other occupation, but only to know the LORD" (Maimonides).

The Sabbath is a hallmark of the coming kingdom. We're all going to be keeping it eventually. So why wait? The Master tells us, "Seek first his kingdom" (Matthew 6:33 NASB)—a task that cannot wait for the kingdom to come, but must instead be undertaken today. If the observance of the Sabbath will be a defining component of the kingdom, then observing the Sabbath is part of seeking the kingdom now.

We don't have to wait for the Second Coming to experience the kingdom's rest. It is available to each one of us today if we consent to keep the Sabbath, to accept that extraordinary gift each week, to partake of the foretaste of the indescribable blessing of the World to Come.